Golden Palaces

HEART OF INDIA SERIES

Silk
Under Eastern Stars
Kingscote

THE GREAT NORTHWEST SERIES

Empire Builders
Winds of Allegiance

ROYAL PAVILION SERIES

Swords and Scimitars
Golden Palaces

Golden Palaces

LINDA CHAIKIN

BETHANY HOUSE PUBLISHERS
MINNEAPOLIS, MINNESOTA 55438

Published by Bethany House Publishers
A Ministry of Bethany Fellowship, Inc.
11300 Hampshire Avenue South
Minneapolis, Minnesota 55438

Printed in the United States of America.

Library of Congress Cataloging-in-Publication Data

Chaikin, L. L.
     Golden palaces / Linda Chaikin.
          p.   cm. — (The royal pavilions ; 2)
     ISBN 1–55661–865–4 (pbk.)
     I. Title.
II. Series: Chaikin, L. L., Royal pavilions trilogy ; bk. 2.
PS3553.H2427G65   1996
813'.54—dc20   96–25295
                                                                    CIP

LINDA CHAIKIN is a full-time, best-selling author. She is a graduate of Multnomah School of the Bible in Portland, Oregon. She and her husband, Steve, are involved with a church-planting mission among Hindus in Kerala, India. They make their home in California.

Fictional Characters

Tancred Redwan, the hero, a Norman warrior, scholar, and seeker of Truth

Mosul, the Moor, and assassin; cousin to Tancred, and archenemy

Helena of the Nobility, Daughter of the Purple Belt, the beautiful Byzantine heroine

Nicholas, the maverick warrior-bishop, friend of Tancred, and Helena's uncle

Philip the Noble, Minister of War in Constantinople

Lady Irene, the aunt and enemy of Helena, the mother of Philip

Bishop Constantine in Constantinople, enemy of Nicholas

Bardas, the Greek eunuch slave belonging to Helena

Hakeem, the Moor from Palermo, and Tancred's faithful friend

al-Kareem, the Moorish grandfather of Tancred

Derek Redwan, deceased half brother of Tancred

Walter of Sicily, uncle of Tancred

Count Dreux Redwan, deceased father of Tancred

Count Rolf Redwan, uncle and adoptive father of Tancred

Ivan, the bodyguard of Walter of Sicily

Modestine, the French village girl, who joins the crusade

Wolfric, the brigand Rhinelander

Leupold, the Rhinelander

Turill, the archbishop

Prince Kalid, son of the emir of Antioch

Rufus, captain of Lady Irene's personal bodyguard

Adrianna, Helena's mother

Andronicus, brother of Nicholas

Historical Characters

Alexius Comnenus, Emperor of Byzantium, A.D. 1081–1118

Pope Urban II, who called for the First Crusade

Peter the Hermit, leader of the peasant-crusaders

Walter Sans-Avoir, the Frankish knight, first crusader to arrive at Nish

Bohemond I, Norman prince of Taranto

Count Raymond of Toulouse

Roger I, the Great Count of Norman Sicily

Godfrey of Bouillon, Duke of Lower Lorraine

Hugh, Count of Vermandois, brother of King Philip of France

Robert, Duke of Normandy, son of William the Conqueror

Emich (Emicho), robber-baron of Leiningen, persecutor of the Jews in the German Crusade

"The Goose" of Emich

Volkmar, persecutor of the Jews in the German Crusade

Gottschalk, a renegade priest, persecutor of the Jews in the German Crusade

Bishop of Worms

King Coloman of Hungary

Governor of Wieselburg

Nicetas, Governor of Nish

Adehemar, Bishop of Le Puy, and official Papal Legate on the Crusade

Raymond of Aguilers, a chronicler of the First Crusade

Henry IV, Emperor of Germany

Kerbogha, commander of Seljuk warriors

"The Red Lion of the Desert," Seljuk commander

Nicephorus, Emperor of Byzantium, A.D. 963–969

Basil II, Emperor of Byzantium, A.D. 976–1025

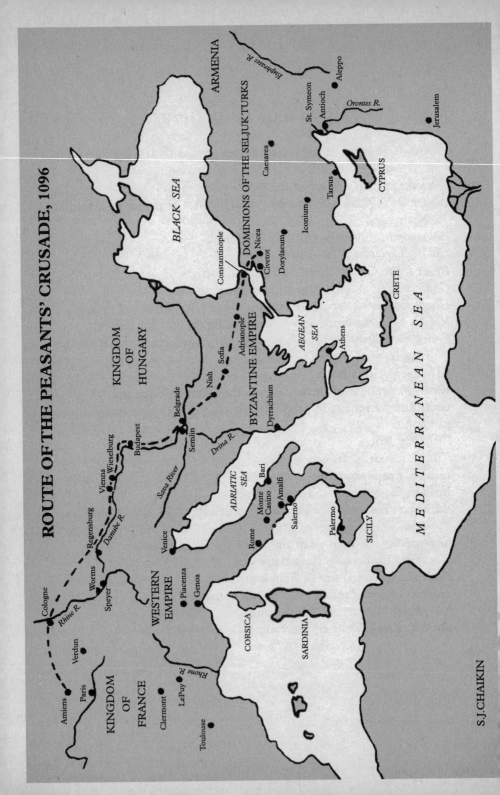

ROUTE OF THE PEASANTS' CRUSADE, 1096

ARMENIA

DOMINIONS OF THE SELJUK TURKS

Euphrates R.

Aleppo

St. Symeon
Antioch

Orontes R.

Jerusalem

Caesarea

BLACK SEA

Tarsus

CYPRUS

Iconium

Nicea
Civetot
Dorylaeum

Constantinople

KINGDOM
OF
HUNGARY

CRETE

Adrianople

AEGEAN
SEA

MEDITERRANEAN SEA

Sofia

Nish

Athens

Belgrade

BYZANTINE EMPIRE

Semlin

Drina R.

Dyrrachium

Vienna
Wieselburg

Budapest

Savu River

Bari

ADRIATIC
SEA

Regensburg

Danube R.

Venice

Monte
Casino

Amalfi

Salerno

Palermo

SICILY

Worms

Speyer

WESTERN
EMPIRE

Piacenza

Genoa

Rome

Cologne

Rhine R.

CORSICA

SARDINIA

Verdun

Amiens
Paris

KINGDOM
OF
FRANCE

Clermont

LePuy

Rhone R.

Toulouse

S.J.CHAIKIN

PROLOGUE

Helena moaned in her sleep, bound hand and foot by a mystical spell of enchantment. The handsome knight had woven a cord out of strange green leaves removed from a physician's satchel.

"Turn me loose, Sir Knight!"

"Madame," he said wearily. "How long? You have only to surrender. Freedom awaits us both the moment our lips shall meet, but you must do so willingly."

"Nay! Never!"

Was he a dragon? A knave? A gallant knight willing to die for her honor?

Though she floundered, his masculine gaze vowed his devotion, his passion, his sword. "Helena," he whispered, "Helena, awaken to me, my beloved. . . ."

She gasped and bolted upright, her heart pounding. A glance about revealed that she was secure within her darkened chamber.

A foolish dream? she wondered. *Or a premonition . . .*

CHAPTER 1
Trapped

The Sacred Palace,
Constantinople
Spring 1097

In a wash of pale moonlight, young Helena of the Nobility, Daughter of the Purple Belt, moved silently across the marble floor between two Corinthian columns in the wide palace pavilion facing the Sea of Marmara. Her heart pounded in her ears as she took momentary refuge behind one of the slim white pillars. A silent prayer touched her lips: *Please, Most Merciful Christ in heaven, do not permit the guards to see me.*

Once concealed, Helena's spicy brown eyes, as tender as the Byzantium night, glanced back over her shoulder into the vast palace hall with its intricately arranged ivory arches, gold ornamentation, and vibrant mosaics. From the enormous walls, dancing torchlight spilled down and onto the carved marble busts of the Greek idol-gods Zeus and Athena.

Helena shivered as her gaze locked with an emblem of her aunt's vile Zodiac religion, by which she influenced certain members within the emperor's senate who trusted her counsel in interpreting the stars and planets. The disc appeared to stare menacingly at Helena, causing a shiver to slither up the back of her neck like a tiny serpent.

She waited, listening for the threatening echo of a guard's iron-studded sandals, the clink of chain mesh, the rattle of a sword. Only a supple evening breeze whispered among the heavy clusters of white Judas Tree blossoms in the garden below the pavilion steps.

The house slaves, too, must be avoided . . . for they were anxious to better their positions by reporting every suspicious move she made to her aunt by marriage, Lady Irene of Troy. The cool and ambitious Irene had been made Helena's legal guardian soon after her mother's arrest and her father's death in battle against the Moslem kingdom of the Seljuk Turks. As her guardian, Lady Irene set into play a nefarious plan to arrange Helena's political marriage to Moslem Prince Kalid, thereby guaranteeing the return of the great walled city of Manzikert to the Byzantine Empire, lost to the Turks in 1071.

Raw twilight hung suspended in a web of expectant silence, broken only by the Sea of Marmara lapping against the granite foundation of the palace seawall. The palace, once belonging to her father, was now under the authority of Irene.

Irene's beauty, unyielded to God, had become a curse to those influenced by it. Her tentacles of power now reached inside the royal bedchamber to the empress herself, who saw Irene's dark enchantments as the advice of a trusted counselor. Helena knew differently. Her aunt had no concern for the empress; it was the emperor she wished to control, and then the throne for her son, Philip.

Oh, Philip, Helena thought with aching fear. *If you would believe me, we might yet escape together to safety, to the Castle of Hohms!*

Her dark eyes caught the last fading golden rays against the purple hills of the Arabic East, and she envisioned the phantoms of war rushing across those mysterious hills, echoing "Allah! Allah! Allah!" to the answering shout of the western crusaders, "God wills it!" The clash of the western sword and the eastern scimitar rang through her head with feverish zeal.

What is to be my fate? Helena shuddered and ran her palms

over her arms. How alone she felt, how abandoned. There was no one left within the Lysander family to whom she might turn except her banished uncle, and her hopes, once as bright as the torches that lined the hippodrome, were growing dim with the passage of time.

Helena's eyes narrowed. *I will not go to Antioch to marry Kalid.*

Contrary to her aunt's wishes, she had made plans to escape to the Castle of Hohms, her inheritance upon marriage. There she would wait for her uncle Nicholas, a bishop from the university and monastery of Monte Casino near Rome. Even now, Nicholas might be among the barbarian Norman crusaders who rode under the crimson *gonfanon* of the grandson of William the Conqueror from southern Italy and the Norman kingdom of Sicily.

Soon, thought Helena, thousands of western knights would be arriving outside the massive walls of Constantinople to swear their vassalage to the emperor for the expedition to reclaim Jerusalem from the Moslems.

But the crusade meant little to her now, as her personal dilemma wrapped itself like dungeon chains about her heart. How could she escape to the castle alone when her every action was under surveillance? What source of strength did her God provide in answer to her ceaseless prayer for deliverance? What strong warrior could she trust to protect her until Nicholas arrived?

Tonight, her faithful eunuch slave Bardas would bring secret information about the Norman mercenary Tancred Redwan. Thinking of Tancred brought a ripple of unease. Visions of his dark Moorish features, along with the icy blue eyes of the Vikings, brought no comfort.

Yet, I must risk further relationship and seek to hire him, despite his barbarian arrogance, she told herself.

As Helena glanced about the palace hall, neither guard nor slave were within view, and she took this grace for an answer to her earlier prayers. Silence kept vigilance in the aromatic night as she held the letter that Bardas must deliver to Tancred.

Donned in white silk embroidered with purple thread and

13

gems, she picked up her wide hem and sped across the open portico. She hurried down the wide marble steps, ran breathlessly into the garden where the blue-tiled walkway led toward the St. Barbara Gate. Just beyond the ancient seawall, the Bosporus glimmered beneath the eastern stars.

Ahead, she could glimpse the little caiques sprinkled across the water, their red and blue glass lanterns swinging from the narrow rowboats and winking like the emperor's crown.

A moist breeze from the waterway touched her face as she rushed to keep her secret rendezvous with Bardas, holding the precious letter to Tancred against her pounding heart.

A thousand stars peered down from the darkness like twinkling eyes of angels guarding her feet from stumbling in haste. She consoled her wounded heart with the thought that although the doom of becoming Prince Kalid's bride loomed as unconquerable as a gladiator in the hippodrome, her future was not left to the battering schemes of the ambitious. The sovereign God's plans for His followers remained secure, unmolested by those who vainly exercised their own independent might.

Yet knowing all this did not quench her temptation to tremble with weakness as she contemplated becoming the bride of a Moslem emir in the golden palace of Antioch. Her private concerns spiraled out of control, shattering her peace.

Helena stood tensely by the singing fountain with cascading water tumbling over polished stones, silvery in the moonlight. Her hand clutched the emblem of her Christian faith—a Byzantine cross hammered from a heavy nugget of gold, encrusted with flashing green emeralds and blood red rubies. The cross, cherished because it had belonged to her mother, had been given to Helena many years earlier on a desolate night at the family villa located in the countryside outside Athens.

Her mother, a banner of calm faith despite her arrest for treason against the emperor, had pressed it into Helena's young hands. . . .

"Trust not the emblem itself, but the One who triumphed on the cross and broke the chains of death," her mother had whispered. *"Christ will be with you always, my fair Helena, even when I cannot."*

Torn as a child from her mother's final embrace, she had clutched the cross while watching her being escorted away by imperial guards in black-and-crimson uniforms.

Etched in her memory, Helena could still hear the echo of the chariot wheels as the guards drove from the villa with her mother—doomed for the dungeon, and then death by plague in the convent.

An unlikely smile formed on Helena's lips. . . . *But she is not dead as they believe. She lives! And I will find her.*

Soon after her husband's death, Lady Adrianna Lysander had been accused of treason against the emperor, but sedition was a vicious lie hatched by Lady Irene. Even so, the throbbing memory of her loss was not assuaged by the lifeless emblem she clutched so tightly. Instead, the spring breeze cooled her fevered emotions, reminding her of God's mastery over the intensity of the storm blowing against her soul.

Helena walked ahead to where the plantain trees grew green and thick.

"Bardas?" she whispered urgently. "Are you there?"

Shadows clustered among the flowering vines, and the garden pavilion eased into a sleepy hush. A bird, tucked securely in for the night beneath its overspreading leaves, offered a call for her courage.

Again, she listened intently for the sound of Bardas, praying that he had not been intercepted by guards. She stole a quick backward glance toward the lighted portico, and the movement of her head caused the silky net of pearls covering her ebony coil of braids to reflect the torchlight. Lady Irene was not home and her lazy and frivolous young cousin Zoe was asleep, but a slave might appear at any moment. If discovered here, Irene could send her to a dungeon until her departure for Antioch.

Helena's frightened mind remembered another dank dungeon where she had spent time as a child, though she could not remember when or why. She remembered only the rats with lemon eyes and white teeth that puttered about in the stale darkness. Eventually, Lady Irene had come down the chiseled steps looking like a golden savior and had taken her away.

15

"You will answer to me now, Helena. You will grow up with my son Philip and your cousin Zoe."

The breeze nudged the vines where she stood now, and Helena's restive glance swept the seawall. *Bardas,* she thought again, *what could be delaying him?* She gripped the letter.

As though he had flown to her on a magic carpet, there came a stir, a gust of wind, a rustle of leaves. From farther ahead a large, muscled man wearing a hooded black cowl ducked beneath the overhanging tangle of vines and stepped out into the moonlight. A breath of relief escaped her.

The big bodyguard lifted a square hand that was scarred from his service to her deceased father in the last war and threw back his cowl. He revealed a shaven head glistening with oil and a left eyebrow partially removed by a scimitar—the wicked curved blade wielded by the Moslems. His broad face wore the scowl she had been accustomed to since a girl at the villa, but so pleased was she to see him that it might have been a grin.

She hurried in his direction like a chick seeking the wings of its mother hen. Other than her beloved uncle Nicholas, whom she had not seen since before her mother's arrest, Bardas was her one source of protection, and he was as dear to her as any kin. He had willingly become a eunuch after her father's death to keep a vow he had made on the battlefield to guard Helena unto death, and his body retained all the form of a muscled warrior. His ancestry, he boasted, bore the blood of the Spartans, but his culture was classical Greek—a matter of tiresome pride on his part, causing him to scorn the arriving crusaders from the West as "savage barbarians and gluttonous cretins. Men without education, fit for little else except to clean the emperor's bear cages."

Helena's relief spilled over in a scolding whisper. "You are late. Where have you been? I feared you'd been detained to harm."

He sniffed with disdain and looked about suspiciously. "Your fears have roots. While I was prowling among the bazaars seeking information on the Norman barbarian, whom should come by in her gilded chariot but Lady Irene?"

At the news, Helena's heart wanted to cease its persistent pounding. "She saw you?"

"She has eyes like a falcon, that one. She ordered the captain of her bodyguard to hail me to her side, demanding to know if you were with me and what I was about."

"You said nothing of the cause which brought you there?"

His one eyebrow shot up. "And betray the daughter of General Lysander? Did I not kneel on the desert sand to swear oath to him?" He pulled on his walrus mustache. "Nay, they will need cut my tongue from my mouth before I betray your cause." His scowl turned into a crafty grin. "I convinced her I was on my way to tell her you wished to attend the emperor's garden banquet for the Daughters of the Purple Belt tomorrow."

Helena remained skeptical of the ruse. "And she believed you? She is as wise as a serpent."

His black marble eyes sparkled with smug satisfaction. "And a hungry serpent as well, who swallowed the baited rat. She is convinced you wish to attend, and now bids you voyage in her caique tomorrow."

The news, however, was intimidating. "Oh, Bardas, how could you? I would rather row to the palace in the company of the emperor's hungry bears."

He looked offended over her lack of appreciation for his cleverness, and knowing how easily his pride of devotion was injured, she hastened, "What did you discover about Tancred Redwan? Did you locate him at the armory?"

Swift disapproval at the mention of his name carved his broad face into a stonelike mask. She had sent Bardas to the Street of Bazaars to secretly discover what he could about Tancred's past, hoping to validate his trustworthiness as a hired mercenary, but the look on Bardas's face declared his disapproval unchanged.

"Redwan is an insidious barbarian, a wanted assassin who slew his brother with a poisonous dagger over a Moorish beauty in Palermo named Kamila." Bardas gazed at her for emphasis, making certain the weight of his words left their intended mark on her confidence in the Norman.

Helena had not expected to hear about a Moorish beauty, but

she did know about the death of his half brother. Several weeks ago in Philip's chamber, Tancred had explained to her of his search for the real assassin.

"He is the heir to his Norman father's wealth but is unable to assume his baronial lands due to his brother's murder. With help from his wily Moorish friend, Hakeem, who is equally a snake to be distrusted, Tancred escaped his castle in Palermo, Sicily. Cold-blooded Norman wolves who are his cousins are searching for him, determined he will stand trial according to a Norman custom called 'craven.' "

She remembered Tancred's words—*"In the Norman kingdom of Sicily, I am heir to castle, lands, and galleons. And I know your uncle well. Nicholas saved my life when I was a boy. For a time he raised me at the monastery of Monte Casino. All that I know of Christ, Nicholas taught me from his own copy of the Greek New Testament."*

Was it true? she wondered. "So he does have a castle and lands in Sicily as he told me?" she gently coaxed, hoping to win his trust in Tancred, but Bardas refused to be impressed.

"So it is claimed. It is said that he killed his brother for the inheritance."

Helena considered that possibility, but somehow Tancred did not appear the ambitious and covetous sort. "Was he not gallant to save me from capture by the Rhinelanders?"

Bardas sniffed. "Only because he has his own wicked plans to have you."

The notion brought her a bewildered pleasure, but she swiftly dismissed it. "He is arrogant and conceited and looks upon me with indifference—it is well that he does, since it is only his sword I wish to hire."

Bardas's expression, however, remained dour. "He cannot be trusted, little mistress. What would your father say if he were alive? It is unseemly for a woman of your aristocracy to even speak to such an uncivilized dog! But to deliberately seek him out—"

"If I seek him," she quickly interrupted, "it is only because he is a knight who is needed at this hour of my abandonment by Philip."

The cool mention of Irene's son—the minister of war and the man whom she had once hoped to marry—prompted Bardas to rush to his defense. "Forbid! Master Philip will surely awaken to his honor and intervene in the evil scheme to send you to Antioch. Long you have been promised to him in marriage, and he will not stand by and see you given to Kalid."

She wondered. Remembering the pain on which she and Philip had parted weeks earlier reopened the wound of bitter disappointment in his lack of courage to stand against the plans of his mother.

"Yet he bartered me to Kalid for his own ambition's sake. No, Bardas, I cannot wait. Who else can I turn to now but Tancred? Your loyalty is esteemed," she hastened to soothe his fatherly pride, "your sword proven true in wars past, but your arm . . ." and she hesitated, her voice trailing off, knowing how it grieved him to be reminded of his permanent injury.

"I admit Redwan is not entirely the uneducated barbarian I first took him for," he grumbled reluctantly, and Helena snatched at the opportunity to convince him of Tancred's usefulness in their cause. "You see? You were wrong! The knight is worthy of my hire! What did you learn?"

He folded his arms stubbornly across his broad chest. "That his knowledge is a danger."

"Danger? But—"

"He has made use of the famed Royal Library, translating some manner of document from Latin into Greek."

"Latin into Greek . . ." Helena marveled despite herself. Tancred had informed her in that suave but cynical way of his that he was a "scholar equal to any translator in the Royal Library." She had laughed at his arrogance—for what else could his boast be but that?—and he had smiled, undaunted by her scorn. Now she wondered if she might have laughed too soon.

"And," said Bardas in wary tone, "he made a map of the environs of Antioch. Some say Prince Kalid is a cousin."

A cousin? Her eyes darted to his.

Looking self-satisfied, Bardas continued. "Might not that map also include the domain of the Castle of Hohms? Do not the Norman wolves wish to control the stronghold for their own attack on Antioch? It is no secret how they wish to conquer and rule the city, not for Byzantium, but for themselves. And who is the seigneur in charge of the castle? A Norman! A Redwan! A man whom this Tancred claims as his adoptive father!" He looked at her, confident. "Ah, mistress, is it not obvious that he is in league with him? Together they wait for the other Normans to arrive. I say he cannot be trusted. He is a spy."

A spy. Was it possible? What did she know about Tancred except what he claimed? And why would he make a map of Antioch and the castle? Yet she needed him! If she gave Bardas a hint that she mistrusted Tancred, her doubts would only serve to strengthen his resolve against hiring him.

She smiled ruefully, deliberately making light of his suggestion. "And I suppose because Nicholas rides with the Normans that he too is in alliance with them? Yet he is no spy and we know it. Neither is Tancred. Think again! He claims to be a count," she reminded him.

"Then I am King of the Spartans!" mocked Bardas, pulling on his long black mustache speckled with gray.

She sighed. "Oh, Bardas—whether a count or not, he is one man in Constantinople who hasn't been bought by my enemies."

He leaned toward her. "Can you be so certain?"

Helena couldn't, of course, and yet . . .

He must have seen the flicker of hesitation in her eyes for he urged, "He would keep his motives hidden, little one. And his claim to being some great lord from the Norman kingdom of Sicily is surely spurious."

"Maybe, but I need his strength as a knight. I could look for a hired sword among the Normans in all the bazaars and not find a man half as adept as he. He may be arrogant," she said wryly, "but you must admit he is brave."

"Because he is clever and hatches schemes of his own."

"Even if I could hire another, news of my action would find its way back here to the palace. My message is likely to remain secret if given to him. No," she stated firmly. "I must hire him. Irene does not own him."

"You may be in error. Lady Irene knows the barbarian is being sought by his Norman cousins for the assassination of his elder brother."

The news was unsettling. Irene often used coercion to force certain warriors into her service to benefit her ambitions, or Philip's. Her methods were cruel, and Helena loathed her for them. Yet, somehow, Tancred did not seem the manner of warrior to be manipulated by threats or enticements.

"And if the vileness of his brother's death staining his honor is not enough to change your mind, I have learned that his mother too was a Moor, a devout Moslem, and he carries a copy of the Koran."

She mused over the Koran, for Tancred had implied allegiance to Christianity, or had she misunderstood?

"How do you know about the Koran?" she whispered.

"A Varangian guard told me. He has friends among them," he said stiffly, not wishing to admit it.

So . . . the esteemed Varangian Guard knew Tancred. Giants clothed in scarlet and bronzed helmets with plumes, the hand-picked Vikings served as the personal bodyguard of the emperor, and were as strong as gladiators, as loyal as blooded sons. That they knew Tancred well enough to offer information to Bardas spoke well of his abilities as a warrior and reinforced the wisdom of Helena's decision to hire him, although it did not offer an explanation for the Koran. Had he not said that his grandfather was al-Kareem, a man of political and religious power in Palermo, with contacts among the sultans from Cairo to Nicaea?

In recalling their conversation, she also visualized Tancred lounging behind the drape during her romantic confrontation with Philip in his chamber. Philip had chosen to pursue his ambitions in the emperor's service rather than risk intervening in the political decision to send Helena to Antioch. And the arrogant Tancred had overheard it all!

The memory overwhelmed her with embarrassment, but her present situation was too perilous to concern herself with injured vanity. Perhaps he had forgotten that dreadful night.

"Koran or not, Tancred claims Christian training by Uncle Nicholas at the abbey of Monte Casino," she argued. "And until the assassination of his brother, he studied as a student physician at Salerno."

She was not certain if she believed all this, but her dilemma demanded that she trust someone. Nor had she forgotten the night along the Danube months earlier when he had saved her from capture by the rowdy Germanic brigands called "Rhinelanders." Nor the fact that he had returned her family jewels to her when Philip was willing to use them to bribe the leader of the Rhinelanders not to attack the Hungarian fortress on the Danube. However, the truth of whether he was a knight of chivalry must await an hour when she was safely at the castle.

Bardas's expression did not soften as she reminded him of the brigands' attack upon Philip's entourage. Both she and Bardas had been with Philip at the time, hoping to locate Nicholas, but the report of her uncle's arrival with the peasant-crusaders had proven to be false.

She resorted to her sheltered upbringing by lifting her chin to show him that the discourse about Tancred was over and that her will must prevail. "Enough. I have listened to your concerns and they are well taken, but I have made up my mind. I must endure the educated barbarian. He is a Norman and will prove invaluable to us. Deliver this letter to him at once," and she pressed the sealed parchment into his big hand, even while she glanced back toward the portico to make certain her absence remained undiscovered.

"If Irene now expects me to accompany her to the royal gardens tomorrow, I must attend. When the Norman reads my letter, tell him to meet me at the rear garden wall near the outer street. I will make my escape with him then. See that horses and supplies are ready. We will journey to the castle."

"As you wish," he said sullenly. "But what if he refuses to come?"

Not come? The idea that Tancred would ignore any command she gave was unthinkable to a young woman born of Greek nobility who wore the privileged Purple Belt of royalty, especially when his position was inferior. She frowned. Tancred was a difficult man to understand—not like Philip. No, he was nothing like her beloved cousin Philip Lysander.

"He has his own plans," said Bardas. "He is not as quick to hearken to your wishes as others. It is my opinion he finds your superiority of race and position a goad to his barbaric ways."

It was true that she had tasted his arrogance toward her status in the past. She had smarted on several occasions from his casual refusals and the malicious amusement garnered from rankling her pride. She knew he could prove difficult and she hesitated, rethinking the wording of her letter. Tancred was not likely to submit easily to her wishes. She must force him to bend his stubborn knee.

Notwithstanding, she had not intended to sound like a princess commanding a slave. Authority was ingrained in her upbringing, and she knew little else except a born privilege to command others. And those from the West were looked upon as strangers and barbarians by the proud Greek civilization.

Her dark brows tightened together as she reconsidered her tactics. "Well . . . then tell him it is most urgent. That I . . . well . . ." she ignored the expression of disdain forming lines on Bardas's forehead. "Tell him that I bid him come with . . . gratitude."

Bardas gave her a surreptitious glance. "It may be that however gracious your tone in bidding the mongrel, he will remain a dog disinterested in your treat. The man may have other plans."

Something in his tone alerted her. He was not telling her everything he knew. "What do you mean, 'other plans'?"

Bardas cleared his throat. "Master Philip has already hired him. He holds a worthy position in the imperial cavalry."

Imperial cavalry! And he had not told her until now?

The imperial cavalry served the emperor, and any member who rode the magnificent horses was considered to be lordly. She wondered that Philip would have allowed this when he disliked him as much as Bardas did. She decided that to have Tancred in his service must be deemed of benefit to his position as minister of war. Philip did not have the compassion to throw a morsel of bread to a starving beggar without receiving some personal gain in return. It was a characteristic of his that troubled her—but this weakness was no doubt due to his mother, she told herself.

"Then I shall outbid Philip for the warrior's sword," she stated firmly. "Better to pay a hefty price than be sent to Antioch."

"He is not a man to be bought easily, and somehow I think he has deliberately remained in the emperor's service waiting for you to call upon him. Yet, no matter the price you offer him for his swordly endeavors, he is likely to refuse, holding out for the castle and," he warned, "for your hand in marriage."

"Marriage!" she gasped, then gave an absurd little laugh, but it came off sounding more excited than she had wished. "Do not be absurd, Bardas. I would not have him if he were the last man in Constantinople, nor does he entertain thoughts of marriage. He is a rogue."

"Agreed, but I ask you—if it is true he seeks this 'phantom' assassin of his half brother, why does he tarry? His appearances at the entertainments are said to be cloaked with boredom. Nor has he love for the emperor. His allegiance is to the West. And there is no woman but you that he too casually inquires about."

Her face turned warm as she contemplated, but not for long. Why did he serve in the imperial cavalry? She remembered Tancred's smooth insistence that he was not for personal hire. His determination was a match for her own, she was certain of that, but this was one game she must win.

"He may be swift with the blade and smooth with the tongue, but he is a ruthless man with aims of his own," warned Bardas, obviously refusing to acknowledge her determination in the matter.

Ruthless, was he? Perhaps . . . but not in the manner that Bardas insisted. "Go," she said.

Bardas dubiously relented and placed the letter inside his cloak.

"Tomorrow at the back gate," she reminded him.

Helena stood in the stone courtyard watching as he slipped away into the vines from which he had come, past the seawall where the little boats were tied at anchor. Then she turned toward the broad marble steps, her Grecian profile lighted by the spring's full moon that turned the pearls in her dark hair into an iridescent white-blue. Her hopes renewed, she sped softly across the court and back toward the lighted marble pavilion. She must return to her chamber above, unseen by guards or slaves.

She rushed toward the pavilion steps but stopped suddenly, gasping with surprise. There on the topmost step stood a dark form silhouetted against the backdrop of the pavilion's blazing torches. It was Bishop Constantine, the man who had worked closely with her aunt to convince the emperor of the expediency of her political marriage to Kalid.

Did he see Bardas?

Her fingers tightened about the weighty gold cross.

Fed by the threat of danger, her imagination envisioned not the fire of the torches surrounding Constantine, but the rising flames of hades.

CHAPTER 2
The Dark Rook in Bishop's Robe

All her instincts warned her to flee, but it was necessary to appear unharried over the arrival of Nicholas's masterful adversary.

It could not be proven whether or not Constantine had usurped the ecclesiastical office of her uncle years earlier by lending support to political enemies who had schemed to have him banished from Constantinople. Usurper or not, Helena questioned the sincerity of his reverence for the things of God as he pursued the privilege offered by association with the emperor.

Only a reprobate would hide behind a cleric's robe, cloaking his personal objectives, she thought. Excluding political gain, just what were his aims?

She observed Constantine standing on the wide step, garbed in black-and-silver brocade. On his head was a fashionable high-crowned turban with a brim of glittering gems. His short reddish beard was fastidiously groomed and oiled, giving his narrow chin but wide forehead a shrewd appearance.

"How much like your mother you look tonight, fair Helena."

The inflection in Constantine's voice when he mentioned her mother prickled her nerves. Could he know that she was alive after all? Helena concealed the undercurrent of her fears with outward confidence and, with a silent prayer on her lips, walked forward, head erect.

"Why . . . my Lord Bishop, your unexpected arrival, so late and without announcement, must surely bring a cause for care." She ascended the wide marble steps, her Byzantine tunic shimmering in the torchlight.

He removed his hat, his red hair glinting, and offered a bow of his head. "I regret to intrude upon you at this hour, my child, but matters will not await the morning. I will be gone a few weeks on urgent business to Antioch."

Antioch!

Her expression of alarm was met by his cool smile beneath his mustache. "No need for immediate concern. You will not be leaving with me to marry Prince Kalid." His smile vanished. "Not yet."

"You go there at the wishes of the emperor to speak with Prince Kalid?"

"No, the prince is in Cairo to attend a meeting of the sultans. Civil war occupies the various Seljuk princes from Jerusalem to the Caspian." He looked pleased. "Disunity is to Byzantium's favor and will bolster the western barbarian princes in recapturing territory lost to the Moslems, including Antioch.

"No, dear Helena, I am here tonight because of another matter that concerns both of us," he stated. "One that is more important than the return of Antioch to the Eastern Empire. Do not look alarmed! I come as a friend, in peace."

What did he know of true peace! He had come for ill purposes, of that she was certain. Helena climbed the remaining steps, her doubtful gaze spurning his words of assurance.

"Peace, my Lord Bishop?" and her brow lifted dubiously. "And does this peace you so generously offer me share the blessing of Lady Irene?"

The mention of her name evoked a flicker in his eyes, but it wasn't clear if thinking of Irene of Troy brought him pleasure or rage, although she had been the calculating mind behind his rise to power, even as she was now, with Philip.

Helena already knew about their disagreements over the direction of Philip's future as minister of war. Those arguments had grown more bitter with the passing weeks. Irene insisted that her son was to be in command of the Greek forces that would travel with the crusaders to bring a siege against Antioch and receive the surrender personally from Prince Kalid. But Constantine insisted that the honor should be his, since he was the emperor's legate.

"I have come on my own initiative," he said. "Irene does not know I am here." His voice turned scornful. "She spends her waking hours plotting how she might trap the handsome Norman named Tancred into willing subservience."

Helena knew what he meant, that her aunt had an eye for every new warrior in the imperial guard. Irene's shameless behavior remained a cause for grief, but the news irritated her more than it would have had the guard been someone other than Tancred.

Helena was also aware that other women were speaking of him, including Mary the Alan, the emperor's mistress. Thus far, it was said he had avoided their clutches like a slippery goldfish from Cathay.

Helena paused on the step below Constantine, uncertain how she should accept his words of peace.

"Was it your peace and blessing that was offered when you took away my uncle and saw him banished to Bari?"

"So you still blame me? At the time of his banishment I held no vested authority to have him undone, yet he will seek to return in the gall of bitterness to strike vengeance against me. It will do him no good and lead to his ruin."

As he stood on the step in the torchlight looking down at her, his motives remained obscure. She did not believe him about Uncle Nicholas. On the afternoon that guards had brought him in chains to the harbor for a Greek vessel bound for Bari, she had heard him promise Constantine that he would one day return.

"You will pay for this betrayal, Constantine," he had shouted. "Let my memory haunt your dreams! Look for me behind every shadow, within the very cloister!"

Since that dark hour when Constantine stood in silence on the Golden Horn watching the guards escort Nicholas to the ship, he and Irene had come far in the imperial palace through the internecine struggle for power. Yet Helena saw his expression turn bitter, as though remembering the past brought memories that robbed him of satisfaction.

"Do not waste words of sentiment on Nicholas," he said. "It

29

was not he but I who was first banished, not from the empire, but from the Lysander family."

She wondered what he meant. "Banished, you?"

Mockery shimmered like live coals in his prominent eyes, but his voice was soft, even soothing.

"Yes, it was I who was first called upon to bear the title of an outcast. In the noble Lysander family, so close to the heart of the emperor, I was the deformed sheep rejected from the fold. It did not matter that I too was a cousin of Nicholas, that I bore family blood. I was nothing in their eyes except a bodyguard to the Lysander women, fit only to escort their chariot to the circus! I had no heart, no soul, an immobile face in a uniform, a decoration to keep the door, to walk behind them like a moving statue."

A cousin to Nicholas? A bodyguard to the family daughters? Helena had not heard this before.

He looked at her. "I was assigned to your mother's chariot. I protected her day and night."

There was something in his voice, a hint of secrecy that set her on edge.

"I guarded her bedchamber door."

Her eyes turned cool even as they searched his, wondering what to make of his words and whether she dare trust them.

He then spoke to her gently, yet with a kind of mild scorn. "Nicholas, whom you esteem so highly, came between the love your mother and I once shared."

His eyes flickered at the thought, and Helena's breath sucked in as audibly as though he had struck her.

Love? Her mother and Constantine? That was not possible. . . .

His smile mocked her surprise. "Adrianna wished to marry *me*, not Lysander. We met often, in secret." He smiled.

She took a step down and her voice trembled. "You lie."

"I have no cause to lie. Our love was very deep," and a strange gentleness thickened his voice, and when it did, her heart sank as reality gripped her.

His eyes became granite. "She did not see me as a mindless bodyguard, but as a man. But Nicholas! That fool! He forbade her to see me again. He convinced the family to send her to Athens to marry General Romanus Lysander—a man old enough to be her father."

Her lungs tightened as she tried to breathe. *No . . .*

Constantine turned his head and looked out toward the sea wall where distant lanterns glowed and danced like living jewels on the water, and his voice was a memory, pathetic and yet angry.

"Adrianna was always obedient to her family's wishes. I begged her to run away with me—even as you begged Philip to flee with you." He looked at her. "I knew he would not hearken to you, even as she refused me. Position meant more to both of them. It is the Byzantine way . . . but it is not mine." He looked at her. "Nor is it yours."

Could he know I expect to hire Tancred and escape?

He walked to the other side of the portico where the shadows clung to the Judas Tree blossoms. "We never saw each other again—except from afar. Saint that she was she would not favor me with a glance, though I knew she loved me still."

The pathos of his voice made her uncomfortable. Her beloved and godly mother in love with Constantine? Nay! Never! How could such a tale be true?

Desperate to deny his confession, her mind ran back to her girlhood at the villa where her mother had retired from aristocratic life. Helena recalled that when she would come upon her each morning in the olive tree garden, her mother would be sitting on the stone bench reading works from the Royal Library, but on several occasions she remembered seeing letters as well. Helena had thought them to come from her father, who was away fighting many distant wars against the Seljuk Turks infringing on Byzantine territory.

In her memory she could hear the pigeons calling "coo-ra-cooo—" as her lovely mother sat upon the bench, so still that Helena believed her in prayer. Once a letter had fallen from a warm brown leather book edged with gold, and when Helena rushed to retrieve it, hoping to please her, her scolding voice had stunned her: *"No, Helena!"*

She looked at Constantine, dismayed. *No.* He appeared to read her thoughts and smiled disdainfully.

"My dear, you are disappointed she would love one like me?"

Helena could not speak. Bardas, who had served her father in the war with the Turks, had told her a different story. Her mother had written Romanus of a certain wayward cousin with "the dark ways of hades, who plagues my every step," until in fear of his romantic madness, she had fled secretly with her child Helena from the palace to the villa. At the time Helena did not know that Constantine was related, but if what he said tonight was true, could he not be that wayward cousin?

Yes, thought Helena in fear, watching Constantine's oddly tortured expression in the torchlight. If she placed that twisted mask on matters, it made more sense than what he was telling her now.

And yet . . .

I will not believe him. Who was he to barge into her cherished memory of her parents and sow seeds of evil suspicions? If he could provoke her to turn against her mother, he might tempt her to trust in Irene.

Then—with a dart of consternation, she searched his face, half hidden now in the flickering shadows of the flames. Could he have discovered that she believed her mother to be alive and that she was searching for her whereabouts? Was he trying to convince her of his love for her mother as a ruse to discover what she might know?

It is Irene he serves, and she would send him to trap me into divulging precious information.

She would not listen to the serpent in the garden. Of this she was certain: though her mother's marriage to General Lysander had been arranged, they had loved each other.

To throw him from the trail of her thoughts, she resorted to the airs of injury.

"I will hear no more scandal to darken the reputation of my mother and father. Was it not enough she was accused of treason against the emperor? And falsely! And for what cause do you bother me now that I am about to be sent to Antioch to marry Prince Kalid?"

She came swiftly up the steps, and Constantine moved to one side, allowing her to pass. Helena sailed by into the pavilion where the torches on the high marble walls spilled their light onto the smooth Greek statues. Despite her demeanor, panic gnawed her insides.

Helena walked with trailing silk hem between the slim pillars toward the outer balustrade and stood staring out at the waterway glistening in the moonlight. In the distance, the eastern stars hung above the camel-humped mountains of the mysterious Moslem world, and in her haunting dreams she heard the high-pitched wail from the domed mosques. Despite her plans to hire Tancred and escape, anxiety washed over her soul as she imagined her mother a slave in a sultan's harem. How could she find her and free her? How could she avoid her own destiny in the ruthless arms of Kalid?

Constantine had followed her, lingering beside the pillar, the breeze moving his circular cloak.

"You are so much like your mother," his wistful voice repeated.

She stiffened and turned her head away.

"Make what you will of my confession. It is true, and I loved her . . . I love her still," he said.

She must not feed his allegations by respecting them with her concern. "I choose to make nothing of your words."

"At first, she too was suspicious of my motives."

She whirled, eyes snapping. "And you wished to cloak her with your protection! Yet she was arrested and sent to the dungeon."

His jaw flexed. "I ever remain her loyal admirer."

She pretended not to catch the present tense of his words. She moved away from him. "Perhaps she had excellent cause to mistrust. Both you and Irene were her enemies. If you loved her as you now suggest, why did you not rescue her after she was sent to the convent when the illness spread? Why did you leave her to die at the wish of Lady Irene?"

She caught the shadow that crossed his face, the tiny leap of flame in the hard eyes as though a woman's sharp nails had clawed his heart, but it vanished as if a cold wind had blown down upon them from Mount Athos.

She watched him covertly but saw no sign that he knew Adrianna lived, lived on in some unreachable desert tent where warm nights and tambourines beat rhythms in the hot dry darkness, beneath these same stars, perhaps in the unwanted embrace of a sultan.

Constantine walked to the balustrade, his footsteps clicking on the polished stone, and he too was looking eastward.

"I had no choice. I could do nothing until it was too late. For years I did not know Irene was involved in her fate."

"Then you admit it at last. My aunt did betray her."

"Whom has the golden goddess not betrayed—with her potions and astrology?"

"How light and excusable you make her ways sound, as though her stargazing is a harmless diversion. It is vile and leads even the senators astray to bow before the altar of Babylon. How you still choose to defend her, like a guard his queen," she accused, "you— declared a representative of Christ. Do you think I do not know that she also poisoned Basil to empty his seat as minister of war for Philip?"

His lip curled. "Only a fool would fling such unwise words about for all to hear. Be glad, my dear, that I am not easily shocked by your boldness. For your sake, let us hope slaves with sharp ears and tongues are not close by. As for her tactics, betrayal is the way of Byzantium. It will always be so. The strong survive on the carcass of the weak."

She shuddered. "You are content to accept evil because it exists, but I am not. Christ is stronger. His truth, His will shall yet prevail over those who scorn His ways and flaunt His righteousness. He has His soldiers to intervene—"

He laughed. "And you, my gullible damsel, think Nicholas is one of them? Poor deluded Nicholas will soon be trapped!" and he flicked the shiny spider's web crocheted between the gallery rails that held a moth, beating its wings helplessly.

In revulsion for his hardened speech she snatched the moth free from its sticky prison.

"Yes," he laughed softly, "so much like your mother."

"You say all this now about Uncle Nicholas because you fear him," she challenged.

He looked at her, surprised, then laughed again. "Fear him?"

"Yes, and Irene does too, though I do not know why," and she turned away wearily.

His smile turned cynical. "Shall I tell you?"

Helena wished to avoid his answer, suspecting more information that smelled of treachery and sin. "I care not to feed my mind upon the vile entertainments of the deluded. I know her immoral weakness, but to hear of it vicariously is also evil."

"She resents him because Nicholas is the only man she has ever truly wanted and cannot have. He rejected her for what she was years ago. She has not forgotten. Not all her conniving nor her tempting beauty can lure him to her bedchamber!"

"Stop it." She jerked her head away.

"He scorned her. She hates him for it yet loves him in her own selfish way. It is more than I ever received from her," he stated bitterly.

"Your ways insult heaven, you who wear the robe of bishop. I will not hear more," and she tried to walk past him, but he stepped in front of her.

"Look at how she fills Philip's soul with prideful dreams of his destiny! 'The stars have woven an emperor's crown for Philip,' she has told him since a child, and like the child he is, he believes it possible."

"No, he will yet see the truth of God; he will tear himself from her schemes, and yours. You will see that he yet has honor and courage."

Constantine appeared not to hear and said of Nicholas, "He unwisely returns. Does he hope to regain the favor of the emperor? He has not learned yet that Byzantium outwits him at every turn. If Nicholas has audience with the emperor, his wild ravings will crackle like fire among dried thorns and come to nothing. Perhaps he envisions himself a Moses, prepared to storm the palace of pharaoh, threatening plagues!"

Her heart beat with righteous indignation. "I suggest, my Lord Bishop, that my uncle is neither to be pitied nor discounted as religiously deluded, though you may hope him to be so for your sake."

He looked scornful. "We shall soon find out. Let us forget him. I have not come to discuss Nicholas. I have come as your friend with advice."

She might have laughed at his excuse for offering advice but she dare not mock. There were too many obstacles remaining in the road leading to her escape. Constantine was a powerful man with soldiers who could move against Tancred if she hired him. Yet she must not crumble now. Constantine respected her resolve to remain strong, even as he had admired her mother. A moment of weakness now would be to his advantage.

Helena watched him as he walked across the polished floor veined with gold and came to the balustrade, where he stared out across the sea. The flash of a white tail from a meteor left traces of light against the hills of Moslem-held territory once belonging to the empire.

"Adrianna is alive," he said quietly. "We both know it. Let us not pretend otherwise. And you expect Nicholas to find her." He turned his head and his gaze was even. "A mistake. One I must thwart. For my sake and hers."

Helena's icy fingers wrapped tightly around the balustrade.

He waved his hand with scorn. "You have me to thank that your stupid informer, so clumsy and gullible, did not keep his appointment with Bardas on the Street of Bazaars."

"Have you to thank—" began Helena, dazed.

"Irene was suspicious," he explained shortly. "She had guards loitering, waiting. Both you and your infantile informer would have been caught. And by now, Adrianna would have met with an assassin's dagger."

He steadied her with an iron grip. She was too weak to pull away.

"Your informer is dead," he said cryptically. "I could not trust him to live and fall into her hands. He would have talked, even as he confessed to me." His eyes flashed. "Yes, Adrianna is alive," he whispered.

"You already knew?" said Helena, stunned.

"I have known for months. She was seen in Jerusalem, but she is no longer there. Yet I will find her. I have my own spies searching. And neither you nor Nicholas will impede my plans. Is that understood?"

"You must tell me where she is, Constantine! Please! If my spy told you, then—"

"Your informer knew nothing more than I just told you. Until

I find her, no word of this must reach Irene."

"Do you think my mother will ever love the man who sold me to Antioch? She will loathe you for it, even as she does Irene who betrayed her."

"Perhaps, my dear Helena, but Kalid will tell me where she is. His prize is you and the Castle of Hohms."

"Kalid knows?" For a moment she could only stare at him. "Are you saying my mother is in Antioch?"

"I wish it were so easy. No, she is not there, but he has access to the sultans, and if he wishes to have you and the castle"—and his smile turned brittle—"he will find out. And, if you wish to see your mother bought from slavery, you will cooperate with me."

She trembled, her emotions straining in opposing directions. "Irene knows everything; her spies are everywhere. What if—"

"Her mind is consumed with other suspicions. She also worries about Nicholas arriving. She may suspect you of wishing to escape before your dromond leaves for St. Symeon. We will permit her to think so. She will be distracted from learning the truth. In the meantime you will keep silent. There will be no more paid informers, do you understand? If you breathe a word of this to Bardas, I will have him disposed of."

Her eyes anxiously searched his. "I will say nothing."

The silence thickened between them, becoming a wall as he scrutinized her face.

"And—should you free my mother, what then?"

He made no answer, and when he turned to walk away, she ran after him clutching his arm. "Constantine!"

He flung her hand loose, his eyes hard. "Dramatics do not become you."

In the silence they stared at each other, and under his gaze she felt her soul wither. Then he turned and walked away.

She listened to his steps echo among the pillars until the sound died away and silence surrounded her pounding heart.

The moments swept by until her mind shouted, "I *must* hire Tancred."

Her mind worked feverishly. If Kalid could gain information about her mother from the sultans, then could not Tancred do the same?

Yes! Of course! Why had she not thought of this before?

She walked to the balustrade and looked out toward the water with the lanterns flickering on the caiques, a new hope bringing strength to her wearied spirits. Did Tancred not say that his mother had been a Moorish beauty from within the mysterious alabaster walls of Palermo? Then, as her son, he too would have access to his Moorish cousins! Even Kalid was related—and that dreadful assassin he had called Mosul.

And wonder of wonders, tomorrow night Tancred would be waiting for her with Bardas outside the wall of the emperor's garden! It was true that her aunt would accompany her to the emperor's banquet for the Daughters of the Purple Belt, but somehow she would slip away from her to meet Tancred. And when she did . . .

Helena's heart sang out with joy as her eyes lifted with praise toward the starry heavens. By tomorrow night at this time, she would have hired Tancred's sword to help her escape Kalid—and to locate her beloved mother.

CHAPTER 3
The Rook's Golden Mistress

The flotilla of caiques bringing young women of the aristocracy to the emperor's garden banquet were strewn across the placid liquid blue like a string of floating pearls.

With its gilt-edged frame glimmering like wet gold, Helena's caique glided across the surface of the Marmara as ships from distant shores floated in and out of the Golden Horn on the magical Persian wind. The afternoon sun scattered red-gold rays upon the water, and Helena lifted her fringed parasol of purple silk above her head and rested upon the daybed cushion opposite her guardian and aunt by marriage, Irene of Troy.

Helena noted how the pristine but cold white of Irene's outer silk tunic complemented the thick golden braids coiled about her head like a serpentine tiara. Her aunt's beauty was unquestioned, and was the ruin of nobles and barbarian lords alike, whom she thought little of using to her advantage. Her appearance was a misleading weapon, for beneath that outward fairness there reigned the strong will of a woman proud enough to believe she would one day become empress and determined enough to eliminate any who stood in her path. There were times when Helena believed that Irene would accomplish her life's ambition.

Death by poisoning . . . The elimination of one's enemies within the secretive walls of the golden palaces of Byzantium and the Moslem East were often carried to success on the slippered feet of assassins walking delicately upon marble floors. Death might come by potions, an assassin's dagger, a certain rare silk.

It was whispered that the caterpillars were fed a certain leaf that was poisonous to humans but not to them. The poison was most effective when the silk was worn directly against the skin. The main buyers of this silk were nobility in line for a throne or women in harems who sought to eliminate a rival. Irene of Troy had her own purposes, but her ambitions in the Sacred Palace also included her son, Philip the Noble.

Helena had retained her composure earlier that afternoon when accepting the birthday gift of a shimmering silk scarf from her aunt. She had affected pleasure but the dart of suspicion remained—did the silk contain poison? Irene must not guess she suspected her of having used this method of poison in the past.

She has her spies everywhere. They've become slaves to her drugs and astrology and perform her orders without question. If she suspects I have plans, the life of Tancred will fare no better than my own, or that of my mother before me. Please, Merciful Christ, do not let her guess my plans.

Aware of her aunt's gaze, and cautious lest her expression reveal her doubt about the silk, Helena laid the rare cloth against the side of her cheek. "It's lovely, madame."

Irene smiled as she lounged back against the cushions. "The color brings out your beauty. Raven's tresses! Eyes like black gold! I was indeed wise to bring you to the attention of Kalid. How else would we have gotten his cooperation to negotiate the rule of Antioch? You have proved a great benefit to the empire, Helena."

To the empire, or her own plans? thought Helena, but said with a calmness she did not feel, "How can you be certain Kalid will keep his part of the bargain? Once marriage to me is accomplished and he has the Castle of Hohms, he may scorn the treaty he signed."

"He has no choice. He is shrewd enough to understand that without unity among the sultans he will have no army of Moslems strong enough to withstand the onslaught of the coming western barbarians." Irene's musings on her successful negotiations brought a smile to her mouth. "I've little doubt the barbarians will conquer Antioch in battle. They are like gladiators. But before they take the city, it's been arranged for Kalid to negotiate a settlement with Philip, who will then return to the emperor in military triumph! The barbarians are our pawns, gladiators to fight our battles while we use our wits to gather in the booty."

"Your clever plan will surely be hailed by those in the senate," praised Helena, her heart beating with reproach for her aunt's ways. "I shudder, however, to think what the barbarians will do when they realize their military victory has been stolen from them at the crowning moment, whisked away by Philip to the emperor."

Irene lifted a golden brow as if to weigh the motive behind her toneless words. "Do I detect sympathy for the barbarians? The emperor shall pay his vassals well enough."

Helena had heard that the Byzantine coffers were dwindling as the emperor paid out gold to buy off the enemies of Constantinople or to hire mercenary armies.

"I have no sympathy for the barbarians, my aunt. Am I not devoted to the emperor? And the acclaimed victories of Philip pleasure me even as they do you."

Irene smiled with amused tolerance. "Come, cease your spoiled fretting. Antioch isn't as dreadful as you wish to think. In his day Emperor Justinian added Greek magnificence to the city, and Caesar built hanging gardens there. Marriage to the son of its emir will occupy you with many diversions."

As if entertainment were all that mattered to me. In order to cool the pulse throbbing in her temples, Helena looked across the water slipping past them beneath a twilight of dusky rose. She fingered the silk. *Often the wearers of the poisonous silk die in a fit of madness. . . .*

Irene's laughter interrupted. "What a child you are, Helena."

She swiftly turned her head and inquired innocently, "My aunt? You were saying?"

Irene looked scornful. "As if I'd poison my niece."

Helena felt two blotches of warm color stain her cheeks. "No . . . I . . ."

Irene silenced her with a lift of a jeweled hand. "You think too much on the vices of the families of the Roman Caesars. You and your dusty manuscripts and trips to the Royal Library! Your learning breeds suspicions in your intellect like little foxes. Does not the emperor need you in Antioch? Not to mention my fondness for you! As soon as you arrive I shall be in contact with you by spies. You will have your orders to perform, and certain information you must gather."

There was little reason to pretend now. "And if I refuse to cooperate in the emir's palace?"

"Did you not say you were loyal to the emperor?" came Irene's lightly mocking voice. "But of course you are, my dear Helena. You are not like your mother. You will cooperate." And she added quietly but firmly, "Otherwise you will remain in Antioch until you are an old woman." She reached to the basket of purple grapes and plucked the fat morsels, biting and sucking their juice. She threw the skins into the water and gestured a bejeweled hand toward the scarf. "If you have any hopes of ever having Philip, you will do what is required of you. The sooner Antioch surrenders, the sooner you will be free of Kalid and able to return to Constantinople. Then we will discuss a marriage to Philip."

Helena's heart pounded with indignation. As if she could marry one man to betray him, then marry Philip as if no stain blotched her soul. Under the cool amber eyes of her aunt, Helena's grip tightened on her parasol.

"You expect me to spy? To marry Kalid, then thrust a dagger into his heart?"

"Nothing so dramatic. You haven't the will. Your religious devotion weakens you." Irene gestured to the silk scarf. "The silk you fear proves your childishness."

Helena tossed the piece aside. "I put nothing past your desires, madame. Though you may have wanted me in Antioch a month ago, your ambitions where I am concerned are as changeable as the spring sunshine."

"And so you think I would poison you?" In scorn Irene lifted her goblet and drank.

"I consider being sold to a Moslem palace little better than poison. Some would prefer death. And to betray a husband with lying words and kisses—even a man I do not wish to marry—is worse than vile."

Irene leaned her head back, resting. "You are too strong of heart to use the excuse of a weak and sentimental girl. You will survive Antioch. And Kalid is a handsome man. . . . You will do what is required of you."

"I do not change husbands as one changes garments. That is your way, madame, not mine. If Philip cares nothing of my marriage to Kalid, then there will be nothing more said between us—whether Antioch is surrendered or not."

"Do not speak foolishly. You are young. You will change your mind. Once the barbarians terrify the city with their threats, the sultan will surrender. You will have played your role well, and there will be no reason why you cannot proceed with your life."

Helena stared at her, struggling to control her emotions. "My life will be ruined, and you say there will be reason to go on as if nothing has happened?"

"If Philip is not disturbed, why should you be?"

Helena stared at her, speechless and angry.

She turned her face to the soft spring breezes and sought to cool her heated emotions. For one fleeting moment Helena imagined floating away on the gentle wind, freeing herself from her aunt and the strictures of the most hierarchical society the civilized world had ever known.

Her thoughts were jolted as one of the emperor's guard galleys beat past them with slave oars dipping full speed in unison, their deep voices echoing to the cadence of the slave-driver's drumbeat.

Helena turned on her cushion to look after them, seeing humble Greek fishermen on flat barks make haste to pull their nets out of the way of the rush of indifferent soldiers. Why were they in such a hurry? she wondered. The guard castle was an important link with the imperial cavalry guarding the old Roman road from Dyrrachium in Byzantine territory. What military information could the guard galley wish to deliver to Herion with such speed?

Also alert, Irene sat forward, shading her eyes to follow the galley as it surged ahead across the water.

Helena noticed her expression. "A military envoy?"

Irene's face reflected concern, but she remained silent.

Helena pressed for more information with casual indifference. "They row in the direction of the guard castle at Herion."

A conclave of Byzantine war dromonds were moored against the bank, and Helena believed the guard galley had been sent by them to Herion. One dromond in particular interested her, for it bore the flag of a military commander. Her aunt too must have thought the same, for she turned on her daybed to her head slave.

"Quickly. Row to that dromond," she ordered.

As their caique approached the convoy, Helena scanned the long hulls of the imperial galleys with crimson pennants snapping. Her gaze fixed upon the lead dromond with its carved dragon masthead, which could spume forth famed "Greek fire"—that mysterious Byzantine weapon that burned even upon the face of the water. "Greek fire" had delivered Constantinople on more than one occasion from enemy ships entering the Golden Horn, and had turned back the Huns and Visigoths, as well as the Normans.

As the slaves rowed toward the dromond, Helena recognized Philip's ship. A man in the uniform of an imperial officer saw them and walked to the rail as the slaves maneuvered the caique closer to the galley's side. Helena rebuked her pounding heart. She had not seen Philip since their last meeting in his private palace chambers when he had refused to contest her marriage to Prince Kalid. Was he aboard?

CHAPTER 4
Knights and Barbarians

A cautious and disappointed glance along the deck told her that Philip was not on the ship. She watched in mute silence as Lady Irene smiled up at the imperial officer, allowing the veil to fall from her golden hair set aglow from sapphire stones. Helena was repulsed to see how swiftly her aunt's icy dictatorial nature pretended to melt into a false helplessness, when she could easily receive the information she sought by simply inquiring.

"It is you, General Taticus," she called up, her tone flattering and tinkling like a musical wind chime. "With the barbarians so near to the walls of our city, your presence in Constantinople brings comfort to the ladies at court."

"Madame, your words cheer me, albeit, I shall not be long in the city."

"A regret! With hordes of brute beasts soon to camp before our gates?"

"I am informed that His Excellency is already planning to call the imperial cavalry back within the city walls. Though the barbarians openly attack, they can easily be beaten back. Food may be withheld to bring them under control. Yet it will not come to that, madame. As soon as the western princes swear their fealty to the emperor, we shall ferry them over the water into Anatolia to face the Moslems."

"I am certain you are far wiser in these matters than I, General Taticus. Your confidence brings me relief." She gestured a delicate pale hand winking with jewels. "But I couldn't help notice the military courier racing toward the guard castle of Herion. Do tell! Is there to be trouble so soon?"

"Imperial guards serving on the frontier have sent word the Normans are within three days of Constantinople. The guard galley, madame, brings news of their approach, no mean matter seeing how their feudal prince is related to William the Conqueror."

"Yet called for by the emperor!" said Irene, as though in disbelief that such a thing could be. "His name is Bohemond, is it not?"

As if she didn't know, thought Helena.

"Bohemond is the son of Robert Guiscard," offered the general gravely. "It was Robert whose very army was outside these walls but ten years ago hoping to take Constantinople. Perhaps of more importance, Bohemond brings many in his entourage from the Norman kingdom of Sicily and Monte Casino."

The mention of Monte Casino, a university and monastery near Rome, set Helena's heart racing with expectation. If Normans from Monte Casino were approaching the city, there was a good chance that her stalwart uncle would be among them. A casual glance at her aunt suggested that she had come to the same conclusion.

Then I may see Nicholas any day now, thought Helena, careful to portray disinterest at the news of the western barbarians. Until she was safe with her uncle, danger continued to surround her.

Irene's concern over the news of the Normans became visible in the taut lines showing around her mouth. Helena remembered what Constantine had told her about her aunt and Nicholas.

Helena pretended boredom. "On such a pleasant day when all Constantinople smells of romance and blossoms, must we concern ourselves with the barbarians?" and she smoothed the glimmering golden cloth at her wrists as though the only thing that mattered to her was the upcoming celebrations.

"Helena is right," said Irene to General Taticus. "We must not ruin the season with fearful talk of war," and she turned, giving an airy wave of her hand to her chief slave. "Until tonight, General.

Aleko! Row us to the St. Barbara Gate."

As the caique skimmed across the water, Irene lapsed into musing silence and Helena covertly watched her. She remembered her aunt's previous warning not to be foolish enough to suppose she could appeal to Nicholas for help.

"If Nicholas is so bold as to show his face in Constantinople after being exiled, he will soon find himself arrested by the emperor."

The flotilla of caiques arrived on the threshold of the St. Barbara Gate, and slaves unrolled bolts of cloth for the young Greek women to walk upon. Stone-faced guards stood at attention while the veiled aristocracy strolled past them to attend the garden festivities. Red-robed eunuchs—always plentiful where women congregated—bowed low as Helena and Lady Irene passed through the gate.

The younger women of imperial families formed small cliques and spread through the garden laughing and talking excitedly of the long courting season ahead. *How many of them know that I am to be given to Prince Kalid, a Moslem?* wondered Helena dully.

The display of garments adorned the late afternoon as brilliantly as did the manifold blooms of the extensive flower garden. Today Helena wore a chemise of patterned rose and blue silk squares, while her outer robe was stiff with tapestry-work and gold embroidery, with loose, billowing sleeves gathered at her wrists. The silk was of excellent quality, produced by the city's ancient guild. Part of her dowry was a silk and perfume shop on the Street of a Thousand Bazaars. It was told her that Byzantine silk had come by way of caterpillar eggs smuggled from China in the hollow bamboo walking staffs of missionary monks.

Indian pearls from Hind were intricately worked throughout her rich dark hair and culminated with a stylish strand draped down each side of her head to her shoulders, shimmering creamy white as they moved with each motion of her head.

Imperial Byzantium even dictated what she wore and when. This evening of the garden banquet, Helena had her role to play as a daughter born of the Purple Belt with no more serious thought on her young mind than the dainties she would dine on at the banquet, or which of the handsome Greek nobles she might add to her countless admirers. Also like the other daughters, she was dressed according to status. In Constantinople and throughout the empire, status was dictated by the imperial color of purple. The rare and costly dye used to color their silk was first discovered in shellfish and was restricted from the time of the Babylonians for use by royalty and other high-ranking officials.

Only men of senatorial rank could wear the purple inset in their robes; only the emperor and empress were entitled to robe entirely in that color, while the emperor alone had the honor of wearing hose and boots of royal purple.

But today such display meant nothing to her and was only a cumbersome reminder that she would need to remove them before escaping the city with Tancred.

"Such impudence," stated Irene scornfully.

"W-what?" murmured Helena, fearing her aunt had guessed her plans after all. In turning, she saw that Lady Irene was not speaking of her. Helena followed her gaze across the garden to the sea-gallery of the Mangana Palace. There, overlooking the grove of plantain trees, stood Mary the Alan, staring boldly down at Irene, her rival. Helena stirred uncomfortably. She had heard by rumor that the emperor had given the Mangana Palace to his mistress.

"See how she flaunts herself," said Irene resentfully. "As though born in the purple chamber of royalty." Her amber eyes glowed with envy. "Like Jezebel she should be thrown down for dog meat!"

Helena masked a wince. It surprised her when Irene could look so harshly upon the character of a woman so much like herself.

"She only married poor Nicephorus because she hoped to place her son in line for the crown," stated Irene. She gave a short laugh. "How cunning of him to deceive her. He chose another son. But she had her vengeance too. The hyena cast her eyes upon the new emperor and won!"

While aware of Byzantine debauchery within the palace, Helena never ceased to be affronted by its careless evil.

Nicephorus had been the emperor until deposed by the present emperor, Alexius, who had him consigned to spend the remainder of his years in the monastery. Nicephorus once informed Alexius that he missed little about being emperor except his meat.

Helena supposed that being sent to a monastery prison was better than being torn limb from limb in the hippodrome, the usual fate reserved for deposed rulers when their popularity waned with the public.

"Do not wander far," said Irene. "I shall expect you to accompany the other maidens to the lighting of the church candles at dusk."

"Yes . . . of course."

Irene regarded her sternly. "The news of the soon arrival of the Normans must of necessity hasten your departure to Antioch. I am pleased you appear resigned to your destiny and do not intend to resist the will of the emperor. You will be rewarded in the end. I shall see to it."

Helena's throat constricted. She recovered, pretending to accept her fate, and remained serene. "Yes, madame."

Irene appeared satisfied, then turned and walked toward the palace.

Helena's dark eyes narrowed and her heart began to pound. She stood watching until her aunt disappeared inside the portico on some mysterious mission of her own, then turned quickly and strolled ahead toward the trees on the outer rim of the garden where Tancred and Bardas would be waiting in secret.

Tamed birds with plumage the color of a flaming sunset promenaded across the walkway and into the shrubs. As Helena passed some young women, she picked up snatches of meaningless conversation.

"They say the new cloth brought by the Venetian merchants has been ordered by Princess Anna."

"Have you heard? A new shipment of pearls arrived from Hind. They say the general will have his wife's palanquin embedded with them."

"Is she truly his *wife*?" came a sneer.

Helena lowered her thin veil across her face so that none of the girls would recognize her and call out, forcing her to stop and explain her fate in being sent to Antioch. Many of them knew of her long-made plans to marry Philip, and some, who were her jealous enemies, would rejoice over her dark future.

Above the bird trills, pleasant voices of trained African singers fell as softly as evening dew on the garden. Slaves meandered about with trays of refreshment: cherries, chilled by the snow brought down from Mount Athos; small, round honey cakes made with sesame seeds; and silver goblets of rose-scented water.

Whenever the emperor played host to the young women of aristocracy, it was a custom that wine could not be served, not even the white wine of Chios. For at twilight—when the young women would customarily follow the emperor's procession to the Church of Hagia Sophia and the incense was lit to spiral upward about his high seat in the church's dome—the Eastern Roman emperor claimed to be not only the imperial head of Eastern Rome, but the embodiment of deity.

When Helena reached the shrubs, she hastened her steps along the marble walkway past the rows of plantain trees, hearing the laughter of female voices drifting on the breeze. Once certain she was out of sight, she picked up her hem and ran toward the trees lining the outer wall.

Loyal as always, Bardas waited in the evening shadows and followed her into the cloister of trees, where branches drooped low with white flowers.

"Where is Tancred?"

He cleared his throat with scorn. "The barbarian did not come. I was right when I said he was clever and could not be bought easily."

"What do you mean!"

"He has maneuvered his way into the hire of the auspicious emperor himself."

"The emperor!" Troubled, she asked, "Where is Tancred now?"

"He is not in Constantinople. He left days ago."

"Not in—" Her hopes shattered.

"I've learned from the Varangian Guard that Master Philip met with him in the Baths of Zeuxippus weeks ago. The barbarian has mistakenly been made liaison for the emperor. And Philip will bid him ride to meet with the prince of the Norman army before it arrives outside the city walls."

Her relief gave way to a laugh. "Then we have more cause to celebrate. Nicholas rides with the Norman prince, and it is my plan that we ride with Tancred to meet him. Will he return to receive his orders from Philip?"

A ridge formed on his brow at her apparent disregard for his news. "I do not know," he said.

Helena's impatience grew. "What do you mean, you don't know? Did you deliver him my letter?"

"I did. Before the barbarian rode out for Herion."

Herion! Then there is little time.

Helena swiftly told him about seeing the guard galley on the Marmara and about the information General Taticus had given her aunt.

"A courier is now being sent to inform Philip of the approach of the Normans. We must leave tonight before Tancred receives his orders."

"Ride to the guard castle? Mistress, are you mad? The Norman went to Herion to appease another of the western princes, a man who arrogantly claims himself some great person in the West—a duke he calls himself, from Lorraine. There is trouble between his men and the emperor's soldiers."

She already knew about the man called Godfrey of Bouillon, who was encamped across the Herion bridge on the other side of the Bosporus waiting impatiently for the other crusader armies to arrive. *So Tancred was sent there to mediate peace. . . .*

"This said duke has command of seven thousand choice knights, besides a foot army of many thousands more," protested Bardas. "To find Tancred Redwan—"

Seven thousand. . . . A chill ran through Helena. The emperor was right—the duke commanded a formidable army, and if joined with the soon-arriving Normans—

"Who can trust such a barbaric force?" said Bardas, as though reading her thoughts.

Her eyes rushed to his. "They might indeed become an enemy to Byzantium, but perhaps an ally if they move east against the Moslems."

He frowned, disbelieving. "They have plans of their own."

"Maybe, but . . ." She made up her mind swiftly. The guard galley would soon arrive at Herion and Tancred would be given new orders.

"I will risk the ride to Herion. If not, my doom is cast." She told him what Irene had said about sending her to Antioch sooner. "By the time Nicholas arrives, I will be aboard a dromond on my way to St. Symeon."

"There is fighting in the towns along the Bosporus, and the duke is displeased with the emperor. What if they turn on us? Who can trust these wily brutes?"

Helena would not think about it. She could not, for her courage would falter. She remembered the horror of the Rhinelanders along the Danube River. If Tancred had not rescued her . . .

"If I must choose between danger or marriage to Prince Kalid, I shall journey to find Tancred."

Bardas grudgingly relented. "I will do that which is deemed best for your safety. If you must go to Herion, we will, but it is best to make our escape in the darkness."

She smiled. "I will go with the women to the candlelighting tonight at the church, then slip away unseen."

"Take caution; you will be watched by madame's guards."

"They will be too busy watching the emperor to notice me."

"I shall be waiting down the street from Hagia Sophia with a chariot. And if we are seen, alas, it will mean the dungeon for you . . . and for me? Death."

"Nothing must happen to you, my faithful friend! But do you not see that it is the only way?"

"I see nothing but trouble when it comes to the barbarian," he grumbled, then sighed. "If it must be, think not of my life. You can depend on me."

Helena smiled and touched his arm. "I shall be there soon after the candlelighting. Go in peace, quickly."

As the final rays of the purple sunset faded over the Golden Horn, Helena and the youthful aristocracy were escorted by members of the guard to the candlelighting.

Lights gleamed from the embrasures in the walls of the high monasteries, and the armed servitors tramped through the shadows toward the magnificently built church. On the water, the sails of the fishing fleet were seen moving in toward the shore after a day of fruitful toil with their nets.

Before the imperial palace, evening mantled the Marmara, where slaves knelt to light the colored lanterns on the waiting caiques belonging to the aristocracy. As the night would wear on, the nobles and citizens would embark upon the same entertainment that had filled its glittering walls for a millennium.

The drowsy pigeons, having flown to safety within the domes of the hundreds of churches dotting the city's horizon, closed their eyes upon it all, bored with man's vaunted display.

Helena was anything but bored as the possibility of her escape loomed like opened gates before her. She felt the excitement in the warm breeze brushing against her face as she walked with her candle amid the other young Greek beauties.

So far, she had avoided the trap awaiting her at Antioch. There was much to be grateful for on this night. She would soon find Tancred, and then her beloved uncle. Nicholas, as a bishop, was expected to wield sword and lance as proficiently as any Norman warrior. Standing between her uncle and Tancred, she would find security at the Castle of Hohms.

Thankfully, Helena lifted her thoughts in praise to Christ while her dark eyes shone above the clear flame of her candle.

CHAPTER 5
Assassin, or Gallant Knight?

Rain clouds marshaled together above the dark waters of the Bosporus, and the spring night settled in with a fine drizzle. Wearing the black-and-crimson uniform of the emperor's imperial guard, Tancred's boot steps rang across the stone floor as he walked to where his winter cloak hung from a peg on a rock wall in an upper chamber of the guard castle.

Accepting his helmet from a young serving boy, Tancred stepped out onto a steep flight of chiseled steps leading down to the outer courtyard.

The Byzantine guard castle was built near a stone bridge that crossed over a long crook of the Golden Horn waterway. It brought him no pleasure in knowing that his mission would bring him to the other side of the bridge where stone castles and wooden structures were scattered amid the little towns along the Bosporus. For waiting in one of the castles was the first of the crusader princes to have arrived earlier that spring, Godfrey of Bouillon, Duke of Lower Lorraine. He had brought an army of seven thousand armored knights, mailed horsemen, and foot soldiers, and was known to be a proud and difficult man to appease. Tancred again wondered that he had allowed himself to become involved in a cause that was not his own.

He knew why he was involved, of course. He was in Constantinople waiting for news to reach him on the true assassin of his half brother Derek. He was also waiting for Nicholas to arrive . . . and then there was his niece, the spoiled and willful Helena.

Envisioning Helena brought an unlikely frown to his face—a face both rugged and sensitive, bearing the masculine features that belonged to his Norman father and the dark Moorish good looks of his mother. His appearance often found him in too much favor with women who were far more appreciative than the somewhat haughty Helena.

Tancred's stormy blue-gray eyes smoldered with irritation beneath heavy lashes dusted with the same flattering brownish gold of his thick and somewhat curling hair. He did not know exactly why it should be, but he felt a mild irritation whenever he thought of her—which was a pastime he refused to engage in. Perhaps he was as stubborn as she was in keeping emotional distance. He was determined to avoid becoming entangled. By the standards of Greek civilization, he was considered ruthless—a barbarian—and perhaps what goaded his pride the most, an "ignorant savage."

It mattered not that his learning was equal to any in the Eastern Empire, or that he bore the skilled hand of a physician. He was seen as a warrior from the West, fit only for the gladiator arena or for service to the emperor against his blood cousins of the Moslem East.

It rankled him that Helena blindly doted upon the "wonders" of Philip the Noble, despite his being an obvious coward and an ambitious man with little honor. That he refused to fight for her and was apparently willing to turn her over to Kalid of Antioch seemed to do little to extinguish the flame in her heart that burned for him. What did she see in this Greek?

Tancred frowned. *Am I as conceited and arrogant as she claims?* He impatiently drew the collar of his dark cloak around his neck and glanced up at the heavy clouds. *Enough of her*, he thought. He had his own work—to find an assassin and bring him back to Sicily to stand trial. He had a life to return to as count and heir to the castle and Redwan galleons.

A dozen Byzantine soldiers stood along the front of the bridge holding flaring torches, and again Tancred wondered how he had permitted himself to become foolishly involved in the difficulty that lay ahead of him in trying to cool the riled temper of Duke Godfrey. What of his own ill temper; who would soothe him?

The heavier rain began to descend and glistened in the torch-light pelting the hides of the horses mounted with imperial guardsmen under his command—as if he wanted them! He was a loner and wished to remain so. What did he care of Greek soldiers?

The muscled black stallion named Apollo, belonging to Helena, stood saddled and waiting for him beside Hakeem, his Moorish friend from Sicily—perhaps the only man he could trust in all the empire. Hakeem, cynical as ever, sat with barely a smile on his lean, savage face astride his "infidel" horse, an Arabian mare.

Tancred came down the guard castle steps, his iron-strapped boots crunching on the stone. He was followed by his commanding officer, Philip, equally garbed in baronial uniform. Philip, disdainful and elegantly handsome, tossed a swatch of dark hair from his aristocratic forehead and eyed Tancred with masked dislike. Tancred knew he hated him; they had clashed from the moment they had met on the Danube River when Helena had come between them. Yet Philip needed Tancred to safeguard his position. Their dislike for each other was militarily cloaked with muted indifference as they walked through the rain and toward the bridge where the unit of soldiers waited. At the bridge, they paused.

Philip had recently been promoted to fill the position of minister of war, secured not by his military experience and wisdom, but by court intrigue, and perhaps poison as well. Tancred heard through members of the imperial guard that Irene of Troy was the power behind Philip. For her purposes she could wield poison as skillfully as a knight did his sword.

Tancred was aware of the risk coming from the leopard-eyed woman who cornered her quarry. Recently, it had taken more of his skill to avoid her seductive traps than it had to escape the Red-wan Castle in Sicily with a dozen guards on his trail. However, it was now to his advantage that the flaxen-haired Irene needed him to deal with the Normans, for it granted him opportunity to gain information on his enemies.

Although Philip's abilities were in question, Tancred wisely kept his feelings for the man as inscrutable as he did his response to Irene when too often called to her side on some question she wished answered, or as an escort for her chariot. He wondered if Helena had heard of their frequent company and what she might make of it.

As for Philip, Tancred had no confidence in his leadership. He remembered the incident on the road to Wieselburg by the Danube River months earlier. At that time, Philip was risking the lives of the men under him and putting Helena at risk of capture by the ruthless Rhinelander brigands. And now, in order to become minister of war, Philip had surrendered her to the prince of Antioch.

What manner of coward would give up the woman he truly wanted? Tancred believed that Philip did want Helena, and that in his own selfish way he may even love her. The thought was disturbing. What would Helena do if Philip unexpectedly forsook all to run away with her?

No chance of that. Philip was not that heroic, thought Tancred as he put on his helmet, hearing the drops of rain pelting against the steel. He drew the chin strap and fastened it, his eyes meeting Philip's.

Philip smirked, the cleft in his chin showing. "You are under orders to convince Duke Godfrey to swear his military allegiance to the emperor."

"He will not vow his fealty," said Tancred too easily. "It is not their way. They are proud and independent."

Philip's jaw tightened. "He must swear. Enough death and fighting. Tell him we shall cut off all food supplies to his army if he does not return with you in peace to the imperial palace."

Tancred showed none of the disdain he felt as he looked out across the dark waters toward the distant castles where Godfrey and his knights were housed and waiting for the imminent arrival of the other princes and their armies. The emperor had already sipped the bitter cup of his first military run-in with the Ironmen of the West.

The knights were not like the superstitious horde of peasants who had followed the monk named Peter the Hermit as he rode his donkey across Europe. The peasant crusade under Peter had met with a massacre by the Turks months earlier, but the Ironmen were deadly knights in steel, riding chargers and carrying powerful long blades. One vicious and powerful swipe of that Norman long blade could lop an opponent in half.

Now there was impatience among Godfrey's nobles and knights to be about the business of war for which they had left their home castles. There was a lack of supplies, misunderstanding between the duke and the emperor, and now the emperor had cut off the food supplies in order to force their leader into becoming his sworn vassal-son, something Godfrey refused to do.

Since Tancred was considered by the emperor and Philip to be of the same western mindset, they appealed to him to make his fellow knight yield to terms of peace.

Philip's dark eyes gazed coolly at Tancred as the rain dripped off his hat. "The emperor cannot state too strongly the seriousness with which he looks upon the duke's recent attack on a squad of imperial soldiers. They were sent to watch his rowdy men. Godfrey's men attacked, leaving not one of the emperor's soldiers alive."

Tancred watched him calmly, remaining silent.

"Godfrey is now master of the open country around Constantinople," continued Philip. "At the same time he refuses to take the oath of vassalage to the emperor."

"I'll do what I can." Tancred walked to Apollo, and taking the reins from a sober-faced Hakeem, he placed his boot into the stirrup and mounted.

Philip appeared furious with his calm. "Do not report back to me unless you bring the barbarian."

Tancred scanned him and was about to ride across the bridge when someone shouted from behind on the road. He waited, and Philip turned as a horseman galloped up. In the torchlight the courier was seen bearing the wet and drooping flag of the guard castle of Herion. He rode to Philip, saluting.

"News on the Norman army, Excellency."

Tancred exchanged quick glances with Hakeem. At last! The news they had been long anticipating.

"The army of Prince Bohemond remained in Kastur for many days while they entertained their prayers and feasting. But the towns of Pelagonia, hearing that Bohemond was coming, did fear and fortify themselves, expecting trouble, remembering the crusaders under the monk Peter the Hermit."

"Cannot these wolves restrain their warfare for even a day?" demanded Philip.

"Word has arrived of fighting and a town was burnt. Whose fault it was is unclear."

"Where are they now?" inquired Tancred, unable to restrain his keen interest.

"They crossed the river Vardar."

"And the emperor's forces are there?" asked Philip.

"The Turks and Petchenegs were waiting. They engaged him in a heavy battle."

Philip's mouth tightened. "How did it fare?"

"The imperial force was beaten back—and this same Bohemond is now but days from Constantinople."

Tancred was not surprised that so much information was known about Bohemond, since the emperor's spies were posted along the route to watch for his coming. He wondered what had provoked the Normans to attack the town.

The courier leaned toward Philip with a letter. "From General Taticus."

Tancred looked on in silence as Philip read the message beneath the flickering firelight. A minute later he looked up at him and excitement stirred hotly in his dark eyes.

"Your business with Godfrey must be consummated hastily. As the emperor's liaison you will ride to greet the Norman lord as soon as possible. He must be convinced to enter Constantinople alone, except for a bodyguard."

Tancred wondered if convincing Bohemond to ride in alone was possible, but he affected confidence. "I shall ride to Bohemond as soon as I meet with Godfrey."

He rode with the others across the wet bridge, the horses' hoofs echoing upon the planks. Apollo's black mane glistened beneath the flickering torches carried by the soldiers.

Hakeem leaned toward him, his eyes twinkling with malicious humor. "Can the Greek king trust you, master, you being a rapacious barbarian Norman?"

Tancred grinned at him. "It is you, infidel, who had best watch his turbaned head when we ride into Godfrey's camp. They may decide to spit and roast you over their fire."

Hakeem grinned back, his white teeth showing, and he patted his scimitar. "Then I must teach them a few Moorish tricks."

Tancred sobered. "Better yet, save your tricks for Antioch. I will need all the help I can get when we arrive, just the two of us within its walls. Do not forget the true cause for which we have come from Sicily."

Hakeem's humor dampened. "I have not forgotten your cousin Mosul. Perhaps it is best that I slip silently away to Antioch and await you there."

"The very thing I was to suggest, Father of Spies. Do nothing to alert Mosul. Wait for me. But keep your eye on him until I arrive."

Hakeem scanned him. "Will you come as a Norman?"

Tancred thought of the crusader army ahead of him bearing the crimson cross. "It is my intention to arrive before Antioch is under Norman siege, but who knows what fortune may come upon me between now and then? One thing is certain, I shall soon lay aside the uniform of the Greek and seek to come as a Moor."

Hakeem grinned and lifted a casual salute as he pulled back, riding to the side and allowing the contingent of soldiers to pass by.

Tancred's meeting in the castle with Godfrey of Bouillon went as he had expected. For several hours the truce he had requested between Godfrey's forces and the emperor's held, but the crusader refused to capitulate to the emperor's terms as distrust grew. He paced an upper chamber where torches mounted on the walls cast fleeting light upon the rugs from Tabriz.

Duke Godfrey was in his thirties and his appearance measured up to the standards of the canons of beauty held in the *chansons de geste* for a knightly liege. Tall with broad shoulders and narrow hips, his eyes were a fierce gray; his hair, the color of reddish gold, brushed the edge of the collar on his tunic. The crusader's crimson cross was embroidered above his heart on the thick leather tunic.

A handsome and arrogant Frenchman was also present. Prince

Hugh, brother of the king of France, was aligning himself with Tancred in trying to convince the duke to relent and swear his fealty to the emperor. As Tancred had suspected, the duke would not be influenced. While Tancred rested his muscular frame against the stone wall near a small window looking below into the castle courtyard, the duke turned hotly to Hugh, his gray eyes smoldering.

"You, a French prince! You did leave your own country as a king with wealth and strong following. Now look at you!" he gestured impatiently. "You have come down from that dignity like a slave. You come here like a man who has won a great thing from the emperor because he gives you meager gifts, to bid me do the same. Nay! Are we not lords in our own western realms?"

Hugh looked at him crossly and emptied his goblet, setting it down noisily. "We ought to have remained at home and not meddled in matters here."

"It is too late to think of that!"

"But since we are here, in a strange land without supplies, we have sore need of the emperor's good favor. If we do not gain it, matters will go ill with us."

Bored, Tancred watched the two proud warriors butting wills. His Norman ancestry had accustomed him to many such disagreements between proud men who were not quick to compromise when oversized egos were threatened.

Of the two crusader nobles before him, Hugh was pragmatic and more inclined to prefer the comforts he had left behind in France. Godfrey, however, felt scorn for the favors of the emperor, seeing them as trifles which insulted his honor. How could he swear to fight for the emperor when he had already taken oath to the religious call? he insisted. Had not his sword been blessed by the Church? He was a knight of Christ on a great journey of deprivation, and he insisted that he battled for the honor of Christianity and the freedom of Jerusalem from the mocking infidel!

A cynic, Tancred suspected that Godfrey's selfless fervor might also envision carving out a kingdom of his own in the Holy Land. Weary of wasting time with bickering nobles, his own quest for locating Mosul gnawed at him, and he was anxious to meet Nicholas. For Helena's sake, Tancred could not bring himself to break his obligation to Philip and ride out a free man to join Hak-eem.

Godfrey said with scorn, "I have sworn my vassalship to King Henry of the Holy Roman Empire! I have taken the cross to fight the enemies of Christ! And shall I bow to this Greek emperor as some slave? Nay!"

"What choice have you?" interrupted Tancred. "Remember, the emperor has the upper hand. The crusaders will need the emperor as you battle for Jerusalem. Despite your intentions to avoid an oath of vassalage, your army is held captive as long as he holds the bread basket. What will you do? The fields are bare. There is naught to forage until summer. In the meantime the emperor has refused you the liberty to buy food. If not for your sake, or your knights, then think of your chargers. If the horses and mules and oxen are in weak condition before you even cross the Bosporus, how shall you face the blazing heat and drought of summer? Your chargers and men will faint before the arrows and scimitars of the Turks."

"He is right," pressed Hugh. "An army cannot fight in heavy armor without food and water."

The duke looked with irritation on Tancred. "If I did not know you to be a Norman with a reputation for courage, we would also suspect you, our brother," said Godfrey. "For what are these men out in the courtyard guarding your horses but weak Greeks?"

"I am not here to defend the emperor's soldiers. They can defend their own honor. And if I did not know you to be a knight, I would take offense."

Godfrey seemed about to relent when the sound of galloping horses interrupted. Tancred looked down through the window, expecting trouble. In the torchlight a group of foot soldiers carried some of the duke's wounded men toward the front of the castle. Godfrey now had his opportunity to refuse negotiations with the emperor.

Within minutes after Tancred gathered with the others in the castle hall below, Godfrey's brother, Prince Baldwin, anxious for battle, called for revenge.

"Was not our situation already ominous before this night? And yet the emperor has insulted good men even more by sending

Moslem infidels here to police us in the towns we occupy until our western brothers arrive."

"What happened?" demanded Tancred, suspecting Godfrey's men of initiating trouble.

Prince Baldwin looked at him sharply, noting his Byzantine uniform, but realizing he was the son of Count Dreux Redwan, he grudgingly showed respect. "They attacked us like ravenous wolves, cutting off a party of our most trusted men." He looked at his older brother, who was scowling.

No matter that Godfrey's men may have deserved to be halted by the Byzantine guard, it was seen as a knight's duty to defend his soiled honor. Any call for reason and calm would be swiftly rejected. He saw Godfrey looking at him from across the hall.

"You see how the emperor has broken his own truce. Byzantine treachery! You ask me to return to the city with you to bow the knee and surrender to his demands like a groveling piglet." He turned to a wounded Rhinelander who sat up from the floor, holding his arm and leaning against the wall.

"What befell you?" demanded Godfrey.

The Rhinelander wiped his sweating face on his sleeve and pushed back his matted black hair. "The attack was unprovoked, my liege. Many good men are dead. Men who would fight the infidels for Jerusalem. Others are sorely wounded. Some of our esquires are now captives! Avenge your honor, my liege."

Tancred took him in, judging him a troublemaker. He remembered all too well the Rhinelanders' attack on the Jews in Worms, Cologne, and the other towns along the Danube, and he felt the man could not be trusted.

"It is not Duke Godfrey's honor that is tarnished, but plunderers," Tancred insisted. "Do you swear to an unprovoked attack?"

The knight's eyes noticed him for the first time and turned hard, scanning the black-and-crimson uniform of the imperial cavalry.

"You question me, Greek! Those of same uniform attacked our esquires out foraging for food in one of the towns. We rode swiftly to their rescue, but the Greeks outnumbered us and beat us down with their swords."

Tancred took him in. "Foraging for food and ready to pay the Greek farmers for their toil? Or were your esquires plundering their daughters as well as bread?"

The Rhinelander tried in anger to get to his feet, but Godfrey gestured for another man to hold him back.

"These esquires, where be they?" said Godfrey.

The knight was staring angrily at Tancred. "Outside, dead. If my word is questioned, my liege, then call the French knight waiting outside. It was he and a band of his footmen who came upon me and others left to die in the field."

Godfrey impatiently gestured to an esquire. "Bring the Frenchman in."

A moment later Tancred gazed on a wounded esquire and a French knight, their faces smeared with dried sweat and blood.

"Monsieur," breathed the knight. "He speaks truth. I and a body of knights sworn to the king of France did come upon a band of esquires under attack. We fought to aid them but killed only twenty of the attackers. We brought back your own for Christian burial, and this wounded Rhinelander."

Godfrey, frowning, turned to his brothers and several lead knights to discuss the situation, while the injured French esquire and knight both slumped to the floor. Tancred went to attend the knight first.

The Rhinelander remained sprawled on the floor watching him sullenly. "My liege, will you make plans before this man who serves the Greek king?"

Tancred refused to respond, concentrating instead on stopping the bleeding from the gash across the knight's shoulder.

"He is a Norman," snapped Godfrey. "A friend, a cousin of Prince Bohemond."

"A Norman! In a Greek uniform?" The French knight looked over at him, taking the flagon of wine offered him by another esquire. "Speak not ill of a brother-knight in his presence, Rhinelander," he snarled. "Lest he cut you in pieces. See how he doth aid me who bleeds and is ready to die?"

The Rhinelander fell into sullen silence, but Tancred felt his angry gaze.

True to Godfrey's desire for retribution, the crusaders made plans to ride out for a successful ambush.

"The Turkish infidels who are in their hire as mercenaries will be distributed to our knights as captives," said Godfrey's brother Baldwin.

Tancred walked up to Duke Godfrey. "The Rhinelander is lying."

"How do you know?"

"I know them. They were out stealing and terrorizing the farms. Any revenge now and the emperor will attack and withhold food. He is also a soldier of the blood. He once fought the Normans near Thessalonica. He will not overlook an injustice done to his men."

"Injustice to our honor has already been done," argued Baldwin, but Godfrey was grave.

"We will talk alone in the upper chamber," he told Tancred.

There was so much depending on this night, thought Helena, her heart beating chaotically. She did not expect her daring venture to go uncontested. Doubts thwarted her attempts at calm. When she and Bardas rode across the bridge toward the castle where Duke Godfrey and his chief princes and nobles had set up their headquarters, it was late in the evening and the rains had ceased.

The stone streets of the town were noisy with western warriors and she scanned the throng wearing various pieces of armor, most of which she did not recognize. She was completely covered in a deep-hooded cloak of patterned blue-and-gold brocade, but that she was Byzantine, as well as the chariot, must have been obvious to all. They stared in cautious silence, some with suspicion as their eyes swept Bardas, who looked about with concern.

"Beneath a thin veneer of gallantry, they are uncivilized," Bardas murmured.

She shuddered beneath her cloak. "There are princes and nobles among them also. Belted knights, I hear, who would fight and die for a lady. But you are right. We must get past the common peasant-soldiers to the blooded princes and knights of the French and Normans."

Bardas showed his skepticism as he glanced about. "Even Redwan claims to be a count. They all boast of kingly blood, but who were their fathers? Savages from the frozen North and tribes of barbarians from the thick forests of the West."

Their chariot moved noisily down the stone street, and the horses snorted to a rumbling halt before the castle fortress. Helena sensed the smell of battle in the smoky air that drifted from the cooking fires along the water's edge where the foot soldiers had set up camp.

Bardas cast his circular cloak of crimson over his wide shoulder and steadied Helena's arm as she stepped down from the chariot.

A rugged knight emerged into the torchlight from the darkened steps where he'd been keeping watch. His shoulder-length black hair was vainly groomed. With a measuring appraisal of Bardas, his gaze then moved to Helena.

Bardas spoke in pompous Latin: "I bring a woman of the highest nobility to the safety of the castle of Duke Godfrey of Bouillon. It is important she speak with the emperor's liaison, Tancred Redwan."

"Count Redwan holds counsel with our liege. Who shall I say calls upon him?"

"The daughter of the notable Greek general."

The knight appeared humored. "And of which notable Greek general do you speak?"

Bardas took a step forward, but Helena lay hold of his arm. "No, Bardas," she whispered.

The knight offered an exaggerated bow. "I will send word to our liege posthaste. Come, Byzantine, do enter the castle with your honorable lady."

She heard Bardas grumble about scornful manners, but Helena was far less worried about homage than finding Tancred. She gathered her cloak about her snugly and walked ahead with Bardas close behind.

Helena had not proceeded far when the door opened and several warriors strode from the castle. They cast appreciative glances, first at the chariot and fine horses, then at Helena, curiosity reflecting in their tanned faces.

Bardas kept his hand on the hilt of his sheathed sword, but there was no mistaking the challenge in his voice. "Step aside," he ordered. "The lady wishes to pass."

The warriors glanced at one another, and as though his superior attitude amused them, they exchanged brief smiles. Bardas glowered menacingly, and several threw back their heads and laughed outright, while another spoke something in French. The warriors all seemed to chorus their approval.

Helena believed them to be conceited Frenchmen, and under safer conditions and farther at bay, she would have been curious about them. These were quite different from the Rhinelanders she had met along the Danube River. These knights were even taller than Bardas and darkly handsome. All wore their hair long and looked to have dangerous appetites and bold dark eyes. And they carried a host of dreadful-looking weapons.

While neither she nor Bardas could understand their speech, there was no mistaking the amusement in their laughter. The idea could easily have rankled her pride, except for her urgent mission.

A powerful man donned in a fur-lined cloak appeared in the doorway. He must have been a nobleman, for the others turned as his demanding voice interrupted their laughter.

Seeing their smiles and exaggerated bows, Helena swept past them with dignity into the castle hall, feeling the nerves along her spine tighten.

The large hall was lit with flaming torches. Wood burned in the wall-sized hearth. A roasted pig hung on a spit and its fat sputtered and sizzled, becoming the only sound in the hall as the men fell silent at her entry.

She glanced about cautiously. More knights congregated at a long trestle table at the back wall or stood leisurely near the hearth with flagons of wine. There were noblemen wearing fur-collared cloaks; all were impeccably groomed, and their rugged faces bore some hint of kingly bloodline. Eyes, alert with musing interest, pondered her. Several shifted their gaze to Bardas, measuring his strength, as all knights do when meeting a new warrior.

Helena noticed another grouping of men and took heart. Friars in brown or black cowls sat in a small circle reading from a parchment, and their young male attendants carried amber rosaries.

Whether friars, knights, or noblemen, all of them wore the same red cross sewn onto their tunics, and all had weapons.

Helena's presence created an uneasy silence; then the noblemen began to speak among themselves in low tones, either in northern French or German. The low guttural voices of the Rhinelanders kindled a raw memory of the frightening hour months earlier when she had hidden in the forest along the Danube. Philip's entourage had been savagely attacked, with many killed. She shivered, remembering.

Like a tiger with its cub, Bardas stepped closer to her side, his marble eyes taking them all in slowly and with obvious distrust, as though they were a pack of hungry dogs with one bone to be fought over. Just then, the French nobleman who had escorted them reached a hand to grasp hold of her arm. She didn't know if he merely intended to lead her to the chiseled steps and up to the chamber where the Duke of Lower Lorraine waited with Tancred, for the moment he touched her, Bardas's sword whispered from his scabbard.

"Foul fingers greased with pig fat! Do you touch the daughter of General Lysander?"

Helena's breath caught with alarm. Whether or not the nobleman understood his speech was unclear, but he understood the meaning of the drawn blade. His dark eyes snapping like embers from the hearth, he too unsheathed his sword, tossed aside his cloak, and stepped back.

He barked in French what must have been a disdainful challenge to Bardas. The other men moved back against the wall to watch. At once, Helena rushed between them to avert death. Did the nobleman understand Latin? "No, this man is my bodyguard! He acted to protect me."

He looked at her sullenly. "Bodyguard or nay, the Greek has vilified my honor!"

"I have the blood of a Spartan!" hissed Bardas proudly.

The Frenchman gave him a dissecting rake. "A Spartan? You? By the wings of a falcon you are a weak woman! Look—" He called to his fellows, pointing mockingly at Bardas. "He wears silk leggings—red—with pretty gold strings!"

Laughter echoed and bounced against the castle walls.

"Do stay your sword, Sir Knight!" demanded Helena. "Bardas—step back at once!"

"I am Robert of Paris, and there are few knights in all my country who are willing to fight me. I once waited beside the road from sunup to sunset, and none would venture forth to contest. And will this pretty fellow in red silk insult my honor by waving his sword in my face? Surely it is stained in goat's milk and not infidel blood!"

"Let him come, mistress. I shall undo him at once! I shall leave one side for the ravens, the other for rats."

Although Helena's heart sounded in her ears, she was able to conceal her trembling knees with a pretended regal lift of her chin. "Silence, both of you," her eyes coming squarely to the Frenchman. "I do not doubt your valor or strength, Sir Knight, nor do your fellow warriors. But I am related to the royal family in Constantinople. And I shall have any man here thrown into a dungeon to keep company with hungry bears if you lift a hand against my bodyguard."

Uncertainty reigned in the chamber, then turned to appreciative laughter as Helena stood her ground between them, appearing undaunted. *Tancred, where are you!*

A command sounded forth on the stairs above her and she turned hopefully, her deep brown eyes wide and warm.

"That was ill done, Robert. Am I your true liege, or but a mongrel in the goat field that you deign to treat my guests like enemies?"

Helena stared up at the man, speechless, for he was obviously Duke Godfrey and his appearance was not what she had expected.

The French knight called Robert of Paris gestured impatiently toward Bardas. "My liege, this Greek in woman's dress has insulted my sword!"

"I am a Spartan," boasted Bardas again. "And I fought beside General Lysander against the Moslem hordes. And I slew twenty infidels with my sword before my master fell to his death, a saint! And if this barbarian doth not like my red cloth—then I challenge him to take it from me!"

Godfrey stood, hands on hips, surveying one warrior, then the other. Rousing anger colored his face.

Helena had heard that he was from the lineage of Charlemagne, the first leader in Western Europe after the fall of the Roman Empire to bring the warring factions together. Charlemagne had died in the eighth century and the Holy Roman Empire had again split into numerous kingdoms. Henry was now the emperor, and though he had not come on the crusade to the Holy Land, he had sent his relative Duke Godfrey.

Godfrey was a handsome man, one who was comfortable with his airs of dignity, yet unquestionably a warrior. He looked anything but the wild barbarian Helena had been told to expect.

He came down the stone steps in a long mantle of fur, his gray eyes swerving from the Frenchman to the immobile Bardas.

"You, Spartan!" he spoke to Bardas. "The color of your cloth is of no concern to me. But you enter my castle boldly waving your sword. For that alone, I myself could take your head! I forbear for the sake of the lady. Speak! At whose bidding do you come?"

Bardas's eyes narrowed and he glanced at Helena. She discreetly lifted her hand, though the gesture was not lost on the duke. That Godfrey already believed himself insulted by the emperor was clear, and she guessed that he had been discussing that injury with Tancred before she arrived.

Helena stepped forward. "Your pardon, sir, but the bodyguard is mine. He is rash—but sworn to protect me. The vow lies heavily upon his heart and oft times prompts him to move too quickly." Her eyes begged his silence as she looked at Bardas. His gaze averted, the veins protruding on his wide neck betraying internal turmoil, yet he remained silent and sheathed his sword with an energetic thrust. The French knight reluctantly turned his back, then strode to the table and snatched up a flagon of wine.

"The emperor does not know I am here," said Helena to the duke. "I have come of my own initiative, alone and through dangerous territory with naught but my bodyguard. I must of dire necessity speak to the Norman they call Tancred Redwan."

Godfrey looked mildly curious as he studied her. Helena drew back her hood, showing thick and shiny ebony tresses embedded with a lavish display of creamy pearls. The lovely Greek contour to her face and the look of nobility once again brought silence to the chamber.

"I am Helena Lysander, daughter of the deceased General Lysander, nephew of the empress."

She walked toward him where he stood on the steps above her and held her head high. When she stopped below the steps she deliberately lowered her head with deference to his title, knowing well how much honor and esteem meant to the princes, barons, and feudal lords of the West.

"I bring you greeting, Duke Godfrey. My venture to come here this late hour is wrought with many risks, but I rejoice now to be safely in your presence and with your company of honorable knights." She looked about at the circle of strong men who also watched her with avid interest. The noblemen looked flattered and smiled, their white teeth showing.

"Your servants, demoiselle," they echoed smoothly one by one, bowing low toward her.

Helena smiled sweetly at each one, and sighs filled the hall. One rushed forward and knelt at her feet. "Demoiselle, I am yours! To die for you!"

Laughter erupted from the others over their mesmerized fellow knight.

Helena had salvaged the moment from further tension, even if she had resorted to flattery to do so—a deed not altogether noble.

"Be on guard, mademoiselle," came a voice from the gallery above her. "Your charms may get more than you bargained for. You will soon have them drinking from your slipper and marching to bring you the head of Kalid."

Helena's head turned swiftly from the kneeling knight to look up at Tancred. Her heart felt an odd lurch as her eyes rested upon him. The black-and-crimson uniform of the emperor's imperial guard only enhanced his veritable good looks.

The duke glanced toward the upper gallery where Tancred lounged against a pillar. "You know the general's daughter, Tancred?"

"We are related."

Helena's surprise showed at his daring remark, obviously offered in ironic amusement. Even Godfrey paused at the unlikely suggestion.

A hint of a smile formed on Tancred's mouth. "She is the niece of Bishop Nicholas Lysander, my esteemed and beloved godfather," came Tancred's reply.

Such temerity! Even if he knew Nicholas, they were not related.

"Then if Nicholas rides beside Bohemond, his niece is also our friend." Godfrey looked at Helena. "You shall be well cared for while under our protection, Lady."

Helena thanked him and expected Tancred to leave the gallery and come down the steps to meet her. When he did not, she looked at him.

"I wish to speak with you, my *kinsman*. I have traversed a worthy distance in the rain."

He offered a gallant bow. "As you wish, my lady. Shall I come down to you, or would you come up to me?"

There was a chuckle from the knights, but Helena ignored it and ascended the steps, her cloak trailing behind like the train of a princess. "I wish to speak with you alone."

"Your every wish, Lady, is my command."

The rogue. "You are indeed gallant, Sir Knight. Bardas, you may come with me."

Halfway up the steps, Bardas looked down on the unpleasant faces watching him, but Helena determinedly climbed the rough stone toward an upper meeting chamber.

Outside the door, Helena paused and drew in a breath. *Lord, guide my way*, she prayed, then turned to Bardas and whispered, "Wait here."

CHAPTER 6
Knave of Hearts

Shielding her inner trembling with a pose of dignity and a calmness of soul, Helena swept into the chamber with its vaulted ceiling and flaring torches encircling the wall. A fire sizzled in the stone hearth. A flash of lightning illuminated the small open window, followed by a lionlike rumble from the region of the dark Bosporus.

Tancred shut the heavy door laden with straps of iron and turned to face Helena, his stormy blue-gray eyes fixed evenly upon her. Now that they were alone he did not mask his irritation over her presence.

"It is dangerous to have come. Do you make it an ambition to place yourself in peril, or dare I instead permit the conceited thought you could not endure another day without seeing me?"

His audacity never ceased to amaze her, and under his gaze, she fought to keep back the emotion welling up in her heart.

Pretending indifference, she went past him to the hearth. "How ill of you to flatter your sense of worth, sir. You are quite like the rest of your egotistical kin downstairs," and she glanced at him coolly, scanning him, "except of course, you do not vainly parade about in fragrantly oiled hair."

His brow lifted in reply, then he folded his arms and leaned against the door. "If I permitted my hair to grow like Samson, madame, would you be more inclined to soothe my head on your skirts?"

Helena whipped about, her eyes sparking, a stain of warmth on her fair cheeks.

Tancred affected gravity at her insult, again bowing.

"I am woefully in error, damsel. My daring has distressed you. I have offended your superior position, and rightly so! I forget I am but a barbarian, whereas you, fair damsel, are a noble Byzantine, and I am not fit but to bow as a bondslave before your glimmering slippers."

He looked at her with a faint smile.

"Surely," he said, "is there naught I can do to win your slightest favor?"

"Hold your tongue, sir. There is one thing you can do," Helena rushed indignantly, and when he straightened from the door and gave her an inquiring look, she snapped, "You can vow your service to me instead of Philip."

He looked as if to muse. "A matter to consider. Is there a dragon you would send me forth to slay for the favor of your merest glance?"

Helena dare not think of the effect of her favor upon him and tore her eyes from his. She walked to the trestle table and ran her hand over its rough surface. She found this man attractive—too much so—and she didn't like it.

"As I thought," he said with mock disappointment. "Then pray tell whose head do you wish as a trophy in a basket? Philip's?" he inquired innocently.

She turned abruptly at the tone in his voice.

"Another disappointment," he said. "I see by your righteous indignation how you unwisely uphold him in your memory despite his cowardice. Ah, then! It must be—yes, the head of the 'golden goddess' you wish!"

Helena flounced toward the door as if to leave, but he stepped in her path, bowing deeply at the waist.

Tancred's eyes flickered with malicious amusement. "A raw jest, uncalled for. Pardon. We both know how fond you are of dear Lady Irene."

It was on her tongue to make a quip about his own reported interest in her aunt, but she would only favor his conceit by allowing him to know that the slave girls whispered of his popularity with Lady Irene.

"I wish to hire you," she stated flatly.

He visibly winced. "I bleed at your voice. Such an utterly unbecoming tone you take in wooing my heart—"

"I do not 'woo' your affections, sir, nor would I be so foolish as to be concerned with your heart!"

"Foolish indeed."

"I wish to buy your sword!"

His masculine presence seemed to challenge her. "Could so fair and sweet a face hold such a biting little tongue? Such an un-Christian attitude . . ." and he sighed. "I cannot sell my sword. The very thought offends my knightly honor."

Her eyes narrowed. He was deliberately frustrating her, of course, but why?

"Your pride is most unbecoming, madame."

Her eyes widened at his temerity. "My pride, sir? Did you say *my* pride? Such false humility on your part! Such arrogance! What of yours!"

Helena's retort did not scathe him, and because his gaze was earthy and distracting, she went to the hearth and held her cold palms toward the embers.

The silence became uncomfortable.

"As for risk, Sir Knight, I have lived and breathed it since a child. Confronting one of your arrogant friends below when I arrived was naught else but what I expected from barbarian men who think of nothing but their prowess with sword and lance."

She turned her head slightly to study him.

His brow lifted. "Your tongue lashes me, Lady."

"Good. I wish it so."

"Yes. No doubt. You would have me beg and plead for the trifles of your benign mercies. Which makes me wonder why you came here at all, seeing I am a barbarian dog hardly fit for your favor."

She remembered the sighs from Zoe and other silly women in

the nobility. "Surely I did not come because of your handsome face, sir."

"That you suggest you notice sends my blood pounding, madame."

She stared stiffly at the fire. "How you presume."

Tancred leaned against the door. "Then presumptions aside, let us talk openly." He walked to the hearth where he could see her face. "I trust your hot-tempered bodyguard to have warned you against coming here. Surely you know of the fighting between the duke and your emperor? You have arrived at a moment of danger."

"I am aware. It was necessary."

"It was not. I sent word through Bardas that I would contact you when I returned to Constantinople."

The gold threads in her Byzantine tunic glimmered with importance. "And I, sir, sent word to you at the Venetian quarter along the Golden Horn as you bid me!"

A lone brow lifted. "Yes, and I received your command."

"Did you indeed! And yet you did not come?"

Tancred's smile was faintly sardonic. His gaze briefly took her in with apparent disinterest. "I did not choose to come."

She met his challenge evenly until bright spots of color formed in her cheeks.

"Might I hope you were languishing with disappointment?"

She gave a laugh. "Personal disappointment? Oh, indeed, hardly!" She turned and threw off her cloak, folding her arms indifferently. "It is your services I long for."

"Ardently?"

"Has it escaped you in your duties to Philip that I am soon to be given to a Moslem prince in Antioch? A detestable rogue as conceited as you, a man whom I have since discovered to be one of your cousins? It appears you have many—one whom you claim to be an assassin."

He turned serious. "I do not claim. Mosul is so. A ruthless swordsman, a murderer."

His words brought a moment of sobriety to the chamber. How could he treat her plight so casually? "And Kalid is his cousin also," she said. "I am to be sent there. Or have you forgotten so soon your odious transgression of eavesdropping in Philip's chambers?"

Tancred glanced toward the small open window as though listening for some unwanted sound. Helena too listened but heard only her anxious heart and the noise of guards milling around a communal fire in the courtyard.

"How could I forget so entertaining a spectacle?" He laughed softly. "It is a treasured moment."

"Your gallantry is tainted; your armor rusts. I suggest your boasted friendship and loyalty to my uncle was a bluff," she accused, frustration in her voice. "Else you would not look upon my dire need with such indifference."

"Accuse me of much, but not of looking upon your destiny with indifference. I could, Lady, favor you with my devotion, if you were not so overtly spoiled and intemperate."

"You dare—"

"There is always hope. Nicholas will become your new guardian to teach you manners and charitable graces. If not he, then I may suffice. Perhaps when our futures are more free to intertwine. Now we are both trapped in the times. I could not pursue if you begged me to, for I have no liberty. And you are yet deceived into believing you love Philip."

Astounded by his audacity, Helena could only stare at him.

Tancred smiled. "Then also, my memory of Kalid is always present. A knight does not forget an enemy. Nor will I. Fear not, it is not my intention to surrender anything of esteemed value to an opponent. And Kalid is now that."

She looked at him quickly.

"He harbors the assassin who killed Derek," he explained. "So I must confront Kalid and Mosul both—for different reasons."

"I would hire your sword for protection from Kalid."

"Ah, my sword . . ." and he slipped it from its scabbard and contemplated the weapon as though it were the Holy Grail, yet a faint smile contradicted his awe. "There is none like it in all the West. There are relics in its hilt. Surely it is blessed, ready to fight for a holy cause. But my scimitar!" He sighed. "It was forged by an infidel Saracen! And now what? They are in conflict. I am divided!"

"Perhaps you are forever doomed to contest between the two," she said ruefully.

"Which sword do you come to me seeking?" he quipped.

"Perhaps both!"

"Then it seems you have forgotten," and he went to the window and looked below as if expecting riders.

"Forgotten?"

He looked at her. "Did I not tell you that night in Philip's chamber my sword was not for hire?"

She remembered that humiliating night, but she wished he would forget it. She pretended indifference.

"Nor is my service for hire now, if that is what you have come for." He sheathed his blade.

Helpless at first, she was disarmed. "But I thought . . . you hinted . . . you would help me."

"You did not ask for help. Instead you came demanding, as a haughty princess to a barefoot slave. You wish me to bow, to plead for a kind word, to risk my head for naught but a smile. Such a relationship I find unworthy of us."

It wasn't so! How could she make him understand?

"Not only so," he continued, "but I have a previous obligation to your emperor, one I will fulfill because of honor, for I have sworn to him, although the duty may yet place me at risk."

Helena thought she knew what undertaking would place him in danger: riding into the camp of the approaching Normans as a liaison. Did he think there may be some who knew he had fled from Sicily? Certainly he didn't think Nicholas would turn against him? Unless, as Bardas insisted, he was not truly friendly with her uncle.

"Once I perform my duty as the emperor's liaison I must go. I have delayed too long," he mused, more to himself than to her. "The urgency of my quest cannot wait."

"But you accepted the position as liaison, knowing of the delay."

He looked at her, showing nothing. "Yes."

"Then—" she reasoned, "since you have accepted, and Philip pays you well, I shall pay you even more." She walked toward him, her gown rustling and shimmering. "I will pay you twice the wage of Philip."

"You think everything is bought and sold for a price. I am not a greedy man. Gold? I have enough." He looked back out the window.

"You are not refusing me because of loyalty to the emperor?"

"True, for loyalty is not bought. If I believed in him, and his cause, he would have it for honor's sake, not for gold."

She squelched the emerging flame of admiration. "But you do not believe in him, nor do you believe in Philip," she accused.

"Should I? Selfish ambition feeds the desires of his heart, even as it does the Moslems. Both claim the blessing of heaven. I suggest their zeal is provoked by the fires of hades. And as for Philip, he wants you for his own, yet he does not have the courage to relinquish his position to keep you. He desires the praise of those who bring him false security."

Tancred's failure to compromise aroused a secret spark of awe, yet how could she listen to these lies about Philip? Yes, he had failed her, he had his dreams and ambitions, but her love was not easily extinguished by failure alone, and she nurtured a hope that he would yet rise to the gallantry she knew lodged within his soul.

"But you sold your sword to Philip! Why not to me? If it is wages—"

"If I join him now, it is for a cause of my own."

She wondered that his taunts could provoke her ire. *I should feel nothing more for Philip, yet it is not so*, she thought, hurt. Philip had shamed her by his refusal to run away with her. He was willing for her marriage to Kalid to take place in Antioch. Yet, somehow, she still cared.

Tancred must have read her expression. "You sorely grieve me, madame," he said with mock dismay. "You waste many hours pining for him, though he lacks honor and courage."

"I do not pine!"

"As to why I serve in the imperial guard, it is only for a brief time. The Normans under Prince Bohemond arrive. If I wait a few weeks longer to ride to find the assassin who killed my brother, it is to join with Nicholas and," he added, "to make certain he knows of your arranged marriage to Kalid."

Helena gave him a side glance to try to measure any interest he may have in her future but could not read his thoughts. At least he shared a common interest in her uncle.

"Then you already know that the Normans are near the city."

"I was with Philip when the news was brought to Herion. Is that why you came?"

"I have learned you've been hired as liaison between the emperor and the Norman prince."

"More spies, madame?"

"They are my safeguard, sir. You will ride out soon to meet alone with the one you call Bohemond. I too must escape. I must ride with you to their camp. Bring me to Nicholas and I shall pay you double what Philip pays."

"Taking you with me would put you in greater danger. I ride to meet Bohemond alone."

In desperation she snatched her cloak and removed a small silver cloth bag. "It is full of gold besants." She pressed it into his hand. "After this, there will be more."

Tancred tossed it carelessly onto the stool as though refusing a drink of water. "Thank you, no. I am not to be hired so easily. A bag of gold coins? Even two?"

Her eyes searched his for some hidden meaning behind his apparent indifference. Was it genuine? It couldn't be.

"Then I shall pay you ten times that."

"No."

"Jewels. I have many."

"No."

Frustrated, she stepped back. In the glow of the fire the pearls in her hair blinked like tiny stars.

"The Lysander family owns lands in Athens," she confessed as an idea emerged. "You respect fine-blooded horses. You may keep Apollo, and I shall have Bardas deliver several mares for breeding. They will be worth much."

Still there was no response.

She scanned him. *What does he want?*

She drew in a breath. "And . . . as you know, I am heiress of the Castle of Hohms. If Nicholas agrees . . . I shall make it well worth your sword to bring me to him and then to the castle. Guard us there against our enemies and . . . and . . ." She stopped.

His blue-gray eyes reflected the first glimmer of interest. "And?"

Her expression showed nothing. "And I shall consider making you its seigneur."

The expression of his smile showed faint irony. "My uncle and adoptive father, Rolf Redwan, serves as seigneur. Why should I wish to replace a kin? He is a strong soldier. There are few better than he."

"Yes, but—"

"And as I once told you, I own a castle in Sicily—perhaps two, what would I do with another?"

"I thought, well . . ."

He scanned her casually. "Is not the castle your dowry?"

Her heart pounded madly. "Yes," she murmured.

He mused, watching her. "It is offered to the man who claims you in marriage?"

She busied herself replacing the money purse back into her cape. "You know it is."

The deliberate silence grew loud. Helena felt her cheeks beginning to flame, and frustrated with herself because he had managed to fluster her poise, she deliberately looked up and met his gaze evenly, lifting her chin a little to show she was yet in control— or was she?

Tancred was leaning against the wall, tapping his fingers thoughtfully.

Helena whisked past him, her back toward him, arms folded. "I will not marry you, Sir Knight."

He threw back his head and laughed.

Offended, she whirled. "You laugh at me!"

"I laugh, my lady, because I do not wish to marry you." He straightened, hands on hips, his handsome face amused, his eyes mocking her pride. "When I said I found you attractive, I did not mean to suggest that I would have you as my wife. Nay," he gave a wave of his hand, "I could not bear any woman so vain of face and form! So proud and haughty of spirit!"

She gasped, stung. "Sir! I am not that! I bow the knee to Christ. And my heart is humble before Him."

"An excellent beginning, but you must also show reverence to your earthly lord . . ." and he smiled. "Your husband, damsel. Did not Sarah call Abraham 'lord'?"

She glared at him. "I would never call *you* that."

He shrugged. "Nor would I call you my beloved."

"How dare you!"

"I dare. Now enough of this talk, Lady. I do not care for your castle, nor your trinkets, nor your hand in marriage. I am a knight. And I battle for truth and honor, out of pure gallantry." He lifted a brow. "So far, you have offered me nothing that woos my heart."

In what appeared to be false boredom, he sighed and lowered his muscular frame into the chair and stretched his booted legs before him, flecking a speck of dust from his black-and-scarlet uniform.

Helena had the mad impulse to snatch the bowl of fruit from the trestle table and hurl it at him, but that would have only justified his denunciation of her spoiled ways.

Her heart thudded loudly in her ears. She studied him through her lashes. *The cretin. Well, I will take no more of his smarting words deliberately tossed to see me flinch.*

She turned with dignity. "Then if you will not help me—"

"I did not say that."

Ah . . . he was rather quick to remedy his arrogance. She paused, waiting.

His eyes flickered with subdued amusement. "While I must regretfully decline your offer of marriage—"

She began to protest but he lifted a hand. "Your wishes will be considered further. I will think about the offer again, when I have freedom to give it my best musing."

Helena folded her arms. "You are generous, to be sure, sir. For how long will I need to wait for your answer?"

"You must be patient," he smiled. "I assure you it will be worth it in the end."

"Patient? When Kalid waits with a caravan to bring me to Antioch? I must hurry, and finding Nicholas will not wait."

"I would not worry about Kalid. And winning the castle is hardly what I have in mind. There is something much more valuable I intend to win."

Not worry about Kalid? Why would he say such a thing in so light a tone? Did he expect to confront him over their other cousin, Mosul? What did he expect to win? Something from Antioch?

"If not the castle, I own a perfume shop on the Mese."

"Keep your perfume. There are many in Constantinople you could hire—mercenaries of rare vintage with the sword. Your own Bardas hints of a warrior. Why is he not enough?"

"I wish your services for the same reason as Philip. You are not governed by politics as the Byzantine. You are uninvolved. We can trust you with our cause. As for Bardas, you may not tell by looking at him—but his sword arm was nearly cut off when he fought beside my father years ago. It is weak, but do not let him know I told you so. It never healed properly, so he keeps it covered."

"So that is why he uses his left hand. . . ."

"You noticed then?"

"It is my business to notice such things. For his sake, he must not growl so loudly when one is in your presence of whom he does not approve. All warriors are not as lenient as I."

Tancred, lenient? She might have laughed. Helena tried to read his expression, but it was a deliberate mask. She pressed urgently. "Then we have a truce, Sir Knight? I ask little from you except your service with the sword and to be brought to Nicholas."

His smile was sardonic. "Your estimation of my value is noteworthy. Then I will not disappoint your lofty expectations. The price for my sword, however, will be costly to you."

Her eyes did not waver this time. "I shall meet your price."

"Without hearing what it is?"

"I need your abilities and I am prepared to pay your price in gold, or lands."

He said nothing.

"I wait, Sir Knight. Your price?"

Tancred paused reflectively, and for a brief moment she thought that even he did not know what he wanted, that he was only teasing her to see her outrage at his boldness.

He must have seen her scrutiny, for his face was suddenly as smooth as any mask to shield her probing eyes. He stood, his every movement attractive and as lithe as any panther. "First, I shall hear the reason why your aunt schemes against you, then decide payment."

So! He knows how Irene plots against me? "What assurance will you give me that you will not go to her with information I hold important?"

"You have my promise. Accept it for what it is worth. If not, we will forget we had this meeting."

"We have a bargain, sir," she hastened.

He smiled. "You best sit down. You're looking vexed."

She could have told him why, and that he was part of the reason, but the knowledge would get her nowhere. He had walked to the hearth and offered a chair. Helena sat down as he stooped and lifted another section of wood onto the red coals.

"When you spoke of the Castle of Hohms you mentioned your father. He was General Lysander?"

"A brilliant military man," she said wistfully, remembering the years gone by when as a child she had waited with her mother for his return from war. There would always be a celebration at the villa, and for the season he was home they were happy.

"You spoke of him a moment ago as though he were alive. I was told otherwise."

Her eyes turned to the glowing embers. "He was killed in battle against the Turks. Bardas was with him when he fell wounded. He stayed with my father until the last, making certain his body was brought back to the chariot for Christian burial. For that act of bravery Bardas was wounded and nearly died."

"And he swore to your father that he would guard you until his death?"

She was surprised he knew as much, and he must have read her expression.

"Philip mentioned it," he said. "He also claims Bardas has sworn his undying loyalty to him."

She wondered. Was he hinting that Bardas could not be wholly trusted? "He is loyal to him, yes, but Bardas would never betray me."

"Bardas would see you with Philip no matter the cost to himself or anyone else, including you."

"What are you saying?"

Tancred stooped and, using the iron poker, stirred the coals into a dancing fire. "I would not completely trust him with the information about my willingness to help you reach the castle."

The idea brought concern, but it was preposterous to think Bardas would turn against her. "He would die first. He does not trust you, but he will do as I say in the end."

Tancred remained thoughtful, watching the flames. "I am told the Lysander family is related to the line of Nicephorus."

She felt a measure of pride. "Again, Philip told you?"

He looked at her, all previous lightness gone from his handsomely chiseled face. "No. I did some research in the Royal Library."

She wondered why. Was he curious about her, or did he suspect some treachery to Uncle Nicholas?

"The line of Nicephorus was deposed," she said uncomfortably, thinking of her mother's arrest for treason in supporting him. And yet her mother, as well as Nicholas, became loyal to the present emperor once he assumed power.

"Nicephorus III—the emperor he deposed—he had no sons to threaten the present rule?"

Tancred possessed more education than she had first thought, and he had learned a great deal about her.

"No, I do not believe so. There was a son, but he has not been heard from since Emperor Alexius overthrew Nicephorus some years ago. Anyway, my father was only distantly related to him. He posed no real threat."

"Byzantium has a reputation for not taking chances. Nor do the Normans," he said wryly. "There is a controversy between the grandsons of William the Conqueror, and it's the reason Bohemond has come east hoping to carve out a kingdom for himself here."

She wondered about Tancred. "What of you? Is it a power struggle within the Redwan family that resulted in the murder of your brother Derek?"

"It is always that. For power and riches most of the world's battles are fought." He looked at her. "And for the women they desire."

"And the women have little to say about it."

"I disagree. They are known for their skilled deceit behind the bedchamber door."

She stood. "I assure you, I carry no poison."

He also stood. "They like silk as well. So I am told."

She paled, thinking of her aunt. Did Tancred know the danger of those left to her plans?

"You know about the poisonous silk?"

"You forget. I have another family besides the robust Normans. I spent the other half of my life within the secretive quarters of the Moors. The art of silk poisoning was crafted among the women of the veil. It became an easy and silent way to remove a woman in the zenana."

The conversation was going down a path she did not wish to follow.

Helena abruptly changed the subject back to the Lysanders. "While my father fought faithfully for the new emperor and died, enemies accused my mother of disloyalty and had her arrested."

"When you speak of enemies, do you mean in the palace, or the family?"

"Both, I suppose. Those ruling the Lysander inheritance have married into it. Irene is my aunt by marriage. Her husband was elder brother to Nicholas."

"Why was Nicholas exiled? He never spoke of it."

"I was only a child when it happened. It was soon after my mother's arrest. I suspect greed."

"And after Nicholas was exiled, Irene became your guardian?"

"Yes, and by doing so she gained legal control of my family's wealth and lands. Constantine—another uncle, more so of Philip's than mine—aided her in her scheme."

"You have proof?"

Helena thought of her meeting with Constantine. She dare not say anything for the sake of her mother.

She sighed. "No. They are too clever. And now they are close to the emperor."

"Was Nicholas ever in love with Irene?"

Startled, she looked at him. "No—he would not, he could not care for such a cold and vicious woman."

"All women do not behave as venomous creatures when they wish to trap a prize."

Her eyes came to his. While she agreed about his summation of Irene, she did not care for his illustration. Did he think of all women as weavers of traps? What did he think of her? Did he see her boldness now in seeking his service as something forced on her by dangerous circumstances?

She frowned to herself. She was not aggressive and conniving.

"Your mother was arrested after your father's death?"

"Yes. Though innocent of conspiracy, she was banished to the dungeon. It was said she died there a month later. I never saw her again."

"Who accused your mother?"

"Irene denies it. Yet I know it was her scheme."

"How does Philip fit into all this, or does he?"

"Irene has grand plans for Philip, as you overheard in his chamber. Emperor, no less. Those plans do not include me."

"And as his mother she would rule through him."

"That is her ambition," she admitted wearily. "And she will not refrain until she achieves her desire."

"Nor will Philip, is my guess."

Helena could not accept this and turned away. She knew him better than even Irene, and Philip would free himself from the crippling crush of the pursuit of pride.

"Who is Philip's father?"

She hesitated, unwilling to betray a secret, and yet she believed that unless she was completely honest with Tancred he would not risk himself to come to her aid now.

"Constantine."

"So I suspected."

She wondered why but did not ask. Had he seen them secretly together? Probably so, since as a security guard at the palace, Tancred had been included in the inner circles.

"I understand about the Castle of Hohms," he said, "and the negotiations between your emperor and Antioch. But what motive do they have in forbidding a marriage between you and their son? I would think it would benefit their cause, since you are heiress to your father's wealth."

"It would have, except Irene has already manipulated to make Philip the heir."

"And you would regain control if you married him."

"Yes. Irene controls everything, including Philip."

"Does he know Constantine is his father?"

"Scandal rarely blushes in Byzantium. Yes, he knows." She looked at him. "But he is a man to whom reputation is important. It is said publicly that Philip is the son of a slain general—an even greater hero than my father. It is the reason he wishes the position of minister of war."

"When built on a foundation of lies, a man's character will soon turn to straw and rubble."

She remembered Philip's military blunders when the Rhine-landers attacked his entourage at Wieselburg. It had been Tancred's victory, but Irene had convinced the emperor otherwise.

She stood, blushing for Philip. "Do not insult him!"

"I do not need to. He unmasks himself."

"Why do you hate him so? Because your own vanity is wounded over the lack of trumpets?"

"Byzantium may keep its shiny trumpets. The tribute means little to me. My heart once knew peace in Sicily before I ever journeyed here."

"You imply your heart is not at peace," she quipped, irked by the indifference he paid to her prized Greek culture.

The blue-gray eyes scanned her face until the awareness between them turned her cheeks warm and she stepped backward.

"You should ask how your beloved Philip can have such apparent peace when he gives up the woman he wants."

"I suppose *you* are a man who would love a woman deeply! You would give up all!"

"If I wanted a woman as much as Philip claims? Nothing could deny her to me. I would face sword and scimitar, and all the golden palaces of the East could not lock her away from me."

The thought of such love sent her heart beating faster. Afraid he might guess, she turned away toward the fire. "Philip does not see it so."

"I am a different man than Philip."

Helena became aware of his nearness. She walked away from

him. "Do you intend to help me or no?"

"Your request is no request at all, but a command. You sound as hard and cold as iron mesh. Now, if you should come to me, look into my eyes, and plead, 'Tancred, I need you!' How could I resist a woman in distress?"

"I am told you have loved another woman—one by the name of Kamila."

She saw his expression harden, and she took it for anger that she had unmasked him.

"So Bardas has been prowling the bazaars asking about my life in Palermo. Why not ask me yourself? Is it mere curiosity about the many extraordinary women I have known?"

"I am not curious!"

"Strange . . . I thought you were."

"You were wrong!"

"You are not curious about Irene?"

No matter what she thought of his conceit, she needed him, and maintained an expression of indifference.

"She is like the woman I once read about in the Scriptures, who wore scarlet and bedecked herself in pearls, and gave her vile cup of wine to many lovers. I am not fool enough to drink. It takes a different kind of woman to woo me, one of purity, who vows her heart to me alone."

"I think this conversation has gone too far—"

"You may tell Bardas I do not care to be followed. He seeks something against me to which he can carry to you. Irene weaves a treacherous plot, and I have no passion to dwell with the dead. But for a woman who only a moment ago couldn't care less about my life, you have had a sudden change of mind."

"Hardly! I am only surprised a man of your character would refuse her."

"And my character you have judged and found guilty."

She tore her eyes from his, her feelings betraying her. She felt a strange pleasure that he had not succumbed, that he was too strong. "I will hear no more."

"As you wish."

Silence followed, then the sound of his steps. She whirled. "Wait! . . . Please!"

Helena sped toward him, catching his arm. "I have been a little unfair," she hastened, managing a smile.

Tancred's eyes were amused at her display.

She sobered. "Yet . . . you have made matters uncomfortable for me from the beginning."

"I was under the impression it was the other way around."

"I won't argue with you. Say what you will. Will you help me?"

"Did I not say earlier I would consider? I will bring you with me to Nicholas."

A swell of relief flooded her heart but ebbed in fear when a shout sounded from below the castle. Tancred left her and peered out the window. She heard horses and angry voices.

"What is it?" She rushed to his side and peered below, her stomach tightening as she saw a ring of horsemen carrying fiery torches and yelling to other men with weapons. "What is happening?"

"Rhinelanders. They ride with Godfrey's army."

"Rhinelanders," she repeated in a whisper, remembering. "They are attacking the castle?"

"No. They battle the imperial soldiers, including the troop under my command." He spoke with angry exasperation.

She glanced at his uniform. He too could be the brunt of their attack if it kept up.

"I suspect your emperor has retaliated against an earlier foray and they come to inform Godfrey. In my opinion they deserved to be attacked. They steal from the Greek farmers, but this is no time to argue justice." He turned and drew her away from the window, and her knees went weak as she thought of being trapped inside the castle.

"It's too late to leave in the chariot. You will fall prey." He frowned to himself, thinking. "Was Philip at Herion when you crossed the bridge to come here?"

"No, the guardhouse appeared empty. We were not questioned."

"Then he must have returned to Constantinople. He should have remained at the castle. Look—there is no choice now. You must wait until I can see you safely across the bridge. If fighting has already begun, it will rampage through the night, maybe for days."

She looked at him, trying to hide her fear.

He frowned. "You should have remained at the Lysander palace."

"I bid you come and you did not."

"I told Bardas I would contact you when it was safe to do so."

Bardas had said nothing to her—had he forgotten?

"You told Bardas?"

He looked at her wryly. "He did not tell you? He located me in the Venetian quarter. Did I not tell you in Philip's chamber you could find me there through Hakeem?"

"Yes, but—" She stopped, not wishing to further antagonize him against Bardas. Surely Bardas had forgotten. . . . There was much on his mind and he had been trailed, or so they both thought, by Irene's spies.

"You might have sent a written message explaining your intentions."

"There was no time. I vowed to Bardas I would come once my mission here was completed. I always keep my word, Helena. That is more than you can say for your gallant Philip."

He had used her name, and it gave her pause, for she found the sound of his voice pleasant in its pronunciation.

The angry voices of the knights carried up to them, and Tancred threw open the chamber door. Helena could not see Bardas. Where had he gone?

She joined Tancred at the gallery rail as more of Duke Godfrey's men entered through the castle door below to report to him.

"Armed horsemen wielding swords and clubs struck a fierce blow against the Rhinelanders. Many are dead, my liege! Tents are set aflame, our precious chargers, slain!"

Helena glanced at Tancred and saw that he was not surprised. She knew that the fragile truce between Godfrey and the emperor was now shattered. She looked below.

The duke was furious, refusing to concede that his own rash use of the sword and inflamed rhetoric had prompted the retaliation.

A second big man, dressed as a nobleman, walked up to the

duke. He was as dark of head as Godfrey was light.

"Who is he?" she whispered to Tancred.

"Baldwin, the duke's younger brother. And not the one to soothe injured pride. He loves nothing better than combat."

Baldwin was speaking: "This time let us teach him a lesson! I and my men will seize the bridge and hold it against his mercenary Turk soldiers."

"He is right," stated the other lords and princes among the knights.

Godfrey paced. "Evacuate the winter quarters. We will burn the castles and houses. But first, we shall thoroughly pillage all he has here!"

Tancred pulled her back from the rail, out of sight.

"Garbed in Byzantine splendor, you are not likely to soothe their hatred for what they believe is your emperor's treachery. Stay out of view. In fact—" he gave her a musing look. "The sooner you abandon your Byzantine costume for the garb of a Norman woman, the safer you will be."

She looked down at her frock with dismay.

"You will do well as my serving woman."

"A maid!"

"Are you not proud to serve me?" Amusement warmed the depths of his eyes.

"Proud—!"

Tancred's mouth turned up at the corners. "Other women I have refused. You are favored. And—becoming a Norman woman for even a short time may teach you a much-needed humility— not to mention submission to a man." His blue-gray eyes held hers. "You need a master."

Helena's eyes narrowed and the warmth flared her cheeks. "And I suppose you Normans are a humble race. You, whose ancestors conquered other kingdoms and tried to storm the walls of my city."

His faint smile was maddening. "Baldwin's young wife is a Norman. I know her. She will be of aid where clothing is concerned. Wait here with Bardas."

"Bardas is gone," she said stiffly. "I do not know where. I bid him wait in the hall."

"He likely went to safeguard the horses at the first sound of trouble."

He turned to leave, but she caught his arm. "Tancred! Your uniform—"

She stopped as his warm hand closed over hers.

"You spoke my name for the first time."

She pulled her hand away, pretending indifference, and placed it behind her, still feeling the warmth from his fingers. It was foolish how that simple touch had made her heart lurch. Because it did, she spoke with a tinge of superiority. "In the fighting none will know you are related to that infamous Norman named Bohemond—or should I say al-Kareem from Palermo?"

He was undisturbed. "You remembered my grandfather's name. You indeed have thought of me. I shall contemplate that."

She laughed carelessly. "How could I forget you are both a Norman and a Moslem infidel—like Prince Kalid? If the true Christian knights knew of your Moorish blood they would roast you below in the hearth instead of their fat piglet."

Tancred's brow lifted and the intense blue-gray eyes only taunted her in return. "Better hope no fool tries, madame. I should loathe to kill a fellow knight. And, should anything happen to me, your own lovely hide will be at risk. But do not fret, I have too many interesting plans to succumb so easily to sword, or to dimpled smiles. Farewell."

The door shut with a resounding thud.

Where is Tancred! He had not yet returned from Prince Baldwin's wife with the Norman garment. *And what of Bardas?* As the night wore on in horror, Helena concealed herself in the chamber, hearing Godfrey's army attacking the Byzantine town, setting their flaming torches to castles and houses.

She stood trembling in the darkened chamber peering out the window, praying that the warriors would not forget that this castle was inhabited by their liege. Not that the duke or his family was here!

Smoke and fire poured forth from nearby castles while wooden houses leaped into flame and sent billows of embers and ash into the air behind the retreating army. She supposed that Godfrey was moving back toward the bridge toward the walls of Constantinople where he would take repossession of his old campsite by the gates and wait for the Norman army under Prince Bohemond. She could imagine the alarm of the emperor at the prospect of the two strong forces joining.

What would she do if men came here to the chamber and found her?

The town was engulfed with the deafening cries of horses and beasts of burden, of men shouting and women screaming. Helena covered her ears. *Merciful Lord, help me! Send Tancred and Bardas, please—*

Now the looters were below, and she could hear their shouting, the sound of running feet, and the crashing of vessels and furniture. They were rushing up the steps. Someone was outside the bolted door. *Please, let it hold—*

Helena winced with each thud of a halberd ripping into the wood braced with straps of iron. She backed away.

The door heaved and shook. Whack! Terrified, she cringed against the wall unable to breathe, tears welling in her eyes. The fire from the town glowed red through the window like the hellish face of a demon. Her cold fingers clutched the Byzantine cross. She brought it to her lips and saw the rubies bleed into the fiery glow.

The door splintered, and she gasped as a warrior entered, his eyes crazed, his face hard and wet with sweat. He looked about and saw her. She was yet in her Byzantine costume, glimmering gold, shouting wealth, superiority. . . .

Tancred has failed me. Where is he, where?

The Rhinelander strode toward her. Her screams echoed horror no one could hear, soon smothered by the thunderous noise of battle. Lifting her like a rag doll, he carried her into the smoking darkness.

CHAPTER 7
Burning Castles

Help me, Lord God! Help me!

"Jesus!" Helena cried out. "Son of the Most High God!"

The Rhinelander flinched. The authority and holiness of that Name reverberated against the high castle walls. As though smitten with a blow from an angel's bright sword, he stumbled clumsily across the floor, Helena with him, and with a heavy jar they rammed into the trestle table. Helena landed hard, muffling a cry.

Sharp pain stabbed her ribs as she clutched at the cold stone floor. Though free of his grip, she was too stunned to move. Gasping, she raised herself up to her hands and knees and crawled from him into the darkness. She struggled to her feet, still clutching the cross her mother gave her.

Helena peered through the haze at the crumpled mass of her attacker, where a trickle of blood shone from the wound at his temple. She swayed—short of breath—pain searing through her right side. In a panic she realized her rib must be broken. Tears of frustration rushed to her eyes, until faith spoke calm to her soul. Had the Lord not just delivered her? Surely He had!

Gritting with pain that soon drenched her body with cold sweat, she inched her way toward the battered door, telling herself she could make it. She must. She could slip unseen down those castle steps into the great hall and escape into the night with all its madness. An angel would lead her; yes, she had seen them in the stained glass art of the Hagia Sophia. Beautiful angels with great white wings!

Once out of the castle she would somehow find Tancred and Bardas, the chariot, the horses . . .

But the angels did not appear. Appalling horror burst upon her eyes as she merged into the alcove above the chiseled steps. Seeds of faith dropped from her hand and scattered, falling between the cracks. It was not the whir of angels' wings but the sound of spiked boots; the shouting baritone voices of more Rhinelanders, their tongues thick with wine! They were everywhere below, a colony of looters, ravaging women and killing imperial soldiers.

In another minute she would be discovered.

The nightmare was real. There was no way out, no way of escape. She could not run with a broken rib, nor could she fight; she could not even hide. She was trapped in the castle with crazed barbarians who thought nothing of slaying anyone who might hint of Byzantium. And she, a princess of nobility, garbed in purple, pearls in her hair.

What a proud little fool she had been to come here brazenly like this! What madness had deceived her better judgment into believing that nothing could harm Helena of the Nobility?

The odor of the Rhinelander's unwashed body clung to her garment like a disease. There were more of them. She was surrounded. If blessed, they would leave her dead.

Fear stalked her once brave spirit like snarling hyenas moving to encircle her. Behind her, the Rhinelander was moving clumsily about the chamber, growling angrily like a wounded bear.

In weakness she edged her way down, one step at a time, each movement bringing pain. She prayed she wouldn't trip on her garment. Haze draped the air. Then, a sudden rush of flames and a shower of red sparks erupted below as pieces of furniture and tapestries smoldered with intense heat, sending forth acrid fumes that stung her eyes and hurt her throat.

Helena halted on the steps, mindless and still, holding her rib until a familiar voice jolted her.

Hope overshadowed her with its mighty wings, promising to

catch her away. "Bardas!" and from the steps, she saw the big man surging his way toward her through the clutter and haze, sword in left hand.

"Mistress! Did they hurt you?"

Her eyes widened. She thought her voice came too weakly to warn him above the hellish din. "Bardas—look out—behind you!" He whirled, firm of stance, meeting a Rhinelander who came at him with a rush, teeth bared.

The two swords smashed with the ring of steel. Helena winced, her emotions feeling the force of rock-solid arms connecting like bulls. The Rhinelander turned his hatred against the Byzantine bodyguard, and Bardas fought for his life. With horror she watched, helpless, as he was struck and forced to one knee, blood filling a gaping wound.

Helena's hands went to her dry mouth, her heart surging in her ears, certain she would see him hacked to death. A knight emerged clothed in black with a leather tunic sewn with rings of iron. He shouted at the Rhinelander, who turned to confront him.

Sickened, Helena watched the knight smash his sword against him with a staggering blow, followed by a second hack that swiped off the hand holding the weapon—but with his other hand the Rhinelander produced an iron ball studded with spikes connected to a strap. He whirled the vicious weapon, but the knight ducked and the ball smashed into one of Godfrey's footmen. Then the knight produced a curved scimitar and with a flash sliced through the Rhinelander's neck.

Helena's knees buckled. She gagged, then sank slowly to the steps, her eyes unmoving from the severed head.

Her mind weaved in and out of sickening darkness.

The knight with the red cross emblazoned on his leather tunic came swiftly to her. She stared blankly into blue-gray eyes which betrayed no emotion as he stepped over the leering head. He caught her up into his arms as easily as the Rhinelander, but this time she felt no terror, only a dazed relief and something like awe. "Tancred?" she gasped.

"Your servant, madame" was all he said.

The street was a panic of soldiers and horses. Fire billowed from a gutted hut, and smoke spiraled from the flames of a thousand torches. She heard Bardas coming behind them.

"The horses," Tancred shouted, "get them!"

Bardas grasped the reins of Apollo, who snorted and pawed, anxious to reach his master. Though injured, Bardas managed to swing himself onto the back of a second horse and gallop toward them, leaning down as Tancred handed Helena to him.

"Easy. Her rib is broken."

"I—I must ride with you to the Norman camp!" Helena gasped, dazed now, her reasoning unclear.

Tancred removed his helmet, showing damp brown hair. He swung his muscular body onto the saddle. "You cannot. A long ride will add to your injury."

"I can! I can!"

"Brave to the end," he said as he reached into the leather satchel on his saddle, quickly searching.

"Redwan is right, little one. The Norman camp will prove no safer than here. Did I not say do not come here? Our hope rests in Master Philip. He will yet make appeal on your behalf, and his, to the emperor."

The mention of Philip brought Helena an unexpected wave of longing as exhaustion claimed her body and emotions. She ached for his embrace and envisioned that it had been Philip, not Tancred, who had swept her away from danger in the castle and was now riding with her to the safety of the family villa.

Tancred's intense gaze interrupted her thoughts, and against her will she looked at him astride Apollo, the rugged and sultry image making swift demands of its own to hold her attention. She saw that he understood her thoughts about Philip and a quick flush came to her cheeks.

He looked at Bardas, who watched him cautiously. "Bring your mistress to the guard castle." He removed a flagon of medicinal wine from his leather satchel and tossed it to Bardas. "Drink some, then see to your mistress. The ride will be rough on her pain."

Bardas thoughtlessly touched his wounded left arm, then drank, still watching him.

"Your minister of war is not at the guard castle," said Tancred, nothing in his voice. "I will bind her broken rib there."

Helena winced at the thought of the ordeal before her. Her discomfort began to wear upon her nerves, and she longed for the release of sleep. Bardas handed her the flagon, but she turned her head away.

"He is right. The ride will be brutal on you, little one."

Wearily she tipped the flagon, grimacing as the liquid burned her throat and set her empty stomach on fire.

They rode from the Byzantine town, and the crusaders were left behind with Godfrey's blue gonfanon now stained with blood. Helena's mind sank into oblivion and she dreamed of dragons and knights, of dark eyes, and masculine stormy blue eyes.

A light rain again began to fall and wet her face. Tancred removed his cloak and, riding closer beside Bardas, handed it to him, and he covered her.

Far behind them the burning castles were turned into dark, odorous shadows of sulfur, billowing upward like giant towers against the eastern sky and the war yet to come.

CHAPTER 8
Sir Knight, Where Are You?

The empire is all important, thought Irene. Her destiny and Philip's depended on enacting harsh measures. She must be strong and carry her plans through to the end, avoiding the entanglements of morality and sentiment; they were only stumbling blocks on the stairs to the throne of Byzantium. Nothing would deter her now. Not even her affection for her son. Philip would one day understand that all she did was for his political good. His weak sentiment for Helena would fade, as all male passion eventually did for the woman of their dreams. Beauty faded, but power lasted into old age and lived on through one's heirs.

Did I not manage to get Philip the coveted position of minister of war? And she had handed it to him with celebration before breaking the news of Helena's marriage to Prince Kalid. She had also convinced Philip the decision to marry Helena to the Moslem prince was made by the emperor rather than through her manipulation.

Irene looked at Philip across the marble pavilion. His dark eyes pensive, his aristocratic face sullen. He lifted his goblet and drank, restlessly running his long fingers through his black oiled hair. He lounged in a palanquin, wearing a brocade tunic of purple and black mosaics. On the agate table between him and Irene sat his high-crowned turbanlike silk hat, its brim thick with gems. His muscular legs wore black hose, and his buskins were also soft black leather.

"Do stop scowling, Philip," she snapped. "Before the surrender of Antioch will come Nicaea. With each military victory you deliver to the emperor, you become more needful to him."

Philip's exuberance at attaining the coveted minister of war position yet lived on in the echo of heralding trumpets; nevertheless, it was obvious to all—including Irene—that the thought of losing Helena remained a source of grief.

Irene looked at Philip impatiently and his whining concerns became an irritation. If only he could be more like her and his father, Constantine, iron-willed and unsympathetic. His weakness was a danger, making him a volatile force she must constantly keep from spilling forth in unexpected ways. In that regard he was like Constantine. He too was volatile, still mourning the loss of his illustrious cousin Adrianna Lysander. She was dead, but Constantine, like a haunted, sick animal, dreamed on. Yes, he too was a force she could not always control.

But Philip . . .

"You are like your father," she said scornfully. "You may have any foolish woman you want in court or out, yet you pine for the one you cannot have."

Irene watched him, as alert to his folly as a leopard to her cub's wandering. He was sick with desire for Helena and foolish enough to try to run away with her.

"Kalid is not the only man interested in Helena," he said moodily. "So is Tancred, though he is wise enough to mask his intentions. That he does so makes him all the more dangerous."

"Leave Tancred to me. I know how to handle men like the Norman. I was informed that his uncle from Sicily is seeking him for the assassination of his half brother. Jealousy and greed, the fight for rulership among the wolfish Normans, will play into my hand. Soon I will have Tancred right where I want him: a slave to me."

Philip drank from his glimmering goblet, uncooperative.

The fact that he was doubled-minded was troublesome. He was like a half-tamed sullen tiger cub; she never knew when he would break out, contesting her will.

Irene sighed, almost as a mew. Little else remained now except to make Philip see that her decision had been logical, that she had done what was wise for him. She lay on the opposite palanquin in front of the hearth, where a fire crackled, and sipped from the jeweled goblet.

They were alone in one of the Lysander chambers, although she soon expected the arrival of Constantine. His recent absence had alerted her suspicions. What information did he seek, prowling about the Arab bazaars on the Mese?

Irene turned her attention back to her son. She had deliberately kept Philip from seeing Helena for the past weeks until he tasted the satisfaction of an ambition realized. Not even his desire for Helena would permit him to turn his back on power.

Yes, she knew Philip well. Much better than did Helena.

"The emperor has called you to banquet with him and the empress tomorrow night. You see how your position in the war department is crucial to him? Do not mope like a dejected puppy. You know as well as I that your ambitions outweigh your love for Helena."

His classical Greek face was moody, his eyes like troubled pools. "You look like the statue of the goddess Medusa entwined with a hundred serpents. Strange that I should think of it now."

She mocked a laugh. "The snarling cub reaches to bat playfully with the leopard. Caution. I do not take kindly to being associated with serpents."

Irene's body was outlined with shimmering silk, and her hair gleamed in the firelight like spun gold. Her eyes, the color of amber, were like burning stones.

"I expected you to be celebrating the emperor's decision, my pet," she crooned. "Instead you look as a dour old man."

He shrugged. "I have been seeking the position of minister of war for years. How could I not be grateful?"

"And now it is yours."

"I am amazed you were able to convince the emperor to select me. He was so pleased with Tarasius."

Her long, delicate fingers curled tightly about the goblet. "Yes. A pity Tarasius spent too much time in his exotic herb garden." She swirled the wine thoughtfully, watching the crimson flow.

"Poor Tarasius; prolonged illnesses are oft worse than sudden death. Especially when one must leave his seat of authority. The gods are indeed heartless."

"The physician Andronicus suspected poison," Philip said absently.

Irene's face hardened. "That meddling fool from Pergamum. He is always poking his nose about. He has become an irritation to me. I must have the emperor's wife send him away. Here, fill my glass. I do not care to call the slave again."

Philip leaned over the table and, grasping the urn, remarked, "Your interest in Persian poison is becoming a matter of gossip. So is your hold on the empress. She will not plan a journey nor hold a banquet unless you assure her it is wise. You are much in demand, Mother."

Irene's movement was as swift as a leopard. She was on her feet, grasping the glass from his startled hand and flinging it into the fire.

"How oft have I warned you not to call me that? The eyes and ears of slaves see through walls and hear through bolted doors!"

"Everyone knows you are my mother. Only you hold to the foolish notion that it remains a secret." He waved a hand. "I am sorry; it was a mere slip of tongue."

"You must guard your tongue like a warrior his life," she hissed. "If the emperor learns who you really are, we are both finished in the Sacred Palace. Your mother died in Athens while giving you birth. He believes you to be the son of slain General Severius, remember?"

"Yes! I remember! And I shall live up to that title!"

"See that you do. I have worked too hard to get us where we are to have you fumble it away."

"And I?" he demanded passionately. "Have I not worked also? There is none more loyal to the emperor than I."

"Without Constantine and I scattering your name about his throne like rose petals, the emperor would not know you existed. You could sacrifice your life to his honor and he would not blink. It takes more than loyalty, Philip; it takes clever scheming. Do not forget how much you owe me."

"Do you think I am reluctant to pursue my own ambitions?

Without you I could still make a name for myself!"

"Ah! The lioness's whelp dares to growl, but where are your teeth? It is the lioness who brings you the meat! Remember it well. Your success is due to my planning. It is also my security. At least until I get rid of Mary the Alan and become the emperor's mistress. I will not have you lose our future in the Sacred Palace on a wide-eyed damsel who stirs your boyish passions."

Philip smashed the goblet against the marble floor and abruptly stalked to the door.

She jumped to her feet. "Philip. Come back! You dare walk out on me before I have finished?"

"I am going to see Helena."

"I cannot permit you to interfere."

His eyes burned like two fiery coals. "Will you have me also placed under your guards?"

"I will do whatever I must. Always keep that in mind. Your folly will not stand in the way, Philip. Do nothing rash. Too much is at risk to allow you to throw it away now. Helena serves no purpose to your future, or to mine."

His face contorted with sudden anguish, reminding her of a cornered animal. "But at what cost!" he gasped more to himself than to her.

"My son," she soothed suddenly, "come, rest. Calm your soul. You may see Helena; you may even have her to your bedchamber soon. Kalid and Antioch are not forever, only a few months. Until then, cultivate patience. Remember, you may have power *and* Lysander's daughter if you cooperate with me now. But you are distraught. When the sun rises tomorrow, matters will have a way of forming new priorities. You will be better able to see how Constantine and I have done what is best for you, for the three of us. What you need is rest."

He did come to her, sinking like a dejected puppy to the cushions on the rug.

Irene, her back toward him, poured a small amount of wine into another glass and added a pinch of white powder. "Poor Philip, I have been thoughtless, not realizing your disappointment. Drink this, my son, it will help you sleep."

Philip took the potion she often gave him when he was overly dejected.

She sank beside him and drew his dark head down to her soft lap. Her long fingers soothed his tousled hair and caressed the side of his face. "In the morning you will feel rested."

"But Helena? Why must I give her to this wretched Saracen!"

"Did we not agree long ago some things must be sacrificed to gain that which is more important?"

"But I want her," he nearly whined.

"Believe me, Philip, I did everything possible to convince Prince Kalid not to marry her. I offered him gold. I offered him the daughters of many other nobles in Constantinople, but he is a stubborn man. When the emperor insisted I do whatever possible to please him, I had no choice. The price he demanded to surrender the Castle of Hohms was Lysander's daughter."

"What of Nicholas? What will he do when he learns his niece was given to the son of a Moslem emir? You know how Nicholas is devoted to the Christian god."

At the mention of Nicholas her heart leaped. She would not think of the one man who stirred her blood to passion. Nicholas had loved her once, when they were young like Philip and Helena. He had loved her . . . until he returned from his clerical studies at Athens and found that in his two-year absence she had become the emperor's mistress. He had turned his back and walked away from her. She had begged him to come back, even promising to change, but he had not listened. And so she had turned to Constantine, and to a host of others in and out of the palace.

Nicholas would love her again. She could lure him back. There were few men who could resist her. She had made Constantine, Philip, and even Helena believe that she intended to have Nicholas arrested, but it was not his end she planned for, but their reconciliation at the expense of Constantine.

"Do not speak of him," she said with pretended bitterness. "There is little he can do. And he will not come back to Constantinople. It would not do," she said smoothly, "for Nicholas to be accused of treason. And neither must you risk the emperor's displeasure," she warned. "Your position is the beginning of that which will bring you respect and fear. I know how much both mean to you. Someday you will show Byzantium who Philip really is. As emperor you will rival the memory of Justinian and Basil."

"At the moment I prefer position, and Helena."

"Selfish to the end. Then console your wounds, my son. If you still mourn Helena a year from now, you can always go to Antioch and bargain with the prince."

He brightened. "Do you think so?"

"But of course. I will even assist you if you vow not to do anything rash now. In a year or so the Seljuk will grow weary of her."

He scowled again.

"Dear Philip, do not look so pious. Poor child, am I cruel to your tender feelings? Come! Smile a little and think of your victory over Tarasius. It will make Helena's departure in two weeks easier to bear. And you can look forward to next spring."

Philip had grown drowsy and the empty goblet slipped from his hand onto the rug. Irene waited a minute longer, then took her son's head from her lap and laid it gently on a silk pillow. A minute later she dimmed the lanterns and left the chamber.

But Philip raised himself to an elbow, his eyes fierce and burning as he looked after her. What a fool she took him for. He was not the benign little puppy she still thought him to be. He would destroy her and all in his path one day. He alone would be emperor. And Helena would be his empress. He had plans that Irene knew not of. Clever plans that included the services of Tancred the Norman to bring about his success. And Tancred too would cooperate with him. He would have no choice if he wished the assassin named Mosul to live to bear witness to his innocence.

Philip had poured the drink into a potted palm near at hand. An expert at deceit, he had learned it well from his mother and father. He stood from the cushions, hands on hips, looking anything but the pitiable whining dog she thought him.

Philip left the chamber and called for his personal guards, men loyal to him and not Irene. To his surprise, Bardas was among them. What news did Helena's bodyguard bring him?

CHAPTER 9
Dark Knight, White Knight, Which?

A dull dismal shroud of misting rain imprisoned the guard castle with bone-chilling dampness. Helena's head felt swollen, her ribs so stiff and tightly bound she could hardly move, and she drew her soiled fur cape about her, trying to gather some warmth as she moved awkwardly and painfully about the upper chamber of the "keep"—a tower used as sleeping quarters for the garrison soldiers as well as a watchtower and weapons arsenal.

She peered through a slat in the thick wall laced with arrow loops and felt the wind blow the rain against her face. She drew away, shivering. The singular good that she could find in the bleak weather was that the persistent rain may have smothered the fires in the burning castles across the bridge.

By now, Helena thought, the main section of Godfrey's army would have passed over the bridge to return to their old camp beneath the main city walls. She assumed that Bardas, too, had brought news of the rampage to the imperial palace.

Remembering the horror that had taken place, she winced from more than physical discomfort and moved away from the stone wall to a small portable stone hearth where hot bricks were brought and stacked inside the oven by a serving boy, who had also brought her a bronze urn containing tea from distant Cathay.

On inquiry of the whereabouts of Tancred and Bardas, the lad informed her that Tancred had sent Bardas to General Taticus for reinforcements, and Tancred had ridden back to the bridge to make contact with Duke Godfrey. He was to return that morning.

Helena sipped the bitter brew, trying to restore a measure of alertness to her brain, and took solace in the heat radiating from the bricks.

Her winged dark brows came together. She hardly remembered arriving with Tancred and Bardas on what would have been four to five hours ago. She judged the time by the glimmer of dawn arising in the east.

She remembered lying on a pile of blankets and stirring in and out of a restless sleep. Tancred and Bardas had been nearby, but she could not recall the details of Tancred attending her injury. When she had awakened it was yet dark, some thick white candles burned on the stone ledge; she was alone, and her ribs were bound so tightly that she had difficulty breathing comfortably.

Sitting now by the hot bricks, she mused again over the interesting man who was both warrior, student-physician, and an adventurer seeking spiritual truth—or so he had claimed in Philip's chamber that night in Constantinople. She had not yet been able to ask him about the Koran.

Tancred's skills as a warrior were awesome, she thought, and she closed her eyes against the gruesome memory of the beheaded Rhinelander. Quickly she set her cup of tea down, losing her appetite.

The wind about the stone embrasures sounded its high lonely whine that chilled her with thoughts of future desolation if Tancred refused her offer for hire. In the keep alone, in pain, hearing the wind and feeling the dampness, she already imagined herself a prisoner doomed for that camel caravan to Antioch and the mysterious Moslem palace of the emir.

Helena rested her head between her palms knowing she must not grow weary and faint in courage, surrendering her hope and prayers for God's intervention. After all, it wasn't as though Tancred had utterly refused to help her. He had appeared to relent to her wishes back at Godfrey's castle, and had it not been for the wicked interruption of the horsemen, she might have won his cooperation in bringing her with him to the Norman camp to Nicholas. She groaned at her loss.

And now! She touched her stiff, awkward bandage. What could she do? How could she journey? Nor could she remain here in the keep for long! By now, Irene would be aware of her disappearance and would have sent spies out searching for her. Her aunt would first confront Philip, and not finding her with him, she would begin to search in earnest. *And Philip, what will he think?*

Helena dare not contemplate what would happen if Irene caught her with Tancred while seeking to escape to the Norman camp and to Nicholas.

She lifted her face from her hands, her thoughts again cut short by the pounding of hoofs on stone below. Grimacing, she stood from the chair and edged her way across the chamber to the narrow window slit which looked out toward the cold Bosporus and those dread hills of the Moslem East, appearing like humped camels.

Daylight began to seep and spread across the gray skyline, and through the drizzle in the fading glow from the torches she saw a handful of Byzantine guards on patrol. Had Bardas also returned?

Helena turned, hearing quick footsteps coming up the steep flight of chiseled steps. The door to the chamber opened unexpectedly.

Tancred entered, now garbed in the becoming black-and-crimson uniform of the imperial guard, his woolen wintry riding coat wet with rain. His hair, too, was damp and curled at his neck, and the intense blue-gray eyes swept her, as though surprised she was awake and on her feet. "You should not be walking yet."

Despite her caution, her feelings toward him had softened, for how could it be otherwise? He had saved her at the castle and was now her physician. . . .

"I have begun to think I do not know you at all. I offer you an apology. So you are a physician after all."

He smiled. "Only a student." He walked toward her. "How do you feel? Is the bandage too tight?"

"A little. You set the bone? I hardly recall you doing so."

"The bone will grow again. It is good you do not remember."

Her eyes sought his. "I owe you a great debt. You will allow me to pay you?"

A smile played on his mouth. "In due time."

"You must not forget to remind me," she hastened.

"I will remember to collect at a convenient season."

Tancred walked to the window slit where she stood and looked below, turning sober and thoughtful. "This is a dark matter you find yourself in, Helena. I could wish it were far different. You were made for the fair things of life, not Rhinelanders, broken ribs, and Kalid using you to accomplish his ambitions in Antioch. And I cannot stay much longer," he said quietly.

His statement seemed to mean much more than his departure to meet up with Prince Bohemond and the Norman army, and for a brief cold moment she felt the loss, knowing that he would ride off as knights did, never to return.

It was the first time he had spoken so seriously and sympathetically, and she responded too readily. She tore her gaze away. She too looked thoughtfully out the window, and together they watched a sullen dawn break over the rough water.

Tancred frowned. "Bardas should have returned by now." His eyes calmly questioned her. "He resents your willingness to come to me for help. Let us hope he does not cultivate enough fatherly zeal to warn Philip you came to hire me."

"Warn Philip?" Her surprised gaze searched his, for why would Philip prove a danger to either of them?

"Yes, Philip," he repeated with a wry smile. "Your illustrious noble with purple buskins. It is my opinion that once he mulls matters over, he will want to manage some way of keeping both his position and you."

This was a far cry from his usual denunciation of Philip willingly abandoning her to safeguard his career with the emperor, and she wondered what made him think differently. The idea that Philip might long for her brought a mellow glow to her eyes, and seeing it, Tancred turned wry.

"I would not yearn too deeply, madame."

"I do not *yearn!*"

"Yes . . . you do. Your misplaced devotion is written on your face."

She turned her head away from his penetrating gaze.

"His schemes are likely to crumble at the first earthquake. If I mention Philip at all, it's because I do not trust Bardas to keep your plans hidden from him. He may have run to him with news of your injury and your plans to seek Nicholas."

Her hopes began to rekindle into warm dreams despite Tancred's attempt to smother them. Just what would Philip do if he knew of her desperate attempts?

"If Bardas knew where to find my enemies, I think he would hand me over in shackles," he mused.

Helena glanced at him. "Nay, you saw how he obeyed your commands back at the castle when danger surrounded us. He would not betray you, and since I seek your services, he will cooperate even if he disapproves. You are needed for the present."

A brow lifted. "For the present, I cannot be dispensed with. You are generous. I suppose that offers some comfort. I can at least keep my sword sheathed when I sleep, but tomorrow?" he asked with mock alarm. "I may be tossed to the bears."

She smiled ruefully. "And do you think I also will betray you—to the bears?"

"You just said you needed me," came his too smooth reply. "My hopes grow."

Helena gave him a cautious glance, but he was again peering below, frowning to himself over some more serious thought.

"You obviously cannot ride with me to the Norman camp. When Bardas arrives, have him bring you to your family villa. Wait for me there."

Then he is going to help me after all! "And Nicholas?"

"I will warn him about your precarious situation with Kalid. No doubt Nicholas will wish to come to you at once."

Her gratitude prompted a quick laying of her hand on his arm, but at the feel of the rough rain-damp uniform she became too aware of him and drew her hand away again.

"I knew you would dedicate your sword to my cause. Then you will let me hire you?"

His eyes held hers. "No."

"No? But you just said—"

"I offer my service freely."

She tried to still the beating of her heart, regarding his gaze beneath dark lashes.

"But . . . what about the castle. . . ." she began weakly.

"I thought you told me last night it was reserved as dowry for the man you will marry, unless . . ." And a flicker of malicious amusement showed. "Unless you wish to plead for the opportunity to become my bride."

"Your boldness is unheard of." She rushed on. "The gold besants—"

"I also made it clear last night it is not what I want."

She swiftly lowered herself onto a chair as though in pain and held her hand to her heart. "You have bound me too tightly."

"Then does my lady wish me to loosen the bandage?"

"No," she hastened. "I . . . I shall manage. As you say . . . it must heal." She drew her cape about her as though cold and remembered the other desperate cause for which she hoped to gain his help.

"There is much I need to discuss with you before you leave to meet with the Norman prince. There is news of my mother you must bring to Nicholas. Before you do . . . there is information I desperately need. Information you might gain from your contacts with the Moslem friends of your grandfather." She stood hopefully, her eyes searching his. "You have heard of ibn-Haroun of Jerusalem?"

Tancred gave her a scrutinizing appraisal as though taken off guard by the change in the direction of their conversation and the name of Haroun.

"That you would know of anyone in Jerusalem by that name astounds me. Who told you of him? Philip?"

She wondered why he would bring up Philip. "Philip did not tell me. He does not know. I have not spoken with him since my informer passed me the message about ibn-Haroun some weeks ago. Do you know him, Tancred?"

He paused, as though considering the depth of sincerity in her question and what ulterior motive might be behind it. "I know of him. In Palermo, my grandfather has done business with him. He is not a Turk nor a Moor, but an Arab, and he and his brother are breeders and traders of Arabian horses. He sold a mare to me in

Palermo." His face hardened at the memory. "He first bought her from Kalid. I named her Alzira . . . and the assassin who killed my brother now rides her."

He knew the Arab named ibn-Haroun! Helena's excitement grew.

"Enough of my past," he said swiftly. "How is it you know of him?"

The dreadful moment of truth had come, one of shame and infamy. "I would not know of him at all except my mother is not dead as enemies have told me. She is a slave in the Moslem East. And she served in the household of ibn-Haroun, the breeder of Arabian horses."

In the surprised silence that followed, she heard the wind whipping the rain through the arrow loops.

"You are certain?" came his low voice at last.

"That she lives? Yes. But she is no longer in his household." Her eyes implored his. "She was sold again . . . or taken by force. But surely Haroun or his brother would know who she is with. Oh, Tancred, I must find her and free her from her vile fate or die doing it. I would have done so by now if my own fate had not cruelly intertwined with Kalid and Antioch. You will help me?"

"You say she is a slave. How is it a Lysander woman of nobility finds herself in the Moslem East?"

Her eyes warmed with indignation. "I have no proof, but I believe my aunt was involved."

"And your informer brought news of Haroun? When?"

"Several weeks ago. I met him on the Mese and he passed a message to me, saying that she had been in Jerusalem in the service of one ibn-Haroun."

"But she is no longer there? How do you know?"

"Another message arrived. . . ." Her eyes clouded. "She was bought by a sultan."

"The East is full of sultans," he reminded her.

"Yes, yes, and my informer was to meet Bardas yesterday on the Mese with further news, but both of them were foiled from keeping the appointment. Irene drove by in her chariot and saw Bardas. I now have word my informer is dead."

She thought of her meeting with Constantine and his warning

to keep silent. Avoiding Tancred's searching gaze, she feared he would begin to ask too many questions when all she needed was his contact with ibn-Haroun. She dare not tell even Tancred about Constantine's plans to locate her.

She produced a message from an inner pocket of her cloak and handed it to him. "This is the last message received."

He lifted a candle and studied it thoughtfully.

Helena knew it by heart: *"Your mother is no longer in Jerusalem. She was taken away a year ago and lives in the Moslem tents of the East."*

"Your family has the blood of the Moors," she urged. "You would have other contacts besides Haroun. You would know the emirs in Cairo, Damascus, Baghdad. I must buy her freedom from the sultan who owns her."

Tancred was thoughtful. "It may not be so simple."

"What do you mean?" she asked worriedly.

"You are certain she wishes her freedom?"

The question stunned her. Helena looked at him, noting the seriousness of his gaze. Remembering that he bore the proud blood of al-Kareem and that she had yet to meet a more handsome man, she contemplated for the first time the thought of her beloved Christian mother liking her sultan captor. She swiftly dismissed the thought as outrageous. "You suggest that my mother—Lady Adrianna Lysander—could love a tribal sultan and live in a nomadic black tent?"

He lifted a brow. "The women of the veil would not find my suggestion insulting. I merely asked if it were possible your mother might care for her captor. It has happened."

Helena held her breath, prepared to dismiss the possibility, but then for a brief moment, she saw Tancred not in the uniform of the Byzantine, nor the armor of a Norman knight, but dressed as a Moor of the mysterious desert, a sultan, and his suggestion did not seem so incredible after all.

Helena walked to the small hearth and sat down, warming her hands. He did not follow but remained by the arrow loops.

"Have you told anyone else that your mother lives? It is important. It could place her in danger if your aunt has access to the assassins."

She thought of Constantine and his warnings about Irene, and remembered the poisonous silk.

When Helena did not answer immediately, he walked up to where she sat by the table. When she did not look at him for fear she would give herself away, he picked up the urn and poured himself a cup of tea. He drank, watching her.

"Your silence tells me you have confessed all to your beloved Philip."

Her eyes narrowed slightly and she lifted her chin. "No. That is . . . not about ibn-Haroun."

"No?"

The smooth inflection of his voice betrayed his mistrust. She hastened, "I told him she was alive before the journey to the Danube. It is the only reason he relented and brought me with him from Nish to find Nicholas. But whatever you may think of him, Philip can be trusted to remain silent about my mother."

"You are so confident. And yet, Irene is his mother."

"He will say nothing," she insisted.

He set his empty cup down. Whether or not he believed her was questionable, and from his musing frown, she believed that he was disturbed that she even knew of ibn-Haroun. Obviously the man had some bearing on Tancred's past in Sicily. Did he worry that Philip would learn this from her?

"I have not told him of your Arab acquaintance," she repeated. "What of Kalid? Does he know this breeder of Arabian horses?"

She saw the blue in his eyes harden. "Yes, he knows him. So does Mosul," he said.

The assassin . . .

"And Bardas would also know about your mother having been in Jerusalem, since he prowls the Mese for you. Anyone else?"

She shook her head wearily. "No one else, except—" She stopped as the determined face of Constantine came before her.

"Yes?"

"Nicholas," she said. "Bardas brought him news in Clermont. At that time neither of us knew about Haroun."

"When Bardas returns from General Taticus, do not return to Constantinople. I want both of you to wait at the villa until I arrive with Nicholas. As soon as I can I will be in touch with Hakeem to inquire of Haroun at Jerusalem, but there is little I can do now since Hakeem has ridden to Antioch. In the meantime I will also begin to ask quietly concerning your mother."

Helena stood. "I cannot stay at the villa. Irene is likely to search for me. How long will you be gone?"

"I am leaving now. Expect me in two weeks, no longer. If I do not arrive by then, leave the villa. Have you another place to wait?"

"I have friends at Athens. Nicholas knows of them." She paused, wondering how to broach the next subject, knowing he would disapprove of her actions.

"I . . . I must send Bardas back to Constantinople if only for a day."

"A mistake. It will increase our risk. Are you thinking of your jewels?"

"No . . ." she hesitated, "they are safely disposed of." She wouldn't say where. "But there is another matter I must take care of before leaving permanently with Nicholas for the castle." She turned away, busying herself with the urn as though she wished more tea. "I must talk to Philip."

Tancred was silent. She glanced at him and saw a hot flicker of impatience in his eyes and she rushed to explain. "I said hateful things to him in the chamber. I do not want to leave without telling him—" She stopped.

Beneath his unrelenting gaze she halted.

"That you are unwise enough to love him still?"

She flushed despite herself. "That is my affair, sir."

"And I suggest, madame, that it is mine also, now that I risk my head to secure your safety and inquire among the sultans for Adrianna."

Helena had worked too hard to gain this moment of his co-operation. She dare not lose it now. "I will forever be in your debt."

"Do not misunderstand my protest—it is not your sentimental words of endearment wasted on such a man that provoke my ire," he suggested. "It is your willingness to risk yourself and me by doing so. You would make us both expendable by kissing him good-bye."

She turned away. "You make it sound so light and frivolous, so wasted."

"Frivolous? I think not. Philip would sell you to the bedchamber of my cousin."

A strong voice challenged from the doorway: "We must prove our gallant knight from Sicily wrong, Helena."

Startled, Helena turned toward the door.

Philip stepped into the chamber, darkly handsome, the image of Byzantine splendor. Behind him stood two of his soldiers.

The black eyes sparked a challenge as he looked at Tancred. "You are wrong, my Norman friend. Helena will not be turned over to your untrustworthy cousin Kalid, nor to you, our talented scholar-physician."

The resentment was plain in his voice and she felt the heightened tension in the chamber. What was she to make of this? A cautious glance at Tancred showed that he too thoughtfully studied the change in Philip.

Philip held out both hands toward her, his eyes flickering with warmth and self-reproach. "I drove you to this daring but unwise action, Helena. You were desperate. You might have been killed. When Bardas told me what happened at Godfrey's castle, and of your injury, I came at once."

"Bardas told you?" asked Tancred smoothly.

She remembered his earlier suggestion, but her eyes were only for Philip.

Philip shifted his gaze away from her to Tancred. "Did you not send him? Am I not the minister of war? A dozen men wait below, Redwan. You have your commission to ride to meet the Normans. But do not leave yet. I want you to hear what I have to say to Helena."

Philip was looking at her again, warmly, as though Tancred no longer mattered, and he was speaking the words she had yearned for him to speak.

"When I learned what happened to you last night, I knew clearly for the first time how much you mean to me, Helena, and how thoughtless and self-seeking I have been these past weeks. Tancred was right—I did fail you. It took the fear of your death at the hand of crusading barbarians to shake me."

Her breath wanted to stop as her eyes clung to his. He came toward her, taking hold of her shoulders. "I cannot lose you."

"Kalid is also a warrior who refuses to lose," interjected Tancred.

Philip looked over at him with a cool, dark gaze. "I asked you to stay that you might realize my intentions to marry Helena. Your opinions on Kalid can wait."

Helena's emotions spiraled out of control. That Philip would have the humility to admit his error before Tancred astounded her and made it all the more sweet. Her heart ached for him, knowing the cost to his pride, and yet she felt great pleasure. He was vindicating her as well as himself, and all her words in defense of his strength of character at Tancred's mocking denunciation. She wanted to look at Tancred victoriously but reined in her childish satisfaction, remembering how desperately she yet needed his familiarity with the sultans—something not even Philip could give her.

"Philip . . ." she whispered, "you need say no more now. We can talk later when we are alone."

"I have much to say. I should have known where your desperation would lead you when I failed you that night in my chamber. Beloved, I vow to stand beside you now." He looked at Tancred. "And you are my witness, Norman. If you would rescue Helena from Kalid, your aid is no less needed now."

If his words left her astounded, what did Tancred think? She glanced at him, uncertain she wished to meet that melting gaze head on. He said nothing, but her breath ceased as she caught the glitter in his eyes. She turned her back, facing Philip, and his arm slipped about her protectively.

"I intend to appeal to the emperor as soon as this other matter with Bohemond is taken care of. He will be in a kinder mood once the princes swear their fealty to him and are ushered across the Bosporus. Should he refuse my plea, I will proceed as though we accept the fate that threatens to tear us apart. But I have a plan."

Plan? What plan? she wondered. And would it work?

Philip turned toward Tancred. "I will have you placed in command of the entourage bringing Helena to Antioch. The men under you will be loyal to me. You will take Helena and proceed not to Antioch but to the Castle of Hohms. I will join you there."

Her heart leaped and she gripped his arm.

"And at the Castle of Hohms, then what?" came Tancred's smooth voice. "You will live happily there, the two of you? For how long? Until Irene and Constantine arrive with soldiers on horses to bring you back to the Sacred Palace? What of Helena? Will she then be sent to Kalid—a present after your wedding night?"

She whirled, her breath catching, but Tancred did not seem to care. He watched Philip with a cool, challenging stare that caused her protest to die on her lips.

If she thought his words would provoke Philip to an angry storm, she was wrong, for Philip remained as cool as Tancred. A glimmer of victory showed in his eyes.

"When Helena and I marry, there is no one who will take her from me again. Including Kalid."

"He may have other ideas," said Tancred. "He is a warrior."

Helena caught the suggestion that Philip was not. His insolence amazed her, yet she was more surprised by Philip's behavior. Instead of dismissing him for a Norman barbarian to be sent from his presence, Philip remained oddly calm.

"No, friend Tancred, he will not. Would you like to know why? It is simple. After bringing Helena to the Castle of Hohms, you will go on to Antioch. It's been arranged with a certain Byzantine spy to see you safely inside the city. You will remain there until Antioch is surrendered to the Normans—and then you will make certain that Kalid does not leave alive." His smile hinted of victory. "I have every confidence in you. We both do," and he turned triumphantly toward her. "Do we not, Helena?"

Dazed by his words, she could not reply.

Philip seemed almost jovial. "I am certain, friend Tancred, that Kalid will die when your Norman race of warriors scales the walls and occupies the city."

Helena's eyes swerved from Philip to search Tancred's face. Had he known about this? He could not have, she thought. What she expected to see in Tancred's gaze was unclear even to her, but she was not prepared for the look that passed between him and Philip. A message was communicated—one that eluded her.

"Philip, what is this all about?" she demanded.

When he did not answer immediately she looked at Tancred and saw his jawline flex, the cool, almost brittle glimmer in the depths of his eyes as he raked Philip.

"The success of your intrigue is to be congratulated. You have matched your emperor for cunning," said Tancred.

Helena felt the underlying insult in his smooth voice and glanced at Philip.

He smiled coolly. "Your compliment is noteworthy," Philip told him. "Your own labors on behalf of the emperor have not gone unrewarded."

Tancred watched as Philip removed a letter from beneath his maroon cloak and handed it to him.

"You will not need to concern yourself with Walter of Sicily," said Philip. "The information I give you to bring to Bohemond will make you too important to him. You have earned friends in Byzantium. And for your future service in Antioch, I have another noteworthy prize for you."

The look of victory played on Philip's face. Helena watched him, uncertain, disappointment in what she saw inching its way up her back. For the first time she saw that he had his mother's smile when he believed himself triumphant.

"And this noteworthy prize?" inquired Tancred evenly.

"Your much sought for assassin. Mosul. He is a prisoner of mine. And I may at any given day do what I will with him. I believe," he said too casually, "that you desperately need this man alive to prove your innocence in murdering your brother for the Redwan castle and galleons."

It was Helena who gasped. Tancred made no response and looked at him. But Philip was obviously pleased with himself.

"What is this, Philip? You have Tancred's cousin?"

He slipped his arm about her and his eyes asked her to trust him, to remain silent.

Uncertain, Helena watched Tancred calmly open the letter and read. She waited tensely.

A moment later Tancred looked at Philip. "Who knows of this Armenian spy? Your emperor? Irene, Constantine?"

Philip's mouth turned into a humorless smile. "They do not know of Firouz. The plans to deliver Antioch to Bohemond remain a secret between you and me."

"You will risk treason?" inquired Tancred.

Philip looked at him sharply. "The emperor wishes the city and he shall have it. The means by which he receives it is inconsequential."

"Is it? Not all will agree with your conclusion."

Philip rejected his suggestion with a wave of his hand. "Whether Antioch is restored to the Eastern Empire through Prince Kalid for Helena and the castle or by Firouz to Bohemond matters not."

"The emperor will believe it matters if Bohemond decides to retain the city. Then what?"

Philip seemed to wish to dismiss the subject. "It is enough now that you work with Firouz. For the sake of Helena, I shall take my chances." He drew her to his side. "We both will."

Without knowing the contents of the letter, Helena did not understand their conversation, but she heard enough to know that they spoke of risk, one that concerned Tancred.

"Am I a mindless child that no one explains to me what is going on?" she inquired evenly.

"The plan is simple enough for any Byzantine to understand," said Tancred. He looked at Philip. "Will you tell her, or will I?"

Philip hesitated as though he wished to hold back, but having said so much already, he could not. "There is an Armenian spy in Antioch named Firouz. For reasons of his own he will deliver the city to the crusaders."

"Deliver the city? But how?"

"That is information Tancred will see to when he arrives there to meet with him in secret. As you can see, this plan is different from what Irene and Constantine have previously arranged. They expect Kalid to surrender Antioch to me. And I, of course, to take command in the name of Byzantium."

Bewildered by his wish to do this, she searched his face and saw only the look of satisfaction. "Why are you doing this?" she pressed. "Surrender Antioch to the Normans? Why should this guarantee our freedom?"

Philip looked triumphantly at Tancred. "Tancred will see to it that Kalid dies in the battle."

Tancred's gaze flickered. "That thought should bring you and your bridegroom a peaceful night's rest, madame."

"And . . . you will go ahead and do this?" she inquired, surprised, uncertain about the storm of unrest that was beginning to brew in her soul.

Tancred's gaze held hers and he said nothing.

She turned abruptly to Philip and saw the humorless smile.

"Tancred has little choice," said Philip. "I was able to work with the Turkish commander Kerbogha without the knowledge of Kalid. The assassin Tancred seeks is now held a prisoner inside Antioch, and whether he lives or dies is left to my discretion."

A tiny sick feeling fluttered in her stomach. *He sounds so much like his mother. This is something Irene can do well. But Philip?* He was using coercion to force Tancred to cooperate with his wishes, even as Irene did with other warriors to make them carry out her plans. Tancred needed Mosul alive to testify to his innocence. And Philip could call for Mosul's death if Tancred refused to follow his orders.

She turned to Philip, expecting anything but his triumphant smile. "I will have no part of this," she stated.

Philip seemed surprised. "Do not look alarmed, beloved. What do you care for the life of Kalid? Tancred would have confronted him over you sooner or later. I am merely giving him a better opportunity to do so. The end result remains the same. All, except for you and me. This will mean our freedom to marry, to live in peace in Constantinople as we have so planned all our lives."

Her eyes searched his. "Constantinople? Do you think the emperor will receive us once you permit the Normans to take the city?" she protested.

"Do not concern yourself over Bohemond," said Philip confidently. "He can be appeased. There are many kingdoms in the East, are there not, friend Tancred?"

"You should know," came his smooth voice. "Byzantium is the queen of bribe and tribute."

"It is how we have survived these seven hundred years," said Philip flatly. "I neither condemn nor condone. It is merely a fact."

While her earlier estimation of Philip had vindicated his honor when it came to his love for her, she was not proud of his methods and avoided Tancred's gaze. She knew what she would find in those blue-gray eyes.

Philip walked over to the door and opened it. "And now, my Norman friend, you have much to do. And may you do better in your negotiations with the Normans than you have with Godfrey. So much depends on it," he said meaningfully.

Helena turned her back, refusing to look at Tancred, her emotions deep and complex. She heard him shut the door behind him as he left.

Philip walked up to her, smiling. He laughed, drawing her into his arms. "Well, my beloved Helena, you see how much I love you! And my plans are as clever as anything the emperor himself would scheme upon his throne! I shall make an excellent ruler one day."

Her heart beat uneasily, and there was a sick qualm in her stomach as she gazed up into his amused dark eyes.

"Philip," she whispered, her throat dry. "Is it wise to trap Tancred into carrying out your plans? To bait him with the assassin . . . the thought brings me a cold chill. What if something goes wrong?"

"Nothing will go wrong. I have the entire army behind me. Mosul is under lock and key in Antioch. I know as much as the emperor. No, I know more."

His expression was troubling. "But," she whispered, "surely God does not smile upon this treachery."

"Treachery! Kalid is an enemy of Tancred. He would kill him at once if he could. Did I not tell you that even if I threw away all my plans, Tancred would still confront Kalid? So why not confront him for our happiness? Come! Do not look at me that way, Helena. It is the way of Byzantium. You know it as well as I. And Tancred is learning he must cooperate."

"He will not wish to learn. He resents your whip; I could see it easily. You can push him only so far before he turns on you."

"So you know him well, do you?" His smile vanished.

"Philip!"

"Never mind. You are hurt," he said swiftly. "I shall bring you back to the city. Your injury will work to our advantage. Any delay in being sent to Antioch will give Tancred and me more time to arrange things."

"I cannot go back! Irene knows I escaped the garden banquet."

"You have nothing to fear. I will have Constantine convince her your injury took place at the villa. She knows how you love to ride. Some new horses have been bought, and Constantine will tell her you were with him, insisted on riding one, and fell."

"Constantine?" she tensed. "Why would he wish to make excuses for me?"

"He has his reasons," was all Philip would say, but he appeared confident. "I will ask him to do so."

"Since when will he listen to your wishes and mine?"

"He will," he said flatly. "Matters have changed between us."

"Why? What matters?"

He smiled. "He will convince Irene. Leave the matter to me."

I have no choice, Helena realized. She had made the decision to follow Philip and submit to his headship the moment that she allowed Tancred to walk away. She had chosen Philip, and now she must rest under his lordship as the man she would marry.

She looked at him, troubled. Had she made the right decision? Had she yielded herself and her future to the right man? Philip was worth the risk. How many years she had tried to win his devotion, his commitment! And now she had him. For all he was worth.

Her eyes searched his. "So many lies, Philip, so much scheming . . ."

"We must survive our enemies. And when this is all over and the crusaders have marched on to Jerusalem, we too shall have our peace, our contentment."

"What of Nicholas?" she asked worriedly. "How can there be peace when there are plans to arrest him if he enters the city?"

"There will be no move against your uncle. He will enter the city safely with Tancred."

She stared at him, desperately hoping he was right about peace, but fearful that he was not. Wickedness knew no peace. God's holiness had willed it so, and justly. And would Nicholas be willing to forget the injustice heaped upon him?

He must have seen her doubts, for he took hold of her shoulders, his eyes imploring hers.

"Helena, with the crusaders eliminating our enemies in Antioch and Tancred supporting our cause, we can now have what we want most—each other."

But at what cost to them? she wondered. Whatever the price,

it did not seem to disturb Philip—but it lay like a heavy dread in her heart.

"We can have Nicholas marry us at the castle," he continued.

Philip held her, but unnamed fears arose to nag and spoil her dreams. The moment she had longed for these many years was now in her hand, but the victory was robbed of the splendor she had imagined it would be. Despite his declaration, her heart beat laboriously slow.

What had happened during the interlude in which she had last seen Philip in his chamber? Why was he so confident that he could maneuver those in the Sacred Palace whose plans conflicted with his own? How had he been able to locate Mosul in Antioch? Would his confidence continue? Or would some unforeseen happening bring them both to a dungeon?

And Tancred . . .

"If Tancred is successful in his mission, the western princes will soon arrive in Constantinople to vow their vassalage to the emperor. I will then arrange for Tancred to command the entourage that will escort you to Antioch, but once out of Constantinople he will take a different route to the Castle of Hohms."

"Will Irene allow him to escort me? What if she is suspicious? Especially now, after my coming here."

"I will arrange it somehow as though the emperor wishes it. If I also ride in the entourage, she will be less suspicious. She believes I have come to peace concerning the matter of your marriage to Kalid."

"Hold me, Philip. I am afraid."

Tancred went swiftly down the steep steps, snatching his helmet from the table. Outside the guard castle he felt the chill rain beat against him. His eyes smoldered as he tightened the strap beneath his chin. Was Philip lying about having Mosul? He did not think so. Philip had looked too pleased with himself.

There was one consolation to being trapped by Philip into complying with his wishes; the look of disappointment in Helena's face as she had watched Philip play out his game. Was he right? Had she been repelled?

Across the court he saw Bardas near the open stable, feeding Philip's horses.

Tancred placed the folded paper Philip had given him inside his jacket. How much did Bardas know? No matter that Helena would swear her life to the safekeeping of his hand, he did not trust the big Spartan any farther away than he could watch him. He might confront him now over running to Philip to inform him of how Helena had sought his aid, but he was blind enough in his allegiance to the noble to deny any wrongdoing.

Bardas looked up and saw him. The immobile eyes stared back briefly, then in the essence of subservience he turned back to the horses.

Tancred lifted his gaze toward the guard castle, knowing Helena was in the top of the keep with Philip, blindly permitting herself to be convinced of the devotion that she had planned so long to receive from the fastidious and handsome aristocrat. Well, she had him now. How much did it matter to her that Philip would stoop to such low and dishonorable tactics?

Philip had Mosul, and he had Helena.

That leaves me in the uncomfortable position of vassal, he thought with cool anger. *But not for long.* He must play along with Philip's game for a time, until he had opportunity to discover the whereabouts of Mosul from the Armenian named Firouz. Once in Antioch, he would break with Philip and follow his conscience. He would not kill his cousin Kalid to allow the spineless noble to have Helena. If he confronted Kalid, it must be for her alone.

The strong wind pounded the chill rain against the stalwart guard castle and soaked through his riding cloak. His eyes narrowed as the drops pelted his helmet. Philip had made a mistake, Tancred thought. He had unmasked his ruthless character in front of her. Unless she remained deliberately blind to what he was, she could no longer defend his spotless honor while she hurled stones at his own.

If her disappointment in Philip did not happen soon, it would be too late. A faint smile turned his mouth. His dilemma might be worth it after all.

Placing his boot in the stirrup, Tancred swung himself into the saddle and scanned the group of men who would ride under his authority to meet the coming Norman army. Philip had said that they were loyal to him, and he did not doubt they were hand-picked.

He gave a last glance toward Bardas, who had his back toward him, then started toward the road, the mercenary soldiers falling in behind.

It would be good to see Nicholas! He was the one man whose honor could be trusted.

CHAPTER 10
The White Bishop

Tancred, having left the Byzantine guard castle, followed the trade route used by merchant caravans and religious pilgrims who once journeyed toward Jerusalem on penance before the Turks had taken the beloved city. After two days he noticed more than the usual amount of the emperor's patrols traveling in groups.

"The Normans make camp a day ahead," the lead soldier informed him. "Take caution: they are a dangerous-looking lot."

Tancred smiled, for the soldier did not know that he too was a Norman. He gave orders to the Byzantine guard to wait for him at the frontier outpost and rode ahead alone.

It was afternoon on the following day when he neared the Norman camp. A group of dusty friars traveling with the army paused when they saw him approaching astride Apollo. The religious men were well versed on the makings of war, and their sharp eyes measured his chain mail visible under the dark outer tunic.

"Hail and well met, soldier. Do you come peaceably to the Norman camp?"

Tancred smiled. "When one Norman greets another, what else can there be but peace?"

They laughed but remained doubtful. "You are a Norman?"

"Proudly so. A distant cousin of Prince Bohemond."

They studied him. "But you wear a foreign uniform, soldier, and if your sword is blessed by Saint Michael, where is your proof of purpose?"

"With your leave, friars—" and he slowly unsheathed his sword, aware that they also carried weapons and undoubtedly could use them well enough. He remained grave as he showed them the hilt of his blade with its emblem of Michael the Archangel.

Saint Michael, believed by the western knights to lead the standard for Christian knights into holy battle, remained the favorite of the Normans. They attended the church named after Saint Michael in Le Puy for "sword blessing" before their battles with infidels. War for the knights and their accompanying friars or priests was considered to be religious in nature, and men fought with the idea that war for Christ wrought the tenderness of heaven toward the forgiveness of sin.

The friars eyeing Tancred's sword seemed satisfied that it belonged to a Norman knight, and they scanned him again, curiously, no doubt wondering why he did not wear the leather garb of Bohemond's men.

"We are from the monastery at Reggio in the extreme south," said a friar.

Tancred turned in the saddle to peer ahead of him. He was midway between two traveling groups, and the second was nearing, some walking on foot and others on horseback. To locate Nicholas would not be easy in a multitude this size.

"Are all in your caravan from the monastery at Reggio?"

"Nay, those behind are from Bari."

The news was good, since Nicholas had first set foot on its shores when excommunicated from the eastern branch of the Church and was banished from Constantinople.

"Then I shall proceed on my way. Begging your leave," and he sheathed his sword and rode ahead down the road beaten into muddy ruts by passing cavalries and footmen.

The spring afternoon was chill, a breeze stirred the new green leaves, and birds trilled their mating calls. It was a good day to be alive, and he experienced a rejuvenation that came to his heart from being among his own people again. He understood them, their warlike nature, their sometimes superstitious beliefs mingled with religion. Yet, for the most part, they were dedicated, and there were many good Christians among them whose hearts bowed in reverence before God and His Holy Son. They would fight to the death for Him, believing that by fighting political wars they were extending the shores of His earthly kingdom.

It was a satisfaction to Tancred that Nicholas believed otherwise. He had always been a maverick, a well-respected scholar who could read, write, and speak fluently in Greek and Latin, which gave him access to the Scriptures. He had taught Tancred well, and he loved him for it, but Tancred enjoyed flaunting the fact that he could also do something Nicholas could not—read and write in Arabic. He smiled to himself, remembering the battle of wits he had put both Nicholas and his Moorish grandfather, al-Kareem, through by pitting one against the other.

Nicholas had usually countered by underscoring some fact about the Scriptures:

"There are three hundred prophecies concerning the birth, death, resurrection, and earthly reign of Jesus Christ," Nicholas had told him.

"Three hundred!" As a boy, Tancred had been amazed, for he'd been told Jesus was a prophet like Adam, Noah, Abraham, and Moses, but they were all of less importance than Mohammed, the one true prophet of Allah. "And how many prophecies told about the importance of the coming of Mohammed?"

"There are no prophecies recorded in the Bible or the Koran about the coming of Mohammed. Neither Mohammed nor the Koran existed until hundreds of years after Christ returned to the Father. The New Testament was already written and complete."

"But the angel Gabriel came to Mohammed," said Tancred. "Allah's messages were revealed in speeches given to him at Mecca and Medina."

Nicholas turned in the New Testament to the epistle to the Galatians. "These words were written hundreds of years before Mohammed was born. Read what is warned about receiving messages from angels that contradict the Scriptures."

Tancred read the portion aloud: "But though we, or an angel from heaven, preach any other gospel unto you than that which we have preached unto you, let him be accursed. As we said before, so say I now again, if any preach any other gospel unto you than what you have received, let him be accursed."

The discussions had given Tancred plenty to think about late into the night.

"Christianity is not a religion seeking God, but a revelation of God coming down in love to seek and to save the lost sons and daughters of Adam and Eve," Nicholas had explained.

"If I were drowning in a lake," Nicholas had illustrated, "Mohammed would walk up to the lake and tell me to swim.

" 'I cannot swim,' I would cry.

" 'Start moving your arms and legs,' he would say.

" 'It is too late. I am already drowning, nor can I learn.'

" 'Then you will fail and I cannot help you' is his answer.

"But Jesus Christ came to the lake, removed His outer garments of glory, and swam out to save me from drowning."

Nicholas had looked at him intently. "Do you see the difference? Mohammed says, 'Try to do good enough, so you may live!' But Jesus says, 'I give you eternal life as a gift, and then out of thankfulness you may do good.' "

Tancred had considered well. Islam offered no forgiveness of sins. Each person's lifetime deeds would be weighed on the Judgment Day, and they would merit either heaven or hell. His grandfather al-Kareem had taught him the five statements of faith called the Pillars of Islam. Prayer five times a day; profession of faith—"There is no god but Allah and Mohammed is his prophet"; almsgiving to the poor; fasting from sunrise to sunset on Friday and for the month of Ramadan; and at least one journey to Mecca.

"You must bow and pray toward Mecca," Tancred had told Nicholas.

But Nicholas believed Mohammed had gotten the idea of bowing toward Mecca from the Jews in the Old Testament, who faced east and prayed toward Jerusalem, where the Temple of Solomon had stood.

"But even Israel's King Solomon, who dedicated the temple, knew that the true and living God was omnipresent. 'The heavens cannot contain you,' Solomon had said in his prayer when dedicating the temple. 'How much less this temple I have built?'

"Did not Jesus say to the woman at the well, 'Woman, believe me, the hour comes when you will neither worship at this mountain nor yet in Jerusalem. God is a Spirit and those who worship Him must worship in spirit and in truth.'

"Truth, my son, is what matters in the end, not how religiously sincere we may be."

Tancred had listened politely but kept his distance. Al-Kareem had told him the opposite. It was too painful to choose between his grandfather and Nicholas. He knew that one day he must make his own decision based on truth, not his love for either man. What kind of god was Allah? Was he the true God?

Al-Kareem had told him there were ninety-nine names for Allah. Allah was said to be great, powerful, to determine all things. But Tancred became disturbed when Nicholas asked him which names for Allah spoke of his love, mercy, grace, and forgiveness.

But al-Kareem was indignant when Tancred told him this on a visit to Palermo.

"It is blasphemy, Jehan, to even think of knowing God in a personal way. Such an idea presumes that God comes down and makes himself available to humans. It is beneath Allah's dignity."

"Ah, but that is the wonder of it all," Nicholas had said when Tancred told him of his grandfather's words. "God did come down. He pitched His tent among us. 'He that has seen me has seen the Father,' said Jesus."

Tancred was surprised at that and had said no more. Nevertheless, he never forgot it. And thereafter he had considered and carefully marveled over the words of Jesus in the Gospels.

His grandfather became agitated when Tancred told him what he had learned from the Christian side of the family. Al-Kareem would whistle through his teeth and narrow his eyes, tapping his fingers across his belly. "Jehan. You must not listen to that infidel Nicholas. The Koran is truth. And the Bible is full of errors."

"How do you know, my grandfather?"

His brows had shot up. "Because the Koran is the last revelation from Allah. And since the Bible does not agree with the Koran, the only conceivable explanation, Jehan, is that the Bible has been changed."

"But—Nicholas says that much of the Bible was written about

things that happened a thousand years before Mohammed was even born."

His eyes narrowed. "Nicholas lies."

"Maybe the angel was not Gabriel—maybe—"

"Jehan!" He threw his hands into the air, overcome with horror.

Nicholas had remained calm when Tancred, a boy of twelve, sat cross-legged before him in the monastery school and soberly lectured him to do as al-Kareem said.

"If you will read the Scriptures, Tancred, then I will read your Koran. We shall match our hours spent and report to the other of the wisdom we have learned. We will compare wisdom for wisdom, truth for truth, Allah with God Almighty, and your prophet Mohammed with the matchless Jesus Christ."

"I accept, Bishop Nicholas."

And so the long journey toward truth had begun. . . .

Tancred rode Apollo down the road toward the Norman camp, thinking of the old one named Odo, who had helped him escape from Redwan Castle. Before his death he had given him an object to return to the shrine at Jerusalem. On one occasion he had nearly lost it when taken captive by Rhinelanders. Tancred frowned to himself, making up his mind. He would give the relic to Nicholas to return to Jerusalem.

He had ridden on for several minutes when he approached a richly draped litter slung between two mules and carrying an ancient man in an archbishop's robe with a fur collar. A wide-brimmed hat with a gold tassel sat atop his white head, and Tancred recognized the sign of an esteemed scholar.

The old gentleman held a rolled parchment in his hand and was speaking to a page who hurried along beside him. The young boy wore a short velvet jacket, tight purple hosiery, and a pair of leather shoes with long points that flopped in the dust. Around the cleric rode well-armored knights who served the archbishop, while in front and behind the litter were archers.

A group of friars, with ankle-length tunics tied around the

waist with cord, followed behind.

Tancred held his mount, and Apollo sniffed the wind with his quivering nostrils.

Waiting until the group came closer, Tancred boldly rode into the road and held up his gloved hand.

At once, the knights circled into a protective position, guarding the cleric. The archers notched their bows.

"Peace, father! I beg your interruption," called Tancred.

The old cleric squinted toward him as though blind, cocking his head to hear. The lead soldier, a man with an unflinching countenance, raked Tancred with suspicion.

"Who are you? What do you want?"

"I ask your consideration in the name of Count Dreux Redwan!"

There came a brief silence among the knights, and he felt their hard, scrutinizing gaze.

The old man leaned forward in the litter, steadying himself on the arm of one of the bearers, and cupped his ear toward Tancred.

"Dreux?" he shouted. "Did you say Dreux?"

"I did, honorable sir."

A suspicious glance sized him up. "What do you know of Count Dreux Redwan?"

"I am his son and heir," he stated flatly.

Again, silence followed, and he was certain the old cleric was stunned.

"He lies, my liege," said the soldier in charge. "It is a ruse. Let us be on our way before we are set upon from the woods."

The old one responded cautiously now. "Who is your liege?"

"The Great Count Roger I of Sicily. Bohemond is related to my father's kin."

The soldier leaned impatiently from his saddle toward the litter. "Anyone would know as much. It proves nothing, my liege. Look at his garb; it is anything but Norman."

The old scholar lifted a fragile hand, beckoning. "Come closer, young man. I would look upon your face."

Tancred eased Apollo forward and looked down at the cleric. The man's clear gray eyes appraised him, squinting.

"Perhaps so, perhaps so. You have his goodly appearance."

It was Tancred's turn to be curious. "You knew my father?"

"He died in my arms in St. Peter's Basilica the night Rome was defeated."

Tancred tensed. The memory of that bitter night when flames touched the city sprang up within his heart. He had been there . . . knocked from the saddle of a scholar friend of his father—

Tancred stopped, startled, and stared. "Turill?" he asked.

The thin lips of the old man moved into a melancholy smile. "Yes. It is I, Turill. So it is you after all, Tancred! I lost you that night, my son. I was so intent upon your father that when I turned about to bring you to his final embrace, you were gone."

Tancred clamped his jaw to control his feelings. His father had wanted a last embrace. . . . "The fire and battle was all about me. I ran."

"Praise be to God that it was Nicholas who found you behind the altar."

Yes, thought Tancred, remembering. He had hidden in terror, hearing the screams of a torched city, of priests, of nuns, and of the citizens of Rome being slain.

In the quiet but suffocating chapel, the drape had been suddenly jerked aside, uncovering his hiding place.

Tancred had expected a halberd to come crashing down upon his head, splitting him in two—just as he had seen his father's friends axed and thrust through with lances. Instead, a warrior-priest with bold dark eyes and a rugged face had stared down at him, a look of keen interest ebbing the ferocity from his expression.

"Come out, my son," Nicholas had said. "You are Count Dreux's son, are you not? You will be safe with me. I shall take you to Monte Casino."

"Well, well," Turill was breathing, dragging Tancred's memory back from the fiery past. "So it *is* you, Tancred! How splendid you look. Your father would be proud. And I suppose you are seeking Nicholas? He is in the camp. And you, son of the great Dreux! Why do you wear the uniform of the Eastern Empire? Do you serve with your uncle Rolf at the Castle of Hohms?"

Although he trusted Turill, he was not certain of the men listening. Explanation must wait. He ignored the measured looks directed at him from the lead soldier.

"I am in service to the emperor, who has sent me to meet with Prince Bohemond."

The old archbishop turned his head toward his lead knight. "Sweyn, take this man to Nicholas. If this is Tancred, son of Dreux, he will know. And you," he said turning again to Tancred, "I wish you the benediction of heaven." He raised his hand in the form of a cross.

Tancred bowed his head and performed the required response.

The caravan moved on down the muddy road.

The soldier named Sweyn was silent, probably wondering if he were truly in the presence of the son and heir of Count Dreux Redwan. Tancred questioned his own folly in so quickly announcing who he was.

Sweyn turned his horse to ride and Tancred followed.

Sweyn gave him a sharp glance, scanning him. At once his warrior eyes fell upon the scimitar—any experienced soldier knew that it was not a weapon used by Normans. He studied Apollo, as though judging if the horse were an Arabian mare, also considered to be an "infidel." Normans rode the Great Horse, bred for its strength, stature, and weight in the impressive Norman cavalry charge first used by William the Conqueror.

"You have a fine horse. And you carry a scimitar."

Tancred gave a slow smile. "You are observant. Even though the horse is lighter than we customarily ride as knights, I prefer its agility and speed."

Sweyn obviously did not agree. "In a battle charge, he would be run down."

"You are likely to be right, and if I were in war in the West, or in a joust, I would prefer the Great Horse. But in battle with the Seljuk Turks to take Jerusalem, you will learn quickly that they do not fight according to our custom. They do not charge, but strike with arrows, weaving and falling back. And the weather is different from what we are accustomed to in our own land. Here, the knights' heavy armor and the desert heat will wear out the Great Horse."

Sweyn did not like what he heard and glanced again at the scimitar. "Does the son of the greatest of Normans also prefer an infidel blade?"

"Like my horse, it is swift and certain. But I also use this." And before the soldier could respond, Tancred had unleashed his Norman blade and held it up, clutching the gemmed hilt. He thought longingly of another sword that had belonged to Count Dreux Redwan. Nicholas had given it to him at Monte Casino.

And now, Mosul had it—along with his Arabian mare Alzira.

In the Norman tongue, he quoted by memory from the knight's *Song of Roland*:

"Ah, Durendal! How white and lovely you are, and your golden hilt so full of relics!"

The soldier's expression changed to one of grudging acceptance. The song was the heart and soul of the belief of the Norman knights. To be a knight meant you battled for God as well as your earthly liege. To fight with courage, to die if need be in defeat or victory, meant glory, even heaven. And the infidel was an enemy for the swift blade Durendal to strike into submission.

Tancred had not read of this in Scripture, but the belief among the knights was real enough to go to battle over, should any deny it.

"I see you are truly a Norman knight," said Sweyn. Without another word, he rode toward the camp.

Tancred slipped his sword into its sheath and followed. Apollo tossed his head, as though to claim his place among the larger horses, his mane shining like black gold in the freckled sunlight that fell from the high branches of the trees. And Tancred in good humor imagined the stallion proud of all the boasting he had heaped upon him and the scimitar.

Apollo whinnied and pranced ahead.

It was toward dusk as they threaded their way through a grove of cypress and tangled wild berry vines. Tancred caught a whiff of woodsmoke on the breeze, and the smell was tantalizing. Camp-fires, thousands of them! It would not be long now. He was hungry and he thought of the good things awaiting him around Nicholas's fire.

Coming to a rise, they surprised two hawks who flew up from the clearing. Squawking and flapping their strong wings in the direction of the eastward hills, they disappeared into the glow of a lavender sunset.

They rode a short distance along the rise facing the sea and a Greek ship was at anchor. Tancred suspected the emperor's men were keeping a tight watch on Bohemond by land and sea, reporting daily of his progress toward the walls of Constantinople.

"A beautiful ship," came the wistful voice of the soldier.

"Yes. But no better than our own galleons. As a boy I once sailed all the way to Cathay."

Sweyn marveled. "You have been to fabled Cathay?"

Tancred turned to ride on. "Cathay is as real as Sicily. It lies beyond Hind, beyond the tallest and greatest mountains upon which I have ever laid eyes. They were constantly white with snow."

The soldier said nothing and took the lead again along the rise, and riding together with the sea breeze to their faces, Tancred watched several other ships now in view. They reminded him of falcons patiently waiting to swoop in on the walled seaport.

"Over there," said Sweyn, and gestured with his gloved hand.

Tancred turned to look southeast. He saw the Norman camp and his heart surged, for it seemed to him the entire army of the three lords was spread below him. Scouts had seen them coming from a distance. Far off, he could see a group of horsemen riding to meet them, no doubt wondering if they were friend or foe.

Then Tancred beheld a horse—a magnificent animal of soft gray, one that he remembered. *There cannot be two horses like that in all Sicily.*

The man seated, he knew. It was Norris Redwan, a cousin.

The breeze caught the gonfanon carried by a knight, and Tancred masked his start at seeing the familiar crimson flag with its twin falcons in flight, one white, the other black. He realized that he had blundered upon an envoy from the Redwan family clan.

It was too late to turn back.

CHAPTER 11
Growl of the Northern Wolves

Tancred touched Apollo lightly with his heels and grimly rode to meet the party of horsemen carrying the Redwan family gonfanon.

His cousin Norris saw him coming from a distance and responded with astonishment. Even if his cousins rode with Bohemond for no cause but the expedition to Jerusalem, they knew about Derek. They knew their uncle searched for Tancred.

Tancred rode slowly forward, keeping his hand within reach of his blade. If he fell captive to Norris there would be no audience with Nicholas or Bohemond. His cousin, anxious for fame, would hurry him off to one of the ships to be returned to Sicily.

The soldier Sweyn gave Tancred a sharp glance. "I sense neither of you expected to see the other. You are his enemy?"

"He has made himself mine. He takes more upon himself than he has the right."

"Then you know him?"

"He is a cousin."

Sweyn looked confused, for the expression on Norris's face was anything but one of kindred spirit.

Norris and the handful of esquires attending him rode forward and stopped. "Seize that man!" he ordered, pointing at Tancred.

Tancred unsheathed his blade. "Peace, cousin, let us talk in a council with Nicholas."

"I am on errantry for Turill of Rome," called Sweyn. "There is to be no fighting now. Turill bid me bring this man to Bishop Nicholas."

"Tancred is wanted by our uncle, Walter of Sicily! Take his blade."

"I am innocent of the charge," stated Tancred. "I can explain if brought to Nicholas."

He spoke in the direction of Norris, demanding in a clear, strong voice, "Where is Nicholas of Monte Casino? I am to see the bishop!"

A half-dozen knights heard him, as he intended, and curious now, they moved in around him. Tancred challenged, "Who among you would dare draw sword against the son and heir of Count Dreux Redwan?" He gestured to his cousin, who sat glaring at him. "This cousin of mine will one day owe me his fealty! And does he order my blade to be taken from me? A Redwan does not surrender his weapon."

The Redwan name arrested their attention and caused a hesitation as Tancred expected. His motive was simple: question Norris's right to command, and breed doubt in the minds of the men under him. He remembered that Norris had always been hotheaded, and he suspected these men were not all that favorable toward his rule.

In the awkward silence, Tancred's voice rang out clear and strong: "It is no secret how I am accused of killing Derek, but my hands are clean of my brother's blood. And I will yet prove my innocence. I am the son of Dreux and the rightful heir in Sicily. I am also the adopted son of Rolf Redwan, whom you all know and respect as a great warrior. Do you deny me the simple request to speak with Nicholas?"

Norris was furious, more so because his horsemen hesitated and were listening. "You are also the grandson of al-Kareem. How did you escape the castle? Did your infidel friend Hakeem get you out? He too will pay for his treachery!"

Tancred clasped his sword and turned in the saddle to scan the sober-faced men. Sentimentality was not a noted trait among Norman warriors, and while they would die for him if elevated to his authority, they could as easily kill him if they thought him guilty of treachery against Derek, whom they had loved.

He clasped his sword. Apollo stepped about, head extended, nostrils flaring, smelling a battle, and ready to prove he was equal to the Great Horse. Tancred quieted him and spoke firmly to Sweyn. "I have come with important news for Prince Bohemond. Deny me audience now and you will do him and yourself a grave injustice."

He looked from man to man as they watched him warily. They had not yet moved against him, giving him confidence. Some must doubt the lie his uncle had perpetrated accusing him of Derek's death. Perhaps Nicholas had already spoken out on his behalf during the journey.

"How many of you are loyal to the memory of my father?"

The knights scowled and the esquires on foot cast their eyes downward.

"You know we are all loyal to your father, Tancred," said one of the knights, shifting uncomfortably. "But he is dead. So is Derek."

"And I will bring to our justice the man who threw that dagger. It was not I."

"That is not for them to decide," called Norris. "It is for you to endure craven to prove your guilt or innocence."

"And if I cannot bring you the assassin, I will walk the fire, if it is necessary. As the heir of Count Dreux I have the right to be heard—a right denied me in Sicily. Before any trial is held, Rolf must be present as my adoptive father."

"Until he arrives we are to serve Walter and his son Norris," said the knights.

"It is Mosul Kareem who assassinated Derek Redwan."

There was an exchange of glances, then Norris shouted, "Mosul? Do you ask us to forget that he is your Moorish cousin? Nor will we forget that you bear his blood—and have the heart of an infidel."

Tancred hoped to gain time, for in the discourse Sweyn had moved away, unnoticed, and he believed him to be going to find Nicholas.

Tancred lifted the point of his blade. "For that, my cousin, I could easily take your head."

Norris took the bait and kneed his great charger forward. "Do you challenge me?"

Tancred scanned him. "I would not contest a babe so soon removed from his mother's milk. I have my honor, and it is not to slay lads."

Laughter erupted. Norris looked at the knights angrily and they grew silent. He drew his sword. "By the gods of the Vikings! I shall not waste you on craven—I shall have your blood myself! A joust!"

Tancred affected indifference. "As you wish, Cousin. Will you meet me on horse or on foot?"

Tancred had no desire to harm him, only to unhorse him, a shame that Norris would not lightly forget. The men drew back, moody, looking anything but eager for the fight. Despite the death of Derek, Tancred was the one remaining son of their liege.

Tancred deliberately took his time, leaning over and checking the reins as though he had trouble. Norris had already taken his position and was impatient as always.

Tancred rode Apollo opposite Norris, then turned slowly to face him. Despite his words, he knew that his cousin was a fierce swordsman and owned a more powerful horse for the charge.

He patted Apollo's shining neck. "You have your chance, boy. Will you be bested by a barbarian nag? This one is for your mistress and Byzantium!"

Apollo snorted as if he understood and pawed the earth.

Norris held his sword ready. Tancred unsheathed his blade and gripped it tightly to stand the bludgeoning force.

His cousin's Great Horse gathered speed like a massive avalanche.

"You will need courage, Apollo!"

The sleek stallion raced ahead, as light on its feet as though aided by wings.

The Great Horse headed straight toward Apollo in an attempt to run him down. Tancred held him steady and kept to the rein. As they approached he veered to the side, smashing a solid blow against his cousin's blade. The horses cleared, sweeping past with nostrils flaring. Turning Apollo, who proved more agile, Tancred approached Norris and confronted him.

Tancred lowered his blade. "I wish only to see Nicholas, then I will leave. Stay out of this. You need prove nothing."

Norris laughed, his blue eyes wild with passion.

"You ride well!" he said almost gleefully.

Tancred studied him. *It is madness—he is enjoying this!*

The horses began to warily circle each other. Norris swung. Tancred barely had time to block his blade. They fought, thrusting. Tancred, unwilling to kill him, was using all his skill to simply hold him off. A gratuitous shout went up from the Norman knights as the two men hacked at each other.

Circling again, Tancred delayed, holding him off with his sword until the knights shouted impatiently for action. He struck a ringing blow to the side of his cousin's helmet. Norris let out a stunned gasp as the powerful force rocked him off balance and a shout went up from the knights. Dazed, he slid from his saddle to the dirt. Beaten, Norris lay disabled with wounded pride.

Sweyn had not returned with Nicholas, but a second group of horsemen arrived, and a second cousin—this one, Leif Redwan.

Leif was five years Tancred's senior and unlike their other cousins, a man who preferred the sea and had sailed the northern waters in command of the family galleons. Because of the age difference between them and Leif's long voyages, Tancred had not known him as well as he had the others.

He hardly recognized his maverick cousin. His mother had been a Norman, and unlike Tancred, Leif's hair was golden, his eyes an ice blue. His hair was not short in typical Norman style but formed a thick golden mane that reached to his broad shoulders. It was now tied back with a strip of leather, and the handsome features typical of all the Redwan men were heavily bronzed by the sun.

Leif's halberd was battered from skirmishes across Europe and his clothes were dusty. With the rest of the Redwan cousins he had left Sicily three months earlier to ride under the gonfanon of Prince Bohemond.

His eyes swept Tancred's handsome Byzantine uniform mingled with Norman chain mesh and helmet, and then swerved to

Norris, sprawled on the ground. He lifted a hand to the men with him, and they formed a line of chargers that kept Tancred from passing through the camp.

"You assassinated your brother, and now do you turn on your cousin also?"

Tancred regarded Leif carefully. He was not hotheaded like Norris, and he seemed to have as much question as accusation in his voice.

"If there were more sound reason in our family than the superstitious beliefs of our Viking ancestors, I would not be hunted down and encircled like some crazed beast fit for the kill. I can prove my innocence by capturing Derek's assassin."

"You will have a difficult time finding him if he exists. We are determined to hold you. The clan from Sicily is all here with Bohemond—including our uncle Walter.

"Call it superstition if you will, but as head of the Redwan clan, Walter will demand craven—" He stopped suddenly, looking past Tancred's shoulder, his expression one of alarm, then anger. "Norris! No!"

Tancred turned Apollo's reins but not swiftly enough. Norris had remounted and was riding toward him, a twisted expression on his sweat-stained face.

Tancred had not yet sheathed his sword and lifted it to absorb the blow. Norris struck again, and Tancred felt the chain mesh give.

He struggled to hold his sword as blood ran down his chest from somewhere. He had a glimpse of Norris, sword lifted.

An arrow whizzed, making a sickening impact. Norris gasped, then slumped in the saddle.

Several men ran to help Norris down from his mount and kneel beside him. "He yet lives."

Tancred dismounted and stood, dazed, steadying himself beside Apollo as Leif rode up holding his bow.

"You are good with that."

"I did it not for you but for our customs—you must undergo craven. And I would not wish yet another cousin to be accused of murder."

Tancred met the ice blue gaze as chill as the northern waters and reached to the spot near his collarbone that seeped with blood. His mouth thinned with cynicism. "Thanks. Then you best hope your arrow missed his heart."

"And you?" He looked at the bloodstain growing wider. "You are turning as white as the ice caps of the northland."

"I will live," Tancred said abruptly and snatched his satchel from the back of his saddle. Ignoring Leif, he fumbled with the bag, removing wine and dried sphagnum. Soaking it, he pressed it into his wound, then turned his attention to Norris.

His cousin lay grimacing with pain as he walked up. Even so, Norris glared his rage at both him and Leif.

"I will have both your skulls for this! Just wait until Walter finds out what you have done, Leif! I would have been commended for returning the assassin! And now—"

"Your tongue acts before your brain," interrupted Leif, yet holding his bow. "Thank God you live. And that I am the best archer in Sicily, lest you would be carried by angels to Abraham's bosom."

Tancred enlarged the rip in Norris's shirt with a jerk of impatience. "Are you so certain of his heavenly destiny?" Examining the location of the arrow, he decided it could be withdrawn without internal damage. He took hold with both hands.

Norris glared up at him. "I do not trust you! Let another remove it."

Tancred smirked. "You speak of trust? You who would attack my back?"

Norris turned his head away, sullen. "I was a little angry," he mumbled.

"Only a little?" mocked Tancred. "What do you do when you are in a rage?"

"You humiliated me. You, a physician, unseated me."

"Count your blessings that I was allowed to study medicine at Salerno." Tancred gripped the arrow more tightly.

But Norris would not be consoled and groaned, "Count Roger's own bodyguard made me a knight! I lay all night on my face before the holy altar!"

"It did you little good. I suggest less hours sprawled on the cold floor and more time devoted to learning the Scriptures."

"Cease your sanctified tongue and pull the arrow!"

Tancred smiled with malicious humor. "Think you are man enough to endure it without piercing our eardrums?"

"Me? You are not man enough to make me yell."

"Your boasts are as empty as the wind."

With a smooth and straight pull Tancred produced the arrow, holding it up for inspection while Norris groaned. Tancred smiled down at him. "My skills never cease to amaze me. You can thank me later when I am your liege." He poured in wine as Norris paled. He covered the wound with a clean cloth. "I will consider you for the duties of carrying my medical satchel and weapons."

Norris gritted at him. And Tancred, feeling weaker than he let on, managed to stand, reaching a hand to his own wound. He grew sober. "I forgive you for your treachery, my cousin, but only Christ can forgive your sin."

He turned and walked toward Apollo, struggling to remain on his feet. . . . He must reach Nicholas—

At any moment he expected Leif's order for the men to take him prisoner, but silence followed, as though they wondered why he would aid a kinsman who had sought his death. Nevertheless, he was certain the order would come.

Perhaps they were in no hurry, knowing he could not get far in his condition. He strapped his satchel to the saddle, fumbling now and leaning against Apollo. His head throbbed, his left arm and shoulder numb. Unloosening the strap on his helmet, he pulled it off, his hair damp. Only a moment was all he needed . . . a moment to rest. . . . His helmet fell to the ground—

Leif's voice rang out, "Yohan! Bring our cousin to the tent of Nicholas! Our uncle will want him well before he walks the fire. I will alert Walter of our quarry."

The Norman camp resembled a rambling tent city. Gonfanons bearing various insignias hung on wooden poles outside large tents where nobles loitered with hunting dogs and falcons. Knights from Sicily and southern Italy gathered with those from Normandy, each group eyeing the other with respect mingled with wariness.

Among them stood two tall bishops, each bearing swords.

Troubadours practiced their entertainments and midgets were running through their acrobatic stunts with a trained bear; a lute player performed a lilting tune while an archer practiced shooting into a haystack to the jibe of others who boasted they could do better. Heralds stood outside important tents, ready to dispatch messages. And, as with Duke Godfrey and the other arriving princes, there was a large peasant following in the rear of the camp. Entire families followed their feudal lords wherever they went, doing washing and cooking and tending of animals. And from many tents there came the cry of newborn babes. *What will become of them?* Tancred found himself wondering. Would they grow to knighthood in and around Jerusalem, or be buried in the sand, known only to Christ? He who had been born in a stable and had to flee from His enemy across the Egyptian desert with only the stars for a roof and a mother's breast for a cradle.

The clink of metal, the whinny of a horse, the barking of a dog, the laughter of rough men not yet disillusioned with the task of liberating Jerusalem, brought Tancred's wandering mind back. There were the familiar smells of a large camp on the breeze; of leather, of horses, of woodsmoke. Here, he felt at home, and yet— he also felt a stranger to the cause that fired their souls. He preferred the peaceful chamber of the Royal Library, the smell of parchment and ink, the deep thoughts of great men who had come and gone down the road of the past.

As he looked about the camp he saw clerics as well as soldiers. The nobles—and even some famed knights—had their own personal priest who traveled with them, and the Norman clergy was not exempt from battle. They had developed the calling of the "warrior-bishop" who was also skilled with weapons.

Now inside Nicholas's tent, Tancred rested briefly on the cushions while Nicholas paced, digesting the news he had given him, most of it ill.

The formidable figure of handsome Greek blood hadn't worsened for wear in his journey across Europe, thought Tancred. Over the black woolen tunic he wore fine chain mesh, his scabbard of leather housed a sword, and though he couldn't see it, Tancred believed that a dagger was kept at his left boot top and a small

Moorish dagger was worn in a wrist-sheath strapped along his forearm underneath the mesh—a gift Tancred had given him several years ago.

His thick hair was midnight black with a flattering tinge of iron gray, like the feather tips of a bird wing. His eyes too were dark and robust, and his hard features were well-proportioned according to Greek lines.

"Sweyn told me of your trouble with Norris."

"Norris tried to kill me. I unseated him and his pride was wounded."

Nicholas scowled. "Norris is impulsive. The news of what happened will spread quickly. You know Walter searches for you and all Sicily believes you guilty of Derek's death, even those who knew you best. It was dangerous to come here so boldly."

"Does Bohemond think me guilty also?"

"I have spoken to him of your innocence and I think he is willing to accept my testimony, but not even he will risk defending you from craven."

"The news I bring him will win his favor and his support."

At that, Nicholas ceased his pacing and looked down at him, curious. Tancred reached inside his uniform and brought out a sealed document. "I must speak with Bohemond. I am liaison of the emperor."

Nicholas scrutinized him, surprised, then appeared humored. "Well, indeed!" And he relaxed, as though the news bought them time and protection. He lowered himself onto a chair tossed with a fur, tapping the edge of a rolled parchment against his chin, seemingly digesting the news.

"Liaison of the emperor, you say. You have moved quickly," he commented dryly. "The next thing I will hear is that you have married into Byzantine nobility."

Tancred remained smooth and inscrutable beneath his dark, robust gaze. "Not yet."

Nicholas was quick to catch his eye.

Tancred smiled faintly. "I left Helena in the arms of Philip Lysander."

"Ah, so you have met her. . . ."

"I have met her," came Tancred's indolent voice.

Nicholas watched him. "And what do you think of my niece?"

Tancred reached across the cushions to a skin of water and, meeting Nicholas's musing gaze, drank, aware of the veiled good humor and alert interest in his mentor's face.

"I survived. You never told me you had a niece in all the years I was under your tutelage at Monte Casino."

"You kept me too busy mentally parrying with my opponent, your notable grandfather."

"Helena is spoiled and willful," commented Tancred easily, tossing the skin aside. "Her attitude begs to be tamed and her Byzantine superiority is trying."

Nicholas continued to tap the parchment, his dark eyes flickering with amusement. "I assume you think Philip is not the man to tame her."

"Philip has captured her devotion from childhood. It will take time for her to mature enough to awaken from the illusion that he is a mighty statesman, a hero garbed in gallantry. She was weaned on Byzantine power and Philip represents its greatness. Otherwise," he said, "I have been too busy to actively consider my feelings toward her."

Tancred leaned back against the soft pillows, locking his hands behind his head and staring up at the tent ceiling.

"I am certain you will eventually realize what your true feelings already are," said Nicholas.

Tancred turned his head at the faint suggestion in his voice that he had already made a favorable decision, despite his words to the contrary.

Nicholas showed nothing behind his even gaze and continued to tap the rolled parchment.

Tancred stated firmly, "But this one thing I do know, and I would warn you—Philip cannot be fully trusted where she is concerned. His emotions are volatile. One day he is his own man, vowing her protection from Kalid and Antioch, the next he follows the plans of his mother. He can be sullen and defeated by life, and at the same time imagine himself a great military leader wise enough to become emperor."

Nicholas was grave, as though remembering something that troubled him about Philip, or was it Irene? "If I were you," continued Tancred, "I would not permit her to marry him at the Castle of Hohms. He is not the strong seigneur that she needs."

Nicholas's black brow lifted. "I see you understand the manner of man Philip has become. When he was a boy, he was different. His heart was tender and he had an ear to hear and distinguish truth from error. I was very fond of him. . . ." A troubled frown creased his rugged face, browned by the months of sun while crossing Europe. "Irene has destroyed his soul. It is a curse that children can have parents who mold and shape their minds into believing the devil's lies. Irene has planted the seeds of astrology in his soul and now he is filled with pride and dreams of self-glory."

"Philip believes he will one day become emperor," said Tancred, remembering back to their meeting in the Baths of Zeuxippus. *"I could never leave the service of the emperor—it is my life,"* Philip had said.

Just how sincere was he in telling Helena at the guard castle that he would align himself with her against the wishes of the emperor and Irene?

Tancred's doubts surfaced. Philip expected to use him to accomplish his ends with Kalid, but then what? Even with Kalid dead, would Philip remain committed to Helena should Irene have political cause to contest?

"Philip believes in the stars," Tancred told Nicholas quietly, knowing it must be a grief to him.

"Yes," murmured Nicholas thoughtfully, as if remembering back to his own dealings with Irene. "She is a mouthpiece for the spirits of the ancient Greek gods. She has seen Philip's future written in the zodiac."

"And he believes it," said Tancred with scorn.

"Hmm . . . but Helena does not. Even as a child she warmed to the truth of Christianity. Adrianna taught her well. We both did. But Helena also nurtured the notion of one day marrying Philip. Even Irene agreed until this vile plan for a political marriage to Kalid."

Tancred sat up and winced as he touched his shoulder, feeling sudden irritation toward Norris. "What will you do about Antioch?" he asked.

"I think it best we carry on the plans you have already mentioned. We will bring her to the Castle of Hohms and leave her under the protection of your uncle while you seek the assassin. Seigneur Rolf will have a garrison of strong warriors, able even to defend the castle against a siege if necessary. Once Antioch falls, the plan to marry her off to Kalid will no longer be profitable. We shall then take matters from there, and the future rests with God."

That Helena would be safe at the castle Tancred was certain, but she expected Philip to be there with her—and Nicholas to marry them.

No matter, he thought firmly. He had his own quest to fulfill. Unless Philip was lying, Mosul was even now held a prisoner in Antioch awaiting his own arrival.

Tancred stood, anxiously. "There is much to do. I cannot waste time lounging about while healing. Can you bring me to Bohemond?"

"It is best you are not seen about camp. I will send a message for him to come here."

Nicholas went to the tent opening and called for a boy, and when he turned back, Tancred's gaze fell on the red crusader cross on the left side of his cloak.

"You have taken the cross?" His voice showed surprise, even displeasure.

"Deus vult!" murmured Nicholas to himself, looking at the parchment in his hand. He laid it aside in a satchel and removed a small leather-bound book.

Tancred paid no attention to the book but studied Nicholas, wondering. He could not believe that Nicholas would accept the edict that waging war against the Moslems and liberating the Christian shrines in Jerusalem was of God. Was he wrong? After all, he had not seen Nicholas since before Urban's speech at Clermont.

"I am surprised you would take the vow. For years you told me that God cannot forgive sin apart from the redeeming sacrifice of Christ."

"Thus it is written. I am pleased my patient teaching has rooted in your mind. May it also blossom in your heart."

"It has. But why did you take the cross?"

"Does it offend you? I am the pope's representative to the Norman army, even as Adehemar rides with Count Raymond."

Tancred pondered. He was not satisfied with the too-simple explanation. At Monte Casino, Nicholas had been the maverick spokesman who did not always agree with the teachings of the Church in Rome, insisting more emphasis should be placed on Scripture rather than tradition.

He frowned. "I cannot believe you would sanction *jihad.*"

Nicholas looked at him, surprised. "I do not. Nor do the Scriptures. The one holy war yet to be fought is in the future, when the King of kings rides forth on a white horse."

"Therefore," challenged Tancred, gesturing to the cross, "why did you vow?"

"I have my reasons. What better way to enter Constantinople, avoiding the traps of my enemies? Yet your concern is valid. To wage carnal war in the name of the cross is profane. The cross represents redemption, forgiveness, the love of God for humanity—even," he said with a wry glint in his eyes, "for the infidel Saracen."

"You should preach that truth to Count Emich and the Rhinelanders," said Tancred, remembering the havoc among the Jews. "The People of the Book have reaped a hellish reward from false zealots with crosses sewn to their tunics."

Nicholas was grave. "Yes, the devil has won a victory. I have heard what was done to the Jews by some of the crusaders." His eyes flashed. "They will answer for it. They have lifted sword against the earthly family of our Lord. You know why the devil wishes their destruction? Because Scripture promises Christ will return to reign over them from Jerusalem. To annihilate the Jew would eliminate the very people He is to reign over! Ah, the twisted mind of Satan! How insidious is his hatred for the Jew."

Tancred told him about his journey through Worms, Cologne, and about Count Emich's ridiculous goose that was used to "guide" his Rhinelanders against the Jewish communities. He removed the handwritten booklet he had retrieved from Rachel, its pages worn from her use, and now his own.

"These words are from the New Testament. I translated them at the Royal Library in Constantinople."

Nicholas examined them. "A good work." And he looked at

Tancred, pleased. "I have something for you. I have spent the last two years preparing this. It is a birthday gift." And he handed Tancred the leather-bound book.

Tancred accepted it curiously, feeling the leather. "A book? Aristotle?"

Nicholas smirked. "Open it."

Tancred did so—then stopped. *The New Testament.* The entire New Testament in Greek! His complete personal copy!

His eyes came to Nicholas's, and with a rush of emotion he could not contain, Tancred threw his arms around him.

Nicholas laughed. "Ah! Your heart and soul belong to Christ! I can see that it is so! A thousand prayers have been answered, my son Tancred. I have made intercession and petition for you before His throne since I found you hiding behind the altar in Rome. How I feared that I would fail to win your heart! But now—"

"I discerned much more during those years than you thought. My grandfather knew it when you did not." Tancred's smile faded as he thought of al-Kareem, for he loved him dearly. "He will be grieved."

"But heaven rejoices. Do not be angry or think me hard because I feel no sympathy for your grandfather. May he too come to know the true God."

"Yes . . . and he will always be my beloved grandfather, but I am not certain I will remain his 'precious Jehan.' Not now. You do not know how painful it is to break a family bond when it is held together by a manmade religion. Islam is also a culture. To forsake that religion means the family circle is torn in two. He will now say that I am dead to him."

Nicholas sobered and said gently, "But alive to God. 'This my son was dead, but now lives.' The Father rejoices. And yet I too have experienced pain. I was banned from the Eastern Church and dishonored by my emperor, then sent as a Judas to the barbarian West."

Tancred regarded him. "You rarely showed your sense of loss."

Nicholas shrugged, easing himself back into the chair. "It is better so. But it is not your mother's house alone who will reject you—so does your father's clan. Maybe you should consider remaining in Byzantium. Did you not mention the medical school at Jundi Shapur?"

"Such dreams seem impossible now. There will be war, and I have yet to prove my innocence in killing Derek." Absently, he removed the Koran from his satchel and stared at it, remembering his grandfather, his mother . . .

Nicholas cocked a brow. "Do you still seriously consider the Koran?"

Tancred looked at him with a faint smile. The question was typical of the Nicholas he remembered as a boy. "Thanks to your patience in teaching the writings, I was able upon closer inspection to detect paraphrased Scripture rewritten to fit the cause of Mohammed. But no—I shall one day use this to speak with al-Kareem." Tancred's eyes returned his taunt. "I have another object for you, one to be returned to your holy sepulcher."

"Ah, the Holy Sepulcher! What do you have, the robe of our Lord?"

Tancred smiled and reached for his satchel. "One day if you continue to speak skeptically, you will also be excommunicated from the West. Then what will you do? No—what I offer you is a stolen object. My great-uncle took it when very young, so he told me. His dying wish was that I return it to Jerusalem. I vowed that I would, but since you are going—"

Nicholas dismissed the offered object with a wave of his hand and lounged back in his chair. "No more relics. I have one too many to carry about now. If you vowed to Odo, then you must see to it."

Tancred was disappointed; he had hoped to be done with this burden. "It is enough I must face sword and scimitar in Antioch to deliver Mosul to the clan. But Jerusalem! Who knows when the crusaders will take the city!"

Nicholas looked confident as he stretched out his booted legs, his chain mesh glinting along with the cross. "They will take it," he stated. "But you are right, when indeed?" He sighed and looked at his sword. "It will be a dreadfully bloody war, Tancred."

"One I am not inclined to be involved in," stated Tancred, gesturing toward Nicholas. "It is more fitting you should return the relic. You are a bishop, and you have taken the cross, whereas I have not. I have one mission." *No*, he thought, remembering, *I have two*. Helena's mother and the house of ibn-Haroun in Jerusalem. He had promised her he would seek information, and when told, Nicholas would surely wish to accompany him.

Tancred carefully changed the subject away from the crusade. "I bring you dark news about Lady Adrianna."

Nicholas looked uneasy, as though he expected the worst. "Helena wrote that she lives—is that so?"

"She is alive." And he told him all that Helena had shared at the guard castle.

Nicholas stood, restlessly pacing. "I must find her. Helena is right. There can be no rest until she is safe with us again. Adrianna, my poor sister, may the grace of our Lord sustain you in your impossible situation."

"I have contacts," Tancred assured him. "I may yet locate her." And he removed the signet ring of al-Kareem and placed it on his right hand, remembering his grandfather's words: *"Then take my ring, my son; it will open the mouths of the dumb."*

Nicholas looked at the ring, then at Tancred. "You think ibn-Haroun will cooperate?"

"He is a friend. He will know the chieftain who now has her. There is one thing, Nicholas. I have said nothing to Helena, but it is possible . . . Adrianna may no longer be a slave but a wife or concubine, even a member of a harem—I am sorry."

Nicholas's jaw tensed and the dark eyes glinted. "Say nothing to Helena of that. It is best that she thinks her mother is only a slave."

Tancred thought that Helena already suspected her mother to be in a zenana. "There is something else," he said quietly. "Once back at the Mese I will visit an Arab friend in the bazaars."

"Tancred, your help is a Godsend. For the first time I am thankful you have the heritage of a Moor."

"A Moor who must also accomplish much inside Antioch."

"You are certain Derek's assassin was Mosul?"

"Informers from the House of al-Kareem have sworn it is so. Ibn-Haroun's brother for one. I met him at the black tent at Palermo before I left. Mosul also boasted of his guilt at Le Puy."

"A man who boasts of his sin is the worst fool. Then you will go with the Normans to take Antioch?"

"No. I go alone to find him. It is between him and me. Hakeem waits there now. And as soon as my business with Bohemond and the emperor is finished, I must be about my own quest."

"Then you are right," mused Nicholas. "I must be with the crusaders when they take Jerusalem. More than the fate of the city now weighs on my heart. Ibn-Haroun must be protected. He alone can tell us where Adrianna is."

"Maybe," said Tancred. "There may be others closer at hand. I will do my best."

He told Nicholas how the emperor insisted all the princes must swear their fealty to him before he ferried their armies across the Bosporus into Anatolia.

"He fears Bohemond, and with cause. We both know he has no intention of surrendering any castle taken from the Turks, or any city, least of all Antioch."

"Bohemond," said Nicholas, "will not agree easily to entering the city alone. He has his eye on obtaining a new kingdom."

Tancred shadowed his personal concerns and dislike for the plan, but Nicholas must have guessed.

"And what did Philip offer you to carry out his plan?"

"He has paid me with secret information."

"On the whereabouts of Mosul?"

Tancred's eyes hardened. "I knew he was in Antioch. Rufus, the bodyguard to Lady Irene, informed me weeks ago. Mosul was serving as bodyguard to the Turkish commander Kerbogha."

Nicholas looked concerned. "Was? You mean he is not there now? Then what did Philip offer you?"

Tancred looked at him. "He holds him a prisoner. For the head of Kalid he will deliver him to me. There is also one named Firouz who is willing to betray Antioch to Prince Bohemond."

Nicholas stared at him, astounded.

"I think," said Tancred, "we should call an urgent meeting. Bohemond will find the information tempting enough to cooperate with the emperor."

"This news of the surrender of Antioch must not be hinted to the other princes. They will all want the prize for their own plate."

"I too have a reason to keep the matter secret. It offers me immediate access to Antioch, to Kerbogha, and to Mosul. Without him to swear to my innocence I will wander the rest of my years as a mercenary soldier, unable to return to Sicily. I have no choice but to cooperate with Philip."

And Helena, thought Tancred. She was now convinced Philip had redeemed his valor. Tancred dare not contemplate how her image disturbed his dreams, how the thought of her marriage to the noble brought undeniable disappointment. Why he would feel this strongly was obvious, but he would not openly admit it even to himself. She was the concern of Nicholas now—and soon Philip's prize.

Tancred glanced impatiently toward the tent entrance. "What keeps Bohemond?"

"Bohemond is never rushed. And your injury will not be rushed either. Let us hope Walter of Sicily does not come looking for you now, lest we have a fight on our hands."

"Worry not. With the information I alone have about access to Antioch, I can have Bohemond and his entire army of knights sworn to my freedom. They will never turn me over to craven."

Nicholas smiled. "I had not thought of it. And now! Show me this stolen object we must bring to Jerusalem for the peace of Odo."

"We?" Tancred smiled, then took the object from his satchel and removed the layers of cloth.

Nicholas waited, growing more curious as he noticed Tancred's solemn expression.

"Will you keep me in dark suspense? What have you?"

"It is the ancient head of a lance."

"A lance!"

"Have a look. What do you think? Another presumed relic of import?"

"No doubt."

"There is an inscription in Latin."

"Read it."

Tancred held it to the candle, squinting. As he made out the words and the meaning implied, he hesitated, then looked at Nicholas. "Golgotha, the year of our Lord's crucifixion. The lance of the Roman soldier who pierced His side?"

Nicholas frowned. "It could not be. The spearhead that pierced the heart of Christ?" He leaned back in silence, contemplating.

Tancred resisted the awesome yet superstitious notion to fear it as though it were holy. He wrapped it back into the cloth. "It could not be," he repeated. "It would have rusted through by now."

"Yes, yet we will return it to the Holy Sepulcher," said Nicholas quietly. "Odo was your great-uncle. I assume you wish to keep the vow you gave him at his dying breath?"

Tancred noted the gleam in his eyes. "Have I a choice? I will keep the lance head with me. It has escaped detection on many harrowing escapades across Europe. To whomever it once belonged, we will see it returned from whence it came."

Tancred stood with Nicholas when minutes later Bohemond entered the tent, his bodyguard waiting outside. He stood in a crimson cloak that fell over his armor. His light hair was cut the style of the Normans; short and rounded at the ears. He was a man both big and tall, broad of shoulder and chest, yet lean in flank and loin, an unquestionable warrior in mind and body. His passion was war; he was a man destined to command: implacable, ruthless, courageous.

After they were seated, Tancred delivered him the letter from the emperor and watched Bohemond peruse the message with cunning consideration.

"He expects you to ride into the city alone without your army."

"Am I a fool?" Bohemond was about to toss the letter aside when Tancred said calmly, "You will have your own bodyguard of eight men."

Tancred could see his scorn and reluctance and moved to relay the secret information from Philip about the Armenian spy. "He can aid us from within the city and Antioch will be delivered to you."

Bohemond's iron blue eyes flared with a surge of passion that must have made his heart pound. He smiled, ironically amused.

"Tancred, my kinsman, I have reconsidered. It would grieve me to think of causing the Eastern emperor to toss the night away upon his bed with worry. I will do as he requests of me. I will leave my army here and come with eight men only, and I will bow the knee. I will seek to convince the other princes to do the same, including Godfrey."

"Then we have an agreement. Yet there is a small matter. One concerning a misunderstanding between myself and Walter of Sicily."

"So I have heard."

"He and my cousins believe me guilty of Derek Redwan's death. By now Walter knows I am here, since I have had trouble with a cousin. Walter will request from you the liberty to take me prisoner to stand trial according to Norman custom."

Bohemond scowled, then gave a wave of his sword hand. "Any man who seeks to take you will know my ire. I will dispatch word to Walter at once. As long as you ride under my gonfanon, Tancred, you will be aided."

"Then we have a bargain, seigneur."

"And a war to fight and win."

When Bohemond left the tent, Nicholas laughed softly. "The wolf has been baited."

"Yes. Philip has shown his ability to scheme as successfully as the emperor," Tancred said thoughtfully, disturbed. He did not like to be placed in a situation where he needed Philip. He looked at Nicholas. "You too may be facing a trap, not from Philip but from your enemies in Constantinople who do not wish your return. Is it wise to show yourself in the open?"

"I will be vigilant against their intrigue. Helena insists Irene was involved in the fate of Adrianna. I am aware of Irene's treachery and she knows it. And Constantine once wished me dead. He may try to accomplish it."

Tancred watched him. Was there an unresolved matter concerning Irene? He did not ask him, believing Nicholas would explain if he wished. When it came to a woman and the dregs of a bitter cup, Nicholas was the manner of man to handle it alone.

CHAPTER 12
Gathered Before the Throne

Helena returned to Lysander Palace near the St. Barbara Gate. In her opulent quarters, she recovered well from her injury, a credit to Tancred's skilled care at the castle.

In the days following her return from the burning castles, Helena waited for her dread confrontation with her aunt and wondered at the delay. Had Constantine been able to convince her that she received her injury riding a new horse? Somehow, Helena remained doubtful. Irene was no fool.

Sometimes she would awaken from sleep with the startled realization that she was actually going to marry Philip. The years of crisis in their relationship was at last coming to a satisfactory end, with the final road of escape opening before them. Only the delay in Tancred's bringing Prince Bohemond into the city disturbed her repose and delayed plans.

Daily she walked in the garden hoping to give opportunity to Bardas to bring her any news about Tancred, but the days and nights inched by, adding anxiety to her other concerns.

As soon as all the western princes arrived to vow their loyalty to the emperor at the imperial palace, the sooner she and Philip could escape to the Castle of Hohms.

Surrounded by Lady Irene's loyal slaves, and unable to speak at any length with Bardas, the days crept by and Helena was able to discover little of what was transpiring. Surprisingly it was Zoe who became her welcome eyes and ears, though unwittingly, as they sat in the garden of the summer palace. Zoe, a year younger than Helena, with ebony braids wrapped becomingly about her head, lounged lazily on a sedan chair and ate the sugared fruits brought to them by slaves. Who her parents might have been remained obscure, but the family said she was the daughter of Constantine's brother, Photius.

"The barbarians took possession of their old campsites by the gates."

"You mean Duke Godfrey?"

"I suppose that's his name. After the burning castles and what happened to you, the emperor should send soldiers out to teach them a lesson."

Zoe pursed her lips thoughtfully. "But the beasts are handsome, are they not? They say the duke is a rare specimen, that his hair is red-gold and reaches to his shoulders. Is it true?" she asked, her eyes showing keen interest. "You saw him?"

"Yes, his hair is long; all of them wear it that way. . . . Is there any news of Prince Bohemond yet?"

Zoe's eyes mocked her. "Is it the Norman prince you are interested in or Tancred? Every woman in the palace has noticed him, including you, though you pretend differently," and she tipped her head back and squirted the juice from a lush purple grape onto her tongue.

"Have the Normans approached the city yet? You saw Philip this morning; did he say anything?"

Zoe shrugged and tucked her gold-slippered feet beneath her brocade tunic. "Philip says little. He is plagued by bouts of moodiness."

The news was puzzling after his exalted proposal to her just ten days ago. "Moody? Did he say why?"

Zoe made a bored face. "Philip never explains. He says I am incapable of serious thought." She waved a hand as she always did when changing a subject and not wishing interruption. "They say the duke waits for the Normans, thinking to merge armies and take the city. The emperor fears nothing of the barbarians." She sighed. "He is so handsome."

"The emperor?" Helena scoffed. "You have weak eyes, Zoe. You think every man is handsome."

She looked offended. "Well, not as good-looking as Tancred."

"Tell me of the duke's army—what happened?"

She tossed aside the cluster of grapes. "War, such a boring subject! It is only the men who fight who are exciting—well; while the imperial cavalry continues to harass the duke's foot soldiers, the emperor withholds food supplies to bring him to his senses."

"Has it sufficed?"

"Nay, some of his men attacked one of the gates."

"They stormed the gate?" cried Helena.

"Only a small band. It is not known if the duke even knew of it. It is said they believed several of their princes were being held captive by the emperor. Imagine, they were willing to try to storm the imperial palace to free them! You should have heard the women nearest the gate screaming! They were certain they would be taken and made slaves. The emperor sent archers into the gate towers to kill their horses."

The thought of any horse being wounded angered Helena, and she knew every horse was needed for the upcoming battle against the Moslems.

"Then Duke Godfrey commanded a retreat at sunset. He sits irresolute in his tent pavilion refusing to swear loyalty to the emperor, while his army must forage for food. But there is none to be had in the fields until summer, and the cattle are hidden."

Helena looked from Zoe to a slave who bowed with immobile face. "Madame, Lady Irene asks for you."

Helena sat motionless, looking uneasily toward the portico, and Irene came out onto the wide pavilion, her hair shining like gold in the sunlight.

"Now you are in for a scathing trial," said Zoe. "Aunt believes you ran away to find Tancred."

An hour later in her chamber, Helena sat on the brocade footstool watching her aunt pace, while she tried to hide her alarm at being questioned.

True to Philip's promise at the guard castle, both he and Constantine had come to her defense after her return, but did Irene believe them? What if she discovered Philip's true plans? Helena sat watching her, trying to read her expression as Irene paced the red carpet, her gown with its decorative gold-threaded hem trailing behind. Her hair hung in a looped braid across her back and was woven with red and green gemstones. Her amber-colored eyes, as equally hard as the gems, turned and riveted on Helena, who sat expressionless on the ottoman, hands folded in her lap, praying she would not be discovered.

"So you fell from a horse," she mocked. "You left the emperor's grandiose garden banquet to journey all the way to the villa to ride a horse. Such idiotic fables! And Philip expects me to believe this?"

Irene walked up to her and Helena winced, expecting a sharp slap across the face, but Irene's eyes narrowed into burning slits. "You might as well spare yourself and tell me."

"I have nothing to say, madame."

"Nothing?" derided Irene, arching both thin brows. "You fled to the guard castle. You expected the Norman warrior to bring you to Nicholas." She began her energetic pacing again. "I give credit to the audacious mongrel Godfrey. Rampaging the towns along the Bosporus at least kept you from accomplishing your plans." She stopped and looked at her. "You fool! You might have been carried away by some barbarian!"

Helena's head lowered and she stared at her hands clasped in her lap.

"How much did you pay Tancred to bring you to Nicholas?"

Then she does not know about Philip.

If Helena admitted the cause that brought her to the guard castle, could she divert the discovery of the real purpose to their plans?

She regarded her aunt with serenity. "I offered him twice what Philip pays, but he refused me."

"He refused you! Do you think I am fool enough to believe that?"

"Evidently, madame, some men cannot be bought. He insisted his obligation to the emperor must take precedence over my wishes."

Irene silently stared at her. Helena hid the faint shiver her gaze provoked. It was true that Tancred had refused to be hired. His offer to aid her had come in the form of knightly gallantry. And if Philip had not come . . . she would have ridden with Tancred to meet the Normans. By now she would be safely in the company of Uncle Nicholas.

Helena refused to entertain a small prick of regret. Had she made the right decision to reconcile with Philip? His scheme to coerce Tancred into complying with his strategy over Antioch remained a troublesome matter, one that she had not yet been able to resolve.

She straightened her shoulders as she sat on the footstool, reminding herself that Philip too had been coerced into making desperate decisions. Could she truly blame him for resorting to scheming? Nothing must come between them now.

Irene must not guess that it was Philip and not Tancred who had vowed his heart and strength to see her avoid Prince Kalid and Antioch.

"He refused me," she repeated. "And I've no more interest in the offspring of an uncivilized mongrel," said Helena in an attempt to throw her aunt off her trail.

"Fair speech, but a mongrel wolf can give birth to a fine-blooded cub. A cub only too welcome in the golden chambers of nobility and slave alike."

"I would not know of such matters," said Helena flatly.

Irene looked at her. "He bears the handsome flesh of a prince. Do not think I am unaware of the whispers going on. All speak of the new warrior in the imperial guard."

Including you, she thought but retained her bland expression. "I do not listen to the foolish chatter of mice. If some wish to make themselves into fools by chasing men, who can stop them? It is not my way."

Irene impatiently turned from her and resumed pacing with quick steps. "The world is full of fools. And you've done your own chasing after Philip. Do not misunderstand about Tancred Redwan. Did you think that in questioning you I concerned myself over a girlish romance with a handsome warrior? It is his sword I was confronting you about. Take heed, Helena. If I discover you are being deceptive about Tancred, I will have you locked in your chamber until your departure to Kalid."

Helena knew she must pretend disinterest. "Since Philip also wishes me to marry Kalid, I see little hope but to cooperate until, as you say, my work in Antioch is done and the city has surrendered." She stood to emphasize her resignation.

"That you have decided to cooperate is commendable. The sooner the deed is accomplished, the sooner you will be able to return to the imperial palace. And," she added wearily, "the sooner you may have my son to your bosom."

Helena watched her walk across the chamber to the door and masked the chill that passed through her heart like an arrow.

Irene looked back. "You will rejoice to know that Philip has accomplished a feat for which the emperor has rewarded him with favors. The dread Norman Bohemond will ride into Constantinople without his army. He comes with a bodyguard of eight men to swear his loyalty."

Then Tancred has been successful, Helena thought with excitement. By now Bohemond knew of the Armenian spy who would deliver Antioch to him. And Tancred would soon be leaving Constantinople to quietly enter Antioch unseen. Her thoughts raced to Uncle Nicholas, hoping he rode with Bohemond. She ached to inquire about him, but doing so would alert Irene, and she swallowed back the words on her tongue. Calmly, she watched her aunt, who now appeared occupied with thoughts of her own.

"You will attend the ceremony tomorrow night with your cousin Zoe," she said, and left the chamber.

The next morning, Helena's eyes searched for Nicholas as she stood beside Zoe and the other daughters of the Purple Belt, including Princess Anna Comnenus, the daughter of the emperor. Anna had exclaimed that she would one day write about the western princes and the crusade to take Jerusalem.

They stood on the balcony watching Bohemond and his Norman entourage riding slowly down the Augustaeum past the senate building toward the imperial palace. Tancred too would be riding beside Bohemond, and Helena looked for him astride Apollo, hoping to conceal her interest.

"Look at the barbarian," whispered Zoe, awed. "No wonder they call him 'Bohemond'—behemoth would fit as well. Let's call him Leviathan!"

Helena agreed, for the Norman prince appeared exceedingly tall with broad shoulders and muscled arms. Without a helmet his golden head sat proud and erect, and his tanned face, unlike the Byzantines, was clean shaven. He wore a fur-lined mantle, and there was the look of dignity to him, yet overall, Helena sensed something cunning and fearsome.

She had heard that his journey across Europe was rife with fighting along the road, much of it done with the emperor's mercenary army who patrolled the Byzantine territorial frontier. Now he entered peaceably into the Byzantine Empire with the ambition to accomplish his own ends.

"They say he likes his meat raw and rips it apart with his hands," whispered Zoe, fervor in her eyes.

"That is foolish talk," whispered another, disdainfully. "He is related to Tancred. Does *he* eat raw meat?"

"I would not care if he did," giggled another.

"Your speech bores me," said Helena. "You are like twittering birds with nothing better to do than run about seeking tidbits of refuse to feed upon."

"Pay Helena no mind," scorned Zoe. "She feeds upon her religion and it makes her self-righteous. Look! There are barbarian women!"

Helena was more curious about the Norman women than about Bohemond, for she had heard Tancred mention them favorably.

From the silence that followed their passing, the Daughters of the Purple Belt were disappointed to discover that the Norman women were indeed as grand as their men.

Helena caught sight of a certain young woman riding near Tancred. She sat erect and proud, her flaxen hair elegantly braided. The northern look of fairness, with well-sculptured cheekbones and widely spaced eyes, suggested a woman of boldness and beauty, and Helena eyed her coolly.

These, she thought, must be the wives and daughters of the nobles. They were all blond and, she suspected, blue-eyed, and she was intrigued that they rode bareback on horses and could keep up with the men.

And just who was this royal-looking woman riding with Tancred?

Zoe leaned toward her, her cheeks faintly tinted with excitement. "It seems as if the 'count from Sicily' has an admirer. Who is she, do you think?"

"I have no idea," breezed Helena, "nor do I care."

"Tut, tut—perhaps the daughter of Bohemond?"

"Bohemond is not so old. He looks only thirty-five," said another.

"She is too old," said Zoe, pouting. "Look at her! She grows wrinkled by the eastern sun."

Laughter contradicted. "Old, by Zeus! Look at her—she is as fair as any Daughter of Purple—including you, Zoe."

Zoe made a face at her. Then impulsively grabbing an armful of sweetly scented flowers from the agate urn on the balcony, she boldly tossed them down toward Apollo as Tancred neared the balcony.

Tancred turned Apollo to keep the hoofs from crushing the flowers and looked up. Zoe waved, and some of the others laughed at her boldness, but Helena did not. As his gaze met hers and lingered, Helena sought to reject the odd lurch of her heart.

He smiled, and in spite of herself—and perhaps because the Norman woman also stared at her unsmiling—Helena removed a single white blossom from a vase and tossed it down at him.

"Helena—" gasped Zoe.

The blossom failed to make contact, and she could not tell what he thought, for just then a shadow from the building blocked out his expression.

Realizing her audacity, she wondered at her actions and looked quickly for Uncle Nicholas. Her heart sang! A handsomely rugged man in his forties rode a few horses behind Tancred. He was laughing up at her, evidently having seen her toss the blossom. She laughed too and waved; then snatching many flowers from an urn, she tossed them down. "Uncle Nicholas!"

He waved and called something up to her, but she could not hear.

"Uncle Nicholas!" cried Helena, tears blurring her eyes. "Welcome home!"

Just then she noticed the expression on his face change. Helena turned her head to find Irene standing at the balcony looking down at him, a picture of golden splendor.

Helena, fearful of what she might see in her uncle's face, anxiously sought his eyes, but Nicholas wore a faint sardonic smile as he stared boldly at Irene. He lifted his wide-brimmed black hat with mock decorum.

Helena felt a sickening flutter in her stomach and turned to scrutinize Irene's response. The feral gleam in Irene's amber eyes startled Helena. *It is Irene, not Nicholas, who is moved by emotion.*

For the first time ever, Helena saw something in Irene that she had never witnessed before—a passion that brought a glow to her cheeks.

Helena's breath wanted to stop.

Nicholas watched Irene evenly as he rode by, and Irene walked to the edge of the balustrade, her gaze following after him until he was out of view behind the senate building.

Her hands clenched, Helena stared at her. *She cannot have Nicholas.*

On this special night when the western princes were to vow to the emperor, a dozen royal sedan chairs arrived to bring Helena and the others to the imperial palace. Muscled slaves, bare-chested and glinting with oil, trotted down the royal avenue carrying them past the senate to the city within a city called the Sacred Palace, constructed of numerous marble porticoes, galleries, arcades, and buildings.

The Augustaeum, a magnificent square surrounded by colonnades and segregated on the south and west by the senate building and the imperial palace, was unrivaled for splendor. From the slope cascading down to the Sea of Marmara, there were terraced buildings of marble and tile forming what was called the Sacred Palace. Since the days of the Roman Emperor Constantine, who moved his seat of authority there, each successor to the throne took care to add to the great residence. Palaces, reception halls with gold mosaics, pavilions cloistered in fragrant greenery, barracks for the imperial guard, libraries, famous baths, and churches—the Sacred Palace had all the pomp necessary for the ceremonial life and culture with which Byzantium dazzled her barbarian visitors.

Beneath the stars glimmering down upon her while hearing the excited chatter and laughter of Zoe and the other young women, Helena's heart bubbled with happiness as she watched the shafts of moonlight filtering between puffs of clouds, sprinkling gold dust upon the Sea of Marmara. *Nicholas is here*, her heart throbbed again. And she and Philip had their plans, undetected by Irene. What could go wrong? No matter that a strange tug brought her emotions back to blue-gray eyes, hair the color of autumn wheat, and a smile that stirred strange yearnings—she would not listen. It was Philip she loved. How could it be otherwise? *I have loved him all my life*, she thought. *There can be no other man.*

Her sedan chair stopped before the steps of the palace, and slaves came to assist her down, while the scent of Judas tree blossoms sweetened the night air. The echo of the hoofs of the arriving imperial cavalry brought the laughter to an expectant silence. Helena looked down the avenue, aglow with fiery torches at the arriving guard, resplendent in their black-and-crimson uniforms.

Tancred rode with an assembly of young Greek nobles escorting Philip's arriving chariot. Her eyes reluctantly sought Tancred astride Apollo, and she told herself that it was her horse she wished to glimpse looking so smart in an imperial saddle.

But her eyes fixed on Tancred, his uniform outlining his muscular body well. In cloak and helmet with a royal plume, he rode ahead of Philip's chariot as guard. Her eyes narrowed. *He deliberately flaunts his handsomeness before the other women*, she decided. It was not enough that, as Bardas reported, the emperor's mistress had secretly inquired about him. He must add fuel to the over-heated fire!

Helena lifted her chin when their eyes collided. Tancred did not smile, yet the appraisal he gave her caused her to blush. She rebuked her response, and with difficulty dragged her eyes from his. She must not give him more cause to challenge her commitment to Philip.

Helena tilted her head and swished her royal blue peacock fan.

Lady Irene was arriving in a sedan chair. The giant ebony bodyguard named Rufus, astride a magnificent white horse and wearing chain mesh beneath a gilded cloak, escorted her like a queen across the marble pavilion courtyard to meet Philip.

As though Philip were the emperor, thought Helena, *and she the Queen Mother!*

Guards and slaves were everywhere, serving with trained ease and watchful eye to guard their superiors. The slaves moved with dignity, their heads erect. Chosen for strength and beauty, their presence was as unobtrusive as the magnificent Greek statues showing beneath the burning torchlights and ornate lanterns.

Did Irene hope Nicholas would make a daring appearance? He was too wise to behave so boldly, she comforted herself.

A swift glance about her showed that he was not present. She believed he would play as illusive as a shadow, troubling both Irene and Constantine with uncertainty. Knowing her aunt's reaction to his arrival, Helena expected that there were spies out searching for him.

The emperor's chariot was approaching and the royal guard took their positions. The procession began walking through the gates, and then with escalating pomp ascended the wide street beneath the white walls of the palace. As they neared, trumpets called and male voices thundered, "Hail to the emperor!"

The smart clip of the horses' hoofs echoed in the torchlight processional, and Helena somehow believed that her Apollo was content and proud in his new calling, as well as satisfied with his new master, who now appeared to own him, though she had not yet given the horse to Tancred. She would, of course, at the appropriate moment. Perhaps when they said their last good-bye at the Castle of Hohms.

The majestic horses pranced to a steady drumbeat, their thick glossy manes and tails brushed until they gleamed in the torchlight, adorned with gold and silver ornaments. She glanced toward Tancred, militarily handsome as a member of the guard, and wondered how it would be between them when she spoke her final farewell. She stirred in the warm breeze, refusing to consider why the thought disturbed her. She was a Daughter of the Purple Belt. He was a barbarian!

As the procession neared, the trumpets blasted forth their tribute.

"Hail to Emperor Alexius, always fortunate and victorious! Hail to the emperor!"

Zoe, eyes shining, nudged her awake. It was time to form the receiving line for the entry of their emperor.

"Hail to the emperor!"

Tradition fixed his costume in a purple mantle over one shoulder held in place with a rope of luminescent pearls. His heavy dark hair and short beard were curled and oiled, while his magnificent Greek eyes stared ahead, serious and deep.

The Varangian Guard escorted him through the arched colonnades of carved ivory into the palace receiving hall, where the western princes would be ushered to swear their fealty.

Once inside the palace, Helena stood in studied silence. Her thoughts were now far removed from the business of the empire and lodged within her own turmoil. Any moment Philip and Irene would enter, escorted by Rufus. Still her eyes searched cautiously for Nicholas.

Her heart beat so fast that her dress felt uncomfortably tight about her still tender ribs. Imperial Byzantium dictated what she wore and when, even as it did the emperor, and this evening she must conduct herself according to status.

She wore a chemise of Byzantine-style patterned squares of violet-blue with purple and gold threads interwoven to form delicate crosses throughout. The customary belt-sash of purple silk encircled and graced her slender waist. Pearls were stylishly woven throughout her rich dark hair and culminated with a loop, which hung down each side of her head to her shoulders, a shimmering creamy white rope that danced with each motion of her head.

"She is beautiful," whispered Zoe at her elbow, and Helena followed her cousin's wistful look toward the entranceway. Irene entered in a costume of sheer spun-gold silk worn over a tunic. Multicolored gems flashed from her hair.

"She wishes the emperor to notice," whispered Zoe. "I wonder if Mary the Alan will show tonight? I hear she despises Aunt. Do you blame her?"

Helena, knowing of Irene's carefully laid plans to reach the bedchamber of the emperor, whispered, "It is his wife the emperor should be looking at and appreciating."

"Your Christianity is too condemning. Even Bishop Constantine has his affairs."

"He is no bishop. He is as carnal as the priests serving the ancient idols."

"How self-righteous you sound," mocked Zoe. "And how tiresome and boring."

"True love knows commitment. And it is not boring at all, but exciting and real."

"How do you know?" she mocked.

"Hush, do you think the emperor would even cast a glance at either Irene or Mary if they should unexpectedly become horribly scarred? Will he hold their hand to his lips and vow it is their character he adores? Nay! He would look swiftly enough for new beauties with foolish hearts that are flattered by his frivolous attention."

"You are a fair one to speak so! Does not Philip permit you to bed the Moslem prince without so much as a whine? If love brings commitment, he loves you not!"

Helena looked at Zoe, wishing she might tell her that Philip had rallied to acts of nobility, but she could not.

Zoe's pale eyes were triumphant and her mouth turned smugly as she looked away.

"I will follow in the footsteps of Irene," said Zoe.

"And live to regret how you tossed away your virginity," quipped Helena. "You feed a lust that will not be quenched. What your mind feeds upon will eventually betray your actions—"

"Quell your words. Look, Constantine comes."

He is back from Antioch. Helena turned, feeling the tension choking her breathing. She gazed across the marble floor as the bishop entered, Philip and Tancred with him.

Helena and Zoe lowered their heads with respect as the bishop walked up and greeted them, their voices echoing demurely, "Good evening, Lord Bishop."

Helena was careful to keep her expression serene as she looked into his baronial face with its dark reddish brown beard, remembering, with a chill, their confrontation over her mother several weeks earlier. What had he discovered? Anything? And even if he had, would he tell her? Her eyes searched his, but his thoughts were obscured with shadow.

"My child Helena, I am at peace to see you looking so well after your unfortunate riding accident."

She pretended not to notice the flicker of irony that swam in the pools of his eyes.

He turned to Philip. "I understand you have made suitable arrangements for Helena's travel to Antioch."

Philip's sullen look, tinged with pompous splendor, revealed his constraint in the presence of his father.

"Prince Kalid grows impatient," he said, nothing in his voice. "The delay caused by her injury is not understood. It was needful to appease him by sending her sooner than advised. Kalid affirms the Moslem physicians are more judicious in handling their skills than those in the West, and Helena will be treated with care."

"It seems you also are skilled in the ways of medicine, Tancred," and Constantine turned in his direction. "I understand we have you to thank for coming to the aid of Lady Helena."

Tancred was standing a tactful distance away from the others, playing the role of the disinterested and silent bodyguard. His handsome face reflected anything except subservience as his eyes flicked over Constantine, Philip, and Zoe, coming to rest on Helena. He offered her a brief bow.

"An art learned at Salerno from my Moorish ancestry. That I have proved myself useful to the future princess of Antioch is heartening."

Helena met his gaze as he bowed toward her. "I am in your debt, sir," she murmured, remaining unresponsive.

Zoe stared at him like a hungry lioness. He looked back evenly until her gaze wavered and two red stains showed on her cheeks.

Constantine watched them. "Captain Redwan will journey to Antioch with you, Helena. You will need a trusted bodyguard in charge of the entourage."

Helena did not trust herself to speak. He must not suspect the plan had been arranged by Philip at the guard castle of Herion.

Philip eased the silence by turning toward Tancred. "Your services have proven loyal and noteworthy. As captain of the entourage, the emperor feels assured she will arrive safely."

Tancred again bowed lightly. "Perhaps it would be best if another fulfilled the mission."

Helena nearly gasped. Why was he saying this? He would jeopardize everything if he persisted! Afraid he would ruin matters, she glared at him, but saw that he watched Constantine.

"Kalid is a cousin in my mother's family," Tancred told him. "He and I are enemies. To bring his bride might offend him. Perhaps the emperor would prefer me to ride with the Normans. The city undoubtedly will be conquered for your emperor."

Constantine measured him, as though taken off guard. It was only then that Helena understood why Tancred had spoken as he did. Constantine already knew that he was Kalid's cousin and he had brought it into the open, disarming Constantine.

In the momentary but tense silence that locked them in, she scarcely breathed, waiting.

"There is no need to decline your services, Captain Redwan. Philip has made it clear the emperor wishes you to lead the entourage. Helena's safe arrival and her marriage to Kalid is crucial for the empire."

Constantine now appeared satisfied with himself. "It so happens the emperor also requested I accompany her in your entourage."

Helena could not look at either Philip or Tancred for fear she would give away her despair.

Philip turned stiffly toward his father. "You will ride with us?"

Constantine smiled at him coolly. "You are not pleased?"

Philip's mouth thinned. "Yes—why yes, of course. Your presence will be welcome."

"Good. Then we will leave the city within three days."

Our plans lie in ruin. Helena believed she must look pale and kept her gaze averted.

"We have important contacts in the city, working with Kalid and Commander Kerbogha," continued Constantine. "Any danger of the city falling to the crusaders, and it is agreed upon they will first surrender to you, Philip." He glanced at Helena, then turned back to Philip. "I will stay on in Antioch to work with you. Together, we will make certain of victory."

Something in his gaze flickered, and she watched him, certain he meant more than merely taking the city from the Moslems. He offered no more explanation and bowed, then met the angry stare of his son, who wore a tight white line about his mouth.

"You have proven yourself a skilled diplomat," said Philip, his voice cold.

Constantine looked at him sharply. "I am ever your loyal counselor. It was necessary. We cannot afford to fail, can we?" he stated meaningfully. He gestured across the wide marble floor toward the audience chamber. "The emperor waits for us."

"A hypocrite of shrewd means," came Tancred's low voice, and Helena, startled back to the moment, was reminded she was not alone. Her troubled eyes darted to his, but he watched Bishop Constantine bowing piously toward the nobles gathering for the emperor's arrival.

Tancred turned his head to look down at her, and his stormy blue-gray eyes arrested hers. "He's surely on to his son's plans to escape with you. And he's clever enough to replace Philip's men in the entourage with soldiers loyal to him. We will need to alter our plans."

A shiver, like a chilling wind denying the arrival of summer, passed through her. "No, let it not be. It must not be. All our plans, all our hopes to be dashed yet again!"

A sardonic half-smile appeared. "We? I assure you, madame, grief is the last emotion to wrap its tentacles about me. You should give thanks that the bishop appeared tonight to give himself away, lest we had gone on our way like sheep for the slaughter. At least now we are forewarned."

His words went past her. "Perhaps he does not know," she whispered a protest, for it was devastating to taste the cup of defeat. Perhaps—" she began hopefully, but Tancred firmly interrupted, this time with impatience for her refusal to accept the obvious.

"He knows. Believe me. Why else would he arrange to journey with us? His master plan is conceived and born of his own making. He arranged it himself. No—do not protest. I am sure the emperor has appointed him to go, but Constantine first planted the tare in his mind. It is a way for him to keep his eye on Philip." He gave her a searching look. "Yet I think more compels him. Some cause of his own."

She thought of her mother and unconsciously touched the loop of creamy pearls at the side of her head. "Constantine schemes and sacrifices for Philip. His success means everything, because it also guarantees his own, and Irene's."

Helena could see Tancred was not convinced.

"He may have other plans as well. Have you any idea what they might be?"

She averted her eyes. She dare not risk the wrath of Constantine, not when there was a hope he would locate and free her mother.

"No . . ." she murmured, disliking her lie, for she needed Tancred. Her convictions also warned her to do nothing to betray his trust, his apparent willingness to help her at last. "Why should I have any idea what his personal plans might be?"

He studied her face until she looked away again.

"I thought you might know. You have paid informers."

"No longer," she said flatly. "He is dead. I believe I told you so at the guard castle."

"And I believe you told me it was our sanctified bishop who had the poor wretch killed."

"Please, must we discuss this now?" Her despair grew. "I must be brought to the castle. If he suspects Philip and me of escaping— what can we do?"

An unlikely dash of amusement darkened the vigor of his gaze.

"You might give up your childhood ambition of marrying the noble."

Exasperated, she clenched her hands. "You mock me at a time like this, when I am wounded with worry and fear?"

He was not sympathetic, but smiled pleasantly. "Fear not. As physician I am sworn to your healing. All I need is opportunity, which you deny me."

"Indeed?" she tossed her head, pearls dancing.

"I once told you I do not surrender anything of esteemed value to an enemy. You forget. I too shall be in Antioch. And Kalid and I shall decide your fate together, even as the Normans will decide the fate of the city."

The daring words took her aback. "Assuming I will even be in Antioch," she corrected. "I will not."

"I do have a concern about Antioch, however. Kalid is an impatient man. A warning: you must not goad him. Kalid does not waste time on pretending to be a gentleman. He would as soon see you in his harem than as his princess."

Helena flushed. "My Christian beliefs demand more of me. I will kill myself before I surrender to the immorality of a harem."

"At least give me time to get there. My scimitar will pave a path of escape."

Her eyes narrowed at his audacity. "I will escape aforehand with Philip, somehow, some way."

"Nicholas may deny you marriage to Philip as ferociously as Lady Irene, but for opposite reasons. He is here, and being his beloved godson, I have made known to him my concerns for your future as the wife of the noble."

"How kind of you, Sir Knight. I will ask you to not pry into my private concerns when it comes to the man I wish to marry."

"It is the obligation of a knight to come to the aid of a damsel befuddled and bemused over the false trappings of a war hero."

Her nails dug into her palms. "I am neither befuddled nor be—" She stopped, a breath of pent-up exasperation escaping. She raised her head to reinforce the conclusion that *she* was Helena of the Nobility, born a Daughter of the Purple Belt.

"Where is Nicholas?" she asked swiftly, anxious to escape Tancred's presence. If she were bemused at all, it was over her unwilling response to his masculine good looks.

"He avoids his enemies—Irene the golden goddess being chief of them all, so I suspect," he said dryly. "She has spies out searching now. Nicholas will come to you instead."

"Where can I expect him?"

He glanced in the direction of Lady Irene. "Where she least expects him. Lysander Palace. Bardas waits to bring you there."

While she had the opportunity of slipping away unseen, she turned to make a swift exit.

"Wait," and his hand caught her arm.

Her gaze came doubtfully to his, aware of the strong warmth of his hand. "Warn him of Constantine. About the likelihood of Philip's soldiers being replaced with his own. I will meet you both later tonight at your family's palace. We will need to make new plans."

Her eyes warmed with hope. "Then . . . you have not changed your mind about helping me? You will find a way to bring me to the castle to await Philip?"

"I will help you, yes, and seek to bring you to the castle, but whether or not it is in order to rendezvous with Philip will be left to the discretion of Nicholas."

"Nicholas will approve. You will see. Philip is—"

"And any aid I offer to Philip is not for his sake. Unfortunately for me, madame, the noble and I are bonded together of necessity. You forget. He has the assassin who killed Derek. And he is the only man who can secure my innocence of murder, and hence my future—as Philip knows only too well. As you say," came his sarcastic tone, "he is a gallant and admirable man, one worthy of your devotion, of your highest passion."

Her cheeks flamed. She remembered with a sting how Philip was using the assassin to tighten the screws on Tancred, to try to force his mercenary service to kill Kalid.

"You are certain you invest your devotion wisely?" came his low voice. "He is not worthy of such trust, or love."

She could not meet his eyes. Her heart increased its thumping in her ears.

He took in the rope of pearls. "He is the wrong man for you. As wrong as Kalid."

Against her will an internal flame warmed her. Her emotions threatened to sweep away her will completely. To survive, she withdrew behind Helena of the Nobility. "Surely, Sir Knight, you have not altered your opinion of me?" came her dignified but taunting voice.

A look of disarming innocence came to his attractive smile as he seemed to see through her demeanor. "My opinion of you, Lady? I worship at your feet! I would see the head of Kalid on a pole marched through the streets! Perhaps Philip's head as well. . . . I swear my indubitable service! As a knight, I am willing to be sacrificed upon the altar of Zeus to safeguard the purple hem of your skirt from brushing the common filth of the street! Ask of me what you will—it is yours, to the half of my kingdom!"

She resisted the impulse to laugh at his deliberate absurdity. It had irritated her back at the guard castle when he had lightly stated that he would never wish to marry her. "You are impossible, Tancred. Am I to take this change seriously? You did say at the guard castle that you did not wish to be romantically involved with a spoiled Byzantine damsel. You do remember?"

"I do. However, having twice saved you from Rhinelanders, I feel duty bound to have some say in your destiny—even if I do not want you for myself, I would save you for a knight more worthy than I. Anyone except Philip."

Her eyes narrowed. He persisted in hinting of caring with one breath, then shrugging her off with disinterest in the next.

"A say in who should marry me? Surely you jest," she managed a soft laugh. "Since when would I ever allow *you* to have any say in *my* future?"

He smiled. "Perhaps it is not a matter only of your say, but the decision of Nicholas. I could never permit the niece of my spiritual father to fall prey to despicable dogs in purple or turbans."

"You may forget your chivalrous duty, Sir Knight. I do not want it, nor anything else coming from the barbarian West."

"No? So soon! And only weeks ago you braved Godfrey's army to beg for my service!"

"I did not beg."

"But then, that was before Philip simply turned up and beckoned you to fall at his feet! 'Oh, great one, I love thee!' "

"I did not! He succumbed to me."

"Did he? You swooned in his arms. Philip is moved by little except his vain dreams of glory. He is as much a slave as those you see walking about offering trays of dainties. He could not leave Constantinople and be content to have only you. Can you not see how he schemed to find some diabolic way to keep his favor with the emperor, and you as well? And his ambitious reasoning rallied to his Byzantine nature. I am the bait he will throw to the bears. Like the coward he is, he watches from the arena while I am bidden to kill Kalid for him."

Helena's breath came rapidly. Her hands turned icy, her palms sweating. "I will not hear!"

"I could tell you so much more if you had ears to hear."

"Ears to hear lies, jealousy, envy."

"But I? I have stormed the arena twice to save your fair face, and what small favor have you offered me of your gratitude—a castle! Jewels! Gold!" he mocked.

"Oh—but you are so knightly and honorable, sir, that you wish nothing else from me—remember?" she taunted sweetly.

His gaze left hers to study her lips.

Her hand brought the gilded fan to her face. Her eyes watched him over the rim. "You may keep your duty and your opinions," she murmured breathlessly. "I offer you nothing."

"I must make do with a castle?" came the affected tone of disappointment.

"I will hear no more of your romantic inclinations, Sir Knight."

A brow lifted. "My romantic inclinations you have not yet heard. Should the moment come, I assure you, you will not be disappointed."

"It may be I shall tell Philip to hire another escort to bring me to the Castle of Hohms. You are growing quite bothersome."

"I would be sorely disappointed. It will take me two weeks traveling beneath the desert stars and dining before the firelight to convince you to seek the right man for a lover and lord."

"Only two weeks?" she managed in a lightly mocking voice.

"I will be too busy as your guard to convince you sooner, yes," Tancred said, pretending to consider thoughtfully. "Two weeks."

Her breath ceased—she tore her eyes from his and turning,

walked swiftly toward the door leading to the garden, head high, her ropes of pearls swinging with regal opulence.

Her heart was beating much too fast. In the doorway she paused and looked back at him.

He bowed low at the waist, as though she were the empress.

Helena whipped away and out into the evening fragrance. She breathed in the cool air, fanning herself rapidly.

CHAPTER 13

The Golden Mistress
and the White Bishop

Emperor Alexius Comnenus had managed to keep the western armies separated from each other by receiving the feudal lords one at a time upon their first arrival from Europe. He gave them gifts of gold, then transported their armies across the strait to a designated camp on the Asiatic shore. All this he had managed to accomplish before the Normans arrived. Thus he prevented the armies of the West from uniting in front of his city gates, casting hungry looks toward Byzantine wealth.

Now that Bohemond had arrived, the appointed hour for public assembly of all the princes was announced. More gifts of gold were sent to the princes, while copper tartarons were given freely to the poor on foot traveling under the prince's gonfanon. Then the imperial heralds called the leaders to the grand assembly at the imperial palace.

Tancred stood with feigned gravity in the royal receiving hall glittering with gold and marble.

One by one the stalwart crusader princes were ushered into the hall by the imperial guard—some with sullen faces, others with affected sobriety: Robert, Count of Normandy, son of William the Conqueror; the Norman Lord Bohemond, grandson of the Conqueror; Duke Godfrey of Lower Lorraine with his two brothers,

Princes Baldwin and Eustace; Count Raymond of Toulouse; Hugh, Count of Vermandois and brother to the king of France; Adehemar, Bishop of Le Puy and official papal legate on the crusade; and Peter the Hermit, who had fled the massacre of the peasant army in Anatolia several months earlier.

Tancred watched as they congregated with their honorable men, all of them fitly clad in fine mantles with gold borders and ermine collars, bearing their swords. He knew that most of them were not serious in their task of vowing their vassalage to the emperor, but rather relented out of necessity, many of them grudgingly. Some, like Bohemond, had agreed to vow for his own purposes. Tancred knew Bohemond's mind was set on ruling Antioch.

Except for Count Raymond, the eldest of the crusader princes, most of the fiery warriors had little except secret contempt for Byzantium and its emperor.

Slaves carrying golden wands beat a clear pathway for Duke Godfrey to pass through the crowd that gathered on the white marble Augustaeum near the throne. While distant music echoed its tribute, Emperor Alexius leaned forward on his throne to greet his "new sons" with a kiss of peace.

Tancred watched the arrogant and sullen Duke Godfrey stiffly bend to one knee.

The emperor spoke warmly: "I have heard you are a man to be trusted utterly, the most mighty knight and prince of your land. And so I take thee for my adopted son, and I place my trust in you, that through you my empire may be preserved and my lands restored."

Godfrey, pledging, held his sword and kissed the emperor's knee.

As the duke stood and was escorted into the receiving hall to wait, slaves followed him bearing gifts of gold, fine cloaks, and bottles of wine. Perhaps of more value to the princes than all the gifts were the promised horses and food markets that were to be established as far as possible along the line of their march toward Jerusalem. The emperor vowed that he would "safeguard the crusaders who came after them," and aid them in the battle with Byzantine forces by land and sea.

So he said. Tancred was concerned about the continued support should the princes refuse to yield any conquered lands taken from the Turks. He now understood the mind of the emperor well enough to believe he would not hesitate to cut them off should their loyalties prove false. Should that occur, famine and pestilence would become the grim reaper among the western armies, for the Moslems would burn the harvest fields and destroy the houses in their march before surrendering goods to the despised Christians.

Alert for trouble, Tancred's gaze was arrested by a movement near the entranceway into the pavilion courtyard. It was only a Norman soldier who loitered, casting a glance about the royal hall, but something unpleasant stirred Tancred's memory. He soon found the man watching him.

Their gazes locked. The soldier quickly turned away, then walked back into the courtyard. Tancred grew uneasy and, looking in the direction where Bohemond had stood only moments ago, saw that he and Count Raymond of Toulouse had left with the emperor. It dawned on him then—the soldier loitering near the courtyard had accompanied his cousin Norris back at the camp.

His cousins were here. Perhaps Walter as well. But Bohemond was not present. Apart from the company of the Norman prince, his uncle would not hesitate to make a move to capture him. Tancred might seek the protection of Bohemond, but there was no time.

Tancred slowly edged toward the opposite door. He stopped, confronted by a rawboned Norman with a ruddy complexion and a shock of grayish blond hair falling across his forehead. Walter of Sicily stood watching him, his pale blue eyes relentless. Behind his uncle gathered several Redwan cousins, but neither Norris nor Leif were among them. Did they wait elsewhere? Or were they not privy to what was happening?

Tancred's brief gaze moved across the room to an open terrace that dropped to a garden below. Walter's gaze also shifted to the terrace as though his thoughts followed his, and he looked disturbed. He gestured to his men standing across the wide hall and they began to move hesitantly in that direction, for it was off limits to anyone except the emperor's guards.

Tancred must be cautious. Did they wait near the stables where

Apollo was kept? He must escape on foot and come back for his horse later.

Tancred moved quickly through the crowd toward the window. The Norman soldiers serving Sir Walter swiftly retreated through the entranceway hoping to overtake him in the garden. He swung himself over the balustrade and, grabbing hold of a tree limb, began descending.

If his uncle came upon him now, he would be an easy target. The shrubs below the tree were dark and quiet. He landed on his feet in the garden.

From behind him there was a rush of feet. They were close. Tancred darted through the trees, jumping over shrubs, and came to a wall. It was high—he leaped, catching hold of the top and pulling himself up. He was about to drop to the ground when he froze. Below, a Byzantine guard looked up, startled, then drew his weapon.

"This is a private residence!"

"I am in service to the minister of war. I need your assistance."

The guard stepped toward him, lifting his sword, but hesitated when he noticed the Byzantine uniform. "But you speak with the brogue of a Norman."

"I also speak Greek," he said in the guard's language. "Quickly, which way from here to the barracks?"

He remained suspicious. "The Normans have come. Their prince, Bohemond, has sworn vassalage to the emperor. You also have vowed tonight?"

"With deep devotion!"

The guard lowered his sword and stepped back while Tancred leaped to the ground.

Hearing the sound of running feet from behind the wall, the guard had second thoughts. He was about to call out when a man of the religious order emerged from the trees, donned in a rugged black riding cloak and chain mesh. Using the side of his hand he walloped the back of the guard's head, and he slumped to the grass.

"It is about time you showed up," said Tancred dryly, and Nicholas lifted a dark brow.

"I thought you could handle matters on your own, my son."

Tancred shot him a glance. Nicholas smiled and pulled the unconscious guard into the bushes. He touched Tancred's shoulder. "Come! Helena waits with the horses."

They ran through the garden, ducking under branches until at last they emerged on the other side. There were magnificent buildings with great walls decorated with medallions and huge domes.

"You know where we are?" breathed Tancred.

Nicholas glanced over his shoulder. "You forget I was born and raised a Byzantine!"

"I could never forget that—Helena forever reminds me."

"Walter and your cousins will be out in force looking for you," said Nicholas. "It will be dangerous to return to the barracks."

They walked briskly through the courtyard, glancing cautiously toward the tall hedge where hired assassins might lurk. Suddenly Nicholas turned onto an open walkway lighted by blazing torchlight. Guards were everywhere.

Tancred walked casually beside him, glancing toward the strolling guards. Did he imagine that the eyes of strong men bearing swords were fixed upon him? How many were his true friends? How many would turn on him if given the opportunity? Although he had served their emperor and Philip, he had felt the resentment of some who were jealous of his swift rise to command. "I hope you know what you are doing."

"Trust me."

Had he not known Nicholas so well and believed in his abilities as a warrior, Tancred would have refused to be led. Nicholas, however, was no soft-bellied priest. His half-cleric, half-soldier garb included both the red crusader cross stitched across his black leather vest and a Norman long blade housed comfortably in his scabbard.

Nevertheless, Tancred paused when ahead of them, a big baldheaded man emerged from the cloister of darkened shrubs where he'd been concealed. Nicholas, too, stopped. Tancred's hand went toward his scabbard, but Nicholas lifted an arm to halt him from unsheathing it.

"It is Bardas."

"I do not trust him. He's been a thorn in my side since I first met your niece."

Nicholas chuckled. "The mother bear growls and grumbles for her cub. Pay no mind. I sent for him."

"A mistake," but as Nicholas strode forward, Tancred followed, maintaining his caution.

When Bardas saw Nicholas he came to meet them, and for the first time Tancred saw a warm smile on the eunuch's broad face. He tugged at his walrus mustache with enthusiasm.

"Greetings, Master Nicholas! The gods rejoice at your presence in Constantinople again!"

"One God, Bardas! One true and living God. Remember."

"Yes, Master Nicholas," he hastened, "a slip of the tongue."

Tancred eyed him. He'd never seen Bardas so quick to respond, so willing to pay respect to a man. He sized up the situation and decided that Bardas could be trusted when carrying out any order of Helena's beloved Greek uncle, even those orders which included himself.

To his surprise, Bardas reached behind the hedge and produced Tancred's satchel and gear taken from the barracks, but he did not even seem to notice Tancred as he quickly explained to Nicholas where the horses were hidden and where Helena waited for them.

Tancred briefly searched his things to make certain all was there and decided Nicholas must have ordered Bardas to bring them.

Nicholas stooped beside him and said in a low voice, "Our plans have changed and must be completed tonight. You must go on without me. I trust you with her life."

"She explained about Constantine?"

A sliver of heated anger showed within Nicholas's dark eyes. "Yes, and you were right to mistrust him. Philip also sent a message urging me to leave tonight without him."

He was surprised Philip would rally to such unselfishness. "Where is he?" he inquired cautiously.

"Yet with the emperor. And Constantine and Irene both watch him."

Tancred had doubts about Philip, but he'd already made them clear to Nicholas in the tent at the Norman camp. Any further warning might cause Nicholas to attribute his conclusions to jealousy. Nevertheless, his own lack of confidence in Philip remained.

"But bring her to the camp of the Norman army? Is it wise?"

"There is little choice. Constantine will have the road to the castle watched, ready to ambush. The long journey will grant us time to arrange her safe delivery to the seigneur of the Castle of Hohms when they least expect it."

They stood, the darkness about them. "Rolf Redwan, you will agree, will prove a mighty protector until the crusaders take Antioch," said Nicholas.

Tancred hesitated, yet uncertain. There would be battles along the way, and the army was no place for a woman of Helena's breeding and culture. He imagined she would soon revolt at the hardships of travel and deprivation sure to come upon them.

Tancred considered the possibility of having Byzantine spies in the camp as well as on the road to Antioch, and did not like the plan. Nor had he intended to journey with the Norman army. He could move faster alone and arrive at Antioch before them, undetected by the Seljuk Turks. He was resigned to the fact that Antioch would not simply surrender in the face of the approaching crusaders, however intimidating the masses of knights on Great Horses and foot soldiers would appear from their lookout towers built on the great walls. They surely knew the crusaders were coming, and they would have made provision for a long and terrible siege. He understood the proud minds of the Moslems.

Then there was Helena's mother. . . . Tancred had not forgotten his promise to use his association with the Moslem allies of al-Kareem to seek her whereabouts in the desert tents. Nicaea would be a good place to begin, but should he arrive with Bohemond they would hardly allow him through the gate into the city to visit Asad.

"Helena will be safer among us than on the road alone with you and a few mercenaries," said Nicholas. "Both Irene and Constantine—should the man appear—realize I will not easily surrender her. They will pretend to believe we cooperate together to escort her to Kalid, but in their hearts they know I will refuse the Moslem wedding of my Christian niece."

Tancred remained uneasy, but he could see Nicholas had accepted the plan as their only recourse.

"Once she is in the crusader camp, they will have little cause to contest. It is for you to get her there before they know what we are about."

"Constantine has other plans in mind as well," suggested Tancred, frowning. "Be assured they benefit his ambitions. And his son's."

Nicholas's alert gaze came to his. "Then you know he is the father of Philip?"

"Helena explained." He wondered what Nicholas thought of this.

"It is good that she did. You now understand some of what is happening."

"Enough to know that the sooner I am about my own quest of finding my brother's assassin, the sooner I can return to peace in Sicily."

Nicholas laughed. "Peace? In Sicily? The Normans are at each other's throats. And if you return anytime soon to claim the Redwan castle, you will be fighting Count Roger."

"You underestimate me, Nicholas. When I return, I shall be a free man to direct my life and goals in Palermo. And if I cannot, I will not return," he said with an unexpected determination that surprised even him.

Nicholas appeared to consider, but the gleam in his eyes convinced Tancred he had thoughts of his own. Nicholas was a man who planned well and usually got what he wanted. Just what did he want? He had returned to Constantinople under the cloak of the crusade, but he was not a man to take pleasure in such a war, and neither did he long to retake his position as a bishop in the Eastern branch of the Church.

"You will find your assassin," said Nicholas with more confidence than even Tancred shared. "And I? Constantine and I have much to settle before this campaign to take Jerusalem is over."

Tancred believed that Nicholas was the man to do it.

"I will join you in a few days at Bohemond's camp," said Nicholas. "I will come quietly. Expect me in the shadows of the night."

"What keeps you in the city?" Tancred asked, curious that he would not join them for several days. "Is it wise? Even now Irene's spies are out searching for you."

"Then I must not disappoint her."

Tancred looked at him, but Nicholas's mouth turned into a grim smile. "See to Helena. I will take care of Irene."

"The horses and my mistress wait," Bardas reminded them anxiously.

Tancred hesitated, still uncertain in his own mind about the plan, but what concerned Nicholas, he told himself, concerned him also. He owed him much—at least where his niece was concerned.

"It was not my intention to become involved in this war, nor is it now."

"Your wishes will be carefully guarded."

Tancred regarded him and wondered that the reply did not satisfy, but Nicholas remained as elusive as always.

"We have a destiny to fill at Jerusalem," Nicholas told him. And with that uncomfortable reminder of the holy object to be returned to the sepulcher, he slipped away like a mysterious shadow into the night.

With Nicholas gone, Helena had again been placed in Tancred's charge. Bardas also slipped away, expecting to lead him to where she waited with the horses. And Tancred did not wish to stay—somewhere not far behind, still searching for him, was Walter of Sicily.

Gathering his cloak about him and snatching up his gear, Tancred followed into the darkness.

Nicholas frowned, his mind engrossed in the unpleasant task at hand. He was not anticipating the need to see Irene again. Despite the confidence he had shown over the matter to Tancred, an uneasy dread settled over his heart. He had loved her once, until, like Gomer, the wife of the prophet Hosea, Irene too had behaved the harlot.

His mind wandered back to when, as a younger man, he had left for Athens to enter the Church, a betrothal to Irene fully agreed upon. On that night so long ago they had lingered in the garden sweetness to vow to each other and to God their devotion, their worship, their bodies, even as they vowed purity to each other. He had returned two years later to find Irene the emperor's mistress.

The pain he had felt back then, thought to be dead after twenty years, stirred like sleeping coals coming to life. Only the prophet Hosea could know the anguish he had felt, the desolation, the disappointment, the bitter loss of his pure and beautiful Irene of Troy to the purple robe and pearls of the harlot selling her wares.

Nicholas walked along, stroking his short beard, contemplating. He slipped silently through the palace garden and neared the low walled gate that led in the direction of the Augustaeum.

He strode forward, musing, his dark eyes reflective of the turmoil stirring in his soul. He was unprepared for the soldiers who emerged from the darkness, their swords lifting in the moonlight, flashing silver.

Nicholas halted and had only a moment to respond before he was surrounded. His blade came swiftly from his scabbard, but a wicked blow struck him across the head from behind, and he fell, his face striking the stone floor of the courtyard.

In a moment of down-spiraling consciousness he heard Irene say, "Bring him to the villa. We will be uninterrupted there."

With all his will Nicholas struggled to move, but a surge of darkness swallowed him, and through the haze he heard the click of her heeled slippers close beside his head, felt her fragrant silk skirt brush the side of his face. She stooped, laying a cool palm to the side of his brow. She stroked it. "Poor Nicholas. Poor deluded but beloved Nicholas. You are mine again, at last."

CHAPTER 14
The White Bishop's Secret Past

The daylight stabbed into Nicholas's eyes like daggers. He groaned and tried to move, but his limbs tingled a thousand sharp needles of pain.

"The bear awakens from his long slumber," came Irene's distant voice, sultry and mocking. "If I did not care to ruin my cushions, I would have you splashed awake with water from the pool."

Nicholas agonized to gather his wits, but the effort proved vain. He felt slaves roll him over on his back, and while he tried to resist, he could not. A moment later he felt a cold, startling splash of water, and he shouted his protest as he raised to an elbow, blinking. As his blurred eyes cleared, he saw Irene staring down at him, hands on hips.

"When he has eaten and dressed, bring him to me," she ordered.

Nicholas entered the open tiled courtyard and glanced about at the familiar surroundings of the villa where he had spent his youth with his sister Adrianna and other members of the Lysander family. The court spread out toward the pleasant olive orchard.

Pigeons cooed and water trickled peacefully over the rocks in the tiered fountain. He fought back the bitter memories like demons trying to conquer and defeat him.

Over the dark woolen undertunic he wore chain mesh, and then a second leather tunic. His thick dark hair was still wet and held back by a thong. He knew his looks had not yet declined, even as Irene's subtle beauty had not yet faded, and he was cautious. He threw his cloak over his shoulder and walked to meet her.

She has deliberately chosen the place where we had vowed our love.

His sword and scabbard were missing—but not his dagger, housed safely under his left wrist. Evidently the female slave attending him last night and this morning respected his holy office too much to remove his inner clothing.

His dark, robust eyes saw her, and waiting for him, she arose from the carved bench—not wearing shimmering silk but a plain tunic with a simple belt. Her face was scrubbed of all beauty paints and her hair was covered with a white scarf.

This he had not expected. He had steeled his emotions against the temptation of silk, perfume, and strong seduction; she came to him looking a virgin, her eyes pleading. He stood there while the warm breeze nodded the colorful poppies growing at his feet.

Irene approached him delicately and held out his scabbard with both hands. "You may kill me with your blessed sword if you wish. I would count it a mercy if you would."

His black eyes mocked her. She was a master at deceit.

"You always were dramatic. And if I took your lovely head, would your soul no longer bear the crimson stain of murder?"

"Murder?" she asked innocently, and walked toward him barefoot, her white tunic trailing. A gust of wind blew back her hood, and her pale silky hair swirled about her waist.

He took her in from head to toe and he wondered that his heart beat as coolly as ever. Nothing remained of the passion that had once set him aflame, only a strange dull pity toward her, the same odd emotion he felt for a wounded bird who could no longer fly, or a lily that fell crumpled beneath careless feet. It was always sad when something once lovely died and withered with the blight of sin.

"I wish to die," she sobbed. "If your hands performed the deed, I would find it a mercy."

A smile appeared above his short dark beard. "I know you too well, Irene. You forget that you have lied to me so many times. I could not be tricked again. Your repentance wears the beautiful face of morning mist, but all too soon it vanishes. Do not mock us by pretense."

"It is you who mock me, Nicholas." She walked up to him softly, and her eyes surrendered to his. She knelt before him and laid his sword at his feet. "I am yours, Nicholas. Do with me as you will."

"My will belongs to another Master. The same One you will also answer to," he said gently. "The One you refused, but your rejection was not enough—you also demanded I too walk away from Him. The price of your love, Irene, was always too high."

"Your god—I despise your robe with its cross! How untouchable, how righteous you were in your rejection of me."

"I came to you not as a priest, but as a man who loved you until I discovered what you were. I never rejected you, not even when I returned and found you the emperor's mistress. I wanted to help you, to bring you to Christ. I would have loved you, Irene. You rejected me when you turned to the idols of the zodiac. You demanded I throw away my greatest treasure for you."

"Your god is nothing but an illusion. What has he done for you? Look at you—nothing now but a homeless bishop with a horse and a sword! But I! In turning to the gods of the stars, I will be empress one day."

"Should you reach so far as to grasp the stars, you will yet die as humbly as the lowest slave. And unlike the poorest among men who dies with Christ as Savior, you will be the pauper."

"So I will go to hades, will I? You pity *me*? Your pity is worse than the sword you could plunge through my heart. I hate your god, for he took you away from me."

"Did you hate my brother also? Is that why you poisoned Leo? You schemed to have me banished to Bari, then lied to him about my death. You deceived him into marriage for the Lysander inheritance, only to learn it was mine after all, and not his. Mine and Adrianna's. You had no further use for him so you poisoned him and claimed Constantine. Adrianna found out about Leo, and you schemed against her also."

Irene winced, suddenly frightened. "I did not poison Leo."

"You did," he stated. "Adrianna wrote me. It is the cause for which you plotted her death."

"He killed himself!"

"If he did, it was because you tormented him so badly he was driven to it."

She fell at his feet. "Nicholas," she whispered, and tears filled her amber eyes as she looked up at him. "Nicholas, I have dreamed of you a thousand nights."

"In whose arms did you lie as you dreamed—a slave, or the emperor's?"

"Mock me all you will. I love you still."

"You never loved me at all, nor do you love any man. Not even your own son Philip. You barter him like an Arab barters for camels! You desire power, you love the thrill of keeping others enslaved to your demands. Why it should be, only God knows. Do not cheapen the word of love by speaking it on your tongue."

Her fingers curled hotly about his ankles and moved up his legs. "Nicholas," she whispered. "If you only knew how I have cursed myself these years. Cursed myself until I despise my image in the looking glass."

"Your pride, Irene, would have you sitting before the glass for an hour adoring your face. Do you speak of self-judgment?"

"I only know that I love you, Nicholas. I will be yours alone. Always yours."

He grabbed her arm and yanked her to her feet, shaking her until her hair flew about them, and her sobs wailed.

"Have you no shame at all? What do you know of sacrificial love, the love of God? You cannot love. You desire the ways of a harlot. I knew it even then when we were young, when you were yet a virgin. Even back then, when innocence was on your lips and your cheeks would flush with humility, you would have lain with me before our marriage bed had I asked. I knew it, yet I refused to see it. It did not take you long to throw it away on the first man who would have you! I went to Athens to pray, to seek the mind of God about you—for even then I had doubts. I knew what you were. And when I returned you had already slept with the slave boy. You boast of the emperor? Did you tell him of the slave boy who came first?"

She reached to claw his chest, but he gripped her wrists tightly, holding her away from him.

"And even now your words are still lies. Yes, you are beguiling indeed. You knew you could not come to me with the face of Jezebel. So you subtly adorned yourself with a worse hypocrisy! You come to me as an angel. And why? You would see me fall prey for the sheer joy of having conquered me at last."

Her sobbing ceased and her eyes turned hard and brittle.

"Surely you are a man inside that bishop's cloak! I can see you are. I remember how you once held me, how your lips took mine, how you vowed your love. It is not too late, Nicholas. We can be together now." She reached for him, but he caught her wrist firmly.

Sudden bitterness sparked in his eyes. "You have bludgeoned me a thousand times with your taunts. Do you think I am a boy, that you can tempt me so easily to succumb?"

She pulled away from him, her face hard with rage. "Why did you come back? What do you expect to do about the past, about Leo? Go to the emperor? Convince him to hang me? Force me to live out my days in the convent? He will not listen to you! And if you go to him, he will arrest you."

His eyes ran over her. "Is that why you threw yourself at my feet pretending love? You feared I would haul you before the throne as a murderess? I would not waste you to the laws of Byzantium. Your end will come in its own way. Nay, woman, I came for the villa, for the Lysander inheritance, the Castle of Hohms. It is Helena's, not Philip's."

"The Lysander inheritance! Do you think you can convince the emperor of that?" she scoffed. "He listens to me, to Philip, to Constantine, not to you." Her eyes mocked. "I have firm control over the empress."

"No doubt. Have you enslaved her with your evil drugs and sorcery?"

"I could easily have you killed," she warned. "I have not done so before now because I do care for you, whether you believe it or not. I will always care for you."

"You are never more venomous than when you speak of love. I do not fear you, Irene, nor Constantine." Nicholas let go of her arm and she stepped back, cautiously watching him.

He looked toward the olive orchard, for he knew she had guards. "I will gain the inheritance, eventually. First, I shall lay claim to the family castle at Hohms."

"You will need to stop Kalid first," she said scornfully. "He has bargained Antioch for the castle."

"I expect to stop him," he admitted. "Helena will not marry Kalid."

"You will not be able to stop it. You are a fool if you try. Even now I can have twenty guards in here. Your death would be so simple," she breathed. "I could have your arrogant head on a platter."

"And sleep well for having done so."

She scanned him, her eyes burning with anger and passion. "I do not want your miserable head—I want you. I always have, and I will until I die." She raised her chin, tossing her silken strands. "I will yet have you, Nicholas. You will see. I will never give up."

She moved toward him and slid her arms around his neck, pressing her warm mouth to his.

Nicholas succumbed for a brief moment, then unwrapped her hands from about his neck and held her away from him, with her arms behind her back. He studied her face as her breath came rapidly.

Her eyes gleamed triumphantly and she laughed, holding her head back. "For all your pious talk your heart beats the same as any man's. You do want me," she whispered.

His eyes held hers evenly, then he released her. "You are to be more than pitied," he said, and caught up his cloak from the courtyard. He turned. "I have the deed for the castle."

"You deceive. Leo hid it and no one has ever found it. He would not tell me where it was."

"So you poisoned him? Let this haunt your dreams—he could not tell you. He did not know. You murdered him for nothing. The Lysander deed granted by Emperor Nicephorous was safely hidden all these years at the monastery of Mount Athos."

An ugly look came to her face.

He smiled and carelessly lifted his chin. "That was where I placed it before you and Constantine convinced the emperor I committed treason. It was within your reach all these years." He turned to walk away. "I advise you not to come to Hohms."

"I will come. I will follow you wherever you go, Nicholas. One day I will convince you to stay with me."

He turned and walked away.

"Nicholas!" She ran after him, her voice pleading, even whining, "Nich-o-las!"

He felt nothing but emotional release as he walked, leaving behind damaged emotions that had been buried painfully in his soul for years. *Let God handle the injustice and death,* he thought.

He paused and looked toward the summer sky as blue as a topaz. Consciously he released Irene and Constantine and the murder of his brother to the will of God.

I am now free to pursue the future.

Nicholas walked on, taking in a breath of fresh air, flinging his bishop's cloak to lie across his shoulders. There was one quest now to concern him—not vengeance, but the safety of Helena and Adrianna. He could not have mentioned his sister to Irene, though he had wanted to confront her, for he did not want Irene to know that Adrianna was alive.

He heard Irene's feet running behind him and he imagined a dagger in her fist.

She caught his arm, sobbing. "Wait, Nicholas. It is not true that there is no love in me, no sorrow, no regret. I am a woman; I have my bitter memories. If I could go back—" Her voice cracked with deep emotion. "I swear I would have vowed to follow your god, your life. I would have chosen differently."

He gently removed her hand from his arm and his dark eyes were grave. "I am sorry, Irene. The years have been lived and are forever gone. It is their memory which haunts us in the night; but the fruit will be there to meet us in eternity. While you have an hour left, choose the life He yet offers. There is no sin so crimson that He cannot wash away. You can become as pure as the virgin snow."

Nicholas plucked a blossom from a nearby vine and pressed it into her limp, cold hand. "All too soon the beauty fades. Your beauty too will fade. You will end up one day an old woman with nothing but regrets."

Irene blanched as she looked into his face. "Pity," she whispered. "You dare pity me?" She trembled, clutching the crushed white flower. "I will have an empire," she said hoarsely.

"Ask the ghosts of the Caesars if it was enough."

"I shall make you pay for this," she cried. "No one treats me this way. Do you think you can, Nicholas? If I cannot have you— then, I will see you dead."

"Good-bye, Irene."

Nicholas stepped into the stirrup and mounted his horse, turning the reins to ride toward the Golden Horn. There he would board a boat and sail to the shores of Anatolia. Soon he would join Tancred in the camp of Prince Bohemond. The deed to the castle was in his satchel and his weapons were within easy reach. He rode away, leaving the ghosts behind him.

CHAPTER 15
To Escape the Web

It was night and no light from the lanterns broke through the darkness of the filthy streets. Here, in a squalid section of Constantinople, thieves and beggars were as numerous as the poor who lived in low, cramped houses among the narrow alleys.

It had rained. The mud was deep. The stench of debris hung in the air, crowded with bursts of drunken laughter. Tancred heard a wary movement from above his head. Instinct halted him. At once he touched Bardas's arm and they paused.

Tancred looked up to a small ledge that extended out below a dark window. A man crouched with a dagger, ready to spring. The robber made a desperate lunge at Bardas, hoping to bring him down, but as he did, Bardas knelt and thrust upward through his chest. The weight of the man's body drove the sword to the hilt, sending Bardas sprawling backward into the mud. He shoved him away and wrenched his sword loose.

"Quick, there will be more," said Bardas. "This way."

"Why did you bring her to this foul place to wait?"

"She is guarded with three soldiers loyal to Philip." They came to a dimly lighted shop where food and wine were sold, and Tancred removed his splotched cloak to enter with Bardas.

It was crowded and they took a wooden table in the back.

Within a few minutes the chief bodyguard who served Irene entered alone.

The giant ebony warrior stood as elegantly shaped as if chiseled from marble by an artisan. He boasted the colors of the imperial guard, his rich purple cloak edged with gold.

Tancred was faintly surprised, for he had come to know Rufus rather well in the month he had been in Philip's service. Rufus had proven a friend, and in the past he had alerted him to Irene's plans to control him, even as she controlled Rufus and others. He remembered that Rufus had told him he could not free himself from her mastery because of his son Joseph, who served as a translator at the Royal Library. He had also warned him about Mosul serving the Turkish commander Kerbogha at Antioch.

Tancred watched as the guard's black eyes scanned those seated in the room. He had wisely chosen a section of the city where he was not known and where Lady Irene was not likely to venture. Apparently seeing no one he recognized, Rufus strode up to the table where Tancred and Bardas sat and pulled out a chair to join them.

Although seated, he remained a giant of a man with strong shoulders and big hands, and Tancred noticed several eyes shift his way uneasily and then stare into their cups.

Rufus had told him that he had come from Ethiopia as a boy and worked his way into the mercenary army serving the emperor. Later, he had gone to the Castle of Hohms to serve Tancred's uncle Rolf Redwan. From there, Irene had acquired him. Tancred suspected that there had once been a romance, at Irene's instigation, for there were few men around the palace she did not consort with to gain their usefulness.

Rufus wasted no time. "Despite all care, I believe we were followed. Lady Helena waits in one of the back stalls under guard. You must take precaution. Your enemy is a tigress who stalks her prey."

Tancred lifted a brow at his description of Irene. A fitting one, he thought.

"What of you? You will come with us?"

"An important opportunity I have long awaited is near at hand; otherwise I would accompany you."

His suggestion hinted of more than personal plans. He despised Irene. Did it have anything to do with her? As Tancred measured him with a glance, a mask came down over his face.

"She has my son Joseph."

"I remember. I have been thinking of a plan to secure his freedom."

Rufus smiled for the first time. "As have I. But we have made our plans. One of the Venetian ships has done trade in Ethiopia recently and for the right price will bring Joseph to freedom."

Tancred scanned him. "And you?"

His eyes hardened. "I will remain behind long enough to see he escapes. If there is a trap, I will see madame fall into it."

"Then we understand each other. Yet hate knows no freedom. You would not wish her blood on your hands, Rufus."

His heavy shoulders sagged a little, and for a moment he appeared a man to be pitied, like a majestic eagle on a short chain. Tancred's jaw hardened.

"Do nothing on your own. I fear your hatred will push you to a decision you will live to regret. If something goes wrong with your plans for Joseph, wait for me to return from Antioch. I will see to his freedom, somehow."

Rufus looked at him and tears welled in his magnificent eyes.

"If she were dead the city would be a better place." He picked up the metal cup and in one hand crushed it.

Bardas shifted uneasily and shot a glance toward Tancred.

"Do not kill her. Wait for me."

Rufus slumped, his emotions spent. He said nothing but gestured his head in affirmation.

Tancred lifted his cup and drank. "Nicholas has his own plans where Irene is concerned. I think he will see to them better than you."

Rufus stood, in control of his emotions again, his face immobile. "We dare not meet again until you return from Antioch. It was dangerous for me to come here tonight. I think not of me, but Joseph. She knows that I could not bear harm coming to my son. If anything goes wrong, I can do no more to help Lysander's daughter. You must get out of Constantinople any way you can."

The view from the stall-like chamber of wood was restricted to the narrow street. Helena was standing in a hooded cloak, peering out into the darkness when Tancred entered with Bardas. She turned expectantly, and at seeing him, her manner changed to a guarded look, for awareness of him brought unease.

Tancred deliberately offered a deep bow at the waist. "Your servant, madame. You called?"

She walked up to him like a princess, an attitude most becoming if it had not been used with the usual attempt to make him feel like a servant.

"Does my arrival disturb you, madame?" he inquired smoothly.

"Why should it? It was I who asked Uncle Nicholas to have you escort me to the crusader camp."

"I am, of course, at your beck and call."

She smiled, lifting her dimpled chin, and turned her back toward him, quipping, "And also Philip's. These are his new plans. He is quite adept at such things."

"Then perhaps," said Tancred flatly, "I should leave you here until he arrives to see to your safety."

Helena turned to face him quickly, hand outstretched as though she expected to see him walking toward the door.

Tancred stood waiting for her. He smiled. "Shall we go, princess?"

Her eyes looked into his, questioning, then she too smiled. "I am ready." She turned. "Bardas? You have the horses?"

"Everything is prepared, little one. The sooner we get out of this vile place the better."

"It is hideous. I did not know such places existed in the city."

"Neither does the emperor, evidently," said Tancred.

She looked at him surprised. "The emperor knows everything about his city. Why do you say that?"

The slight pride in her voice irritated him. "Because he does nothing to help his poor peasants. But then, I suppose he is too busy to bother. Along with the nobility, he must grow exhausted attending games, the circus, hiring barbarians to fight his wars."

She brushed past, and he walked beside her, Bardas and a guard in the lead, two more guards in back.

"Of course life for the poor will change for the better once your beloved Philip becomes emperor," he told her.

Helena raised her head. "I am glad you think so. If you do your duties well, soldier, perhaps I will ask him to hire you when that day comes. You may drive our royal chariot as bodyguard."

She stopped at the door and looked at him with an innocent smile.

Tancred reached to open it and bowed her past. Helena swept through and out into the street.

On an impulse he swung her up into his arms. "A Daughter of the Purple Belt must not soil her golden slippers."

"Put me down."

It was dark, but by the rushed tone of her voice he knew she flushed.

"I am your humble and dedicated servant, princess. How could I allow you to walk through the filth as a common peasant?"

He strode with her in mute silence down the narrow alley. She felt good in his arms. "I think you belong here," he said gravely.

Her head turned sharply. "I beg your pardon, Sir Knight!"

"In my arms, madame, not amid the squalor."

They reached the horses and Bardas waited, his eyes cool and hard when he saw Helena in Tancred's arms. He held the reins, and when Tancred set her onto her feet, Bardas moved at once to step between them, holding her stirrup so she could mount.

She sat her horse well and looked to ride even better.

"It is good that you are able to ride," he stated as he mounted Apollo with ease and turned the reins. "It is a long journey to Antioch."

"I am not going there," she countered, "but to my castle to marry Philip."

Tancred scanned her, ignoring the ever-watching eyes of Bardas. "I can see why he marries you—for the castle."

"He does not! But for love."

"The castle is of strategic importance to Philip, but not to me."

They rode forward at a smart trot with guards riding in the lead and flank.

"You already have a castle, remember?" she mocked. "Unless you spoke only from your ego," she laughed. "I doubt there are castles in the barbarian West. I suspect they are dirt hovels."

"Now, a galleon! Ah, that is quite another thing to consider," he went on as though he did not hear her. "I would easily marry a girl for a ship."

"A ship!" she repeated with surprise. "But why?"

His eyes taunted her. "Because I could sail to Cathay, to Hind, to many such exotic places. I could enjoy the peace of a cabin while I read my cherished books and stayed free of her nagging for several years at a time."

She flipped her reins and rode ahead beside Bardas.

When Tancred arrived at the harbor of the Golden Horn he discovered that the Byzantine navy under orders from the emperor was already engaged in the monumental task of ferrying the crusader armies across the Bosporus into Anatolia, also called Asia Minor. Great contingents of ferried knights and soldiers were making their camps on the shore fifty miles from the first Moslem fortress.

Curious as always—for she was, he believed, an intelligent woman—Helena rode up beside him. "What is it? Are we too late?"

"No, the foot soldiers tell me there still remains a large section of the Normans on the Golden Horn."

"What about Walter of Sicily? Suppose he sees you?"

"You are concerned for me?"

"I would not like to lose a good bodyguard," and she rode back to Bardas.

Tancred rode toward the tents, gazing longingly at the ships in the background. He half wished he might buy passage and sail to the other side of the world, forgetting Mosul, and more. He would not, of course. He could not respect himself if he chose the easier path through life.

She was right. He would need to carefully avoid his uncle and cousins. Had Walter decided not to come on the crusade?

Wishful thinking, he told himself dryly. *Like starving wolves they now have my scent and will stalk me to the bitter end.*

An hour later he rode back to where she and the others waited out of sight.

"I've secured private supplies and hired a Levantine. The boat will take our horses aboard. He will bring us to the other side of the Bosporus tonight. In another day or two we will reach the crusaders."

That night under a clear sky with their horses stored amidships, they slipped away from the harbor and down the Golden Horn toward the Bosporus.

Helena stood alone and Tancred knew she watched Constantinople recede into the distance, moonlight glinting on the great domes of Byzantine churches.

"Do you grieve at the loss?"

She had not heard his approach and now turned her head at the sound of his quiet voice. A wistful smile touched her face, and he watched the summer breeze play in her hair.

"No, I think of my mother."

"I would not hope too strongly," he told her casually. "But it may be that I can help Nicholas learn where she is. Once Hakeem reports back to me from Antioch, we will both know more of what to expect concerning our future."

"Our future?" she asked, mistaking his intention. "I did not know we shared one."

"My mistake, princess. We do not. A reason for which to give thanks." And he deliberately left her there.

He went to where the horses were tied and fed Apollo and the others from a canvas bag of apples that he had bought. He knew she was still thinking about his remark and glanced in her direction, amused. As he had guessed, she stood watching him, and he imagined that she was puzzled over his pretended indifference toward her. The more she shielded her emotions with superior pride, the more he would reject her. And if he knew anything about her at all, his indifference baited her interest in him.

Being sought after by men who cared not for her but for her beauty and position, she could not understand why he behaved differently.

He carelessly turned his back toward her, lounging against the side of the boat, and bit into one of the apples.

When they arrived on the other side of the Bosporus in Anatolia, the morning sun was hot and bright in the June sky. As they rode into the crusader camp, Helena recognized the flag, or rather, what Tancred had called a gonfanon of Prince Bohemond. Other feudal lords from Normandy had arrived, and as they stood about, she noticed the same red crosses sewn upon their garments. There were also more soldiers who had recently arrived on Venetian ships, and Helena saw the men gathering near the tent headquarters receiving crosses to be sewn on.

The size of the spreading camp amazed her. She stared, shading her eyes as she rode slowly through the compound between Tancred and Bardas.

Bardas tugged on his flowing mustache and quietly grumbled, "There are even more barbarians here than with Duke Godfrey at the town across the bridge. I hope Master Nicholas was right in bringing you here."

Though Helena did not question Nicholas's decision, the sight before her was intimidating. As far as her eye could see there were tents, horses, donkeys, carts, wagons, and soldiers—thousands of them. And, as Tancred had explained, these men were not the half-starved and tattered mob of deluded peasants who had followed Peter the Hermit to their massacre, believing Christ marched ahead of them to kill the infidels.

These strong-belted knights wore iron-ringed leather, while their chief pieces of armor were kept polished and ready by what Tancred called "esquires," the young lads in training to become knights. She took in the magnificent Great Horse, bred for war.

"They are as important to the knight as his own body," said Tancred, following her gaze. "The horse is kept by a groom near the knight's personal tent and fed and blessed with good foraging." He added, glancing at her with an amused glint, "They are treated better than their women."

"I am most assured of that."

"Each knight usually has six footmen who fight beside him, guarding his horse, or in front of him, hacking away at the enemy." He gestured to another group. "These are the famous archers. And over there—stone slingers. They claim David as their mentor. Then there are foot soldiers. They wield the halberd—an ax on a long shaft that also includes a spearhead in its arsenal, and others carry the morningstar—a heavy iron ball studded with sharp spikes attached to a handle with a chain."

Helena gave him a side glance.

"So you see, madame, you will be well protected." He gestured to the tents of the blacksmiths. Helena heard the ring of steel upon anvils.

"All these weapons and more are kept in readiness," Tancred told her. "The vigil never ends, in order to split an opponent in twain, hack off a nose, or leave a skull crushed."

Helena could not tell by his smooth voice if he were being cynical or deadly serious. "I am profoundly impressed," she murmured.

"You should be. The knights have every wish to kill the Turk—and though told they are sent to do so by heaven, they were not above looting a few Christian towns along the route across Europe. Many of them, especially the princes and nobles, are out for gain—land, gold, especially new kingdoms to rule, and of course, the great adventure."

She gave him a wry glance. "I am surprised you would admit this."

"Why not?"

"They are your kin, your national people."

"So are the Moors. Am I the crusaders' liege? And anyway, it is not my cause to either defend or condemn this expedition."

She scanned him as he rode astride Apollo, and believed he looked every inch the same manner of knight as the rest of them. "Will you join them, then?"

He squinted toward the camel hills of the East, growing ever nearer. "Not if I can avoid it. I was against crusading from the beginning and I still am, but that means nothing to them. They are anxious for battle. Many of the knights and their esquires, along with the common foot soldier, believe they fight for Christ and His honor. They were told their sins would be forgiven, that heaven would open for their immediate entry if they went on crusade and fought under the cross. Their swords were blessed before they journeyed, and they are ready."

She mused. "But you do not believe God has called the Church to destroy unbelievers, even to retake the most sacred Christian city of all, Jerusalem."

"How the bishops can believe that has me puzzled."

"Nicholas does not," she hastened.

"Because he understands the Scriptures better than the common priests. And from what I have read, the last words of Christ before His ascension were to bring the message of hope and forgiveness to the uttermost parts of the world."

"And if they do not receive it?"

"Then they do not receive, to their eternal loss. From what I have read, it is for Christ to ride forth in final judgment against His enemies and bring in His earthly kingdom. The Church will not do it by physical force, for the weapons are not carnal but spiritual."

"And you do not think He rides forth 'spiritually' to judge through the earthly sword of the crusaders?"

Tancred looked at her as though he wondered if her question were sincere. "If He does, then we will never lose a battle. But what of the evil done in His name when many of the crusaders attacked the Jews as they came through Europe? Even those with Peter the Hermit looted and burned, though they denied it when confronted with their guilt."

"I believe you are right about the crusade," she said quietly. "Though I have not thought much about it. I have been too occupied with my own problems. I fear there will be great loss of life between here and Jerusalem."

"Yes" was all he said.

She shivered, considering.

"I am glad you will not join them," she said after a small interlude of silence.

His blue-gray eyes held hers momentarily before she looked about at the tents and soldiers.

"I may have to," he replied tonelessly. "There are times when a man finds himself caught up in circumstances that he cannot avoid. To live, I must battle. No matter what my convictions, I have no wish to surrender my sword and die the martyr's death beneath the scimitar." His smile formed. "Who would save you from the embrace of Kalid?"

She turned her head away, brushing a dark wisp of her hair from her cheek. "You will not need to concern yourself for that. I will marry Philip soon."

"Will you?"

She did not reply, for just then she looked ahead toward Prince Bohemond's tent and said with surprise, "Why—Philip is here." Her breath caught with alarm. "And is that not Constantine standing with him?"

Tancred followed her gaze to the large tent headquarters belonging to Bohemond with its crimson flag staked proudly by the entrance. Both Philip and Bishop Constantine stood waiting for them. And with them, General Taticus, commander of the small Byzantine force journeying with the crusaders.

"What is Constantine doing here?" she whispered. "I wonder if Nicholas knows."

"I am certain he does not. Nor has he arrived yet. And when Nicholas does come, he will do so as quietly as the falcon's wings."

"Until he arrives, Philip will see to my comfort. He will have a few servants and set up a tent for me near his own."

"He would naturally think first of ease and comfort," came Tancred's bored voice. "I hope he survives the long journey to Jerusalem. There may be famine before we gaze upon David's city."

"He will survive! Have you forgotten Philip too is a soldier?"

"Forgotten Wieselburg? I make it my cause to remember well. What of your safety? Will he see to that also?"

She looked at him coolly. "Why you dislike him so is obvious."

"Is it?"

She flipped her reins and rode ahead, Bardas in close pursuit, followed by the three guards. Bardas glanced back at Tancred with a scowl.

Tancred slowed Apollo to a stop and rested his elbow on his saddle. He watched General Taticus, a spy for the emperor, no doubt. It would be his secret ambition to make sure that every fortress taken from the Turks would be returned to Byzantium. The crusader princes had hard lessons to learn about outsmarting the emperor of the Eastern Empire. Alexius had no notion of surrendering past territory taken by the Moslems. By now, the emperor would have spies stationed at every outpost along the way, already trying to make secret deals with the various petty sultans and emirs to surrender to General Taticus instead of the dreaded barbarian lords.

Constantine was a far different matter. Like Nicholas, Tancred believed that his presence meant more than mere devotion to the rule of his emperor, or even seeing his son Philip claim the glory of any upcoming victories. Just what did Constantine want or expect to find on this arduous journey toward Jerusalem?

One thing seemed certain: Helena had not yet told him everything about her mother, Lady Adrianna.

He watched Philip leave the side of General Taticus and come forward to assist Helena down from her horse. They stood for a brief moment, eyes holding, then Philip, behaving as though she were only a friend, turned and walked to Constantine, saying something to him.

Astride Apollo, Tancred walked the stallion toward the impressive gathering of Byzantine officials beneath the canopy boasting the flag showing the doubled-headed eagle looking west and east. Since the days of greater Byzantium, however, Constantinople had lost control over territory in both directions.

Philip left the platform under the canopy and walked up beside Tancred's dusty horse. He seemed as though he would quietly ask about Nicholas, but Constantine joined them, ending the opportunity.

"You are surprised to see us, Captain Redwan?" said Constantine with a thin smile. "I forgot to inform you when last we met that Philip and I have been chosen as the emperor's legates to journey with General Taticus and his Byzantine troop. We will travel with the crusaders on the road to Antioch and Jerusalem. I, however, will journey with Count Raymond of Toulouse."

Tancred looked at Philip, who appeared tense. Had he come for Helena under the ruse of working with General Taticus? Or was his mission a genuine one for the emperor?

"You have safely delivered Helena to our care," said Philip. "Well done, Captain. Any trouble along the way?"

"Was I to expect it?" he asked innocently. Nicholas had been right. Both Constantine and Irene would have their private soldiers hiding in the hills, ready to sweep Helena away to Kalid should his son seek to escape with her.

Philip was silent, but Constantine's hawklike face hardened. "There is always danger. You can expect trouble from here to Jerusalem."

"I will be on guard, Bishop."

Constantine's eyes flickered. He walked to his horse and mounted, turning to ride. "A pity I have missed Nicholas. Does he not ride with your Norman liege? Or has he decided to trail behind like a weak shadow, darting behind the desert rocks?"

Tancred's expression showed nothing except a military response. "Do you wish me to send a rider for Nicholas?" he asked innocently.

A flicker showed in his bold eyes. "There is no need, Redwan. I am certain Nicholas knows I am here among the crusaders. He will find me at Count Raymond's army with Bishop Adehemar when he chooses the moment."

"Then you will be close at hand, no doubt."

Constantine's brief gaze ran over him. "As a legate of the emperor I will always be close to Philip. It is his responsibility to make certain the rest of the princes keep their vow to surrender all territory to the emperor."

"With you here to aid him I am certain neither of you will fail in your task, Bishop."

Constantine's mouth twitched and Tancred turned to Philip, who stood tensely. "With your leave," and lifting a hand, he turned Apollo to ride on.

Tancred stood near one of the pens that kept several of Bohemond's Great Horses. Apollo was kept separated from the others for they were uneasy around him. Tancred was attending its hoofs when a lone, distant whinny carried on the east wind. He straightened, peering off into the black night. As always, his weapons were at hand and he was cautious.

Nicholas arrived in the desert night like a mirage, wearing a Norman-style coif of chain mesh over his head and a short warrior's cloak.

A good-humored smile showed on his rugged tanned face, and he gestured to Apollo. "Do you expect to join a Norman charge riding a spoiled thoroughbred?"

Apollo rolled his eyes and lifted his head as though he understood the insult.

"Do not mind him, Apollo," Tancred said. "He forgets how we intend to ride circles around them all—including his nag."

Nicholas kneed his charger forward and leaned there, resting his arm across the saddle, his black eyes sparkling in the silvery moonlight, his white teeth showing beneath the dark mustache.

"I hear Constantine has been inquiring about me."

"Are you a phantom that you know and hear words when you are not present? Maybe you have other spies besides me," said Tancred.

"Raymond informed me. I visited him before riding here."

"Did you see Constantine?"

"No, but Raymond is burdened down with having several of the emperor's spies traveling with his army, besides Constantine. Where is Helena?"

"She is safe. Her tent is among the Byzantines. I've wondered why Constantine has not spoken to Philip about transferring her to his own entourage? There must be a reason why he's left her unguarded so close to Philip. Maybe," said Tancred thoughtfully, "he has reason to think Philip won't escape with her to the castle after all?"

Nicholas looked off into the starry night as the wind gusted against them, warm and dry. "You think Philip may be cooperating with him more than he's told us? Perhaps. I'm beginning to think he may also have spies reporting to him from inside Nicaea."

Tancred gave him an alert glance. "I too have news from Nicaea. It concerns your sister, Adrianna.''

"Ah! We shall talk in my tent—or am I doomed to sleep among the scorpions and fleas?"

"Your Byzantine blood shows. You retain a fleshly desire for luxury. Yes, you have a tent, a fine one at that. And I am not above appreciation of comfort myself. While it stood empty and waiting, I've taken advantage of it. I will move my gear among the knights."

"There is room for us both, and I wish you near at hand. There is much to discuss." Nichalas swung down from his charger and led it toward the pen where food and water waited and two young peasant lads dozed. They jumped to their feet when they saw the bishop and hastened to greet him. "Christ be praised, Lord Bishop!"

"May He be praised indeed. Take care of my charger—I mean, my 'nag,' " he said, glancing surreptitiously at Tancred, and they walked together into the camp that was bright with myriads of campfires, the wind scattering the smoke across the barren land.

Her spacious tent glowed with lantern light as Helena paced across the floral Tabriz rug, her lustrous dark hair undone and sweeping in tresses down to her small waist. Hearing a "scratching" sound on the entry flap, she wavered and turned, eyes cautious. Surely Tancred would not be so bold to come to her tent so late? She had not spoken to him since their arrival days ago, and she had wondered where he was. Anxious about Nicholas, she had pressed Philip for answers to her questions, but he claimed to be as much in the dark as she. Bardas too had not been able to tell her what Tancred was about—or was it that he did not want to?

She pushed aside the flap and silenced a start of surprise when Nicholas grinned at her, tossing the coif back from his thick black hair.

"Do you have room for two renegades?" he whispered.

Two? She glanced past him and saw Tancred.

Swiftly she drew back the opening and beckoned. "Hurry, I will lower the lantern. They'll think I am asleep." She rushed to turn down one of the lights. "How is it the guards did not see you?"

"Bardas diverted them. A clever Spartan."

She lowered the second lantern. "Philip has my tent watched. He fears Constantine has spies watching us, expecting us to try to slip away to the castle."

"Is that what he told you?" asked Tancred.

She looked at him, catching the veiled doubt in his voice. "Yes, what other reason would he have?"

Tancred didn't explain and drew a second curtain across the entrance to block their shadows, then turned toward her. She noted that he'd exchanged his Byzantine uniform for the rugged leather of the Normans.

She lowered herself to the rug opposite Uncle Nicholas, ignoring Tancred but aware of his presence.

"Shall I call for Philip?" she asked her uncle quietly. "If we discuss our plans—"

"Not yet, Madame," interrupted Tancred's smooth voice, revealing nothing of his motives. Helena thought she already knew them and turned her eyes in his direction. He had lifted a silver urn of fresh fruit that Philip had sent her earlier and inspected the lush produce, choosing a cluster of bright purple grapes. He passed the urn to Nichloas, who was smiling—as though entertained by some though of his own—as he watched their response to each other.

"Tancred is right. Do not call him yet."

To have Nicholas agree so readily with Tancred convinced Helena that the relationship between them was closer than she had thought. Learning this could have been disappointing, since she wished Nicholas to show more approval of Philip. Her uncle had not yet given his blessing on her decision to marry Philip at the castle. In the end, she expected his final approval, but it would have pleased her had he been more enthusiastic. After all, Philip was a relation, and she would expect Nicholas to be proud of his important position as minister of war.

"You have news?" she asked quietly.

She watched him expectantly, but Nicholas drew a dagger

from inside a wrist sheath and began to peel an orange, deep in thought.

She stirred a little uneasily, not certain if it was because of his sudden look of sobriety or the dagger he so comfortably wore. She saw that it bore an engraving of two crossed scimitars and suspected the dagger had been given to him by Tancred.

"Do you have the drawing of Nicaea?" he asked Tancred.

Tancred caught up his satchel and joined them on the carpet, handing his half-eaten cluster of grapes to Nicholas. He removed a drawing, and Helena lifted the lantern down to spread the light.

"As you know, Nicaea is a formidable walled city," Nicholas told her. "Tancred has been inside recently."

The information surprised her, but she was beginning to learn that she should never take Tancred for granted.

"With good reason. It now guards the main road for the supply line for the Crusader armies. To leave a strong Turkish garrison behind them would be deadly."

"So the princes have made plans to attack Nicaea," Nicholas told her. "The news is beneficial to our personal cause."

"What have I to do with it?" she asked uneasily.

"I first hoped to speed you on your way to the castle to Tancred's adoptive father, Seigneur Rolf Redwan, a man of lionlike abilities, but it is not possible to bring you there yet. Constantine expected the move and has soldiers posted. We must wait for the opportune time." He looked at Tancred for explanation. "And your discovery in Nicaea?"

She saw the exchange of glances between them, then Tancred turned to look at her.

"The citadel is ruled by the Sultan, Kilij Arslan," said Tancred. "You know him as the Red Lion. Your mother was last seen riding with him to Nicaea from Jerusalem."

Stunned, she stared at him. *Mother, in Nicaea? So close at hand?*
"You are certain?" she whispered.

"My sources of information are reliable," said Tancred quietly, "but I cannot promise she is still in the citadel."

My mother with the Red Lion of the Desert!

Nicholas reached a sympathetic hand as tears welled in her eyes, despite her effort to hold them back.

"She must be there," she repeated again.

"If she is, we will find her," said Nicholas.

She was on the verge of telling him about Constantine. Did he also know? She remembered his cold warning. Should Constantine locate her mother first, it was crucial that she not anger him by unmasking his plans. At least, not yet.

"You do not believe she is there now?" she asked Tancred.

"I do not know. I was told the Red Lion is not there."

"You are certain?"

"No, but do not hope."

"There is nothing left but hope."

Nicholas drummed his fingers on the carpet, musing to himself. "I am remembering something. . . . When Alexius became emperor, he found it in his interest to make a treaty with the Red Lion—or was it his father?" He looked at Tancred for help.

"His father. Sulieman was caliph of all this region, but he is dead. Since his death the Moslem empire has broken into many warring bands, each with a contesting emir. If the emperor made a treaty, he did so with the Red Lion. Why do you bring it up? Are you thinking of Constantine and Philip?"

"Yes, and if Nicaea is surrendered to the Byzantines, the emperor has vowed in that treaty to safeguard the family and wives of the Red Lion. . . ."

"I see what you mean," said Tancred.

"But I do not!" whispered Helena.

Tancred looked at her. "When the Red Lion left Nicaea, he may have arranged for safe passage of his family to a secret place in Constantinople, according to the treaty."

Helena looked at them, her hands in balled fists, thinking of Irene. She would hear of the arrangement and find her mother. . . .

"Has Philip said anything about the treaty with the Red Lion?" asked Tancred.

"No, I'm certain he doesn't know."

"I beg to differ, Madame, he knows as much as we do, perhaps more."

"Philip? How can you say so!"

"He is minister of war, is he not?" came the smooth reminder. "As such, he is the head of the secret intelligence."

She stared at him, confident he meant something unflattering by his words but not certain what it was. She looked at Nicholas and found him lost in troubling conclusions of his own.

She stood and walked away, icy fingers gripping her heart. She guessed what Tancred was hinting—that Philip might notify Irene of Adrianna's presence in Constantinople. How could Tancred even think he might?

She stood there in emotional isolation, too many thoughts bounding and leaping through her mind to grasp even one of them for long. She sank slowly onto the brocaded stool. *My mother is in Nicaea,* she told herself. *I will find her. God will hear my prayers.*

CHAPTER 16
Knights, Valor, and Courtly Love

The gonfanons of the crusader princes tossed in the Mediterranean wind as the four-day march to Nicaea got underway. The knights rode their Great Horses while soldiers with axes moved out ahead to clear a road through the wooded area for the wagons and the multitude of followers who traversed on foot.

The long, hot days brought them through the hills fringed with pine and cypress trees, marking the border of the present Byzantine Empire, and toward Anatolia—the Seljuk kingdom of Moslem Turks. After the city of Nicaea the warriors would battle against Dorylaeum, Antioch, Edessa, Tripoli, Damascus, Tyre, Acre, Jaffa, Bethlehem, and finally Jerusalem!

Riding some distance behind Bohemond and his chief knights was the small, elite Byzantine entourage consisting of Philip and General Taticus surrounded by a dozen Greek soldiers.

Helena rode between Tancred and Bardas, with Nicholas a horse length ahead beside Bohemond. Friars and monks walked nearby carrying the church standard and their prized relics.

Helena's horse had been rigged with a small canopy of red silk with gold fringe, and as the day wore into the afternoon and the wind grew still, she fanned herself, wishing for a cooling breeze.

"How much farther until we make camp?" she inquired, directing her question to Philip, although Tancred was nearer at hand as guard.

Philip reined his horse back beside her as Bardas made room by dropping a length behind.

"Not weary already?" He smiled at her, then beckoned a serving man to ride forward with refreshment. The servant had been trained in the emperor's assembly and he miraculously balanced a gilded goblet while pouring from a silver urn. Philip sipped first from its rim, meeting her eyes then handing it to her.

Helena smiled and raised the goblet, drinking from where his lips had touched, and as she did, she found herself compelled to glance toward Tancred. He looked pointedly at the goblet, sparkling like a multicolored nugget in the sun's rays. Helena ignored him as he lifted his battered waterskin from the saddle and quenched his thirst, watching her. Once again she was reminded of the immense differences between the two men. Had Philip not ridden beside her she would have expected some smooth but goading remark from Tancred about Byzantine excess.

As Helena topped the side of the rocky ravines and their entourage was greeted by the frontier of Asia Minor, she sucked in her breath, startled by the sight.

Decaying half-skeleton bodies in rotting rags! Bones! Heaps upon heaps of rag-clad bones! And they were grotesquely arranged into fortlike enclosures!

Her hand went to her throat. "Who—are they? Who would mock the dead so?"

Tancred was grim as he followed her horrified gaze. "You are looking at the pitiable remains of the peasant army under Peter the Hermit. Take a long look and consider. This was the first contingent of crusaders who sallied forth with *Deus vult* on their tongues."

Helena looked at Philip for confirmation and he wore a grave expression, staring at the sight.

"Why are they arranged—like that? Into forts? It's revolting!"

"The Moslems have a morbid sense of humor," said Philip.

Tancred glanced casually toward the hilly horizon. "Undoubtedly they know of the advancing crusader army under the princes and wish to encourage us with this monument."

She shuddered, recalling the shameful debacle of months earlier under Peter the Hermit and his misguided peasant mob. The restless and undisciplined horde—arriving before the legitimate armies of the feudal princes—had refused to pay heed to the emperor's advice to abide in the camp by the Bosporus. They had crossed the waterway into Anatolia with little more than mistaken religious zeal, believing Christ would lead them to military victory. Tragically, they had moved against the Seljuk Turks and were horribly massacred. Except for some of the women and children who were carried away as slaves, all were dead.

Helena sobered, thinking of her mother. *She too is a slave, perhaps to the Red Lion.* A shudder went through her, and Helena whispered a prayer that their long journey would not be in vain.

"Nicaea hosted the first universal council on the deity of Jesus Christ," Tancred told Helena on the fourth day as they looked upon the ancient citadel.

Unwillingly, she looked at him—long and hard—and tried to resist the strong pull she felt that seemed to draw her toward him emotionally, physically, and now, spiritually.

She was curious about his faith, and the moment offered a choice opportunity, one free of danger as they rode along, the fringe on her canopy swinging with the horse's rhythm.

"I am surprised you would know. Bardas has seen you reading the Koran, devotedly."

"Devotedly? That is his interpretation. I do not call study a devotion, but a process of learning the vast differences between Christianity and Islam." Tancred reached into his satchel and removed two books: a leather-bound New Testament and the Koran.

"My grandfather gave this to me when I fled Palermo. 'Take it with you and you take wisdom,' he told me. I could not admit to him then that my heart asked questions for which no one gave me answers. I felt a need to search for truth. I already knew the Koran . . . but I wanted to know more about the Bible. At Monte Casino I studied Christ under Nicholas. The school was the only place where there were complete copies of both Old and New Testaments. . . . Hebrew I could not read for myself, but I was taught Greek by Nicholas and Latin at the medical school, and I speak Arabic fluently, so there was opportunity given me that has not come to all."

He placed the Koran back into the satchel and handed her the New Testament. "Nicholas presented this to me at the Norman camp. Take a look. He did the copy work himself."

Helena's fingers accidentally brushed Tancred's as she reached for the Scriptures, and for a moment he held her hand before letting go. She could not tell if the move were deliberate or not and did not meet his eyes. She held the New Testament tightly, awed by the fact that Nicholas had gone to such profound work in preparing this masterpiece for Tancred. It not only spoke well of her uncle, but also revealed his thoughts toward Tancred. The work must have been several years in the making, and she found her heart stirred.

"So that is why you read the Koran—to compare with the words of God," she stated quietly.

"I knew that one day I would study the Bible for myself wherever my travels took me in life, not just sitting in a darkened cloister with the ancient manuscripts consigned to the church vaults. Nicholas has made it possible—or I should say, God heard my heart's longing."

Tancred paused for a moment, deep in thought. "Ultimate truth is not locked away in Rome, nor in Mecca or Medina—nor yet Jerusalem, but in having access to the Word of God itself. The truth of His Word now shines upon my path, and while I may stumble because of my inner weakness, my upbringing, my culture—I know that I am known of God.

"My grandfather gave me the Koran, and I expect one day to use it to show him the truth. If I threw it away—he would never respect me enough to listen to me. In winning him, I must never insult him, but honor him and show unlimited patience. For me, that will be hard to do. I am not ready yet. One day, perhaps I will be."

Helena was touched by his honesty. He had opened a door to reveal his soul, his spiritual quest and deep longings. She felt respected by him because he did so, but something else was ignited within her own heart. Helena fingered the pages, her eyes skimming the Greek she knew so well, mulling over what Tancred had said. Her soul burned with a fervency that expanded far beyond the physical to a spiritual oneness she had never shared with Philip. It kindled a desire far deeper—and mingled with the physical attraction she had long felt for Tancred.

She remained silent, staring at the Testament in her hand as her horse trotted along, the sunlight glinting on its auburn mane. Apollo, his black mane gleaming, his strong neck sprinkled with sweat, seemed to nudge closer to her mare, tossing his head provocatively.

Helena read the words inscribed in fine gold lettering:
For Tancred Jehan Redwan, my son in the common faith.
Nicholas Lysander, Bishop at Monte Casino. A.D. *1097.*

"Nicaea," said Tancred easily, "is rich with history, much of it Christian."

"The Nicaean Council?"

"You know of it?"

She smiled. "Again, it was Nicholas. He taught us when we were children at the villa."

He seemed curious, glancing toward Philip, who rode ahead in conversation with General Taticus. "By 'we,' do you mean Philip?"

"Yes, and Zoe—a cousin. You met her?"

"I remember her."

Helena cast him a glance, but he was replacing the Testament back into his satchel.

"Philip had his own interpretations of Christianity," she said, masking her voice. "I suppose he's adopted the Arian belief."

"Arian?"

She suspected he already knew but found it to his entertainment to hear her expound on the religious subject. Well, if he thought her unlearned about such things—

"At the time of Emperor Constantine there was heated controversy going on in Alexandria, the largest city in Egypt and the center of Christian theological development."

"Egypt? I am surprised!"

She did not believe him and fanned herself as they rode along, staring straight ahead at Nicaea. "The church in North Africa was the center of theology at the time. The controversy was a serious one—it centered around the person of Jesus Christ. Was He God, or was He not? Two churchmen who opposed each other on what the Scriptures taught were Arius and Athanasius.

"To put it most simply for barbarian understanding, Arians believed that God was supreme, but Jesus, while the greatest of all 'created' beings, was inferior to God. The Athanasians taught the truth of Scripture: God, Jesus, and the Holy Spirit are equal members of the Trinity—a Latin word meaning one in three."

"And Emperor Constantine settled the matter by calling for a church council at Nicaea?" Tancred asked innocently.

"He himself presided over it. Bishops were called from all parts of the empire, and they concluded the Bible taught that Jesus Christ was indeed the God of all ages, a member of the Trinity. And the doctrine officially became the view of the universal church."

"You are wiser than I thought—for a woman."

She looked at him. He wore a faint smile.

"For a woman?"

He lifted an indifferent hand. "Islam implies women are spiritually inferior."

Helena looked straight ahead.

"You were made to produce sons," he said.

"Indeed?"

"And to please in the bedchamber."

Her eyes narrowed and turned to his.

He smiled. "Also, to please over the cooking fire."

"Anything else?" she inquired coolly.

"No, that will suffice." He leaned and gave Apollo a good pat on his neck. He looked at her. "In some places in the East, as a follower of Islam, a man would be willing to pay more for this excellent specimen than for a woman. But," he said airily, "a woman is permitted into paradise if her husband agrees and wishes to be bothered with her. Then again—the Koran pictures paradise as a man's delight with many beautiful women pouring wine and keeping his wants satisfied. Why should he bother with a wife who nags and has grown old and fat?"

Tancred's warm blue-gray eyes scanned her. "Kalid expects you to keep him happy."

Helena sucked in her breath.

"Nicaea has important Christian history," he said smoothly, changing the subject. "And the Church believes it has the right to redeem it from the rule of Islam. Nicaea was once also a Roman stronghold. See that masonry wall?"

Helena was still fuming over his earlier comments.

"It was built by Rome," he said. "It's miles long and over six feet thick. And the crusaders will have a difficult time tunneling through, if that is their ambition. I've looked at it when visiting with Hakeem. It's been hardened to impregnable stone under the heat of the desert sun."

Her heart was quickened as she contemplated a hope that even now her mother might wait somewhere inside its walls. "And my mother may be there," she whispered. "Oh, Tancred, do you think she is?"

"If I had only known about her when I visited," he said quietly.

She stared intently at the walls. Had she heard about the coming crusaders? Did she pray for their success? Perhaps she was gazing out the palace window watching the dust trail rising from the tramping of horses and soldiers. Perhaps she heard the slave girls whispering excitedly of the warriors who came from the distant barbarian West.

Philip rode back beside Tancred, gesturing ahead to the city-fortress that was built on the shores of Lake Ascania, with much of its thick wall facing the water. "The gates are all shut up tight against us. The siege will be a long one."

Helena noticed the expression on Tancred's face and believed him suspicious of Philip's presence among the crusaders. Why had he come? Was it to seek a way for their escape to the Castle of Hohms undetected by Irene and Constantine's spies, or to deliver Nicaea to the emperor? She had to admit that thus far on the tiring journey Philip had been more interested in military matters than in discussing their upcoming marriage at the castle.

"I suppose a long siege is what your emperor wishes," said Tancred.

Philip's proud dark head turned sharply. "The emperor wishes success for the crusaders."

Tancred toyed with the reins, his every movement suggesting he rejected his glib words. "Then it will take more than battering rams to break down the walls." He gestured. "Adjacent to the lake there is a forty-foot moat encircling the walls. We need more from the emperor than his good wishes. The princes will need Byzantine weapons. Will you supply them? You are the minister of war."

Something flickered within Philip's eyes. "Do you doubt my sincerity? They have but to ask. Am I at fault because their western ego restrains them? If they wish to camp here till the end of summer, it is their decision, not mine."

"Which makes the delay all the more convenient."

Philip remained undaunted, his dark eyes cool and scornful as he gazed off toward the walls and moat. "The crusaders are not concerned. They already speak of filling in the moat."

Helena considered, glancing at Tancred to judge his response—but he did appear to share his confidence.

"It is useless to even think of scaling a double wall of defense," came his restrained but impatient voice. "Look at the positions of the projected towers. They make for deadly crossfire. With the Seljuk bowmen and their engines of stone-casters, they can easily defend the walls. We could be here for months."

Months! Again, Helena gazed upon what must have been hundreds of towers built with embrasures to defend the open ground.

"Nevertheless, siege is the sensible approach," said Philip stiffly.

"For the emperor? Certainly not for the army. Among the peasants and foot soldiers there is even now scarcity of wheat to make bread."

Helena thought uncomfortably of the abundance of delicacies that Philip had brought for themselves and the Byzantine delegation under General Taticus. No wonder Tancred had glanced mockingly at the splendid goblet. She heard him contesting Philip: "What good will a siege do us? Without boats, can we cut off supplies from being smuggled into the back gates facing the lake?"

"Smugglers?"

"Even the most unmilitary minded among us can guess how

the Turks will continue to supply the city with food under our very noses," he said, bored.

"We have no proof."

"Last night, knowing we neared the city, I rode ahead. On the bank I boldly watched as the Red Lion sent boats carrying food supplies to the gate towers along the wall facing Lake Ascania."

Philip's handsome face was scornful as he reined in his sprightly horse to keep prance with Apollo. "Until this hour their pride is unwilling to take my presence seriously. I suggest you convince the barbarians to cooperate with me. Unless they wish to fight with naught but sticks and stones."

"It is to the benefit of the Moslems and Byzantium to maintain a long siege. If I convince the princes to appeal for siege weapons, are you and Constantine prepared to send to Constantinople for them?"

Philip's eyes flashed. "Do you suggest the emperor wishes the crusaders' defeat? For the Moslems to maintain their stranglehold on Nicaea? That is absurd."

"Perhaps nothing is absurd in Byzantine intrigue. I do more than suggest, I ask bluntly—does your emperor have plans to take the city? His own purpose may not require the same haste as the crusaders', since his table is well supplied with meat and wine, while the monks and the peasants who walk on foot become gaunt."

Philip's nostrils flared and his knuckles showed white as his grip tightened on his reins.

Helena glanced from one man to the other. Philip gave him a cold appraisal, then turned his horse. "I will see that your emaciated monks have meat." And as he rode ahead, Helena's eyes followed him to the side of General Taticus.

"You enjoy goading him," she chided.

Tancred looked at her with faint surprise.

Her brows drew together as she studied him. "Philip did attend military training at a Greek school. But you scorn his expertise as though it belongs to a student."

"Maybe. He needs to be reminded. His pride is an obstacle."

"And you, Sir Knight, are not what I would call humble!"

"And will you always be the mother hen rushing to defend

235

your chick?" His mouth turned. "Fear not—your emperor has *arranged* for his victory. And if not, you can be certain Constantine and Irene have done so."

"What do you mean, *his* victory? Is it not to the benefit of the crusaders that Nicaea fall?"

"It is. And they will not be pleased to turn over their spoils to Philip. It will be their soldiers who die to win the victory."

It was mid-May, and the weeks wore on. The morning was warm and turning desperately hot beneath the eastern sun in the long valley surrounded by ridges of distant scrub pine. Nicaea, with its yellowing walls, was well under siege. The princes with their armies, each bearing their own gonfanon, had set up siege lines against the citadel, whose gates were shut and barred.

Tancred mounted Apollo, and with Nicholas, they rode from the Norman's sector and took the dusty, rutted road in the direction from which Count Raymond of Toulouse was expected to arrive shortly from the court of Constantinople.

Much to his irritation, a fellow knight named Erich who rode with them continued his habit of making up riddle songs and sharing them loudly with a thankless but captive audience.

> . . . *her hair so gold,*
> *she wept when I left*
> *with my sword so bold—*

"You should have been a troubadour," Tancred interrupted. "On second thought, they wouldn't have you. Can you not do better than that? 'Sword so bold'!"

Nicholas chuckled, but the young knight scowled at Tancred. "I suppose you could do better, Redwan?"

"If you don't keep your eyes open you may need your sword to be bold. Are you certain you saw a foraging party of Turks near here?"

"Am I dimwitted and blind? I saw them. More than a dozen infidels prowling about on horseback. I have never seen more odd-looking fellows."

"You will see a good deal many more before you reach Jerusalem."

"These have vanished," said Nicholas. "We best ride back."

Erich's pride was wounded. "With your leave, Bishop Nicholas, I will ride to the south and see if I can find their trail."

"And lose your head if they come upon you," warned Tancred.

But Nicholas lifted a hand. "Let him go. We will ride east. If there are Turks spying out our defenses, Bohemond wishes to know."

"They are about," said Tancred. His past experience made him cautious. "They will eventually wish to test our fighting abilities to discover if we are as weak as the peasants under the Hermit."

The knight named Erich gave a smirk and rode ahead, determined to prove he was not imagining things. Tancred reluctantly followed Nicholas on a rutted road into a field.

They rode for a distance in silence, the sun becoming hotter as it climbed. Nicholas gestured to a tree and they stopped beneath its branches for reprieve from the sun. Tancred shaded his eyes.

"The camp of Count Raymond is ahead."

The blue gonfanon of Toulouse fluttered proudly. Behind the siege lines where there was a measure of safety, horses and pack animals grazed contentedly, and children were busy filling water jugs as women attended tables. The sight of women, children, and even the aged and sick among the crusaders disturbed Tancred. Many of them had brought along their entire families and belongings—a declaration that they had no intention of returning to Europe and relinquishing any territory taken in the war. One of those determined not to return to Europe was Count Raymond.

"He swore an oath never again to set foot on western soil," Nicholas told him. "He has brought his wife, his child, his riches, and I think he has a secret desire to rule Antioch or Jerusalem."

"He will need to contend with Bohemond when it comes to Antioch."

As they rested in the shade of a cypress grove, which proved to be a Moslem cemetery, an old monk from Raymond's camp sat on a gravestone unawares.

"A delightful morning," said the old one to Tancred and Nicholas.

Tancred cautiously scanned the wooded heights near the road. "Think so?" he breathed.

The monk eyed Tancred curiously. "Ah, a very well-equipped warrior. You are no foot soldier, and you look more than a knight."

Tancred looked down at him, smiling. He nodded to the gravestone. "The bones of the Moslem are so insulted at your presence the ground rumbles beneath you."

Nicholas smiled as the monk stood at once and shook his robe as though contacting some uncleanness. He looked down at the stone and squinted, seeing what it was for the first time, then up at Tancred with a strange expression. "Did you hear voices?"

Tancred tensed, glancing from the monk toward the hills. "Yes . . . but not of the dead."

Distant cries! Tancred saw lines of Moslem horsemen emerging from the wooded heights and trotting in a warlike stance toward Count Raymond's camp. At the same time, Erich charged his horse madly in their direction shouting, "Infidels!"

Nicholas drew the horn on his saddle and sounded an alarm that rolled across the camp of Count Raymond. The knights rushed from their tents to stare.

Tancred looked in the direction of the Moslems. In the rolling dust clouds the Seljuk cavalry approached with swinging scimitars, their short bows loaded and ready. Yelping shouts of "Allah il-Allahu! Allah il-Allah!" broke through the hot afternoon.

Tancred believed they were the advance of a stronger cavalry under the Red Lion, who intended to break the siege.

"There rides Raymond," said Nicholas. "To the battle, Tancred!"

"Sire," the old monk shouted as Count Raymond rode forth with his chief knights. "God aid thee!"

Tancred unsheathed his sword and rode beside Nicholas to join Count Raymond, the crusader cross blaring red and bold on the standard.

The Moslems rushed forward intending to throw the camp into confusion. They were halfway to the camp when Tancred rode to meet them, Nicholas at his left and Erich beside him. The knights under Raymond scrambled for their weapons and horses and were soon in the field without armor or saddle. The foot soldiers stumbled forward in their haste to reach their captains and protect the chief knight and their Great Horses.

The Great Horses of the knights were a force unmatched in an all-out charge. They gathered speed, the dirt flying, their armor glinting like flashes of silver as they rode toward the open field of battle. Among the shouts of fury, swords and battle maces struck and the Turks fell from their horses under the crushing hoofs of the Great Horses.

Tancred's sword struck a blow against the light shield of his attacker, cutting through it and leaving him defenseless. Tancred followed with a heavy blow that slashed through the Turk's chest. The long swords of the knights swung above their heads, gathering force and crashing down upon heads and hacking the warriors into pieces.

The Moslems, surprised by such strong resistance, retreated back toward the hills.

"We have beaten them," yelled Erich jubilantly.

"Do not underestimate them," warned Tancred. "They wished only to test your skills. They will return."

Word of the earlier attack brought groups of knights from the other feudal lords who rallied to Raymond's blue standard. By early afternoon, as Tancred had said, the Moslems gathered again on the ridge, this time quiet and sober, weapons ready.

"Hold your line!" shouted Count Raymond, riding before his knights.

The Turkish horsemen rushed straight forward, scimitars swinging, the name of Allah on the wind.

"Christ be praised!" shouted Bishop Adehemar beside Count Raymond.

The priests shouted, raising the cross. "There is no God but the Living God, Father of our Lord and Savior Jesus Christ!"

Tancred drew his sword and entered the battle with Nicholas, dust flying, shouts and opposing screams smothering the afternoon.

The two opposing forces struck with equal religious fury, swords halting scimitars; scimitars slashing through the line of knights to behead the priests who ran into the battle armed with nothing but the cross they clutched. Tancred battled to protect them, angry at the scene and compelled to make a stand.

With savage determination they fought—pain, blood, and screams of death filling their ears. As suddenly as the attack came, it broke. Again, to the bewilderment of the Moslems, the western Christian knights held fast. There would be no heaps of bodies left to rot in the sun as the peasants under the Hermit had been left.

The knights briefly rested as the monks and even women and children rushed to them with buckets of water. The priests knelt in the dust, praying and evoking the sign of the cross. The wounded were carried back to the tents, and new foot soldiers ran to take their positions to guard the Great Horses.

The Moslems also regrouped and struck for the third time with their green standards bearing the crossed scimitars. The Moslems withdrew, only to close in again, yelping praises to Allah, followed by a barrage of arrows from the Turkish short bow, whizzed from behind round shields.

The field was now soaked with blood of Christian and Moslem, and dead and wounded littered the ground. Friars ran to the dying knights to pray but fell under the deadly arrows before reaching them. Priests crawled with their last breath toward the weeping knights crying out for forgiveness where their wounded horses had fallen.

Tancred looked about for Nicholas; he had lost sight of him in the battle. Nor did he see Erich. But as he turned in his saddle he felt an arrow strike his helmet, and for a moment he was stunned, but the famed steel held, saving his life. Caught off guard, he could not respond to the Seljuk rider who charged past him, his scimitar tearing through the links of his chain mesh, leaving Tancred wounded and bleeding. Nicholas emerged from the dust, his heavy charger bearing down, his Norman long blade hacking into the enemy's round shield and knocking him with great force from his lean horse.

"Ride back, Tancred!"

But again the battle broke with both sides thundering forward and he had no time.

The Seljuk cavalry, unable to scatter the knights, rode back toward the hills, and the crusaders shouted their victory as Count Raymond and Bishop Adehemar led in pursuit until the last rays of the setting sun slipped behind the horizon.

⬦

Tancred awoke to find himself resting on blankets in a quiet tent in the company of a familiar young woman named Adele, whom he had first met in Bohemond's camp. He had no notion how he had come to be brought to her tent and assumed that he was in the camp of Count Raymond. Her gold braids were wound about her head and her blue eyes watched him gravely. She handed him a flask of water.

"Do not be weary, brave knight. You shall prevail mightily."

Norman women took great pleasure in the knightly abilities of their men. He wanted to smile his irony but did not, and reached a hand to his wound and found that it had already been attended.

"Your words cheer me, Adele. You are sure of this?"

She looked gravely puzzled that he would question her statement. "Seigneur?"

"I am a knight who moans and groans," he said as he struggled to an elbow, wincing, for he knew that there was romance on her mind, and he wished to discourage her infatuation with his bravery as a knight.

"As you can see, I am no champion. And so . . . I should like to know who brought me to your tent?"

Her eyes fixed upon him with awestruck devotion. "You are surely wrong, Count Redwan. My uncle has told me how brave and valiant you are. And Nicholas firmly agrees."

He did not need Nicholas sounding his praises before starstruck young women. "He did, did he? And just where is Bishop Nicholas? Or has he left me here as an invalid to be cared for by you?"

"Nicholas is with Count Raymond asking questions about the Byzantine bishop named Constantine. It seems he has disappeared."

"Not dead, I hope?" he asked flatly.

"No. He broke tent and with his dozen guards rode away."

The news was disturbing. "He has left?"

"Yes, a day before the battle. No one knows where."

241

Had he returned to Constantinople having become weary with the siege? Tancred suspected otherwise—he may have gotten inside Nicaea by the help of officials loyal to the Red Lion.

"There is no Norman knight as worthy as you," she murmured, leaning toward him, and he felt her hand move to his bare shoulder.

His eyes flickered across her face to her full, rounded mouth. "And . . . what would Bishop Adehemar do if he knew his niece was rubbing the shoulder of an assassin wanted in Sicily?"

She pulled away, shocked into sobriety.

"There is no more unworthy knight than I, except Erich. And I advise you not to try to rub his back. He is more cooperative than I. And I would like you to send for him—we need to talk."

"I have met Erich. I do not see how he is unworthy. He was very gallant and rescued me at the field. He is the one who brought you here at Bishop Adehemar's orders. And as for you—your smile tells me you are no villain."

"I cannot help my smile." Tancred tried to sit up. "I am a villain." He held her away. "Madame, you do sorely try me. Where is your father?"

"I have no mother or father."

"I was afraid of that," he murmured.

"You spoke, seigneur?"

"My tunic," he said gesturing. "And my armor—I have no time to rest here."

She placed her palms on his shoulders and pushed him back, smiling. "You must rest, my count. I am Adele, remember?"

"I remember well."

"I met you in the Norman camp. Bishop Adehemar is a relative." She smiled. "So, shall I also have Adehemar come and see you here?"

Tancred visualized the stalwart warrior-bishop coming to unwanted conclusions about his relationship with Adele, and so when she started to jump to her feet, he caught her wrist, wincing weakly from pain as his shoulder moved. "Wait. Please."

She looked at him curiously. He added wryly, "He will not come. He is too busy out hunting Turkish heads. We will wait."

"Do not grow despondent," she said, mistaking his cynicism

for regret that he was not out doing the same. "You too will soon be better again, and chasing infidel heads. You are very strong," she murmured, scanning his chest.

Tancred fell back against the pillow. Outside, he heard horses carrying singing knights arriving back at the camp after their first victory over the Turks. Erich came in as proud and arrogant as a young cock, singing the song of Raymond.

"Spare me your wretched singing. You sound like a mule with an aching throat."

The girl threw her hands over her mouth and giggled silently, but Erich was undaunted. "The infidels have run away," he boasted.

Tancred corrected, "They always scatter, but they will regroup and return to fight you all the way to Jerusalem, being joined by others who are not as weary as we. They have the advantage of fresh soldiers, and we fight in a land they know far better than we."

"Your Moorish blood tells. Nay, they fled like feeble rabbits below a circling hawk. We took a prisoner. He says that the Red Lion has sent word to his garrison in Nicaea that he cannot aid them from without. And so the knights sing."

The news was interesting, and as Tancred considered it, Erich turned his complete attention on Adele, something he did very well.

"I am glad you are cheered," said Tancred, reading his smitten expression. "I am not. Hand me my tunic. The Red Lion may have learned the manner of warrior they are up against, but he is no fool. And," he concluded, "the walls of the city still stand."

"Not for long. The city has been encouraged to surrender."

When Tancred's eyes questioned him, Erich added with a toothy smile, "We catapulted some infidel heads over the walls and pinned others before the gate. They will see them in the morning."

As Tancred prepared to ride back to Bohemond's camp in the morning, nothing moved but the warm wind against the tent. The sound of a horse was followed by a low voice asking questions of Erich.

Alert, Tancred raised himself to an elbow and looked toward the tent opening, reaching for his weapons. The flap pushed back and Helena entered wearing a hooded riding cloak. She threw it back revealing intricately worked dark clusters of curls woven with golden cloth. Her luminous spicy brown eyes glanced about.

"I heard you were wounded and . . ." She stopped, the words trailing off into silence as her eyes fell on Adele, who stood up from beside Tancred's bed.

The two women stared at each other. Tancred leisurely weighed their expressions. Adele looked bold and confident, hands on hips as she took Helena in from head to toe. But it was Helena whom Tancred watched with concealed satisfaction. He managed to keep from smiling at her expression as she stared at Adele. A faint color warmed Helena's lovely features. Her mouth tightened and her shock swiftly altered into confusion. Her eyes rushed to his.

Tancred held her gaze until with satisfaction he saw what he was searching for. Those eyes that could send his heart pounding betrayed the jealous anger she felt over finding him in the care of Adele.

This, I must drag out. . . . He pretended to reach for the water-skin and fail, as though too weak from his injury. As he expected, Adele rushed to bring it to him, kneeling beside the bed.

"Water, seigneur?" she asked swiftly.

"I die of thirst, damsel. Are you real, or do I envision an angel?"

Adele blushed and Tancred acted too weak to lift his head. She slipped a hand beneath his head and brought the skin to his mouth, her arms wrapped about him. He drank, watching Helena through his lashes.

She stood staring, eyes flickering over them both.

"Did you come to seek Nicholas?" he asked a moment later, resting his head against Adele's arm.

Helena faltered, then stepped backward. "No, I thought—I mean, I was mistaken, Sir Knight. When news reached the camp of the battle, someone said you were gravely injured and I thought you might need help. I see you have all that you need, and more."

Adele looked at her evenly. Tancred affected sobriety. "Your generosity is appreciated, madame. It is not often a barbarian can expect a Byzantine Daughter of the Purple Belt to grace his humble tent, but as you see, her hands well attend me," he said of Adele.

"Yes, so I see!"

"This is Adele," he said. "A Norman woman. Adele, this is Lady Helena, a Byzantine."

The two women exchanged appraisals, and Helena stood as though she expected Adele to acknowledge a lesser position and leave the tent, but she did not and turned her back to make certain Tancred's wound was clean and covered.

Helena glanced about; then with a flicker of pain in her eyes she turned to leave.

It has gone far enough. Tancred suddenly appeared to regain his waning strength and, pushing Adele aside, managed to get to his feet, though needing to steady himself on a pole.

"Wait, Helena. I intend to return to the Norman camp with you and Nicholas."

He snatched his tunic and slipped it on over his muscled chest, wincing as he did. Adele watched boldly, but Helena rushed through the tent flap and into the night.

Tancred caught up his weapons and did not respond to Adele, who took hold of his arm, her eyes searching his.

"Let her go, seigneur. She is not the manner of woman to please you."

"I am in service to the Byzantine minister of war. If Nicholas comes searching for me, tell him I have returned with Helena."

Adele's hand dropped with resignation.

Outside, the warm wind came against him and stirred his hair pleasantly. A thousand stars illuminated the black heavens, writing a new message of desire upon his heart. He saw that Helena had reached her horse and was prepared to mount and ride.

A quick glance told him that Bardas had not accompanied her. She had come to him alone. Tancred strode ahead, catching her wrist and pulling her back around to face him. "Helena, you cannot ride back alone. It is dangerous. There are soldiers everywhere."

She shook his hand free and stepped back, then whipped

about, placing her foot into the stirrup and mounting with the air of a princess. She snatched her reins, then looked down at him, her eyes hot and bright. "Return to your Norman woman. Does she not wait with adoring breath?"

Helena turned to ride, but he caught and jerked the reins from her grasp, holding her mount steady. "For a woman who insists she is in love with Philip, you behave strangely. You show me the raw sparks of jealousy, madame. And I like it. It shows in your eyes, in the lovely warmth of your cheeks. Get down."

"Cretin," she hissed. "Nay."

"Get down. Look at you, you are trembling."

Helena tried to lash him with the reins. "I am not. Jealous? Such presumption. I . . . I came out of Christian charity. And, Philip and I will yet need you to bring us safely to the castle." She took him in. "You need anything but consoling, lounging about without cloth to cover your chest. It was revolting."

She tugged at the reins. "I see you are well enough to live, Sir Knight, so—with your leave."

He held them firmly, irritated, considering hauling her down and taking her into his arms. The moonlight fell on the Byzantine cross she wore around her neck and the rubies glimmered like blood. As though rebuked by heaven, he looked at the cross again, then at Helena. Her face was pale in the moonlight and he noticed the anxiety in her eyes for the first time. It struck him then that she was more overcome than he had realized.

She tugged violently, the sound of tears in her voice, tears of fright. "Turn loose my reins or I shall scream for Nicholas."

Tancred sobered. "You will indeed need to do so, because I will not permit you to ride alone through camp. Relax, madame. Now," he said quietly, "please dismount, or will I need to lift you down?"

She grew suddenly still, but he could see her breath came rapidly. The moments slipped away, then she smiled unpleasantly. "Your company is forced upon me. I do not wish it."

Her words stung and prompted a gritted retort. "Don't you? Your insult makes me want to prove you wrong. But I will not. I have too much respect for the One we both adhere to. I would not breach His laws. I will wait until you wish to bestow it."

"You will wait until your hair is gray and your muscles turn to fat."

A sardonic smile touched his mouth. "Your words are discouraging indeed."

She turned her head away.

Tancred studied her, and against his will saw her lovely in the starlight, the contour of her face soft and sweetly alluring, the wind tossing her dark tresses like silken strands. An ache raged through his heart, but it turned to frustration.

"The high princess Helena!"

She said nothing, her hands clutched in her lap, one lone tear slipping down her cheek.

"When will you be honest enough to look at your heart?" he asked.

Helena looked straight ahead. "Very well. You insist on backing me into a corner. Have your way. I will wait for you to escort me."

Tancred hesitated, cautious, wondering if she meant it, then released her reins. "I will only be a moment. I must saddle Apollo."

He whistled for the stallion, who trotted forward, but before he knew it she flipped the reins and galloped away.

Tancred gritted his teeth, his blue-gray eyes flashing frustration as he looked after her.

CHAPTER 17

The Knight and Helena's Tent

The siege of Nicaea dragged on. Gathered before its walls were about fifty thousand knights and foot soldiers, the largest army that Tancred had yet seen put into the battle. Still, the impregnable fortress held out against the determined crusaders.

Their past experience—limited to the destruction of wooden ramparts and the breaking down of smaller gate towers or the single large tower of a castle—was no match for this.

Tancred, while healing from his injury, listened as Nicholas reported on the crusaders' tenacity.

"It is admirable indeed. So is the creativity of Raymond of Toulouse. He has taken your advice."

"How goes it?"

"He built screens of woven aspens and willows to shield his archers and engineers from the Turkish garrison in the towers above the walls. He built a low shed open at the ground, and moved his men up against the eastern tower at the corner. They mined the walls and lit fires in them so the tower would collapse. Unfortunately, it did so during the night." He gave a short laugh. "The wily Turks worked through the darkness and rebuilt the stonework so effectively that entrance is now impossible."

Nicholas paced. "We cannot abandon the siege and march toward Antioch. Nicaea lies across the direct route to Jerusalem. Leaving a fortified Turkish garrison intact behind us would cut off our supply line from Constantinople. We need Byzantine siege equipment: portable fortresses that can be wheeled to the walls, scaling ladders, and mangonels."

"But it is to Philip's benefit to see the siege protracted, so he does not request them."

Nicholas looked at him, alert. "You share my thoughts. There is more. We received a message from Rufus."

Tancred was wide awake now. He remembered the secret plans of Irene's bodyguard to try to escape with his son Joseph.

"What message?"

Nicholas removed a piece of paper from under his tunic, tapping it on his chin. His eyes glinted with musing displeasure and suspicion as he handed it to Tancred.

Nicholas resumed his pacing. "Rufus informs us that Constantine has quietly returned to the imperial palace where he meets with the emperor."

Tancred read the brief message. Nicholas was right to be disturbed. Why had he left the camp?

"Constantine suspected Philip of making plans to escape secretly with Helena. I find it a matter of curiosity that he has now left them unguarded," said Tancred.

"Maybe not so odd after all . . . if his return to the imperial palace has something to do with Philip's plans for Nicaea."

Tancred stood and slipped into an undercloak of light maroon cloth. Over it he placed the chain mesh and then a black tunic. He belted on his scabbard and looked over at Nicholas. "Did you not say the emperor made a treaty some years ago with the sultan?"

"I have been thinking much of that. . . ."

"With good cause. It dawns on me now that we may have our reason for Constantine's disappearance. He could arrange for the secret surrender of Nicaea to Philip."

"Yes, and it makes sense. But I cannot help thinking there is something more, Tancred. It eats in my bones like burrowing worms. My enemy has some cause of his own besides Philip's . . . but what?"

Tancred filled a cup with steaming broth and drank thoughtfully. He would speak again to Helena.

Erich arrived, entering the tent. "The princes hold an urgent meeting and ask that you both attend."

During the night the jackmen had busied themselves with timber and rope, building a rough pavilion in the center of camp. The council was underway as the hot June wind rippled the proud gonfanons of the western princes who gathered beneath the pavilion canopy with their chief knights. While united in cause, their temperament and ego provided a bristling atmosphere. When Tancred arrived with Nicholas, the mood between the princes crackled with the energy of the fat thunderclouds forming over the distant eastern hills.

Nicholas took his seat beside Bishop Adehemar serving with Count Raymond of Toulouse. Tancred, who continued to represent Byzantium, chose to stand, leaning against a wooden post.

Count Raymond, perhaps the most pious and sincere in the Christian cause, was somewhere in his fifties, the eldest of the crusader princes. His well-groomed silver hair and short beard was oiled, and his deep-set eyes looked with impatience upon the younger and easily riled Duke Godfrey.

"We have little choice except to appeal to the emperor to send war engines. We have all heard of their Greek fire and flaming missiles! If we could fire projectiles over the walls of the Moslem citadel—"

"Has this Greek beguiled you as well?" Godfrey cut in, his temper as warm as the color of the red-gold hair brushing his shoulders. "I have had dealings with their conniving ways before. We cannot trust their face, for while they smile with brotherly cause, they plot to gain the advantage. Any weapons manned by the Byzantines will muster their demand that we yield the infidel fortress to General Taticus."

Count Raymond, however, was at least partially determined to honor his vow to the emperor. He had been better received than the other princes whom the emperor did not trust as genuine in their vow. The emperor believed the Count of Toulouse, along with Bishop Adehemar, to be the true leaders of the crusaders, and he had come to trust and respect them.

"There is no other way. We have already wasted weeks in a siege. If the emperor has artillerists, let us ask for them. Did we not vow to cooperate with him?"

"It was forced upon us." Duke Godfrey looked at the other princes. "It is *our* blood that will be spilt fighting Christ's enemies. And where is this minister of war and his weak general who follow our armies like spies among us? They sit in tents eating dainties and sipping from silver goblets! But look at us! We are soiled with sweat, our hands are bruised and bloodied, our reputation as lordly knights of valor is mocked by the infidels who gaze down upon us from the walls! Let us rise up and as one man scale these walls. Is God among us to bless, or not?"

In the silence that followed his outburst, Prince Bohemond stood to seize the moment for his advantage. The lordly Norman, looking the cool wolf that he was, walked to the center of the platform, his crimson cloak moving about his boots.

"Who among you does not know how my father fought this same wily emperor and nearly prevailed? Had it not been that we Normans are soldiers of the Church and were called back to Rome to defend the pope against the German empire"—and he looked at Godfrey—"my father would rule Constantinople to this day!"

Duke Godfrey wore a faint ruddy tint to his cheeks. Tancred recalled that Godfrey had zealously served King Henry of the German empire in the war against the pope over the right to appoint bishops. And Godfrey had been the first to climb the walls of Rome and bear arms against the pope.

"The Byzantines may scheme, yet we will insist on our right to rule Nicaea," declared Bohemond.

"And who among us will claim this prize?" came Count Raymond's cool voice. "Will you, Bohemond?"

The Norman's blue eyes glittered. Then he laughed, a snorting sound that matched his height and broad shoulders.

"I think only of us all—of our vow to liberate this land from the infidels. Are there not enough kingdoms waiting for us all, Raymond? If it is Nicaea you crave, then take it. As for us Normans, we will remember our vow to see the gates of Jerusalem fall to its true liege, even Christ."

Nicholas left his seat beside Adehemar and looked about at the others, his lively dark eyes glinting. "Some of you came to me at Le Puy and bent the knee, offering your sword for blessing, your hearts as servant-soldiers of the Church. And now will you permit inter-rivalry and envy to divide and conquer your great strength as Christian knights? We could lay siege against Nicaea until winter sets and starve doing so—only fifty miles from Constantinople. What of Jerusalem? Siege engines are needed! Let us send Tancred at once to the minister of war with a request for the emperor's help! Have we not sat here long enough? It is a thousand miles to Jerusalem!"

Bishop Adehemar laid a strong hand on Nicholas's shoulder. "Hearken! He speaks the words of truth and valor. Let the noble cause for which we have all set forth on this expedition shine as a light before us. The Moslem has scorned the true king of Jerusalem, even Christ. They have defamed our holy places and denied us access. We have come to liberate Jerusalem!"

The barons and knights glanced at each other, then Duke Godfrey walked forward and knelt to one knee, bowing his head. The others followed suit, and soon a sobriety settled over the meeting as prayer was offered and confession was made for the sin of self-seeking and envy.

The princes stood and embraced, and soon a pleasant mood circulated. Several men walked over to join Tancred.

"You have served these months in the imperial guard," said Duke Godfrey. "What is your opinion of the Byzantine equipment?"

Tancred straightened from the post. "I have little doubt that a battery of ballista could break through the citadel. The engines I have seen can shoot heavy iron arrows with great force."

The idea commanded Godfrey's attention as well as the others. And Bohemond was already acquainted with Greek weaponry from his father's war against Byzantium. "What of the lake?" he reminded Tancred. "It is as troublesome as the walls. The Turks are able to bring in supplies on boats. Until this is halted, our siege will fail."

"The emperor can prepare a fleet of shallow draught vessels. I have seen them in Civitote. The minister of war can also request iron arrows, boats, and siege weapons from the emperor."

Bohemond turned to the princes, and they spoke quietly among themselves as he assured them Tancred's description matched what he had seen in the earlier war. They spoke to Bishop Adehemar and Nicholas, then turned to Tancred.

"We are of one mind. Seek to arrange for the Byzantine engines of war."

On the other side of the camp near the Byzantine headquarters, Tancred secured Apollo beneath a cypress tree and looked toward Helena's tent, frowning to himself. As expected, Bardas was on watch, but the day was hot, without a breeze, and he sat outside the tent cross-legged on a cushion, dozing. Tancred's frown turned to a faintly amused smile.

He walked up silently, but Bardas continued his snoring. Wryly, Tancred lifted his foot to nudge the old bear awake but changed his mind. It would teach him a good lesson in diligence to find that he had been able to slip past him.

Tancred quietly entered the regal tent and glanced about the bright silk cushions and rugs for Helena. She was seated before a small ivory vanity table with a mirror, braiding her dark tresses.

Helena glimpsed him through her mirror and her eyes widened over his temerity. Swiftly she stood and turned to face him, holding a gilded hairbrush.

Tancred offered an exaggerated bow, saying with too much humility, "A thousand pardons at my intrusion, madame, but it is necessary I speak with you alone. I beg your grace!"

He straightened to see her eyes run over him, and it brought him a moment's pleasure. Surprisingly, she did not appear indignant over his intrusion.

"Well, indeed, could it be?" she whispered mockingly. "Why yes—I believe it is so—it is the knight who allows the Norman woman to keep him comforted and consoled in her tent."

He stood staring at her. "Your memory is keen and active. You have thought about it much."

She tossed her jeweled brush down carelessly and walked toward him, this time with an unflinching gaze, as though memory of their previous encounter, and her fluster, left her determined to behave otherwise this time.

"Do you carry a dagger?" he asked dryly.

"With such a bold and strong knight to overpower me?" she asked innocently. "What good a dagger? I doubt that the Norman woman carries one. I suspect she deliberately hides your scimitar, hoping you will try to take advantage of her."

"Dare I hope you too have reconsidered?"

"I have not wasted time thinking of you. How did you get past Bardas?" she whispered.

He resumed his informality now, and to show her that her royal position did not intimidate him, he tossed his riding cloak on a chair as though he were at home.

"A snoring watchdog does not bark a warning to his mistress." He gestured his head toward the opening. "You will need to hire a better guard to keep me at bay. But if I deem it necessary to see you, nothing could deter me."

Her eyes unwillingly responded, but she was quick to retreat behind her armor, turning a shoulder toward him.

"After your uncomely behavior in that woman's tent, I can think of nothing which needs to be said."

"Uncomely, you say? That she attended my wound? I flinch at your heartlessness—and after you braved a lone ride through camp to do the same!"

"Only because I needed your sword."

He laughed softly. "Do you blame me still, because I awoke from unconsciousness in her tent? Would you prefer I bled to death on the battlefield so you would need not be jealous?"

"You appeared to be quite at home in her tent."

"I would have preferred yours. I still do."

"Sir, you forget yourself!"

"Not at all. How could I in your presence? Now, as for Adele; she is a noble damsel, related to Bishop Adehemar who watches her every move."

"Enough, knight," she said breezily. "I have no wish to discuss your relationship with her."

"There is no relationship. I confess," he sighed, "I wait for you to grow weary of the haughty and ambitious Philip and turn your yearning attentions upon me."

"We will not speak of that," she said airily.

Despite her denial Tancred noticed that she looked pleased to learn that Adele was the relative of a bishop.

Helena walked past him, trailing a long golden scarf from her shoulder to her ankles. "You best go at once, or I shall awaken Bardas." And she made as though she would sweep past him toward the opening.

Swiftly he intercepted her but kept his distance. "Nay, my lady, I can think of a great deal that needs to be said."

"What makes you think I wish to hear?"

"Your eyes—they betray you."

She looked at him, her delicate dark brow forming a dignified rebuttal. She folded her arms calmly, tilting her head. "You are so certain of yourself. So utterly conceited as to think—"

"As you wish." He stepped back and bowed, with an arm extended toward the opening of her tent. "If you wish to scream, do so. Alert Philip and the entire Byzantine guard and they will come rushing in. They will be certain to detain me—if that's what you want."

For a moment he thought she would call his bluff, for she walked toward the opening. She paused.

Tancred smiled to himself, but his expression became inscrutable when she turned about to look at him, a rueful smile on her lips.

"What a pleasure it would be to see you detained until *I* wish to convince Philip you meant no harm in coming here."

"Yes . . . I am certain you wish me at your feet. But you will not betray me."

Helena seemed to consider his boldness, then slowly walked to the crimson cushions on the rug and sank comfortably into them. "Perhaps I shall consider showing grace."

Tancred's wry smile was disarming. "I am in your debt, fair damsel. It is your grace for which I long, like a dying man, water."

She leaned forward to the urn, poured a goblet of water, and handed it to him, her eyes amused. "I always show mercy. Drink."

He took the goblet, refusing to permit his restraint to crack. He finished it in one gulp, watching her evenly.

She relented first, looking away to the bowl of fruit. As though intrigued by what she saw, she chose a plum. "If you wish to explain about that barbarian girl, I assure you, I have no further interest."

"It is well you do not wish to know, because I had no intention of a long explanation. I did not come about Adele." He gestured. "May I join you on the cushions?"

"No." She lifted several and tossed them at his feet. "Do stay your distance."

Tancred's irritation began to climb. He caught up the cushions, abruptly arranging them for his ease, and sat down, tossing the empty goblet toward her as though it bored him. She looked at it, shimmering with jewels. Snatching it, she set it down firmly.

He rested his arm across his knee, watching her steadily. Her long hair fell across her shoulder, down past her waist.

"If you have words to speak, do so," she urged. She avoided his gaze, nibbling the plum.

His voice came, quiet and toneless as he watched her. "Gathered about Nicaea is the largest number of crusaders that have ever been put into the field. Yet the siege lingers with no hope of surrender, and summer is upon us. One thing could end that siege—boats from the emperor to patrol the lake in order to halt supplies from being brought into the city by the Red Lion. We also need siege weapons to scale the walls. You heard me mention all this to Philip weeks ago when we rode in."

"Yes, I remember." She looked at him, troubled. "And if my mother waits in Nicaea in the palace of the Red Lion, each day longer adds to my agony. I believe you are right, but why do you say this to me and not again to General Taticus?"

"Because the general answers to Philip. You can get those supplies by convincing him. As you say, it is also to your benefit if your mother is there."

"Me, convince Philip?"

"Why not?"

"But you are in his service! Oh, I know he wishes to pretend he does not pay heed to your words, but he listens more than you think." She tossed the nibbled plum aside. "If he behaves superior at times, it is because he is afraid of his own inadequacies."

"I am astounded you would admit this."

She shrugged. "I do not think less of him because of it. He must achieve a high level of military success—he dare not fail."

"My conclusion exactly. Except he does not have my sympathy. If he wishes success it is for himself, because he is a slave to self-adulation. He wishes to build a monument to himself and all he has achieved. And he doesn't mind trampling on thousands to make his causeway to the pinnacle."

"I refuse to entertain your insulting words."

"Then think on this; why does Philip wish to prolong the siege? Is it at the emperor's orders, or Constantine's?"

At the mention of those names she picked up her gilded fan and swished it uneasily. "Even if Byzantium wishes to prolong it, Philip has broken with my aunt and Constantine. We have our own plans now. In due season we will escape to the castle."

"You are certain that a favorable season will arrive? It seems to me that Philip shows no impatience. For an ardent groom, he is content to sit in his tent and scheme with General Taticus."

Helena snapped her fan shut. "Need I remind you that it is Nicholas who bids us wait because Constantine has guards watching the escape route to the castle? What can Philip do but cooperate?"

"Constantine is no longer with Count Raymond. The bishop has returned quietly to the imperial palace. What would you say if I told you Philip knows this? He also knows you could escape now to the Castle of Hohms."

A flicker of alarm showed in her eyes, but he could see that she tried to mask her feelings.

"Philip does not know. If he did, we would leave tonight."

"He does know," he said evenly. "And—as for Constantine, I am certain he brings a message to the emperor, one from Philip, perhaps from the Turkish official inside Nicaea as well. A message that benefits his cause, and Philip's. Constantine will return to Nicaea to negotiate its surrender—not to the crusaders, but to Philip."

Helena hesitated, then a flicker of fear showed in her eyes that alerted him. She was concerned about more than Philip—what was it about Constantine that she was keeping from him?

"How do you know all this? You presume."

He reached inside his tunic next to his chain mesh and removed the message Rufus had sent.

"Nicholas received this earlier." He handed it to her to read.

"I informed you the night I came here with Nicholas that your mother was last seen with the Red Lion, and that there was a possibility she was held within Nicaea. There is something more I have not told you, until I could be certain. Because my grandfather is al-Kareem, I have—shall we say—certain unlikely 'friends' within the Moslem world. I had Hakeem prowl the citadel two months ago before I ever decided to take a position with the imperial cavalry. He brought me news that the Red Lion was not at Nicaea, but was warring on his eastern frontier fighting another clan of Turks for the control of a small Christian Armenian state.

"His wives and family, however, are still in the city. So are members of his harem. No—do not interrupt. There is more."

Helena hung on his every word, moving closer to him and placing a hand on his wrist.

"I have also spoken to the Turkish prisoner which Count Raymond took in the recent battle. Though he speaks some Latin, I was able to converse fluently with him in Arabic. He assures me the wives and family of the Red Lion are still within the palace under tight security."

"Then my mother is there!"

"I cannot promise. If I could get inside . . . but friends would have to risk their own lives. . . ." Tancred grew thoughtful.

"Does the emperor know about the sultan's wives?" she whispered.

"Yes. And he will make good use of the information."

She looked alarmed. "So will Constantine. If she is there he will find her. You asked the prisoner about her?"

"I did. I am sorry . . . he did not know of any Adrianna."

Helena stared at him, then said, as if unable to accept the truth,

"She would have a Moslem name by now."

"I thought of that, but he knew nothing more. I went back the next day to bribe him, but he had escaped—at the same time Constantine left Count Raymond's camp."

"You think he set him free?"

"Or had him killed to protect the information he wished only for himself. It is what the emperor knows that disturbs me as well. Do you recall Nicholas saying that the emperor made a treaty with the Red Lion after the Christian defeat at Manzikert?"

"Yes, but what has this to do with my mother or Constantine?"

"The emperor could send a secret negotiator by ship to the other side of Nicaea to meet with the ruling Turkish officials serving the Red Lion. He will bring a message from the imperial palace saying that they will be slaughtered by cannibalistic barbarians if they do not surrender first to him. This way he bargains for the surrender of the city before the crusaders can take it. I believe Bishop Constantine is that secret negotiator."

"Constantine must not enter the citadel first—he will find her," she whispered, frightened.

"What is it?" he asked. "What have you not told me?"

She buried her face in her hands. "I . . . I could not tell you. He threatened me."

He took hold of her wrists, lowering her palms so he could see her face, drawing her toward him. "Who?" he demanded quietly. "Philip?"

"No! No! He does not know. . . ." She hesitated, and as their gaze held, she let out a breath of resignation. "Constantine. He knows about my mother. He came to me weeks ago before I ever spoke to you at the castle."

"Explain."

"He told me he knew I searched for her, that he too searched. That—that they were passionately in love and always had been."

Tancred saw the flicker of pain as she struggled to accept what must have been to her incredible.

"Then Constantine believes your mother is held in the Red Lion's palace?"

Helena nodded. "He must. And if he is inside the citadel as you say . . ." Her voice with its concern trailed off.

"How did he learn she was alive? Earlier you told me both he and Irene believed her to have died in a plague at the convent."

"He intercepted my informer on the Mese. I begged Constantine to tell me where she was, but he refused. If I had known then that it was Nicaea—but I had no idea. I thought of Tabriz, or Baghdad. And then I was told it was Jerusalem with ibn-Haroun. And all this time she has been but fifty miles from Constantinople!"

"I have doubts, but Constantine may believe it. Philip must also think so. . . ."

"No, he does not know!"

His grip on her wrists tightened. "When will you awaken to the truth that Philip plans first for himself, and not for your best interest? Why else do you think he wishes this siege to be prolonged? His presence among us is a ruse. He and Taticus are here to watch, to play the Byzantine game of chess. And they expect to win. It fits his plans—perhaps better than he first anticipated. And he expects Nicaea to surrender to him, not the crusaders. How all this affects Constantine's personal plans to locate Adrianna, I do not know, but they work together."

"Philip would never keep such information from me."

Tancred's mouth turned. "Madame, if you would trust me half as much as you do the noble, we—"

"I do trust you, Tancred. Did I not share my fears just now about Constantine's plans?"

"Then trust me explicitly. There is something you must do. The crusaders must take the citadel. Any secret surrender to Philip must be foiled."

He saw her stir uneasily at the thought of denying him a victory.

Helena followed his line of thinking and stiffened. "I will do as you require, but what makes you think Philip will listen to me?"

"You must try. There is no one else to get through to him. He knows we need boats and weapons. As minister of war he can write an official request and they will be sent at once."

He held her arms, aware of her, but she seemed unconscious of their nearness. Her fragrance was heady, so were her eyes, her hair . . .

Tancred withdrew and pushed himself up from the cushions. He grabbed his cloak, avoiding looking at her. "I will leave Philip to you," and he prided himself that his voice was calmly indifferent. "If he cares for you as you insist, there is nothing he will not do for you, including writing that request for boats."

Helena scrambled to her feet. He turned now, his eyes meeting hers, and he knew she was puzzled, wondering if she had imagined the moment earlier.

"Are you suggesting I deceive him? . . . the man I am soon to marry?"

Tancred masked his anger with her childish romantic inclinations. "Whether or not you marry him is uncertain. As for deceiving him, it is the other way around."

In frustration, she walked away, her back toward him, arms folded.

"I will leave you with one consideration. If a man loves a woman, he will risk his life for her. He will be ever anxious to carry her off to his castle as his beloved. I ask you to decide why he prefers to sit in his tent and connive with General Taticus when you would marry him this moment, with Nicholas performing the ceremony."

She turned to look at him, and Tancred gestured toward the tent opening. "I will need to get past Bardas again."

She hesitated. "No, wait. It is best he doesn't know." She went to the veil that led into her bedchamber and drew it aside. "There is another way out."

He followed her past more bed cushions, ivory bottles of perfume, and bundles of silk clothing to the back of the tent. She drew aside a tall woven basket to reveal an opening. "You may leave this way and not be seen."

"My expectations of the Byzantine mind have not been disappointed. Only a Daughter of the Purple Belt would have a secret exit in a tent."

Philip has sent an official request through General Taticus to the emperor for engines of war and other weaponry.

Tancred looked up from the written message. "Return, Bardas, and tell your mistress the crusaders are in her debt, though it may be too late."

Bardas showed his puzzlement as Tancred left the camp and went to join Nicholas at the lake as he had requested. After three weeks of stalemate, the crusaders planned an attack for the following day, June nineteenth.

The night was still and black, yet moonlight shimmered on the distant water near Nicaea's walls. Tancred took a silent position beside Nicholas, who stared ahead. Within a short time they heard the distant lapping of the water as boat oars cut through the Lake of Ascania in the direction of Constantinople.

Tancred squinted into the darkness and was able to make out the silhouette of small Byzantine boats, each guarded by soldiers. As they skimmed beneath the amber moon, he caught a glimpse of Turkish turbans, gilded cloth, and scimitars strangely mingling with the familiar uniform of the imperial guard. Seated in several boats were a number of veiled women.

Tancred turned his head toward Nicholas, whose hard brown face wore a bleak smile.

"The Red Lion's wives and family," said Tancred.

"And by morning the flag of Byzantium will fly over the gates of Nicaea."

Tancred watched the distant boats silently slip away into the night, his thoughts turning to Helena. She would be bitterly disappointed. Was her mother among those veiled women?

As June nineteenth broke over the hills, dawn lifted above the horizon and the sky bled with a mixture of gold and crimson. A cry of alarm surged through the crusader camp like a rolling trumpet blast.

Emerging from their tents, princes, knights, footmen, and peasants awoke to find the bold insignia of the Eastern Empire gazing down upon them from Nicaea. Flags, boasting the double-headed eagle, waved victoriously from the high city towers.

The news spread like fire. The treacherous Greeks have betrayed us!

The news of surrender was followed by a swift and determined Byzantine edict:

"The emperor has issued orders that all Turkish inhabitants of Nicaea may be granted safe conduct to Constantinople. There will be no entry into the city of any persons except those of notable excellence as determined by the Byzantium authorities."

The announcement, made first to the sullen princes, knights, and nobles under the gonfanons, soon made its way among the commonfolk. Armed Greek soldiers on horseback rode through the camp reading the official paper in Latin to the priests, who in turn sought to calm the anger of the people, who believed themselves cheated.

Stunned, Helena learned the news from Bardas.

"During the night, the emperor sailed a flotilla of his boats out on the lake. A surrender treaty was signed with the Turkish garrison serving the Red Lion."

"Where is Philip?" she cried.

"He sent word bidding me bring you at once into Nicaea. He waits at the Moslem palace."

Her heart pounded with equal amounts of fear and hope. "He has located her?" she whispered.

"I could not find out. He does not seem pleased." Bardas scowled. "I do not like this, mistress. Perhaps you should not go."

"When Philip requests my presence? He will have news, Bardas. Come. And what of Bishop Constantine? Is there any news of his arrival?"

"Master Philip said nothing."

Had he been a member of the delegation sent by the emperor to sign the treaty with the Turkish garrison? Could Tancred have been wrong about him? What if he were not involved in the negotiations? Then Philip and not Constantine would be the first official to enter the citadel! Hope flooded Helena with renewed strength as she rode under guard across the drawbridge and over the moat into Nicaea.

What of Tancred and Nicholas, did they know of the surrender? They must, yet she saw none of the crusaders in the nearly empty street now patrolled by Byzantine soldiers on horseback. Her eyes scanned the domed mosques, the minarets, the alabaster screens on the windows of two-story stone houses and small singular palaces. The palace of the Red Lion stood golden in the June sunlight, but she paid scarce attention to the dazzling sights as Philip's guards led her down a gilded hall. She was escorted into a receiving room where there was a crimson drape surrounding a raised dais. The sultan's seat was empty, but not the chamber.

"Helena."

She turned at Philip's tense voice.

He walked toward her, his handsome face drawn, his dark eyes warning her—of what? she wondered, suddenly becoming rigid.

Standing farther behind him and near a lattice-worked terrace of ivory, she saw only the familiar members of his entourage. Moving forward in her direction was General Taticus, and holding to his arm was a woman.

Helena's heart surged with expectation, then drained from her and she paled as her aunt greeted her warmly.

"My dearest Helena, you have fared well indeed through this ordeal," came Lady Irene's musical voice. "A few weeks resting here in the palace, however, will renew your vigor for the happy arrival of Prince Kalid."

Irene's smile was unpleasant but victorious, and her amber eyes laughed at what Helena believed must be her own ashen expression.

"Philip my son, bring a goblet of wine to your cousin Helena. She looks faint—it must be the heat." She smiled at Helena. "You will be pleased to know I have sent word to Kalid that you wait for him here in the palace of the Red Lion. It will save you a wearisome journey by camel. The marriage will take place here amid the beautiful surroundings of the new Byzantine Nicaea."

CHAPTER 18
The Unexpected Summons

The crusader princes, feeling the brunt of what they considered to be not only treachery but insult to their knightly honor, wasted no time. A second council meeting was convened. Tancred paced, waiting for Nicholas to arrive. A sense of restlessness nagged at him. He had heard that Helena was in the company of Philip and the Byzantine officials in the palace of the Red Lion.

As he had suspected, Nicaea surrendered with trumpets and flags to Philip Lysander, Minister of War, Legate of the Emperor. Constantine had stood at his right, Lady Irene on his left, and with her, General Taticus and some three thousand of his regiment that now patrolled Nicaea.

Debate raged as the princes discussed alternatives to what they considered was the rotting fruit of deceit.

"Did I not say, never trust a cunning Byzantine?" grumbled Duke Godfrey.

"He is right," said Bohemond. "There is naught left for us to do except leave this place and set out toward Antioch."

Tancred was no longer listening. Minutes earlier a peasant had brought him a hastily written letter from Bardas.

Master Nicholas has disappeared and I fear he is a prisoner of Constantine. I am searching for him now. My mistress is in

267

danger within the palace of the Red Lion of the Desert. She bids you come to her with all speed. Meet me in the Court of the Oranges.

Bardas

Philip's hurriedly written message had reached Helena through a slave soon after she had been escorted under guard to a chamber in the sultan's palace. *Tonight we will escape.* The two of them would ride as far as a certain olive grove near the family villa and meet up with Nicholas. From there they would ride to the Castle of Hohms and remain within its secure walls until the Normans liberated Antioch.

She shivered. Kalid was to arrive at the palace. Was he even now on his way?

The changes in plans spoke of danger, but she consoled herself, remembering that Philip would arrange for their escape.

Her mind wandered to Tancred. . . . Did he know she was being kept in the sultan's palace?

Inside the tent he shared with Nicholas, Tancred changed into his black-and-crimson uniform, then mounting Apollo, he rode slowly beside the high walls of the citadel until nearing a drawbridge over the moat to a gate of Nicaea.

The day was sultry without a breath of air coming from the lake. Before him the gate yawned open and guards kept watch on any and all entering or leaving. This was the moment of failure or success. His Imperial Cavalry uniform and the half-hearted position he still held with Philip offered a cover, but it could easily wear thin.

Several soldiers loitered, watching, but Tancred rode Apollo forward and past them. Then ahead, he heard a familiar voice.

"None of the barbarians are to enter the city. That includes the knights. Understood? It is the order of the minister of war."

It was Rufus!

Tancred continued riding forward and glanced at him. He saw him and their eyes held, then Rufus turned away and gave an order to one of the guards. The fact that he had pretended not to recognize him warned of danger.

There was no choice. Helena and Nicholas were both in peril. He could seek out the secret friends of al-Kareem—but not in the garb of a Byzantine!

With a taste of irony he realized how he must balance his identity. Inside his pack he carried the clothing of the Moors, and also the rugged leather of a Norman. But the heart and soul of Tancred Redwan, who was he truly?

He rode into the side streets where he would be less noticed by guards. He knew of the court where he would meet Bardas for he had come here before with Hakeem. How long ago those few short months seemed.

Late afternoon shadows clung to the sides of ancient stone buildings and latticed windows, where heat seeped from stone baked by the day's intense sunlight.

He dismounted, leading Apollo behind, hearing his hoofs echo on the ancient cobbles. As he walked, he wondered that Bardas would have him come to the Court of the Oranges. . . . What did Bardas know of this public court? Perhaps Helena had learned of it in the short time she was in the sultan's palace.

He turned a corner where the street ended with a high iron gate that was shut and surrounded by a high stone wall cooled by green vines and purple flowers. There was another street that turned and widened, leading into a maze of buildings. A glimpse beyond revealed cypress trees—a favorite of Moslems who considered them sacred. There were gardens green with vegetation and a colonnade of Moorish arches. Beyond the arches lay the public court, full of orange trees, their boughs heavy with the juice-laden fruit.

Tancred secured Apollo, then walked across the courtyard, his feet crushing the fallen orange blossoms until the overly sweet scent filled his senses. The shadows were deepening and the strollway was deserted where on any other day but this day of defeat, the Turks and Arabs would walk toward the fountains, or to the places of prayer.

Tancred stopped—as though a haunting voice from his Moorish past came calling him across the court. The *muezzin* was calling from his balcony, and the faithful hastened to cleanse themselves and kneel. . . .

Allah is almighty—Allah is almighty. . . . I witness that there is no other god but Allah—I witness that Muhammad is his prophet. . . . Come to prayer—come to prayer . . . come to the house of praise. Allah is almighty—Allah is almighty. . . . There is no god but Allah!

His eyes flickered with memory. *No god but Allah?*

As though compelled, he reached into his satchel and drew out the leather-bound New Testament. Nicholas had written a personal message of God's attribute of love and concluded it with several verses from the prophet Isaiah. His eyes searched until they found the words he sought.

He read them aloud, his voice a whisper but the words echoing across eternity:

I am the Lord, and there is none else. . . . And there is no other God besides Me, a righteous God and a Savior; there is none except Me. Turn to Me, and be saved, all the ends of the earth! For I am God, and there is no other. I have sworn by Myself, the word has gone forth from My mouth in righteousness, and will not turn back, that to Me every knee will bow, every tongue will swear allegiance. They will say of Me, 'Only in the Lord are righteousness and strength.' Men will come to Him. . . .

"Redwan!" came an anxious, low voice. Bardas hovered in the shadows of the grove, concealing himself with a dark hooded cowl.

Tancred walked toward him. Maintaining his caution, he paused, but Bardas gestured over his shoulder where the domed palace roof was visible in the golden twilight.

"Prince Kalid has unexpectedly arrived."

Kalid! It had been several months since Tancred's last unpleasant meeting with him in the armory at Constantinople. He was certain Kalid had befriended their cousin Mosul and that Kalid was now his avowed enemy.

Tancred had doubts about Bardas. He searched his marblelike eyes that shielded inner thoughts. How would Kalid know the siege had ended? How could he arrive so quickly?

"He expects your mistress to be brought to St. Symeon. Why would he come to Nicaea?"

"He was sent for by Lady Irene. The marriage will take place in the palace of the Red Lion."

Tancred's jaw flexed. "Where is Kalid now?"

"In the Red Lion's palace. He makes plans to travel with her to Aleppo instead of Antioch, but Master Philip has arranged for their escape."

"Philip is with her now?"

"They both bid me urgently to send for you. They have horses waiting and will leave for the Castle of Hohms tonight."

Tancred hesitated. "What of Nicholas? Has he shown himself?"

Bardas stood rigid. "He will join us at the gate. He comes by a boat."

Tancred watched him, fingering the hilt of his sword.

Bardas stepped backward into the deeper shadows. "Would you have me bring Apollo here to you? Where have you left him?"

Bardas had not shown this much cooperation before—was it because Philip also requested his presence? They would need another man with a sword, and perhaps Bardas was concerned with the threat so near in the presence of Kalid, and yet . . .

"Yes, bring him. He is back at the gate. Be quick."

Bardas disappeared into the shadows, and Tancred looked after him, stroking his chin.

The fragrance of blossoms hung sweet in the evening air, but the stark silence walled him in, adding to his growing tension. Was he a fool? Minutes slipped by, narrowing his chances of escape as he left himself at risk, and all because of a princess with warm, vulnerable eyes.

Tancred noticed the gate in the garden wall. It stood ajar, where once it had been shut.

He unsheathed his blade and stepped back into the shadowed vines.

From behind him came a faint clink of metal. He turned, but at the same moment three men emerged through the gate, swords drawn.

Before and behind, Byzantine soldiers encircled him.

"You should have left when you had opportunity," said Rufus, no emotion betraying his voice. "Unfortunately, I am under orders to arrest you."

"Whose orders? Irene's? She is *here*?"

"Yes, but it is Constantine who has ordered you to be brought to him. I have no choice, Redwan. Come."

"Since when do you serve the bishop instead of Irene?"

"Since he offers hope for the freedom of my son Joseph."

Tancred lifted the point of his blade. "I am sorry, my friend, but I have no interest in becoming the sacrifice for the release of your son. It is important I ride from here tonight."

"My son's freedom cannot wait. That ship I told you about? It leaves for Ethiopia, and we will both be on it. Sheathe your blade. You have no chance against so many."

Rufus gestured to the soldiers. "Take Redwan to the boat—"

A voice from the darkness interrupted sharply: "You will pay for your treachery against me, Rufus. Release Tancred Redwan!"

Tancred's head turned sharply toward the familiar voice. Rufus also turned, and for a moment his shoulders stooped with defeat.

"You heard me," Irene demanded angrily, a dozen soldiers at her side. "All of you—sheathe your swords. You are outnumbered. You! Rufus! So you think to serve Constantine? I shall deal with you later."

Rufus stood rigid as Irene warned, "I have Joseph in my control. Have you forgotten? I will yet need you for future battles. If you are wise, you will not contest me." She said more gently, "If you serve well, I shall send you both freely to the Castle of Hohms. Constantine's promise of a Venetian ship to Ethiopia is a lie. He is a traitor to me and the emperor."

Tancred listened, alert. Did this mean the relationship between her and Constantine had come to a dark end at last? Had she learned that he was searching for Adrianna?

Rufus and the guards sheathed their blades.

"All of you, return to your duties," she said scornfully. "Except you, Rufus. Stay there."

The guards melted away into the darkness, and Tancred and Rufus were left standing alone.

"Both of you—come at once," she commanded.

Mercenary soldiers appeared on horseback with immobile faces, their eyes empty as they stared ahead. Tancred guessed they were in a similar position as Rufus, unable to break free from her iron web.

Rufus walked forward and took his place resolutely behind the chariot reins. Seated in back, Irene smiled pleasantly toward Tancred.

"My handsome Norman—or should I say Moor? You will join me?"

Tancred bowed suavely. "Madame, do I have a choice?"

"None," she said sweetly. Then her smile faded and her voice hardened. "Unless you wish to die here."

"Thank you, no."

"I agree it would be a pity. I have important plans for you."

"And if I refuse them?"

"You are too wise to do so," she said confidently. "Unless you wish me to turn you over to Walter of Sicily?"

Tancred looked at her sharply.

"He waits near a postern gate where Bardas foolishly hoped to lead you."

So the old warrior betrayed me after all.

"Where is Bardas?"

"He escaped, but that is of no concern now. You have me to thank for intervening and sending soldiers to thwart your ambitious uncle. For my generosity, I expect a good return."

"I have no doubt of that."

Tancred walked up to the side of the chariot and eased himself into the comfortable leather seat beside her. The chariot moved ahead, followed by guards on horseback.

Now what? he thought wryly.

He pondered Bardas. What had prompted his betrayal? What had he hoped to gain by turning him over to the Redwan clan? And what of the information about the disappearance of Nicholas, of Helena and Philip escaping—had it been a ruse? *Bardas has learned well the art of the Byzantine,* he thought bitterly.

He must escape, but how? And what did the "lioness" want of him?

A casual glance over his shoulder convinced him there was no chance of bounding from the chariot and making a run into the dark shrubs.

Irene sat closely beside him with a faint smile, her amber eyes warm and bold. Her fragrance was strong, provocative, and meant to be. She wore shimmering gold silk beneath a white fur cape, but he imagined that armor would fit her better.

"This is a unique situation—to be the prisoner of a woman," he said with an imperceptible smile. "I feel as though I am in even more danger."

"Would you prefer Walter of Sicily?"

"If it comes to a choice, I find your chariot lush and comfortable, but I prefer my freedom," he said lightly. "I was about to congratulate you and the emperor on a successful surrender of Nicaea, and take my crusading spirit elsewhere. If you permit—"

"Permission refused. You have something I want." Her eyes mocked him. "Information."

Tancred lounged back in the seat, arms behind his head, and gazed up at the vivid stars in the black sky.

He sighed. "Ah, yes, information. . . . For a foolish moment I forgot the favorite pastime of the Byzantine. Since you collect spies as some women collect pretty slippers, what information could I possibly have that you do not already possess?" He looked at her with a smile.

Irene's eyes toyed with his. "You may rest assured you are valuable, Tancred, or I would not have arrested you."

"Yes, of course, forbid such a foolish thought. Surely you do not wish my skills with a sword. You have Rufus and the others. What, then? Does it concern Philip?"

Her eyes hardened and she settled back in the seat. "I make it my ambition to know everything Philip does. My son is a charming boy, but irrational and given to foolish changes in mood."

"Very risky for a minister of war! But I am sure the emperor will have no need for concern since he does have your stability to lean upon."

"I suppose Helena sought once again to hire you to bring her and Philip to the Castle of Hohms?"

He believed her too cunning to deceive now, but could he lead her to a false conclusion?

"She did. Like Philip, she too is a charming girl, but irrational. Your niece holds no romantic inclinations for my cousin Kalid. She wished to escape to Athens, but I could not help her. I have my own quest. As you saw tonight, my uncle seeks me for the death of my brother. The assassin is in Antioch and I must find him."

"I have known about your escape from Sicily and the death of Derek Redwan for weeks. It may be that I can help you locate Mosul—for the right price."

That she knew was no surprise. Rufus had already informed him of the danger connected with Irene's informers. However, she did not know that Philip had Mosul incarcerated until his work with the Armenian spy was finished to his satisfaction.

"You know of Mosul?" he asked, pretending innocence.

"As you said, I make such matters my ambition. There is one thing you do not know, Tancred, for Mosul is no longer in Antioch." She smiled. "Your expression gives you away. You are surprised? No doubt you would be."

He had not expected this turn. Mosul not in Antioch! Had Philip lied, or had Kerbogha moved him to a more secure place? The news unsettled him, for unless Mosul was in Antioch there would be little chance to find him until Philip kept his bargain; and he did not trust Philip or Kerbogha.

Irene settled back, her jewels flashing. "Kalid warned Mosul and he escaped, but I have access to secret information and I can tell you where he is if you cooperate."

His heart thudded. He felt the python of temptation slowly encircling his soul. What information did she want from him now? Could he give it without compromising the safety of Helena and Nicholas?

"I have effective ways of dealing with Helena," Irene was saying. "Philip as well. So do not think I need you to explain their foolish plan to run away. It will do them no good. Kalid will come here to Nicaea." She turned her riveting gaze on him. "No, the information I want from you concerns the whereabouts of Adrianna Lysander."

Her words could not have struck him harder had she slapped

him. He watched her, his expression deliberately inscrutable. He must delay. . . .

"She did tell you about her mother?" inquired Irene, watching him intently. "At the guard castle of Herion, I suppose?"

"Her mother? She told me she died several years ago during her incarceration in a convent."

"Am I a fool that you think you can mock me? I have learned she is alive, and a threat to me and my son as long as she lives. You too know Adrianna lives. Helena would have told you. Nicholas knows as well."

"Then you admit Philip is your son?"

"Helena would have told you that also. She delights to play the victim, to indulge in vicious gossip about me. It is no secret she despises me because Philip listens to my counsel. Not that her gossip about his birth disturbs me, nor will it ruin my plans for his career. Why should I deny it? Yes, he is my son. And one day he will be emperor of Byzantium. It is written in the stars."

"When a boy, Nicholas would bring me to a great rock on a summer's night when the sky was cloudless and bright with ten thousand stars and planets. 'Why trust the stars? Trust the Maker of the stars!' he would say. 'The heavens declare the glory of God.' He quoted the greatest writing of all time—the Scriptures. Your zodiac astrology was born in ancient Babylon and was the religion of the Tower of Babel. Since it was cursed by God, any message you think to receive from the alignment of the planets is foolishness. If Philip becomes emperor, it will be because his mother is adept at poison."

"You audacious fool! Do you dare speak to me like this? I could have you killed at once and there would be none to question me."

"The One who flung the stars into space, madame, remains in final control of my destiny, but perhaps the one appeal for staying your hand is a lesser consideration—the need for the information you insist I have. Kill me, and your plans will falter."

Her eyes were cool. Then she gave a short laugh. "Nicholas and his devotion to Christianity has also misshaped your sound judgment. He was always a determined man, but also misguided by devotion to his God. He threw away the opportunity to become emperor, and so—" She stopped as if having said too much.

Tancred followed her twisted logic. "And so you reread your astrology and decided your calculation was in error; the crown you claim to see belongs not to Nicholas but to Philip! Very convenient, madame. When prophecies prove false, simply change their meaning. But God's truth does not change." He looked at her, his gaze mocking. "I am surprised you did not convince Constantine that the crown belongs to him. Is it because he is not as easily manipulated as Philip?"

"Like his father, Constantine is devoted."

"Devoted to his own ambitions, or Philip's?"

"They are one in the same. It is Philip who is bent toward a wayward path, and his father and I must keep him on the ordained path. We cannot permit his marriage to Lysander's daughter . . . at least, not yet."

"His marriage to Helena would mean the end of your control over her inheritance."

She shrugged. "You might as well know, yes."

"And Lady Adrianna?"

"If Adrianna lives to return to Constantinople, we will all lose our positions close to the emperor. I have worked too devotedly to ensure Philip's reign to permit such a mistake to happen. Enough of your questions! It is you who must answer to me. I want to know where she is."

"And if I do not tell you?"

"Then—before this night is over, you will." Her eyes grew scornful. "Come, Tancred, you are a clever man, and no fool. You are far too experienced with danger to play games with a woman of my determination. You know I will not hesitate to have you strangled if you refuse to tell me her whereabouts."

"I am disappointed. I would expect you to come up with a more extraordinary way of disposing of an enemy."

Her smile was brittle. "To make you talk? I have Helena at my disposal. A gallant knight will face torture and death to retain his honor; but would he see his damsel arrested and punished?" Her smile came, calm and cool. "I see by your angry expression that you are beginning to understand. It need not happen, of course. And for a worthy prize I shall tell you where you can find the assassin."

CHAPTER 19
Dark Shadows of the Zodiac

In the audience hall of the Red Lion's palace, Irene sat upon low cushions before a crimson curtain of silk. Tancred watched her, wondering how long he could hold out. What would she do if she found out he did not know where Adrianna was? He was playing for time. And if Helena was also a prisoner somewhere in the palace, what could he do?

He watched Irene, as cool and methodical as a stalking leopard. Was she bluffing? For the first time he found himself hoping that Philip had roused himself in time to have already escaped with Helena. *And Nicholas.* Obviously Bardas had lied about his being in trouble just to lure him here. Then where was he?

"Dungeons are ugly places," Irene reminded him, and when he remained ambiguous, her gaze raked him. "Not that I expect to waste time on your imprisonment. You would stubbornly resist me to the end. No, in order to make you talk I must bait you with information on Mosul, or use one weaker than you as leverage. Helena is fearful of dungeons and has a phobia about rats."

Her lips curled. "As intended, my suggestion has located its vulnerable spot. I am sorry. I hate to be cruel." Irene stood and walked to a low table where she filled a golden goblet with wine. "She braved a dungeon once. It was dark, the air stale and cold.

Rats were everywhere. Very large, hungry ones." She looked over at him. "Helena was a child then. She was nearly crazed with fear. It took me several months to bring her mind from the horror."

Tancred remained without expression. She was even more of a shrew than he had thought. No wonder Nicholas had rejected her in the end.

Her amber eyes glistened. "If you tell me the location of her mother, the tragedy need not repeat itself."

The silence lingered. The advantage of permitting her to believe he knew of Adrianna's whereabouts gained him time, but little else.

"Kalid will have something to say about this breach in your bargain. If he discovers his bride pines away in a dungeon, he will not cooperate in the surrender of Antioch to Philip."

"That is why I offer you the whereabouts of Mosul. Think of your own freedom. You could return to Palermo if you wish, or settle in Constantinople. The emperor thinks well of you. I could arrange for a seat of power. You could even have Helena. I could arrange even that—after Kalid."

Tancred lifted his goblet and took a mouthful. The witch!

"You will not cooperate, or do you muse? Believe me," she warned, "I will not deliver her to Antioch at all if it becomes a necessary choice between finding Adrianna and the surrender of Antioch!" She threw her goblet at him and he ducked. It smashed against the tile mosaics.

Her face was white and her eyes were hot. "I will find some other way to get what I want! Do not underestimate me. If I must, I am willing to lose much of my present plans. Locating Adrianna is far more important." She paced, the silk swirling about her dainty slippers. "I can always make new plans," she said to herself. "There will be other cities to reclaim from the Seljuk Turks to insure the success of Philip. Nicaea is a prize to please the emperor, and it is Philip's gift to him. Look at this palace! It's fat with riches."

"And Philip?" Tancred warned. "He will stand by and see you put her into a dungeon? He may surrender his will to yours, but he is also selfish. He wants Helena as much as Kalid."

"And as much as you. I am no fool when it comes to men. I

have seen the way you look at her." Her golden brows lifted. "Philip will have Helena, one day. He is patient enough to wait, knowing his position is also secure. Like the gods—two horses pull him apart."

Irene walked toward him, her body seething with energy. "I must find what pulls you apart. And when I do, you will do as I wish, when I wish, and for as long as I insist."

Tancred drew in a breath and lifted a brow. "Madame, you frighten me!"

She laughed. "Do I?" She reached a cold, slithering hand and wrapped it around his neck, then the other arm, drawing his head down toward hers.

He reached and untwined her arms. "You leave me cold."

She shrugged. "It is just as well. I would prefer distance. The others whom I control, however, wish it otherwise."

"All except Nicholas?"

At the mention of Nicholas an ashen look glazed across her eyes. She turned and walked back to the cushions and sank onto them, lounging there, an arm draped across a pillow, her shimmering tunic catching the torchlight. She looked unreal, like a statue of some pagan idol from Troy.

"There is no need for Philip to know I have her in a dungeon, not yet. As far as he knows, I may have already sent her to Prince Kalid. And when he does find out, well, I can arrange an illness for Helena and pretend I kept it from him, knowing how precious she was to him. I did not want him to suffer." She reached over and picked up the wine, pouring a second goblet.

Tancred thought of his options. He had his sword, but against so many guards what chance would he have?

Holding her goblet, she sipped as she arose, walking toward him. "I suppose you may wonder why I have not confronted her on the whereabouts of her mother, but I am quite certain she does not know, nor does Nicholas. The answer rests with you, and Constantine." Her lips curled. "That fool. Constantine betrayed me. He's escaped to find her, so that leaves only you."

So Constantine had escaped. "He loves her?"

"He was always an idiot about Adrianna. I believe him to be mentally unstable. He used to follow her wherever she went and make wild claims of how she met with him and wished to marry him. None of it is true. Adrianna," she said with disgust, "is too much the saint to care for a man of Constantine's appetites and spiritual hypocrisy. Even as Nicholas scorns me. He looks on me with sympathy—can you imagine?" She threw back her head and laughed. "He pities me, he said. He thinks when I die I will go to hades!" She looked at Tancred thoughtfully, and her smiled faded. "Do you think so too?"

Constantine is not the only one in the family who could be said to be insane.

"Probably so, madame," he said silkily.

She laughed. "My other warrior pets would say, 'You, madame? Spend eternity in hades? Oh no, madame. Not you!' I like you, Tancred—it is true, you are not afraid of me. Neither is Nicholas."

She sank into a chair, looking unexpectedly weary. "I could bribe Kalid to tell me where she is. Even the Red Lion, but it would take time. Weeks. Constantine would find her first."

"Then he knows where Lady Adrianna is?"

"Yes." She lifted the goblet and stared at it. "Even if Helena knew where her mother is being held, she is foolish enough to resist me, though a dungeon await her. She is a child who clings to sentiment. Her 'beloved Christian mother' is worth her own death."

Again Irene stood, as restless as a trapped cat.

"Your niece is a woman of valor," said Tancred. "I suspect the same of her mother."

Irene turned and looked at him, angry, as though the complement enraged her.

"Do they not spoil your morning when you rise to look at yourself in the mirror, madame? Or are you so vain as to think your beauty is enough to win the devotion of a man?"

"When I wish a man's service, I may obtain it as easily through fear as through devotion."

He thought of Rufus and the other warriors bound to her.

"But you would do well to heed caution; when given a chance, the half-starved dogs may not hesitate to devour their Jezebel."

Her palm whipped across the side of his face like the dart of an adder. Her nostrils flared.

Tancred rubbed his chin, watching her. As cool and heartless as she was, she did not like to be compared to the Jezebel of the Old Testament.

"I was a lady too, once." Her eyes turned toward the open balustrade where the horizon glowed as though the hills were on fire.

"Once," she repeated, "I was as innocent and sweet as Helena, as religiously devout to the Church as Adrianna. Nicholas knew me then . . . loved me then. Then he went away to study at Athens. And I, well . . . I changed. I could see my meekness got me nowhere, while others less talented were called to the chamber of the emperor. . . . Why shouldn't I go there? I thought. It is the only way to get what I want."

Irene looked at him, nothing in her face. "And I went. When Nicholas returned two years later I was the emperor's mistress. He said nothing to me, he simply looked at me with that insufferable pity of his and walked away! Oh, I hated him for that superior pity!" Her voice broke and a strangled gasp came to her throat, as though tears had come to her eyes. Swiftly she brought her hand to her throat to force back the emotion.

She turned toward him, and for the first time he could see the lines of age stand out on her stricken face. She appeared vulnerable, and yes, a woman he too could pity.

Tancred lowered his gaze and concentrated on his goblet, studded with emeralds and rubies and sapphires. It all meant nothing in the end. Character, a woman's soul, her self-respect—these were the virtues that mattered, that drew men like himself and Nicholas.

Silence filled the gilded chamber. Irene had gained control and slipped behind her Byzantine mask again, her emotions encased in armor.

"Despite your cool attempts at shrouding your disciplined emotions, I know you find Helena a woman of particular interest. Therefore, I offer you a choice."

"A choice?" he asked flatly.

"Yes. An exchange of information. I will give you the whereabouts of Mosul and Helena's freedom from the dungeon if you will tell me where to find Adrianna before Constantine."

Tancred glanced casually toward the terrace.

She followed his glance and read his mind. "Do not try it. Guards await." Abruptly she turned. "Rufus!" she called.

The giant bodyguard appeared from the outer hall, his features taut.

"Come here!"

Tancred tensed when Rufus did not move but watched her. An unease crept through Tancred when he saw the rabid hatred that sprang to life in the Ethiopian's face.

Irene did not seem frightened. She smiled. "Come, Rufus. Or the guards who hold Joseph will flog him. Do you think I fear you, Rufus? Not as long as my presence back in Constantinople means that Joseph will live. If anything happens to me—he will die. You know that. Now," she said. "Come to me."

Tancred could not bear the scene and turned away, his shoulder leaning against the column. He heard Rufus walk forward, heard her laugh. "Bend the knee," she mocked. "That is so—very good. You are very handsome, Rufus."

Tancred let out a breath and looked up at the ceiling with disgust.

"Our Norman friend must be convinced. Have the guard bring Helena here," said Irene.

Tancred unsheathed his sword.

She turned sharply. "Do not be a fool. I have a dozen soldiers. And, like Rufus, they are all my slaves. They may despise me, but they can do nothing to help you."

They came into the chamber, lean, tough men with drawn blades, hard faces, and glazed eyes.

"Now—sheathe your sword," she ordered Tancred. "It will do you no good here." She turned to the guards. "Take him away. I will call for him when Helena arrives. Where is the minister of war? How is it I cannot find him?"

"He is meeting with the officials."

"Send for him. I have no more patience left in me tonight for fools!"

As several guards left to carry out her orders, others led Tancred up the steps to a chamber. Irene called, "I am certain if you rest awhile, Tancred, you will see the wisdom of cooperation. I will let you ride free as soon as I am certain your information is accurate. If not, you will be turned over to Walter of Sicily."

Rufus brought him to a stone chamber. Tancred turned away from him with impatience and walked to the one small window.

"There is no way of escape," stated Rufus, following him to the window. "She has made certain. And now you know why I have been unable to throw off her chains. She thinks of everything," and he gestured below.

Tancred peered into the courtyard. It was enclosed with a high, insurmountable wall. He saw something else—two leopards pacing nervously in the enclosure.

"A dozen guards serve her obediently—she has control of their wives and children. If they serve faithfully, she rewards the family with gifts and bounty, keeping them at peace and happy. If we turned against her—she would see to our ruin."

"If we all move in unison—"

But Rufus turned away. "She has spies among us. We do not know whom to trust. The risk to our loved ones is too great."

"I would choose death before a life of servitude to her."

"So you say now. What will you do when she brings Lysander's daughter?"

Tancred wondered. *God*, he prayed, *there must be some way!*

"Find Nicholas," he told Rufus. "He must be somewhere in the Norman army. Tell him of Helena."

"What you ask is impossible! I cannot leave the city." He turned his back to walk out. His black eyes smoldered with bitter frustration. "She has Joseph somewhere in the city and I know not where. If I betray her again—she will turn against him." He strode out the door and a heavy bolt jammed into place.

Tancred made careful search of the chamber, though he was nearly certain he was trapped. There was no ledge on the outside wall facing the window.

Frustrated at his impotence, he threw himself down on the bed and tried to sleep, but he kept thinking of Helena. Longingly he thought of Hakeem and his falcon, but by now his Moorish ally would be in Antioch waiting for him. He was not likely to know that Mosul had already fled!

Angrily he stood. He pushed a table aside that blocked his pacing. *The shrew!* She not only tempted him with information on Mosul, but threatened harm to Helena.

Could she be lying about Mosul? No, for her information matched Philip's. He could not think of Mosul while the dilemma of Helena gnawed at him. What a fool he had been to allow Bardas to detain him. His fingers wrapped around the window bars.

And Bardas, just where was the foul betrayer?

He saw torches flickering below. What if he continued his ruse and offered Irene false information? She would keep him a prisoner until her work was done, and still send Helena to Kalid. By the time he was free and able to go to Antioch, she would be Kalid's reluctant bride—or just another woman in his harem.

Think, I must think. But for the first time in his life he was trapped, not by his Norman uncle and wolfish cousins, but by a woman of delicate beauty with a reprobate conscience and the iron will of a gladiator.

His eyes darkened beneath his lashes as the image of Helena came to mind. No, he was not trapped by Irene, but by his feelings for Helena. He could easily get out of his situation if he wished to betray her. He would even find Mosul and avoid the danger of entering Antioch as a spy, avoid the blood-soaked battles ahead of him before the gates of Jerusalem opened wide.

It was time to admit to himself that she had captured his heart. Tancred turned from the window and, seeing the chair in front of him, booted it across the chamber.

Dawn broke above the hills and ushered in the Moslem call to prayer. Tancred watched as a guard walked the courtyard wall and heaved several hunks of red meat to the leopards.

Tancred mused with a cynical expression, then came alert. *The leopards are being fed.* It could mean that Irene did not expect to use them as a threat. Had she discovered something in the late hours of the night that altered her plans?

He turned toward the door, hearing heavy footsteps in the passageway and a moment later the key being turned in the lock. The door swung open on creaking hinges and Rufus stood there alone, immobile.

"Irene has left. You are free to go. Apollo waits at the gate."

Free to leave? The unexpected change in circumstances troubled him, and he stared at Rufus evenly, searching his grim face. "What happened!"

Rufus's eyes flickered with heated emotion. "You are no longer needed, but do not tarry lest she change her mind."

"Not needed, why?"

The dislike Rufus felt spilled over in his voice. "The minister of war gave her the information she wanted."

Philip . . . "Where is Helena now?"

"Locked in a chamber until Prince Kalid arrives."

"Kalid—coming here? When?"

He shrugged. "A week, two weeks, who knows?"

"I must speak with her."

Rufus turned stiffly. "There is nothing I can do. Your horse waits at the back gate." He paused, adding quietly, "Philip has sent a secret message to her, saying that he plans their escape tonight."

"She knows this and expects him?"

"Yes."

"He is a coward," Tancred said disdainfully. "He will not risk it. Together we can help her."

Rufus shook his head. "No. I can do nothing."

"Then take me to her chamber. I must see her before Philip arrives, if only for a moment."

Rufus considered this as he glanced down the hall, uncertain. "All right. . . . For you, I will do this. For the memory of your father. I cannot leave you in her chamber for long."

Tancred strapped on his scabbard and threw his cloak over his shoulder, then followed Rufus down the passage and up a flight of marble steps.

They came to a door. Beside it stood another guard. Rufus spoke to him quietly. Tancred watched a gold besant fall into the guard's hand. The key turned in the lock, it opened, and Tancred stepped inside. A moment later he heard the rattle of the key locking him in.

The chamber was lavishly decorated with purple hangings and thick rugs. He glanced about for Helena. She had been asleep in a chair covered with a silk coverlet, but at the sound of his entry she awakened.

CHAPTER 20
A Knight's Honor

Helena must have thought him to be a slave bringing her a breakfast tray, for she did not look at him. "I am not hungry. Please go away."

Tancred leaned his shoulder against the door, watching her. In the uninterrupted stillness, she must have sensed his presence, for she stirred and lifted her head.

Her eyes widened, then settled with a rush of cool anger, and something else that puzzled him—disappointment?

Bewildered by this response, he wondered whether Irene told her of his incarceration.

"Good morning," he said, and extended her a bow.

She jumped to her feet, tossing the cover aside. "Get out," she whispered, hands in balled fists at her sides.

He studied her expression, trying to read her mind. "Are you always so ill-tempered upon rising? Or am I to blame for the fall of Nicaea? If you had listened to me at the tent—"

"Silence." Helena walked toward him.

Tancred straightened from the door. "I've about had my fill of women cracking the whip over my head."

She stopped in front of him. "So you are gallant, are you? A man of integrity? Of honor? A knight? A man I could trust with

289

my life, with secret information about my mother?"

He remained calm and thoughtful, rubbing his chin.

"You traitor! You barbarian! You—you—" She drew back her arm and he caught it.

"Venom must run in the family. Your aunt also packs a wallop. I dare not think what storm rages you against me."

Helena jerked her arm free, her breath heaving.

"I am leaving. I decided to say good-bye," he said.

She turned her back toward him.

Tancred scanned her rigid stance. "I will be joining the Norman knights under Bohemond," and he waited for her response. "We will be leaving soon for Antioch. So I will not see you for some time. There will be the war—"

"I care not what you do, barbarian," she said over her shoulder. "And I hope a scimitar takes your head before you ever reach Antioch." She reached past him to open the door and found it locked.

"Do you have the key?" she demanded.

He was becoming irritated, all romantic inclinations swiftly turning to ashes beneath her scorn. He threw his riding cloak on a nearby chair and stood, hands on hips, scanning her.

"Now just why would I have control of the key? Am I your captor?"

"Oh no, never that—but you are *her* captive, are you not?" she hissed meaningfully.

"Of what do you accuse me? If you knew what I've been through trying to save my hide and protect you at the same time—"

"As if you did not know of what I accuse you. Who let you in my private chamber?"

"Irene's bodyguard, but I regret asking to see you. I would rather stare into the icy eyes of a poisonous adder. As for Rufus, trust him. He may prove a good friend."

"I trust no one," Helena spat. "Not now. You will not see me in Antioch, nor anywhere else. After you vowed to find my mother and learned all you needed to know—you betrayed her whereabouts to Irene last night so you could find Mosul."

He grew still, watching her, and felt an ache in the pit of his soul. "I must be a fool," he said quietly. "I thought I would be the last one you would accuse of treachery. I see I am the first."

"The first? Yes, Bardas was right about you; so was Philip. And no—do not try to explain. Your smooth excuses will not deceive me this time. I have heard one too many."

She whisked past him toward the open terrace. Swiftly he pulled her back and against him. "Not so fast. Not this time."

Helena's heart leaped at the impact of their touch, and she grew taut. She pushed against his chest with both palms, turning her head away. "Let go."

"Stop struggling."

"Do you want me to scream? I will!" Her voice shook and it made her angry that it did.

"For what it is worth, I did not betray your mother. I do not yet know where she is, but Constantine does. He has left to find her. Irene thought I knew and she hopes to thwart him."

Helena could still envision her aunt's smug smile when telling her how she had gained the information from Tancred. The shock of disappointment she had felt when told the lurid details still weighed with a sickening force in her mind and heart.

"Do you know me so little as to think I would betray you?"

"I suppose you think I will believe you if you deny it?"

"She did not get the information from me. Did she tell you she did? And you believe her witness against mine?"

As Helena stared into his eyes she faltered. She did not know what she believed. Confusion stalked her spirit, bringing grief.

"No? Then how did she learn? Not from Constantine. He escaped last night on one of the boats. And not from Bardas—"

"Bardas! That traitor! Next time I see him I will wring his neck. Ask Philip how his mother received the information."

She read the accusation in his smoldering gaze and rejected it at once. "Philip? He would never tell. You are mad."

"Philip! I am as weary of him as I am of your childish trust in him!"

Helena fought in vain to pull free. "You betrayed us for information on Mosul. I know what it means to you to find him—and you spent the night with Irene; she told me so."

Tancred released her so abruptly she took a staggering step back.

He watched her, his intense blue-gray eyes holding hers. "You do not know me at all."

The quiet disappointment of his voice startled her to sobriety. In the silence she searched his face.

"Irene boasted, she said that—"

"And you believed her?" came his ironic voice. "A woman you have long lamented to me about being your nemesis? You will swallow her lies and refuse the truth I give you?"

She faltered. "I . . . do not know . . . how else would she find out but through you?"

He bowed with exaggerated cynicism. "Thank you, princess. Your high opinion of my character overwhelms me. It so happens I risked a great deal that is important to me to protect you and your mother. She did offer me more than you might suppose and I turned it down—bed and all, including information on the whereabouts of Mosul. Information that would have freed me from servitude to Philip. Mosul is not even in Antioch, yet Philip sends me there to accomplish his cowardly work for him."

Helena stared at him, his anger giving her cause to reconsider. Against her will, she began to wonder if perhaps Irene might not have lied simply to hurt her. She struggled against bewildering feelings that were beginning to flow through her soul, warming her like a fire on a frosty morning.

"The formative years you have spent in the palace have made you cynical about men, Helena. You think every man will sell his soul for ambition, greed, or lust. I must do something to restore your trust. Especially in me."

She resisted his intense gaze, for it was proving as dangerous as her dilemma in the Red Lion's palace.

"I spent the night behind a bolted door. Alone. By choice."

"Perhaps so, but that does not make you innocent about my mother, and furthermore—I do not care where you slept."

"You are contradictory and impossible to understand. One minute you accuse me of evil, and when I deny it, you reject me and say you do not care."

"Because I do not care!"

"However," he continued, "I do care what you think. And while I was alone, it was you who consumed my restless thoughts and longings."

Helena whirled away, fear coursing through her. "Please stop. I will not listen. . . ."

"Yes you will—" Tancred came to her, turning her about and drawing her to him again. As he bent toward her lips she jerked her head away.

He pretended dismay. "And to think you would turn me down for Philip! A betrayer, a coward!"

She broke free, backing away from the danger of his embrace. Her eyes narrowed. "You only despise him because he is everything you are not."

"The day I envy Philip, I cease to be a man."

"Your ego is unbearable."

"I do envy him something. Your indomitable trust and devotion."

Dare she believe him? Dare she risk the strange, confusing yearning in her heart?

"After your betrayal? I wish you would fall in love with me so I could tear your heart into pieces."

He stared at her, and suddenly, Helena felt a dart of fear, of regret. Why had she spoken thus? Why did she deliberately seek to hurt him, to ruin anything between them?

"I think you truly mean that, Helena," he said so quietly that she turned cold.

No, she wished to cry out, *I do not mean it, Tancred!*

"I thought you may be a different woman under that armor of superiority, but now I begin to wonder if I have been deceived. I shall remember to protect my vulnerability from your claws."

Tancred's hands loosened from her shoulders and he gently held her away from him.

Pain sprang like fire to her heart, burning and hurting. She stepped back, then under his cool, distant gaze, she felt the chill wind blow across her soul. *What have I done?*

She walked to the terrace, keeping her back to him, feeling

weak. There she waited, expecting to hear the door shut behind him. Gone, forever . . .

He did not leave.

She turned, pale and emotionally weary, holding to the back of a chair. "Well? You are going to war, like the mercenary you are. Go! And may your betrayal of my mother come back on your head a hundredfold."

"I am going, fear not, but I cannot bear to leave you with the satisfaction of believing that it was I who betrayed Adrianna. Did you tell your dauntless hero about the Red Lion?"

"If you speak of Philip, yes. Of course I told him. I can trust him," she said coolly. "That is more than I can say of others who claim to be gallant. Philip is to be my husband. Should I keep secrets from him?"

He laughed, leaning against the door. "A miserable husband he would be. You will never know if what you whisper in his ear in bed finds its way to Irene."

Her eyes narrowed. "Get out."

"With Philip as minister of war you do well to keep your deepest secrets locked in your heart—especially if they could bring greater success to him and Irene."

"Do you think I would ever believe Philip betrayed my mother?"

"No, because you wish to think I did."

Helena met his gaze steadily. "Philip and I are to be married tonight. He has decided to leave Constantinople and his position. That proves your estimation of matters false. He had no reason to betray me. He no longer needs the power and glory of the imperial palace."

"Philip will need it as long as he breathes. It is his reason to live, his god."

She winced, for the words penetrated her armor and touched something frightening inside of her, something that caused her to recoil because it might be true.

"Philip is free now, is he? Do you truly believe that about him? Even if he left with you, and you became his bride, you would soon learn that he can never be content without Byzantium. He will wither and die."

Helena swallowed, staring at him, her heart thumping and aching.

"He gave the information about Adrianna to his mother. Ask Rufus. He will tell you the truth; he has no reason to lie, nor to defend me. And since it was Philip who cooperated with Irene last night, ask yourself why he did so, if he truly wishes to give up his position with the emperor. I thought you were wiser than this."

She found no words to answer him and looked out upon the terrace. The hot morning air poured over the ancient stones and sapped her faltering strength. "I don't know," she murmured.

"You do not love him, Helena. You have only convinced yourself, because all these years you knew nothing else existed in life except Philip, Byzantium, your dreams."

Helena shut her eyes against his words. "I don't know," she murmured again. "Go away from me. Please."

"How do you expect to escape the guards?"

She looked at him. "Do you think I would tell you how we expect to escape? It is enough that Philip has arranged everything."

"I do not know what he has in mind, but I would not trust him. He will not come for you. You will travel to Antioch. And I will find you there."

She shook her head. "He will come, as he promised."

Tancred walked toward her where she stood on the terrace, his eyes troubled, but there was something else smoldering in their depths, something that halted her tongue and held her fixed to his gaze.

"Please . . . stay away from me," she whispered.

"No . . . I cannot stay away. I told you at the castle that night when you came to me that neither I nor my sword can be bought cheaply. Willingly I offered you my help, but you rejected it when Philip arrived. Now you wish to think that same allegiance can be bought cheaply by Irene. You hope it is so, because such thoughts about me make it easier for you to reject your feelings."

Helena stirred, moving away from her smoldering emotions. "My feelings?" she asked innocently. "You insult Philip. You tell me I am a child who does not know what she wants, then you are conceited enough to tell me it is you I really want."

"You just said you wanted me; I did not."

"I could never have any feeling toward you except disappointment and pity for what you have done."

"Pity! Spare me, madame!" He followed her across the terrace as she backed away. "I insist that you are deceiving yourself. You are afraid of the feeling between us. It is strong, is it not? Like the ceaseless pounding of the surf, like drawing wind tugging irresistibly."

"Do you fancy yourself a poet?" she mocked in a whisper, hoping her expression appeared calm, her voice steady.

"With you in my arms? I could be anything you wish."

Philip did not ignite such wild pounding of her heart, nor did he vow such passion.

"Admit it," he said. "We were attracted to each other from the beginning, from the moment we met on the road near the Danube. For me, such attraction has not come before. No matter what you insist about Philip, I do not think it comes any easier for you. You only imagine you love Philip."

Helena tried to smile, appearing bored by the words that drew her to surrender to his embrace, an embrace upon which he did not insist.

"But it is you I really love?" she asked.

"One day I will hear you say, 'Tancred, it is you I love.' "

"This has gone far enough. Leave me at once!"

"Do not marry Philip. Wait for me. I will come to you at Antioch."

"I will not be there."

"You still think he will come?"

"Yes. Regardless of your conceit, I am in love with him."

Tancred's arms went around her. "I will make you forget him. You have only to ask for my utter devotion, and I will give it."

She grew confused and uncertain as heated emotions rampaged through her heart. "Since when does the invulnerable Tancred Redwan ask a woman for anything?"

"I am not so invulnerable. Not when it comes to the one woman I want."

"Did Kamila ask you to love her?"

"Yes."

"Did you—love her, I mean?"

"No . . ."

"I will never ask you to stay."

"Suppose I am determined to see that you do. If not now, one day. And, if it is the last thing I do, I will be with the Normans when they take the city. And I will kill the Seljuk who owns you and take you to myself. Is that in keeping with my reputation as a barbarian?"

Tancred's determination, and the desire he showed toward her, was both strangely thrilling and unnerving, and her voice trembled. "I think you have suddenly gone mad."

"Do you? Perhaps so. For the first time I am mad about a face I see at night when I close my eyes, a form so lovely she moves with the wind . . . and I will make her my bride, my friend, my lover, the mother of my children, the—"

"Stop," she whispered. "Please . . . go."

"Do you really want me to?"

"Yes . . . yes!"

"Never to see each other again?"

Her eyes turned to meet his and she weakened, though words would not come.

"I have no choice but to leave for a time, for Walter of Sicily searches for me. Before I can ever know peace, before I can ever offer you my devotion, there is something I must do. If I can prove my innocence I will be free. But before I go, there is something for which I have yearned from the moment I saw you. . . ."

I can't bear this . . . she thought.

"You would not begrudge a simpleminded barbarian the memory of the touch of your lips on mine, would you? Should I die in battle, I would have your memory to comfort me."

"No . . ."

"Your eyes say yes. Which shall I believe?"

Her breath paused. He bent toward her.

"Shall we say . . ." Tancred hesitated, "that it is a Byzantine generosity? You know in your heart I would die for you."

What manner of request is this? What manner of challenge robed in false humility?

"You once asked me the price for my sword, my devotion to you and your cause. I now make known my price. A simple kiss."

She could not move as they stood so near, his hands resting lightly on her arms.

Why did she not pull away and denounce the entire thing as foolishness? Because she had secretly dreamed of this—perhaps as much as he?

Helena told herself to refuse him, that it was a trap as carefully laid as any Byzantine plot. He could be dangerous; she knew that. Still . . . was she to be the first woman to own the feelings of the elusive Tancred Redwan? And what was a small kiss?

"Your request is minor payment, Sir Knight. After all, you did save me from the Rhinelanders."

"And became your dedicated physician."

"Yes . . ."

"Then . . . with your permission, madame."

Her eyes closed and she pursed her lips.

"I am humbled, fair damsel," he teased, "to think that Helena of the Nobility would permit me to take such a memory with me to war. Perhaps you also will remember?"

Helena's eyes opened at the bold suggestion, but then his lips touched hers and her heart raced loudly in her ears.

The brief exchange was over too quickly. She wondered, puzzled, and looked at him cautiously from beneath her lashes.

His eyes were amused.

Her arms moved around him, drawing his head to hers, and he swept her into his embrace.

Her head went back against his arm, and uncounted blissful moments blew away.

"What was it that Solomon said . . ." he whispered. "You are all fair, my love, there is no spot in thee. Your lips are sweeter than the nectar of the vines, your—"

She breathed, "Enough . . . you must go now. . . ."

"Come with me to Cordoba, or to the end of the world. If you wish to run away, then do so with me. One day I will claim ships, lands, a castle. I will build you a castle worthy of your beauty; you will have servants, jewels—anything you want."

The drugging words roamed through her mind and emotions until they did not seem absurd at all, but right. His eyes were blue . . . she thought. No, they were like cobalt . . . like a storm on the sea sweeping away everything in its path.

"You would not lie to me, Tancred?"

"Do you think I would do anything to hurt you?"

His tender voice and manner was anything but what she had expected.

"You did not betray my mother?"

"I would die to protect you, to guard your secret."

"And Philip? You believe he will not come to me? He lied?"

"He will not come. He met with Irene last night and gave her the information she requested."

"Where will you take me?"

His embrace tightened, and their lips met again. "Beloved Helena. To the Castle of Hohms, and we will find Nicholas. Marry me there?" he whispered.

She kissed him. "Yes . . ."

The trotting of horse hoofs echoed below the open terrace.

"Someone is coming," she murmured.

A familiar voice called out a command to a guard. Helena stiffened. *Philip!*

But . . . Tancred just told her that he would not come—

Her eyes darted to his. Tancred was wrong. And if he had deceived her about this, what about the betrayal of her mother? What about the promise of his devotion, his love? Who knew what he actually had in mind for her, or the castle? Perhaps Bardas had been right after all. Tancred was a spy for the Normans!

Under her deliberating gaze, he was unreadable. Tancred walked over and looked below, and she saw his expression harden. Helena rushed to his side and peered into the courtyard.

Below, Philip dismounted his fine horse, tossing the reins to a servant and giving orders.

Turning swiftly, Tancred started for the door, but she rushed ahead of him and whirled to confront him. For a moment they stared at each other.

She slapped him harshly. There! That would tell him what she thought of his deceit.

"I meant every word, Helena."

"Until you had what you wanted. Your clever words come smoothly enough and I was a fool to believe them—but then, you have had so much practice speaking them to any woman who will allow you. Including Irene last night! Why did I ever listen to you? I am only indignant with myself for having believed you. You lied about Philip, trying to make me think he would not come."

She rushed to the door and found it unlocked. Rufus must know that Philip had arrived. She flung it open.

"I will tell Philip how you insulted me. How you forced me into your arms."

"Was that what it was? I rather thought we were both willing victims."

"I shall always remember that you lied. That you accused Philip of betraying Adrianna. What did you expect to do with me at the castle? Sell me to Kalid for information on Mosul? Get out. I will tell Philip, and he will kill you."

His eyes glimmered with anger. "Or I will kill him."

"Touch him and I will despise you until I die."

He studied her for a moment and her expression must have revealed her fury. His jaw tensed, then he bowed obligingly and walked past her into the passageway. Before he could turn, she shut the heavy door as loudly as possible.

Tancred leaned there, his fury boiling over. He had gone to the emotional heights only to fall and splatter on the rocks below. Resentment burned like a branding iron on his heart.

He contemplated what he thought to be her willful, spoiled emotions running out of control. He had bared his heart and she had slapped his face. Yet she would trust Philip over and over again. She went running back to him like a bird with clipped wings.

He felt his heart harden. Very well. If that was the way she wished it, so be it.

Rufus strode quickly toward him from his lookout down the passageway. "Be swift, Redwan. Philip comes. Your horse awaits at the back gate. If he finds you here, he will order your arrest, and mine for allowing you to speak with her. Follow me."

Cold reason flooded back into Tancred's brain. Enough of dungeons and threats! Enough of this impossible woman!

He snatched up his helmet and satchel and took the back steps down to a door which Rufus threw open.

"May the wind bring you to freedom also," Tancred told him.

At the gate he found Apollo, the friendly whinny giving him some solace. Tancred mounted and looked back toward the palace fortress, considering. It was one thing to tell her good-bye, a far different matter when he found that her memory would ride with him wherever he went.

"Adieu, fairest of damsels," he said wistfully, and rode Apollo through the open gate.

CHAPTER 21
Bound by Enchantment

Philip entered the room and came to her swiftly, burying his lips in her hair. "I went mad when I realized what they might do to you."

He turned her face to his and kissed her. Helena felt cold and tired and blamed her fears, but at her lack of response, his dark gaze sharply arrested hers and held it until a tiny flush warmed her cheeks.

Her emotions gave her away, proving once again that Tancred held more control over her heart than she wished, or would admit to herself.

"I am afraid," she whispered. "What if Irene expects us to escape?"

His jaw tensed with determination. "She will not find out. Everything is arranged. We will not ride toward the castle. It is the first place she will send soldiers searching. We will return to Constantinople, then ride to the villa. Once I gather more loyal soldiers, we will leave for Hohms."

"We must find Nicholas first—how can I leave without him? You must send word to the Norman camp."

The alarm in his eyes set her on edge. "He is not with the princes. We will send word once we arrive at the castle. There is much to concern us and little time to see our plans to fruition. If we do not leave now it will be too late for us."

She held him, frightened, her mind in a whirl.

"I thought Constantine might have discovered our plans, but his mind is so consumed with finding Adrianna that he has blundered," he said. "His failure is our success. We have our moment."

Her head raised from his chest and she looked at him, searching his face. "Then you know?"

Impatience etched lines on his face. "Know? Know what? About Irene arresting you last night? Of course I know! And I came here as soon as I could. I would have taken you from the dungeon no matter what her evil plans. She told me everything."

"But I did not tell you about Constantine searching for my mother." She watched him, troubled. "How did you know? Irene says Constantine disappeared last night. She is furious and searches for him."

A flicker of impatience hardened his face. "For the sake of Zeus! Am I on trial? I am the minister of war! There is little going on I do not know about!"

"Yes, and you knew I searched for her," she accused faintly. "And I also told you that she had been with the Red Lion."

"Oh, that!" He waved an impatient hand. "I too have searched for her for your sake, knowing that you believed she was alive. But I never expected to discover her whereabouts. Constantine, unfortunately, came across the information. I am sorry, beloved. Yet I believe he cares for her. He will find her before Irene. There is nothing to fear. He is a determined man and he will not be bested by anyone, not even her."

"I am not as certain as you. And if you searched for her all these months, why could you not tell me? We could have worked together."

"There was too much risk to your safety. Your informer is dead."

"So Constantine told me," she said coldly. "Is he an assassin also?"

Philip's face went taut. "He is my father. Do not speak of him so flippantly."

"You knew all this about the Red Lion through your post as minister of war. Yet you allowed precious time to elapse. They may have brought her elsewhere."

"Can we not discuss all this later?"

"No, Philip. We cannot. I want to know now."

His dark eyes flickered impatiently. "Of what do you mean to accuse me? Do you think it was I who told Irene where to find Adrianna?"

The bluntness of his question shocked her back into emotional retreat. Helena felt ashamed and realized that for a short time she had allowed herself to seriously consider the possibility. She had attacked him, backing him into a corner as though he actually were guilty. She realized that Tancred's accusations against him had been successful in planting seeds of doubt.

She rushed to pluck the suspicions from her heart. "Oh, Philip! I am sorry. I do not accuse you of anything. How could I? I was just surprised that you knew. . . ." She turned away bewildered and walked toward the terrace.

"Everything is happening too quickly," she confessed. "I am worried, uncertain about . . . about how I feel, about so many things."

She looked at him sadly, and his face was pinched with anxiety. Her heart felt pity for him.

Dare she explain the reason for her outburst? Should she confess Tancred's accusations? But he did not know that she had seen Tancred and somehow she feared to admit it, remembering his embrace, his kiss. . . .

Her eyes closed and she turned away. "I am so confused."

Philip walked swiftly up behind her, taking hold of her shoulders and turning her to face him. "Helena, I have long known Constantine cared for Adrianna. I thought it a matter to upset you. I knew how you disliked him, how you believed he and Irene betrayed her and Nicholas. So I found no cause until now to mention it, not wanting to burden you with more worry."

Helena searched his eyes and saw his sincerity.

"There is hope, for Constantine will find her before Irene is able to carry out her evil schemes. And we too must flee. If we are caught, it will be the end of us, Helena."

"She would not harm you. You are her son. Constantine too adores you. It is me they want, and Adrianna. I suppose you know why."

His hands dropped from her and he shrugged impatiently, looking below into the courtyard. "The lands and castle, what else? Why else do families seek to destroy each other?"

"Not all families, Philip. Only the Lysanders."

He gave a scornful laugh. "If you think that, then you are indeed naive. Treachery and greed are everywhere. It is in every ruling family. The empress herself seeks an occasion against the emperor—for she has learned about Irene. And I, as a favorite of the emperor, am fought over by the strong wills of those who would use me to gain power."

He shook his dark head. "My independence is crumbling, Helena. I find myself more and more Irene's slave. What is more troubling, I find myself willing to be that pawn. If I do not escape now, I never will. I am my own worst enemy!"

He turned and gripped her tightly, his hands cold.

Fear also gripped her. "I believe in you," she hastened. "You care for more than power and glory. Do not doubt yourself. If you did not care, you would not have changed your mind about us at the guard castle. Tancred was wrong about you. He . . . he cannot be trusted. You are gallant and honorable."

Philip stared down at her, his face taut and pale, his hands squeezing her shoulders.

"Tancred? When did you see Tancred? What did he tell you about me?" He turned his head sharply and looked toward the chair.

Wondering about his sudden change in action, she followed his gaze. Her stomach tensed.

Tancred's cloak remained where he had carelessly tossed it. Philip walked over and snatched it up, staring. She saw the knuckles of his hands whiten. He looked at her angrily.

"This is Tancred's cloak. The one I sent him."

She drew in a breath. "Yes." Her voice was calm; why should it be otherwise? After all, what did she have to hide? She refused his marriage offer in the end. That was all Philip needed to know.

"He left it," she admitted. "He was in a hurry to escape when he heard you arrive in the courtyard."

A dark expression held his face. "He was *here*?"

"Yes. Irene arrested him. She sought information about my mother and he claims he refused to tell her, but I do not believe him."

Philip merely stared at her.

She went on to explain in a dull voice. "Mosul is no longer in Antioch. Irene bribed Tancred with secret information in return for my mother's whereabouts."

He stood in utter silence, watching her, his dark eyes flickering.

As the silence grew, she wondered at his response. At last he spoke, and when he did his voice had lost the emotion that had driven him until now.

"Anything else?" he asked quietly.

Should she tell him? She sank weakly into the chair.

"Yes. Tancred insisted it was you who betrayed my trust to Irene. He told me you would not come to me, that you would not leave Constantinople, that you would be, now and always, a slave to power and glory."

Philip's lean jaw tightened; his mouth thinned. Unexpectedly angry, he threw the cloak down.

"What else could we expect from the Norman wolves? It is my fault. It was a mistake to have ever hired him."

"What about Bohemond? What about Antioch? What of the plans to have Tancred contact the spy?"

"Unfortunately we have no choice but to go through with it. Without Tancred, Kalid will survive. Only in his downfall will we be free to return to the emperor with Antioch as a gift and the Castle of Hohms in our command. The fact that we escaped and married will be overlooked if we deliver Antioch to the emperor."

Philip drew her toward him. "No more can be said now, beloved. We will go to the villa."

"They will never find us. We will have each other, and a new life."

"Yes, we will be happy."

"Of course we will, Philip."

The momentary silence brought a tight smile to her mouth.

Something was dying between them and she feared to admit it. She grasped his arm. "Remember when we were children at the villa? How we used to sit at the window and watch Bardas training the horses? You said you would ride as emperor. And I, with eyes shining with pride, told you I would be in the hippodrome cheering for you?"

"Yes . . . I remember, Helena."

"Philip, I still want to cheer you on to be the man you can be, the man God wants you to be. You do not need the adulation of the people. How fickle their love is! Anger them, disappoint them, and they could dethrone you and cast you to the chariot wheels."

"Yes, I know, I know," he said, and looked toward the terrace.

"A man must respect himself and know that there are values he believes in that are worth living for, dying for if necessary. God, honor, courage to do right," said Helena, thinking that she had been influenced by Tancred's words.

"Do you espouse the calling of the western knight, Helena?" he asked quietly.

Her eyes rushed to his. "If you hint of Tancred—no. I espouse your own integrity."

A half-smile touched his face. He took hold of her arm. "The horses await. So does our destiny. Or as you would say, the guidance of God."

"He surely keeps the path of His worshipers. He will keep us," she said, and wondered that she felt so weary.

"Then we will ride forward boldly and with honor," he said with a wistful tone and a sad smile.

"With you, Philip, I am not afraid."

He drew her into his arms suddenly, fiercely, and held her as though she would vanish. "Your words make me want to be all your brightest dreams! We will make it; you will see."

It was late . . . the night very dark . . . yet they could see the horses where guards who were bribed to silence turned their backs. Bardas too was there, waiting and holding her reins.

Helena wore a hooded cloak and walked beside Philip beneath the shower of stars. Not a word was spoken, for everyone knew what to do.

They mounted the horses and rode out the gate where several men waited on horseback to bring them safely on the road toward Constantinople and then on to the family villa. Perhaps by then a message could be sent to Nicholas, who could meet them at the castle, for undoubtedly he would journey on with the crusaders toward Antioch and Jerusalem.

"We will not wait to reach the Castle of Hohms to marry," he said. "We have our opportunity, and nothing must come between us this time, beloved. Time slips through our fingers like stardust."

It was enough for the moment to be with him, to believe again, and they rode in silence.

There was no moon tonight and the stars throbbed with intensity in the black sky. She turned in the saddle to glance back. "I cannot believe we are really leaving," she whispered.

Before and behind them rode the armed guards.

"We must ride all night," he said. "I hope it will not be too much for you."

Helena tried to reach him with her hand. "If I am with you, I will not grow tired."

The road passed large fields and distant farmhouses, and farther behind, the dark mountains of Asia slept like a caravan of camels.

Staring ahead, Helena saw the darkness as a grim reminder of danger. They would be sought—Irene would see to that—they would be hounded until so far exiled from Byzantium that she and Philip would be given up for dead.

Her mind continued to dart in many directions. Her mother? Would Constantine find her? She resigned herself to that fact, for there was little she could do now.

And Tancred—had he made it safely back to the Norman camp? He would surely tell Nicholas that she had escaped with Philip.

Toward dawn, the sky began to lighten over the hills. Weary, cold, and hungry, she rode in silence, her muscles cramped, her mind dull with the need for sleep.

One of the soldiers ahead of them rode back to Philip. "There is an inn. There is room for all the horses and provender."

"We will stay the daylight hours, then ride on to the villa," Philip told her. She nodded, only too glad to have an opportunity for sleep.

Bardas helped Helena down from the horse. "I do not like this place," he whispered for her ears alone.

"It will do," she said, glancing about cautiously.

Travelers were leaving now, soldiers, merchants with camels and donkeys, and a peasant woman with an infant. For the first time Helena wondered what it would be like to be so poor, so helpless, and in this woman's situation with no real home to go to, always wondering if the man you were with could provide shelter and basic food. And the infant. So tiny, so defenseless against great empires, armies, and imperial lords.

Helena's eyes wandered to Philip. His inner strength was not confined to Byzantine life. He would fare well without the culture to which he was accustomed. He would survive, dauntless and content. He would not live in shattered dreams, growing bitter and defeated by change.

Strange that she should be concerned now, on the verge of her wedding. Why had it never plagued her before? She would not admit that Tancred had shaped her thinking of the image of true commitment between a man and woman.

Philip slipped his arm around her and led her toward the inn. "I am sorry to bring you here."

The situation appeared to bother him more than it did her. She smiled and shook her head, thinking of the Virgin Mary giving birth to the Son of God in a cave, having neither attendants, nor a soft bed for herself or the Christ Child—and who was she to murmur over sleeping by a warm hearth in the inn?

Tancred had claimed she was spoiled. Well, she would prove she was not. She could ride a horse and sleep in a common room that smelled of unwashed bodies; she could turn her back on the splendors of the Queen City, and unlike Lot's wife, she had no longing to look back upon the comfortable culture she left behind. Her heart did not cling to the fine things, nor did she take interest in the vulgar. It dawned on her then that Tancred would not know, nor would she see him again. It should not matter to her what he thought. A tiny qualm, like the ripples of a raindrop shattering the stillness of a pool, spread through her heart. It did matter. And would she ever forget him? *I dare not consider such a festering pang!* she thought, surprised and dismayed at her discovery.

When the innkeeper did not wait on them at once, Philip grew scornful.

"Such slothfulness is unheard of in Constantinople. There, my peasant friend, I would see your inn closed until you learned how to treat worthy company. Bring food and wine. Enough for us all."

"Philip, please, he is old and tired. Look at his body—it is bent with years of labor. You need patience."

"I suppose you are right. I must get used to my new position of unimportance."

"You are important to me."

She remembered little else after they had dined. The warmth from the fire on the hearth put her soundly to sleep.

Philip sat at the low wooden table staring into the fire, his mind dull with the wine he had drunk. His lips were tight, his artistic face moody.

"This should not be, Bardas. Look at us! Helena and I, both of us nobility, yet sleeping in a common inn on the floor, hunted like fowl for the table feast!"

He held out his cup. Bardas reluctantly filled it again. "When problems loom large, master, too much wine presents a mirage of escape that is not there. It is a yawning pit of ruin."

"Do you criticize me?"

"I would be a fool to speak ill of you. It is the blood of the barbarians we cannot trust."

Philip wondered about trust. If he had been left alone to find his own purpose in life, far from court, would he not have developed into a far different man? The passion for significance, the love of praise, and all that it seemed to offer could be his downfall.

But how could Helena give up Constantinople with so little regret? Did it mean nothing to her?

"You too must rest, Master Philip."

He watched Helena asleep by the hearth. "What dismal city can compare to the glories of the Queen City?" he murmured. "I tell you, Bardas, though we wander the world and cross the unknown seas, where is there a kingdom such as Byzantium?"

"They say Cordoba is also a queen. And ancient Rome—"

"Rome, bah! The ghosts of the Caesars chase each other among the ruins! Such is the destiny of all civilizations, Bardas. Only ideas survive, and they too perish, unless built on truth and justice—listen to me! One would think I was a philosopher! Bravo!" he mocked, raising his glass. "Tancred the Norman would be proud of me! He has learned honor; he has learned the thinking of the knights!" He pushed his cup toward Bardas. "Fill it. Let us drink to the crusaders! Does not our hope of freedom at the Castle of Hohms rest in them?"

"Surely you jest, master. Are they not dumb dogs ready and anxious for the kill?"

"Do you call Redwan a dead dog?"

Bardas laid a hand on his arm. "Do not speak his name so loudly."

"He would call you out for that. Nay, he would not—he would look upon your insult as the thoughts of a fool blinded by his own prejudice."

Philip smiled ruefully and set his cup down.

"The long road to the villa will soon beckon with the dawn, and you will need your strength."

Philip stood and Bardas assisted him to the blankets and covered him.

Minutes passed and still Bardas stooped beside him, looking down at Philip, a worried line between his eyes. Philip was wrong. The Norman would as likely remove his head with his scimitar as look at him again. *Nay, I did the right thing for Helena,* he thought. Then why did his conscience smite him like the old wound in his arm?

No matter. It is done.

When the sun rose the following day they continued their journey toward the villa. They traveled with a few armed men that Philip told her he would trust with his life, and a favored slave he had known from his childhood. Philip spoke of revolution and the need for a new emperor, becoming moody and intense.

"The house of Comnenus must fall. Was not your father Lysander a relative of the deposed Nicephorus?"

"Do not even whisper such treason, Philip."

"I would not whisper, but shout."

Helena glanced at him, then toward the band of soldiers, noting their immobile expressions.

"You are assured these can be trusted?"

"They would die for me. I have known them since I was a boy."

"Which means little. Did not Tancred's cousins journey across Europe to hunt him down?"

"They had cause."

Philip turned in his saddle to speak briefly to his chief guard. "We will rest ahead. There is a well."

The sun was hot and Helena reined her horse beneath a gnarled tree in the olive grove, and Philip drew up beside her.

In the distance a stone house belonging to Greek farmers stood solid in the sunlight. They watched several men working the field with oxen while a woman operated an oil press.

The silence between them lasted as the pleasant wind swept along the wide field, rippling the grasses. Tomorrow they would be at the villa, she thought. Aware that he watched her, she turned to him and smiled.

"You have thoughts you keep from me. You are not mourning the knight from Sicily, are you?" He permitted his lips to form a smile.

"On the eve of my wedding day?" she mocked, but her conscience was throbbing . . . she *had* been thinking of him . . . and soon, to think of him would be a sin against Philip. . . .

"Why would I think of him?" she asked lightly. "Have not I dreamed of you since a young girl?"

"You are not much more than that now, and a woman grows

and changes. The way of the Norman is more attractive to you than your Byzantine culture will admit. The knights who come are not the ignorant barbarians we envisioned them to be."

She played impatiently with the reins. "I am surprised you would admit it."

"The princes are ruthless, arrogant, yet they have a spirit about them that is fresh and invigorating. We Byzantines grow smug and lethargic. Resting upon the past of ancient Greece, we boast of bringing our civilization to the world. And we did. If Rome built roads and kept the peace," he said wryly, "we gave the world language, art, and the beauty of earthly man touched by the Greek gods. And now! Our vaunted marble statues are no longer a reflection of us, but of the knights from the West!"

She was surprised at his words. This was a Philip she had never heard before, and she found herself agreeing in part.

"Nicholas is the best of both worlds," she said.

Philip studied her. "He thinks well of Tancred."

Helena lifted her face toward the breeze, feeling it stir her dark hair. Tancred had told her the truth. Nicholas was his Christian godfather, and he had shared in his upbringing along with the scowling al-Kareem. He had told her of the long-standing debate between himself and Tancred's Moslem grandfather in Palermo, how they both had sought to win him, and how he had seen through their scheme and enjoyed playing one against the other.

"But it is Christ who has won his mind," Nicholas had told her. *"Now He must have his heart."* But she had doubted his character—what if she had been wrong?

Philip looked absently across the field to the farmhouse. From his expression she knew he had more to tell her and he was weighing the consequences. He dismounted and came around to her, lifting her down beside him.

Something troubled him and because it did, she was also disquieted. Leading their horses they walked slowly through the deep shadow of the olive grove. Ahead, the Greek peasant family would offer them refreshment. She glanced back and saw that the guards remained where they were, leaning back against the tree trunks and letting their horses rest from the long ride.

Emptiness nagged within. She had Philip at last, and they would eventually find their way to the Castle of Hohms, yet sadness restrained her anticipation. All was not as it should be, or perhaps, could be?

"Helena?" Philip's voice was questioning.

"What is it?"

He cupped her face and searched her eyes and she felt that they went to the bottom of her heart.

"I am not at peace," she whispered. "Hold me . . . I am afraid."

"Of our long journey to the castle?"

"It is more than the journey ahead. This is not the way I dreamed it would be, I—"

"Dreams," he said with an indulgent smile. "Wishing does not open the door to the future, beloved. The hours pass, the days, the years, and they leave lines on our faces and discontent in our hearts. Can it be you have loved me with a dream that vanished with the reality of the Norman knight?"

"Philip!" she gasped. "No! No!"

"Then?"

She could not answer him, for her own heart beat painfully with confusion. "I do not know. . . . I think I wanted the two of us together, living in quiet contentment of who we are, with what He has planned for us."

"He? God? *We* choose our destiny. The stars merge with our wills and thus history is written. We can break the force that unites us, but if we do there will be no peace until we find the ordained road again."

"Philip!" she whispered, pain making her voice quaver. "You are yet bound in spirit with the doctrine of Irene! I speak of the Sovereign Creator of the universe! He who flung the stars into space as lights for the night. There is no divinity in the planets; our very souls are in the watchful care of the heavenly Shepherd. . . . What was it Nicholas said? . . ." and she looked toward the hills, a longing on her face. " 'I will lift up my eyes to the hills, from where does my help come? My help comes from the Lord, maker of heaven and earth.'

"I am weary of those who plot and scheme. I have seen the evil done to my father, my mother, to Nicholas—to both of us, and others! For what cause? Castles and thrones built on the minds and souls of slaves! Of ruined lives! I want more. Something of eternal value." She looked at him and saw his impatience.

"You speak with the sheltered voice of the cloister. Life is meant to be lived, Helena! There is the taste of sweat, of blood, of tears, yes—but also the thrill of victory, the shouts of the throng—"

"A throng who quickly can turn into a fickle mob. Hosanna, they cry today! And tomorrow? Crucify him! If they did so to the Christ, how much more to mere princes, kings, and emperors?"

Philip drew her against him. "Helena! What is all this? With what speech has Nicholas filled your ears?"

"I do not mind the taste of salty tears, nor of blood if it must be. I would not hide from life, and I do not speak of a hermit's cave. I speak of the vanity of man's glory, of seeking praise from men rather than from God. Of denying Him for a throne, believing significance is found in any other calling except to know and serve Him as He bids us."

Philip stared down at her and their gaze held, with his searching and hers longing, yet their spirits did not merge as one.

Emotions spent, Helena leaned her head against his arm and closed her eyes.

When she opened them again he still held her quietly and there was no passion in their touch. It was the touch of friends.

She gazed at the small stone farmhouse, the quiet plodding of oxen, the unpretentious labor of the olive press. "I would give anything if we could be as they are now."

Philip held her from him, smiling. "Have you forgotten we are Byzantines and they peasants?"

Weariness crept through her body and mind. Her heart ceased its pounding and the fire of holy zeal was quenched.

"No," she said quietly, "I have not forgotten."

"Since you favor these poor peasants, let us taste of their wine and oil and see if it compares to even one evening in the imperial palace! Come—the priest will arrive this night to make us one."

Purple dusk faded into evening darkness and the stars became visible. An old wooden tower was built near the olive press, and Helena climbed the steps to the small room on a platform encircled with a handrail. Standing at the rail, she looked down and saw Philip, the warm wind moving his short circular cloak. She enjoyed the caress of the wind and thought, dazed, *Tonight I will actually marry Philip.*

In the silence the wood creaked as the gusts struck against it. Below, Philip left the guard and walked toward the flight of steps and began the climb, calling up to her with a smile. Helena walked to the landing to meet him, hands outstretched.

"The priest is here," he called cheerfully. "Are you afraid?"

"I have dreamed of this moment since we were children."

"Children grow up."

"My wedding eve, and look at me! I am dressed in riding tunic and cloak!"

"Excuses to change your mind?" He caught her hands and drew her toward him. "Beautiful Helena, how like the goddess you are."

"Once," she said thoughtfully, softly, "I believed we would walk the marble path of the imperial garden, stepping on rose petals and hearing the choir chant our blessing."

His mouth was rueful. "And now you will marry in the kitchen of a peasant with the smell of garlic and olive oil."

The warm, peaceful night hovered about them while their minds mused the path they were set upon—but their eyes were startled by a rush of flaming torches moving swiftly toward the tower from the direction of the field behind them.

Philip straightened abruptly and scowled.

A cry of alarm split the night. Below in the yard the guard shouted to their small troop.

Bardas came running from the house, and Philip leaned over the rail and called, "The horses, quick!"

Voices on the wind were overrun by the surging thunder of oncoming horses galloping toward them across the field.

"Who are they?" cried Helena as the once-peaceful darkness turned into terror.

"We've been betrayed," he gritted.

Dazed, she watched, eyes wide, as more flames were blazing and leaping through the dry grass and spreading on the escalating wind.

Philip grabbed her and she rushed with him toward the steep steps, but the attackers were swift and drove their lean horses forward at a gallop to encircle the tower. Other warriors holding torches galloped past the house.

Helena heard screams from inside as fiery torches were hurled through windows. Fire spread, quickly catching up all that was not stone with its searing tongue.

"We are trapped," breathed Philip, gripping her arm as the horsemen tightened their circle about the tower.

As the firelight illuminated the riders, Helena's breath caught in her dry throat. She stared at the strange turbanlike helmets, the small round shields, the short bows and quivers of arrows, the deadly curved scimitars slung over their shoulders or carried within easy grasp on their horses.

The leader rode forward on a prized white mare, sitting proud and straight, his lean bronzed face all too familiar. Helena noted the insolent features so well defined beneath the gilded turban. His short, pointed dark beard and mustache were vainly groomed, and he wore a stunning tunic of red-and-gold silk over his military garb.

"Prince Kalid," she said, her breath leaving her, unable to tear her eyes away from him to look at Philip. But how! Yet there was no mistaking the young prince she had seen once before, riding in the emperor's train on the night she had hidden in Philip's chambers. She recognized that haughty face, that same look of ruthless intelligence in the black eyes that looked up at them with satisfaction.

"You have betrayed me, Byzantine!"

Philip pushed Helena back against the wooden wall and drew his sword.

"You have my word as prince of Antioch that I will not kill you!" called Kalid.

"On what condition, that you order your followers to do it?" scorned Philip.

The bright flames and heat were becoming intense and Helena

pressed backward against the wall. *Please, God, help us!*

The nervous prance of the horses moved in closer about the tower, and the curved steel scimitars glinted in the firelight like mocking smiles.

"Your life for the woman promised me by your emperor! Send her down and you will live."

Helena's heart thudded. She looked from Kalid to Philip, who stood angry and grave, gripping his sword.

Kalid turned on his saddle and gestured to his horsemen. There was a stir, and a moment later two of his men dragged forward the priest who had come to marry them, the dust swirling about them. His black robe was torn and his hands cruelly bound. One of the Turks held a dagger point at his throat.

"You intended to betray me, to marry her this night," called Kalid. "This dog who kneels and kisses the idol of the Queen of Heaven will die here and now unless you surrender!"

Helena gasped and rushed to the rail. "Harm him and I shall hate you till you die, Kalid!"

He lifted his proud head and looked at her, his bold dark eyes narrowing as they ran over her, her hair blowing in the wind.

"Let the worshiper of a woman go!"

The two warriors let him fall into the dust.

Kalid looked up at Philip, who stood pale and beaten, his face damp with sweat.

"Why sacrifice your favor with the emperor? Your position as minister of war remains secure. The future is yours. Send her down to me and all this will be forgotten."

Philip stood rigid. "If you take Helena, you must take me first."

Helena whirled to stare at Philip.

"Then I will send up man after man, until one severs your infidel head!"

Kalid turned to the ring of soldiers. "Who will go up first? In the name of Allah, who will take the head of this infidel and bring me the woman?"

Philip grabbed Helena and pushed her through the opening of the small tower.

She held him, her wide eyes imploring his. "No, Philip, this is not necessary. They will kill you and still take me away—"

She stopped, hearing soldiers rushing up the steps behind them. Philip whirled, but with a small cry, Helena darted past him.

Philip lurched after her. "Helena!"

She stumbled to the steps. "Wait! Kalid! Tell them to stop!"

It was Kalid on the steps, scimitar in hand, his eyes fierce and dark as they collided with hers.

She stood breathing heavily, trembling.

"Do not kill him. There is no need. I . . . I will go with you peaceably."

He took her in from head to toe, then shouted for the soldiers to cease.

Helena brushed past him, holding her head high.

The light from the burning house illuminated the yard, and she gazed at the ring of Seljuk Turks on horseback. They stared back impassively.

Kalid went past her to his mare and mounted. He rode his horse forward, his cloak glinting in the fire like blood red rubies until he came up near to where she stood. He removed his foot from the stirrup and held out a hand, his eyes holding hers evenly.

Her gaze faltered and she stepped into the stirrup and stiffened as his arm slid around her waist, drawing her to the saddle in front of him.

Helena clenched her teeth and blinked back the sudden rush of tears. *God, why? Why this! Why me?*

Bardas pushed his way past the horses and struck the guard below Kalid's mare with a blow that sent him to the ground.

"No, Bardas!" she cried, fearing for his life.

A warrior galloped up and kicked Bardas viciously in the face, and he fell backward. The sickening sound brought a cry to her throat as Kalid reared back his mare and they charged forward toward the road. A yelping cry followed from his warriors and they followed with dust flying behind them.

The mare raced on, leaping the low wall, the wind coming cool against Helena's face. It was madness, and trees rushed by like shadowed blurs, the darkened earth flying beneath the mare's feet. The grip about her mending ribs kept her from breathing, and she feared she would faint. Onward they raced into the darkness, away from the heat of the searing flames, away from the road to the villa and toward the distant horizon of the Moslem East, to Antioch.

CHAPTER 22
Swords and Scimitars

The last Byzantine guard tower was left behind and a whole continent lay before the crusaders, as rich in treasure as it was in soil. They had departed Nicaea in late June and by July they were nearing Dorylaeum.

It disturbed Tancred that the various armies did not travel as a unit, especially now as they journeyed deeper into Moslem-held territory. Bohemond and his Normans had journeyed ahead of Godfrey's and Raymond's armies, and due to a poor liaison between the princes they were separated by a half day's journey. Tancred was ever aware that the Red Lion, having learned of the fall of Nicaea, would have had time to gather a great force to confront the barbarians from the West.

Around them stretched red farmland, rolling hills with an abandoned gutted palace, and a half-deserted village on the skyline among gray willows and green oaks.

Mounted men of arms trotted by with a jangle of rein chains and the clink of armor—a gust of laughter drowned in the thudding hoofs. Dust swirled over the bands plodding on foot, the black robes of the priests, jackmen, and sturdy pilgrims. Women clustered together on mules.

Ox carts crawled by, creaking under loads of grain from Byzantium topped with men sprawled out, sleeping in the July heat. For miles through the veil of dust, spear tips flashed in the sunlight, and iron heads rose and sank, like the waves of a dark river rushing on steadily. Faces damp with summer sweat moved by. Somewhere bagpipes wailed and a voice intoned a common chant, made up on the road. Tancred had heard them often enough. They made up new verses every day.

He watched the human tide flow past him before he picked up his reins and turned Apollo toward the head of the column. He had to ride for an hour with Nicholas through the fields before they reached Bohemond and his advance knights with their esquires and foot soldiers.

"We have seen a Moslem cavalry during the day," Erich had reported to them.

"When?" asked Nicholas gravely.

"Peveral, Normandy's standard-bearer, saw them when they crossed a range of low hills."

Tancred gazed across the long plain but saw nothing except a road leading down to a small river. "A good place to make camp for the night," he said to Nicholas. Bohemond must have made similar plans, for the advance column turned off toward the road for the night, avoiding the flat country.

He and Nicholas rode with Erich toward the river. Here the hills formed in a rough semicircle behind them, extending out on either side. An ancient Roman ruin crowned a rocky pinnacle in the plain, and Tancred and Nicholas rode to search it and found it deserted.

Tancred dismounted and walked to the edge of the slope to look about the horizon but saw no sign of the Turks. Looking down toward the river he saw that the young esquires and some peasants and priests were already fishing in the river, hoping for a good supper.

He joined the armed patrols that circled the camp at night and reported to Bohemond that all was quiet on the plain.

"I do not like this," said Nicholas. "Nothing has been heard from the main army with Godfrey and Raymond."

Tancred listened to the river running over the rocks. Above, the stars shone on in the blackness, undisturbed by the events of time.

He awoke before daybreak and found that Nicholas was already up and preparing to lead the morning prayers. Tancred joined him and the Norman leaders at the river. They knelt to one knee and bowed their heads as Nicholas sought the blessing and protection of Christ. Soon the camp was stirring, gathering water, saddling horses, and yoking the beasts to the carts and wagons.

As Tancred cinched the saddle on Apollo and prepared to mount, the young and daring Norman, Pain Peveral, galloped in with several other chief knights.

"My liege, detachments of Turks are advancing toward camp out of the mists."

Tancred looked at Nicholas. "The Red Lion. Who else could it be?"

Soon the news was passed throughout the camp to the multitude. Some of the horsemen, remembering the battle at Nicaea and their victory, were eager to catch sight of the infidels. Others were thronging toward their feudal masters.

Tancred watched, disturbed, as he saw an almost holiday spirit permeate those footmen and knights who had not yet contested the Seljuks. He saw Frenchmen rushing off without their mail, fearing the infidels would run away before they could reach them.

Women crowded to the tops of hillocks, staring up the valley for a clear view. Others climbed on the carts and wagons.

Where are Godfrey and Raymond? wondered Tancred uneasily.

"We may be fifty thousand strong," said Tancred to Nicholas and Erich, "but they are not knights, nor even soldiers. They know no discipline except the kindly restraint of priests and the will of their feudal barons."

Nicholas looked about, troubled as well. "We ought to send a rider to locate Godfrey and Raymond."

Tancred watched as the commoners grouped themselves by the knight who back in Western Europe had been their liege, and the mounted knights sought the standard of their baron, to whom they owed military service. The barons joined one of the leaders and they all rode toward the front of the camp.

"Will Bohemond take command of these, besides his own Normans?" wondered Tancred more to himself than to Nicholas.

"He will find it his duty to protect the commoners. He comes now."

Tancred saw the stalwart warrior already astride his charger riding into the somewhat confused mass of commoners and armed peasants.

"Let all mounted men pass to the front. They will ride with the Norman knights," he repeated again and again as he passed through the camp. "Let all men on foot who are armed follow after. The rest of you set up our camp defense here, at this spot."

Bohemond's own army had already followed, knowing what to do. They quickly aided the mass of commoners to pull wagons into place, unyoke cattle, and lift the heavy tents on poles.

"All men who are unarmed, aged, or ill, with the women and children, take refuge in the back. Archers, and jackmen with pikes and axes, go to the tents to guard them."

The priests, monks, and friars were already swiftly to prayer, bringing out their relics and crosses to evoke the protection and aid of Christ and the angels, and especially Saint Michael and Saint George, who were expected to lead the mounted knights into battle.

Tancred swiftly aided the women and children toward the tents, unloading pack saddles from the animals in the baggage train. Horns were blaring the warning of the approaching Moslem army. Horses neighed, but the Great Horses, bred for war and picking up the mood of their masters, pawed the dust, nostrils flaring and eyes rolling toward the brightening sky. The day would be hot; the sun was already beginning to beat down on the armor of the knights.

Tancred now rode toward the front where Bohemond and the main army of knights waited. The night before, Bohemond had pitched camp beside a wide marsh. The river was shallow, no more than a stream in the summer, and the Seljuk horsemen would have no trouble crossing it, but the marsh would shelter one flank of the encampment, while the rest waited near the foothills.

In front of the tents the men of arms were standing by their horses or forming ranks. Others knelt in the grass to pray quietly, leaning upon their lances, awaiting the moment when the sound would come for the battle to begin.

Tancred joined the section of knights with the standard-bearer Pain Peveral, and a cousin of Bohemond—another young Norman like himself with the same name of "Tancred."

Nicholas too joined them and rode along the front line, reading from his Greek New Testament, translating into northern French, for almost all of the crusaders spoke the language.

"They come," said Tancred.

Across the plain in the early morning light the Norman knights from Sicily and southern Italy and the French knights from Normandy looked with growing but silent dismay on the emerging sight. Never in their wildest imaginations had they expected this.

How many armed Seljuk Turks and mercenary soldiers rode toward them? *A hundred thousand?* wondered Tancred. *No, three hundred thousand or more!*

A breath sounded from the Norman knights. "God aid us."

Astride his horse, Erich leaned toward Tancred. "We are in trouble."

"The Red Lion, no doubt," said Tancred. "And he has gathered Persians, Arabs, and Africans to join his Seljuk warriors."

Nicholas seemed not to notice as he rode back and forth along the first line of knights who would ride forth to meet them, reading the words of Moses to Israel before they entered the battle:

" 'Arise, O God! Let your enemies be scattered!' "

Across the plain, brightly clothed horsemen moved toward them at a trot—lean, tough Moslems with tanned faces, wearing pointed helmets or white turbans. They rode small horses that he knew were swift and maneuverable, their saddles covered with red cloth. Instead of lances or the Norman long blade, they carried ready-strung bows and smaller round shields. Tancred saw their flashing scimitars in the sunlight.

The green banners of the Moslems fluttered—and then he saw what he had been searching for: the standard of Kilij Arslan—the Red Lion.

They neared.

Bohemond, imperious and calm, yet as deadly as a cornered wolf, rode toward his chief knights.

"Seigneurs and knights of Christ—the battle is at hand on

every side and we are greatly outnumbered, with forty thousand noncombatants to protect. Our honor and courage will be tested by the flame of Islam! Go forward!"

They moved in unison around the young Norman standard-bearer Pain Peveral with the crimson gonfanon of Prince Bohemond fluttering in the wind.

Tancred touched his helmet to tighten his chin strap and kneed Apollo forward. Nicholas, also in chain mesh, the red cross clearly showing on his black tunic, rode beside him, armed with sword, lance, and mace.

"What did you do with your Scriptures?" asked Tancred.

Nicholas gave a wolfish smile and patted his heart. "Fear not, and behave yourself wisely—no great feats this day, understood?"

Tancred smiled and lowered his visor.

Suddenly, out of the Moslem horde came the beating of drums and the crash of cymbals.

The knights rode to meet them, the long lances came down, and they shouted as one man while the heavy chargers swept forward: "Deus vult!"

The clamor of the Moslems swelled louder as if to drown out the name of the Christian God. "Allah! Allah! Allah! There is no god but Allah!"

Tancred heard the arrows whipping. His heart sank as the Great Horses began to plunge into the dirt, neighing, wounded. The arrows crashed into the loose-linked armor of their hauberks. Knights toppled to the dust. Far outnumbered, the best were going down. The myriad of Moslems surged forward like a tidal wave ready to sweep away all in their path. The Seljuks' skilled use of the bow was accurate and deadly. Gritting with dismay, Tancred saw the Christian knights being scattered.

"Erich," he gritted, and saw his friend plummeted with arrows yet still fighting with his long sword. Tancred rode furiously to his aid, smashing his blade through a Turk, cutting through the thin armor and toppling him, yet for every Moslem who fell, ten more took his place. They were surrounded. A scimitar struck Erich and in a flash, Tancred saw the blood-soaked knight slipping from his wounded horse into the dust under a hundred pounding hoofs.

"Erich—!"

Nicholas was somewhere beside him, his heavy ax tearing through the armor of the Turks. Wheeling and striking back, Tancred's blade struck again and again.

The Moslems closed in on every side, and the Norman and French swords met them with the ringing clash of steel, but the Seljuks were at their best this hour, attacking as Tancred had known they would, driving, shifting, withdrawing, swiftly returning in a weaving dance, sending a barrage of arrows with every new wave.

The wounded Normans yet astride their chargers were easy targets for the Seljuks, who used hand-hooks to pull the knights down from their saddles to be trampled. Rearing horses and shouting men added to the madness.

The first wave of knights was forced to retreat and the Moslems mocked them with shouts: "There is no god but Allah!"

Bleeding and somber, the Normans rode back to the main line of crusaders, and a second force of knights advanced, shouting, "O Christ our Defender! Thy Name is to be honored above all false gods!"

The strident clashing of cymbals and drums from the Seljuks sounded, and a new wave of Moslems swept in, again outnumbering Bohemond's choice warriors.

Nicholas clenched his fist. "Erich is dead. And the best of our knights are no match for three hundred thousand! Where are Godfrey and Raymond!"

"A rider has been dispatched!" shouted Pain Peveral. "Hold fast, seigneurs! We cannot, we will not, surrender to the infidel!"

Bohemond, looking tense and deadly, rode boldly among them, displaying his bare head. "Fight like the knights you are! Will you allow dogs to defeat you? You who are Normans! Sons of William the Conqueror! You are worth twenty infidels! Go forward! Christ aid thee!"

Sudden singing from the priests and knights swelled louder and louder and the Great Horses shook their sweating manes. The knights gritted with determination and raised their gauntlets. "There is no God but the Living God! In the name of Saint Michael the Archangel, the warrior angel—go forward and conquer!"

Tancred interceded silently in prayer, his jaw set, but Nicholas was in great dismay. "Merciful Father of our Lord and Savior Jesus Christ, when zeal deceives us, when our willfulness is our true enemy, have mercy! These knights sincerely love you, though they are oft misguided and wrongly zealous! They battle for what they believe is your honor among enemies, your glory among the idols! Spare their lives this dark hour! Send us help from your sanctuary on high."

"Monsieur priest, monsieur priest, it is you! It is you," cried a woman's voice, and Tancred turned in his saddle to the woman who came running toward him, carrying a waterskin.

"Modestine?"

Her eyes shone and she smiled, grabbing hold of his booted leg and handing him the water. "Thanks be to God you are here and safe. Our God has brought us together again!"

Tancred smiled for the first time and grasped the hand she thrust boldly toward his.

Modestine took it and held it to her cheek, despite the gauntlet he wore. "God aid thee this day," she said.

"Yes, and how good to see you alive," he said with sincerity. "I thought you and Niles were killed with the peasant crusade under the Hermit."

Her smile faded. "Niles is dead. He died saving me. And I was brought as a slave to Nicaea. My baby also died, monsieur priest," and her eyes flooded with tears as she remembered. "They violated me, monsieur! And my baby, not yet born, died."

He squeezed her hand and, bringing it toward him, saw that it was scarred and callused. He kissed her palm.

"My pity, Modestine. Take heart; your baby and Niles are safe with our Savior. You have lost them to this life, but not in eternity."

"This life," she choked. Her eyes shut tightly and her face contorted with sorrow and depression. "Oh, monsieur, this life is wretched. I wish to die also."

"You must live, Modestine. God has spared your life for a purpose. You are important to Him, to His cause."

She touched her snarled hair and looked up at him, dazed. "Me? Me, monsieur! Important? To the Seigneur Christ?"

"Yes, *you*." And Tancred dismounted, taking both her arms and giving her a friendly hug.

She flushed with joy. "You mean—"

He caught himself swiftly and frowned at her. "I said important to *Him*. To me, you are also important as a friend, but I love another. Understood?"

Her eyes faltered. "Yes, monsieur. . . ." She looked at him quickly, now ready to accept her fate, and she smiled sadly. "It is best, monsieur priest, for I am not good enough."

His heart was thudding from more than battle as he searched her eyes, a hope flaring to life in his mind. "You are good enough. It is only that my love for another is too great for me to ever be fair to you."

She looked about. "She is with you?"

"No," he said flatly. "She is with another. The one she loves."

Modestine looked at him—scanning him boldly, then rolled her eyes toward the sky. "Monsieur, the lady, she must be weak of eyes or mind. How could she want another other than you?"

Tancred smiled and lifted her chin. "Yes, I wonder. How could she?" He grew serious. "You were brought to Nicaea? Did you see other slaves? Other women, like yourself? Women who were not Turkish in blood?"

She pursed her lips, bored. "Many, monsieur. Yes, many. Some very lovely, but they were the blessed ones. They were not with us—they were kept in a different place as wives of important Turkish officials."

His hands tightened on her shoulders. "Did you ever see these women?"

"Many times. Unlike the Turkish wives of the sultan, they did not live inside the Red Lion's palace but in a royal tent. Oh, monsieur," she sighed, throwing up her hands toward the heavens, "it was very beautiful with rugs and vessels and silk. And they all had silk dresses, and gold bracelets, and earrings, and nose rings, and—"

He laid a finger against her lips. "You even know the Seljuk name of Kilij Arslan. Did you ever see a woman of Byzantine nobility, a woman who called herself Adrianna?"

Again she pursed her lips as though the matter were obvious. "Oh yes, monsieur. Many times, I saw that one."

He stared at her, tensing. The unexpected answer left him speechless.

"She was one of the fairest," she said.

"You knew her?" he breathed.

"Oh yes. But she has another name. She is called Safia. She has white skin, with dark brown hair with all manner of jewels. She was the love of his nephew."

His hands gripped her as though afraid he was dreaming and she would vaporize. "Adrianna is called Safia, and she is the wife of the Red Lion's nephew?"

"His name is Sinan."

Sinan. . . . Tancred tried to place that name in his memory but did not know him.

"She is with him now."

He started, looking at her as though he had not clearly heard. "She is with him? Where?"

"In the army of the Red Lion, monsieur—the army you fight. She went with him when they left weeks ago. They heard the barbarian army of the West was coming and so they rode to Aleppo to meet his uncle, the Red Lion."

He was silent. "She went with him gladly?"

She shrugged. "It would not matter. He would not leave without her. She is with child now."

Tancred's breath ceased. His hands left her shoulders and he stared down at her. "You are certain, Modestine?"

She smiled sadly and ran her hands over her stomach as though remembering her baby. "Yes . . . she was newly with child."

Tancred rubbed his chin and glanced off toward the cypress trees, musing. The situation between Helena and her mother, as well as Constantine, was becoming more complex.

He asked simply, "As a woman, Modestine, you would know— did she seem to love Sinan?"

She pursed her lips and looked toward the cypress trees thoughtfully as he had done. "For the life of me, monsieur, I could not say. She is a very good woman. A saint. She prayed much and she was always kind to the other women. Safia was liked by all, even those who should have been her enemies. Love Sinan?" She shook her tangled locks. "Only God knows for sure, monsieur."

"Yes, only God knows."

"I will bring you bread, monsieur." She ran toward the tents and Tancred leaned against Apollo, drinking from the waterskin and musing. He became aware again of the noise of battle, of death. He drank long and rested and wondered. He would have much to tell Nicholas if they survived this battle. And what would he tell Helena?

He remembered with a dart of despair that he would not see her again. By now she would be the bride of Philip.

Tancred left the water and mounted. Giving a pat to Apollo's sweating neck, he encouraged with a whisper, "Bohemond needs every warrior, Apollo. We must fight on. Summon your strength and show yourself equal to any charger!"

Apollo pranced forward, shaking his black mane.

Bohemond rode straight into the masses, his great sword swinging about his golden head, and Tancred followed. Richard of the Principate charged with his men. Robert, Count of Paris, followed with his men and fell wounded, dying among forty French knights on the field. Then Pain Peveral carried forward the standard of Normandy.

The Moslems drew back, then closed in about them. The fighting spread over the plain. With dismay, the western knights, fighting for their lives, saw fresh armies of the enemy coming from the foothills on either flank. Bohemond swiftly sent a courier racing to find the main body of the western army under Count Raymond and Duke Godfrey. "If you wish to take part in this day's battle, ride strongly!"

By noon the battle was worsening. The other princes had not come to aid the Normans.

Moslem horsemen coming by way of the swamps had surged into the civilian camp. Modestine cringed with the other women and children on the wooden platform, terrified, watching as the Seljuks cleared a path through the tents, riding down archers and foot soldiers guarding the defenseless. Modestine watched in horror, hearing the hysterical screams of children and women as the warriors plundered the tents and violated the women, passing their swords through their bodies as they left.

"Oh, monsieur priest," she wept, "where are you?"

Had not the Norman Ironmen driven away the Moslems at Nicaea? Until now nothing had been able to stand against the dread charge of the Normans on their Great Horses. But like a plague of locusts the enemy had flooded the plain and now the camp. Modestine watched, dazed, reliving the horrors of the peasant massacre in Anatolia. As a civilian fell, she saw not the stranger but Niles dying. As a baby screamed, abandoned by the death of its mother, she imagined her own baby lying uncared for in the dust. She watched the Seljuks rushing upon a group of clerics and monks and saw them killed.

Then she turned to see a warrior rushing toward her. No scream would sound from her throat—it died in her heart as the sword pushed through her. She fell. . . .

"Monsieur priest . . ." Her lips moved and then were still.

Bohemond drew back to camp but refused to break and run. With him were the best of the young knights of chivalry who still charged the Moslems on wearied horses. By the standard of Normandy, Nicholas held his position, a strong figure in armor and cleric cloak, holding the symbol of the cross. "Hold fast!" Nicholas shouted to the knights. "Though you cannot drive them back, nor withstand their numbers, God is able!"

The elite held on, dividing into struggling groups, and formed again. They held out, as the sun reached its zenith and the hours slipped by, their long swords and battle maces smashing bones and slashing heads from bodies.

Sinan read the sober expression on the sun-darkened face of Sultan Kilij Arslan, the Red Lion. The dark almond eyes flickered like a heated pool, and the hawklike nose seemed to smell death on the July air. The green banners of Islam fluttered about them as they looked down upon the plain where the battle continued.

Sinan, a young nephew of Arslan, recently come from Cairo, sat proudly on his mare, watching.

"These Ironmen from the West are truly warriors," said the Red Lion.

Sinan reluctantly agreed. It was not a simple thing to do so. He was proud of his own warrior race, who had descended from the nomads of Central Asia. He and his race, newly converted to Islam, rugged and thus far invincible, were noted for courage, and they respected the same tenacity in other races. Differing from the Arabs and Persians, the Seljuk Turks considered themselves superior to the people they conquered, and they held power through a line of illustrious sultans—Toghrul, Alp Arslan, and Malik Shah. Before the crusaders had arrived, Malik Shah had died, and the resulting civil war occupied the various Seljuk sultans from Jerusalem to the Caspian.

Kilij Arslan was a minor prince in their great empire, but few of the crusaders knew it, though Sinan did. His own father was a mightier ruler in Cairo, and Sinan himself was an emir. He wondered what his father and his uncles would say when he returned with his foreign wife, a Byzantine of splendid beauty named Adrianna. What would the mighty Seljuk princes say when he produced his firstborn son?

For the child she bears must be a son, he found himself thinking. *If the infant is a female* . . . But he could not be troubled by such disappointing thoughts now.

He followed his uncle's gaze down onto the blood-soaked plain.

"For the first time," said the Red Lion, "we have met a people like our own. A people who are warriors and who wish to conquer new lands. These men are as steadfast as we. If they would become Moslems we could live in peace with them and permit them to settle here."

The handsome Sinan scoffed, smoothing his black mustache into his short, well-groomed Moslem beard. His white turban was wound proudly about his head and showed crimson at the top, glinting here and there with rubies and pearls.

"The Christian will never bow the knee to Allah," said Sinan, studying his uncle. "There is one hope for their defeat; the reason for which I first came from Cairo to Antioch to meet with you and Prince Kalid." And now Sinan's eyes grew impatient. "All the sultans must unite to destroy these Ironmen before they take Jerusalem. Instead we feud among ourselves."

But his uncle seemed to pay him no heed. "Six hours of combat and they fought on, refusing to yield or run. Against my will I must commend them."

Sinan glanced about the hills, becoming aware of a new threat, and he said sharply, "You may yet need to fight till the sun sets," he gestured. "The standards of more Ironmen."

The Red Lion followed his nephew's gaze toward the foothills. He stood in his stirrups for a better view.

Sinan knew it was the main army of the West under the other lords, for a scout had already reported to him. He had prayed mightily that this would not happen.

"They arrive in good formation," his uncle told him.

Sinan saw the armies of Duke Godfrey, Robert of Flanders, and Prince Hugh, brother of the king of France, riding toward the left flank of the Red Lion's army. And toward their rear, Sinan could see Bishop Adehemar and Count Raymond, leading their army down toward the plain. At the same time, the Normans under Bohemond formed a new line and attacked.

Sinan looked at the Red Lion and read the grudging respect, but also the alarm that flickered in the weathered face. Sinan believed he knew what his uncle was thinking. They were now the outnumbered ones, and they might easily be trapped between two armies if they stayed on to fight. Sinan thought not of the Ironmen, but of his wife in one of the princely tents back in the camp of the sultan. He had not wished to bring Adrianna from Nicaea, but he would not permit her to join the caiques carrying the other women to Constantinople—not when he believed the child she carried would be a son. Anything might happen once she returned to Constantinople, and how would he retrieve his newborn prince? He did not trust the emperor, though Alexius Comnenus often corresponded to his uncle. He had even asked the Red Lion to turn now against the crusaders.

Sinan wondered what the Ironmen would do if they knew the

emperor expected to hire the Red Lion to turn against the very warriors the emperor called his "vassals from the West."

Sinan turned in his saddle, his round shield glinting in the sunlight. He was equipped with bow and scimitar and prided himself to be a warrior of distinction—even as his newborn son would be one day. Sinan gestured to the bodyguard serving his uncle, and the Moor named Mosul rode up.

Mosul's dark eyes were unflinching, and a faint, curling smile was on his lips. "You beckon me, Excellency?"

Sinan did not know why, but there was something in the behavior of Mosul that disturbed him. Prince Kalid of Antioch had sent Mosul to serve the Red Lion, boasting Mosul to be a trusted man of excellent skills with the sword, but sought after by family enemies from the Moorish section of Sicily.

Sinan did not like Mosul, though the warrior had done nothing to warrant his mistrust. It was the look of superiority that Sinan did not like. The Moor was ambitious. Sinan had seen that hungry look before in others.

"The sultan gives orders to withdraw," said Sinan. "Bring word to al-Din at once. Then break for camp. Where is Prince Kalid?"

Was it a look of scorn or merely concern that briefly passed like a shadow across Mosul's face?

"At the royal tent, Excellency. Shall I tell him you wish to see him before the battle?"

"Yes, make haste."

Mosul turned his Arabian horse, Alzira, to ride to the warlord who commanded the army of the sultan.

Tancred watched the orderly retreat of the Turks turn into an unexpected and seemingly mindless flight—back in the direction of the camp of the Red Lion. He turned the reins of Apollo and galloped the distance between himself and Nicholas.

The horse lifted its head and snorted as Tancred pulled rein, facing the rugged and sober face of Nicholas. "The battle is not yet over. We have opportunity to overtake the Red Lion at his camp. Are you strong for the battle?"

Nicholas's dark eyes flickered as he appeared to wonder at his words. "Have you not tasted enough blood and sweat for one day?"

Tancred gestured his head, his blue-gray eyes meeting the friendly challenge. "Does not your heart beat even as Helena's for the freedom of Adrianna?"

Nicholas's head lifted with the strength of a wild goat. "Speak plainly, my son."

Tancred smiled confidently and looked toward the hills. Swiftly he told him of Modestine's words concerning Adrianna. "There is a chance," said Tancred. "But she is with child. It will not prove easy."

Nicholas let out a laugh, looking victoriously toward heaven. He raised the standard of the Church. "Praise be to God! Then we too may slay a lion on a snowy day!" he said, referring to the famous deed of one of David's mighty men. "Onward!"

Duke Godfrey, Robert of Flanders, and Hugh the Great pressed ahead in pursuit of the scattering Seljuk Turks until the raw hot pink of the summer sunset splashed the skyline over the hills. Tancred and Nicholas rode with them.

By sunset they came upon the camp of the Red Lion sprawled in a plain between the flanking hills of Asia Minor.

"Ah," breathed Nicholas. "Like Gideon, we look upon the camp of the Midianites spread out before us like locusts covering the land. And like Gideon we shall plunder their camp and set our Christian captives free."

"God wills it!" shouted Duke Godfrey, his red-gold hair flying in the wind as his Great Horse thundered in the lead. Apollo raced ahead like a flash of black gold, his eyes sparking like fire. Tancred drew his sword. "This one is for Helena," he breathed to Apollo.

So rapidly had the Seljuks retreated and vanished into the hills that the tents were nearly abandoned when the crusaders stormed the camp. Camels, extra horses, goats, and sheep were still penned in their grazing ground. Tancred saw a wounded man crawling in the choking dust, hoping to avoid the trampling hoofs of the crusaders' horses.

The man looked up and Tancred felt a surge of pity. His eyes had been plucked out. Obviously this poor creature was not a Moslem. Tancred swung down from the saddle and stooped beside him, bringing the skin of water to his mouth.

"Peace," he spoke in Arabic. "Are you a follower of God's Son?"

The man's breath caught and then he began to weep, nodding his head. "Yes, yes, bless His name! Are you an angel, sir?"

"That depends on whom you ask," Tancred replied. "Suffice it to say I am His follower as well. Who are you and what do you know about Kilij Arslan the sultan?"

The man gulped the water, clawing at the skin with both eager hands. "I am an Armenian. And I was taken a slave from my goats near Bethlehem a year ago. The sultan did not own me, but a beast of a soldier named Dahir, chief bodyguard of the emir Sinan. For seeking to aid his wife, Adrianna, a Grecian woman, Dahir plucked out my eyes."

Tancred's jaw flexed and he exchanged alert glances with Nicholas, who had stooped beside them, producing a small leather pouch of medicinal eye salve.

"Sinan is the younger son of the caliph of Cairo," Tancred told Nicholas. "He has growing ambitions to replace his father. A warrior and a man to be reckoned with." His eyes held Nicholas's. "He is now your brother-in-law."

Nicholas's mouth turned up with the irony. "Can there be peace in the house of my enemies? What communion hath Christ with belial? Brother-in-law! At whose choice, his or Adrianna's?"

"She wishes escape, my lord! I tried to aid her. . . ." The man began to sob.

Nicholas laid a strong hand on the Armenian's dusty head. "For your courage, my son, I will see you well served. Another shall be your right eye." He stood and called for one of the friars, who came running.

"See well to this fellow," Nicholas told him. "He will go on with us to Jerusalem. He will ride in a wagon and you will feed and bless him with the Scriptures. And when Bethlehem is retaken, he will abide there."

The friar knelt to the Armenian. "Peace, fellow pilgrim. God has sent us to you. Be of good cheer!"

Tancred laid a hand on the Armenian. "Where is Sinan now? And Adrianna?"

"Still in the royal tents. He hopes to escape with her."

A knight rode up. "The Red Lion makes a stand by the tents!"

Tancred and Nicholas mounted and rode swiftly into the foray of frantic warriors, rearing horses, and shouting men, their iron implements smashing and hacking through the skulls of those who rushed to block them. Tancred rode down the foot soldiers seeking to guard the sultan's tent. He fought his way forward through screams and curses, Nicholas surging up beside him swinging the spiked morningstar.

The Seljuks were setting the tents aflame, hoping to discourage the crusaders' advance, but the gonfanons of Godfrey and Count Raymond passed forward and made way for the crusaders' dread mailed horsemen.

"The royal tents!" shouted Nicholas, and they fought their way forward.

The crusaders were shouting as they stumbled victoriously over dead and dying Moslems. They tore into the bundles of booty, hauling out tapestries and rugs, embroidered silk from Baghdad and Cairo, vessels of gold and ivory, and vials full of cinnamon oil and perfumes.

Tancred and Nicholas advanced, glancing about them and glimpsing one of the Turkish princes leading two saddled horses and shouting for help. *Two horses? That man, is he not Emir Sinan?*

"You have him! Be quick, Nicholas!"

Emir Sinan did not see Nicholas and shouted through the burning tents, "Mosul! You filthy insect! Eater of swine's flesh! Betrayer!"

Mosul?

The name stabbed through Tancred's heart. For an instant he could not respond. He wiped the sweat from his face, clearing his vision, his blue-gray eyes seeking a glimpse of his Moorish cousin.

He is here? But where!

He reached to the leather sheath slung over his left shoulder, housing his scimitar. Mosul. *Where!* He wheeled Apollo, looking among the flames, but the evening shadows and smoke coming

338

from the burning tents became a shield to the assassin who had killed Derek.

In a moment a small royal entourage moved forward on horseback through the darkness in a last-minute attempt to escape. Through the haze, a warrior appeared like a ghostly vision from among the fiery tents.

His cousin Mosul rode as one of ten men who made up the bodyguard of the Red Lion. With them were several Moslem princes and a woman.

Tancred stared at Helena, her hands bound behind her as she sat on a mare with a guard keeping the reins. His heart surged with strong, new passion. *She is here! But where is Philip?*

Beside her rode Prince Kalid.

Tancred's eyes narrowed as he readjusted his chin strap on his helmet and his gaze drifted from Kalid to Mosul. Kalid must wait.

Mosul had heard the angry words shouted a moment earlier by Emir Sinan. He now turned in his saddle to look over his shoulder, but as he did, Mosul's startled gaze confronted not Sinan, but Tancred.

For a second their eyes locked. Then Tancred rode Apollo forward over the fallen bodies to cut off his escape route.

Members of the royal entourage turned sharply in his direction. Prince Kalid startled, then tensed, muttering under his breath as his hand gripped the handle of his scimitar, but Helena also saw Tancred and gave a cry, kneeing her horse savagely. The mare leaped forward, breaking loose from the grip of the guard.

Nicholas galloped to intercept the horse, catching up the reins and turning it around.

"She's in the royal tent!" cried Helena. "Loose me!"

Nicholas leaned swiftly, cutting the cord binding her wrist, and Helena dismounted, running through the smoking tents. "Mother! Mother!"

Tancred tore his gaze from Helena's retreating form and shouted to the Red Lion, "The matter between Mosul and me does not concern you. Leave now and I will see that the crusader princes do not seek after you. That goes for you too, Kalid. We shall meet again at Antioch!"

The Red Lion and Prince Kalid spoke together in low voices.

Someone among the bodyguard was heard to protest, but the Red Lion's voice rose above his. A moment later he turned his horse to ride in the other direction, followed by Prince Kalid and his bodyguards.

Mosul cast a calculating glance about him and seemed to guess his dilemma. They had abandoned him and he could not escape Tancred. Mosul's hard face was grim and sweating in the flickering flames. He wheeled Alzira to confront Tancred, weapon in hand.

Tancred came near, reining in Apollo. "It is you and I, Mosul."

"Swine. Take me if you can," and his scimitar slashed boldly at Tancred's throat but missed as Tancred's curved blade blocked the full force.

He followed through with a savage swipe of his own that left Mosul shaken. *I must not kill him!* thought Tancred, restraining his emotions.

The force of their blades connected with a ringing whack, withdrew, then collided again and again.

Mosul was determined to kill him, but Tancred was cool to the point of calm, as though he watched a battle other than his own. He heard the steel caressing, sliding away, smashing again with a force that jolted them both in the saddle.

They fought in the blazing firelight, their horses circling. A soft whinny distracted Tancred's concentration and for a second his gaze shifted—his Arabian mare! She recognized him and had whinnied to her true master.

"Alzira," he breathed.

Mosul took advantage of the unexpected moment and struck. The scimitar cut through Tancred's chain mesh, glancing his left side. Before he could recover and respond, Mosul leaped Alzira past him, and with a last swing of his scimitar struck a ringing blow against Tancred's helmet.

Mosul raced past the collapsing fiery tent and away into the hot black night after the royal entourage who had fled toward Antioch.

Tancred held his side, staring after his sworn enemy, feeling the warm blood seeping through his fingers. Apollo blew through his nostrils and pawed the dust.

Tancred sat there for a minute, trying to clear his head from the deafening blow, his emotions and strength ebbing as he grasped the realization that the lost opportunity could not be captured again soon. Alzira was as swift as the desert wind and not even Apollo could catch his beloved mare now. Mosul and Antioch must wait.

Becoming aware of the burning heat coming from tents all around him, he heard knights shouting over their great victory. They carried and dragged and dumped booty into heaps before Duke Godfrey and Count Raymond. Bishop Adehemar looked on gravely as they brought gold and silver, weapons, saddle horses, donkeys, sheep, cattle, and camels.

Tancred turned his head toward the royal tent. *Helena . . .*

Still astride his Great Horse, Nicholas surged after Helena and toward the tent of Emir Sinan. "Adrianna is there!" His spirit convinced him that it was so, that his prayers and Helena's had been answered. "Thou mighty Christ, strengthen thy servant!"

Wild eyes blazing, a Moslem guard on horseback swept toward him through the shadows to intercept his advance. "Allah Akbar! Allah Akbar!"

He rode straight toward Nicholas, his short bow drawn.

Nicholas raised the church standard and the blood red cross showed in the light from the dancing flames. The arrow whizzed, flying through the standard and disappearing into the darkness behind Nicholas as the rider drove past.

The dust, which arose from the horse's hoofs like scuttling clouds, ascended around Nicholas as he steadily advanced toward the royal tent. The green banner of Islam with the insignia of two interlocked scimitars hung limp in the curling smoke.

Emir Sinan raced out from his tent to where his mare waited. Nicholas rode toward him, formidable in a torn black cleric's cloak worn over chain mesh, and a gleaming lance in one strong hand lifted to hurl straight into him.

Sinan threw himself to the ground, rolling away as Nicholas pitched the weapon with a groan. The lance whisked through the air, missing Sinan by inches, piercing the ground. He scrambled

to his feet, his black eyes smoldering, drawing his weapon. "Idol-
ater!" he spat into the smoke and dust. "Thou worshiper of a weak
woman!" He spun around. "Dahir! Dahir!" and a Seljuk came
bounding forward on foot from somewhere in the flaming darkness where tents blazed hot.

Dahir, seeing Nicholas riding toward them, threw himself beside the Great Horse, hoping to pull its rider down from the saddle, but Nicholas swung his mace with a crushing blow and the
Seljuk impacted the dust in bloody silence.

A giant Turk emerged from the royal tent, carrying a woman
who lifted her voice toward the sky as though her words sought to
climb the ladder to the sovereign throne. "Son of God, have pity
upon thy handmaid!"

Helena raced after the Turkish guard, trying to thwart him,
beating against him with her fists, pulling hopelessly at his huge
arms. "No! No! Mother!"

"Adrianna!" shouted Nicholas, riding up, his voice cutting
through the fiery night.

Her weak head turned toward Nicholas, and the expression on
her contorted face broke his heart. She tried to reach a hand toward him, but Sinan came between them.

Emir Sinan, his eyes fierce and dark, shouted an order to the
guard who carried Adrianna.

Helena threw herself against him, but Sinan struck her hard
with his hand and she stumbled backward. Swiftly he swung himself into the red-gold cloth of his princely saddle and raised his
curved blade as a signal to the giant guard to mount and escape
with Adrianna while he confronted Nicholas.

Nicholas's ragged breath came painfully as the sweat streaked
his dust-stained face. He drew his blade and charged past Sinan,
bludgeoning a blow against the side of the neck of the guard and
sprawling him face down in the dirt. Adrianna stumbled to escape
and fell with a cry.

"Mother—" sobbed Helena. Still dazed from Sinan's blow, she
pushed herself to her feet, swaying dizzily, trying to reach her.

Nicholas dismounted and ran toward his sister, but Helena's throat constricted with terror. Sinan was coming stealthily up behind Nicholas, dagger in hand. At that moment no sound would come from her throat and she could only stare, unable to move.

Firelight reflected on something silver lying in the dirt near her feet. Her gaze fixed upon an abandoned sword shining like the magical sword of Durendal.

With a gasp, as though moving to some unseen call, she caught it up, stealing forward toward Sinan. Helena roused her courage and new strength flowed through her veins. *Nicholas must live!* She lifted the sword high with both hands and brought the sharp edge down, wedging it into the back of Sinan's head.

The sickening thud shuddered through her hands, wrists, and arms. With horror, she let go and staggered a few steps away from him.

Emir Sinan sucked in his breath and fell to one knee, quivering, catching himself on one extended palm. He turned, his feverish eyes full of rage at the sight of her. With teeth bared, he crawled toward her, sweat dripping from his face. His shaking hand fumbled, though still clutching his dagger.

Helena's stomach churned and she slipped to the ground, too weak with shock to move.

"Nicholas!" screamed Adrianna, stretching a hand toward Helena as if to come between her daughter and Sinan.

Nicholas whirled with his weapon, slaying the Moslem just as a sleek black horse galloped up.

In a moment Tancred dismounted and ran toward her—"Helena!" His strong hands enclosed her, grasping and lifting her to her feet. "Beloved, are you all right?"

Helena's dazed heart responded to his vital touch, coming to life again as his blue-gray eyes burned into hers.

"Tancred," she sobbed, reaching both arms to grab him eagerly, fearful that she only imagined him standing there, that her hands would clasp nothing but emptiness. All her foolish pride had long ago fled, and now love surged through her with a pulsating awareness that could no longer be denied. He was no apparition and her fingers clawed into warm muscle.

Her eyes anxiously scanned the blood-soaked tunic, reaching

a hand to lay against his muscled chest. Her gaze lifted to his.

"I'll be all right," he breathed, loosing the chin strap and removing his helmet.

Helena's eyes moistened. His arm tightened about her as though she too would melt away from him into the heated night. She clung to him, shaking.

Holding her gaze, he swung her up into his arms and carried her away from the carnage.

CHAPTER 23
Two Hearts Beat As One

Somewhere in the distance, a lute player had begun his music, and the dark night began to dance with heartrending notes that wrenched the listening soul. In response, the stars filled the endless expanse of summer night with their wordless song. Below in the desert, damp with blood and sweat where lost men scribbled their names in the dust, flickering campfires wove through the night air like little gonfanons.

Helena and Tancred stood outside of the tent, their embrace as fervent with love and desire as the night was saturated with summer heat and throbbing starlight. The noise of revelry and battle had died, but the pounding of their hearts filled their ears.

The lute sang on as its crowning notes ascended, then ceased abruptly, followed by utter silence that intensified their emotions.

"I've been a fool," Helena whispered, weaving her fingers through his damp hair that glinted the warm color of autumn wheat in the firelight. "I was too prideful to admit what I truly feel about you, but I shall be a fool no longer."

Tancred gently wrapped her lush hair around his hand and brought her face closer to his lips. "It can wait," he breathed. "There is only one declaration I wish to hear you speak now. . . ."

Helena's warm eyes held his and a smile touched her lips as her fingers caressed him. "Tancred, it is you I love. . . ."

His eager kiss silenced her lips with passionate longing. Their hearts merged as one, and the sweet haunting melody of the lute began to play again.

When they arrived back at the main camp near the river where the Red Lion first attacked Bohemond's Normans, the dread news of what had happened to the peasants awaited them.

Tancred immediately arranged for Helena and her mother to journey to the Castle of Hohms, accompanied by two dozen soldiers.

"It is not safe for you here, Helena," Tancred urged in response to the unspoken plea in her eyes. "Rolf Redwan will care for you until I return."

"Then you shall return for me?" Helena's gaze betrayed her vulnerability, the false mask of the Byzantine elite stripped away from her in the heat of battle.

Tancred held her close. "My dearest Helena, I vow it. I do not know the day or the hour, but I shall return for you."

Hours later, Tancred buried the body of Modestine beneath a cypress by the quiet, tumbling river. His heart was heavy as he remembered back to the first hour he had met her near the river Rhone in the Auvergne region of France. He seemed to feel the drizzling rain in his memory and hear her voice calling: "Monsieur priest, take me with you."

Tancred thought of the words of Christ upon the cross, only seconds before his death: "It is finished." He stared down at the humble grave. "Adieu, Modestine . . . you who have known sorrow—now laughter." He looked up toward the sky as a small bird winged its way on the summer morning. Then he turned and walked away for the last time, his heart no longer heavy.

Tancred neared Bohemond's tent headquarters with its crimson gonfanon staked proudly by the entrance. The other princes had arrived, and as they stood about he took thoughtful notice of the red crosses sewn upon their garments. There were also new soldiers who had recently arrived from Nicaea. They had come to Constantinople by Venetian ship from Genoa and were gathering near the tent headquarters to wait for Nicholas. This morning he would lead them in the solemn ritual of their vow, and afterward hand them their red crosses to sew on.

Tancred stood there, musing.

Nicholas soon emerged with Bohemond and the newcomers lined up. One by one they bowed the knee to God and accepted a cross cut from the crimson cloth, voicing their allegiance to the Jerusalem expedition.

There was a stealthy movement from the cypress trees. Tancred turned to find his Redwan cousins Leif and Norris. Their blue eyes glinted with gravity beneath golden locks, their bronzed skin damp with sweat. He was about to reach for his sword but noticed their arms were folded across their chests. Slowly they walked toward him—Leif, grave and emotionless; Norris almost smirking.

"We come in peace, cousin," said Norris.

Tancred looked from one to the other, weighing their sincerity.

"Leif has convinced even me that you did not kill Derek," said Norris. "If you had the heart of an assassin you would have left me to die. Instead, you aided me with your medical skills and even forgave me for attacking while your back was turned. I have thought much of it, and I cannot forget it. We come as your kin to aid you in your search for your Moorish cousin."

"The one you call Mosul," added Leif.

Astonished, Tancred searched their faces and saw something in their eyes that convinced him.

He smiled—and it turned to laughter, and they came toward him, their own laughter joining his, each gripping his arms, Roman style.

"The three of us," boasted Norris with a grin. "Who can stand against us?"

"We will find him," said Leif.

"What of Walter and the others?" asked Tancred uneasily. "If you align yourself with me now, you will also be hunted. And if Mosul should die in the war, I may not be able to prove my innocence."

"We no longer follow our uncle from Sicily as our true liege," said Leif. "We believe he is envious of your inheritance and sought an occasion against you by making it appear as though you were guilty of Derek's death."

"We will follow Seigneur Rolf Redwan at the Castle of Hohms," agreed Norris.

"Then we will seek him together," said Tancred. "For we have Antioch to take from the Turks."

Norris frowned, inspecting Tancred's leather tunic for the crusader cross, but not finding it. "What is this, cousin? You have not taken the vow?"

Tancred glanced over at Nicholas and Bohemond and the line of new soldiers. Circumstances had progressed too far to ever turn back now. Willingly or not, he was caught up in the crusade on the long and bloody road to the gates of Jerusalem. And it appeared as if he would accompany Nicholas to return the relic to the Holy Sepulcher after all.

Tancred turned from Nicholas to look at his cousins. For a moment he imagined seeing the smiling, hopeful faces of the peasants, of Niles, Modestine, and Erich. The crosses on the strong shoulders of Leif and Norris stood bright red at noontide. He thought of the pregnant Adrianna carrying the child belonging to the house of the caliph of Baghdad. He thought of Helena. . . .

Tancred removed his dusty riding cloak from his bloodstained tunic and walked across the ground toward Nicholas.

Leif and Norris glanced at each other with a smile, then followed, watching.

Tancred unobtrusively merged into the line of warriors.

Nicholas automatically turned, prepared to pray, but seeing him, he stopped. Their eyes locked.

"What are you doing here?"

"I came to vow," breathed Tancred evenly.

"Are you sincere?"

"At such a time as this? Have you not also taken the cross? On with it, Nicholas!"

Nicholas's eyes searched his. "Yes, but I had my reasons for doing so—in order to enter Constantinople—"

"And I have my reasons."

Nicholas studied Tancred's face, then smiled faintly. "As you wish. But take heed my son; any vow to the Almighty must be taken seriously."

Tancred searched the dark, flashing eyes. "Understood, Lord Bishop. I do not vow lightly."

Nicholas smiled. Tancred placed his battered helmet beneath his arm and knelt to one knee, bowing his head, now damp from the July heat.

He felt Nicholas's hand firmly on his head and heard him praying in Latin, and then quietly in Greek, "May Christ guard you on the road to Antioch, and may we live to see our loved ones again, and Jerusalem!"

Tancred offered his prayer, then his sword for knightly blessing. In return he accepted the crusader cross. "Deus vult," he whispered.

A moment later he stood, and Nicholas returned his sword. They looked at each other, both feeling the summer wind.

"On to Antioch," said Nicholas.

Tancred sheathed his sword. *And Mosul.*

As he walked away he looked off toward the Moslem East, toward Antioch, where Saint Paul and Barnabas had been commissioned by the Holy Spirit to bring the gospel to the Gentiles.

Apollo was impatient, shaking his mane.

Nicholas waited with Leif and Norris astride their chargers.

"Helena," whispered Tancred. "Wait for me! I will return!"

I will pay my vows unto the Lord now in the presence of all his people. In the courts of the Lord's house, in the midst of thee, O Jerusalem.

—Psalm 116:18–19

GLOSSARY

abbey: a group of buildings comprising a monastery.

abbot: the head of a monastery.

arrow loops: slitlike openings that permitted the firing of arrows with full protection.

bailey: a courtyard surrounded by soldiers' quarters, stalls for horses, and food storage rooms.

conical helmet: worn over a hood; the shape of the crown and the smooth metal protected from cutting or thrusting weapons.

craven: a Norman trial to establish guilt or innocence.

donjon: a dungeon

durendal: a name for the sword of Roland in the epic poem "Song of Roland"; a symbol of knightly swords pledged to the service of God.

gonfanon: a banner that hangs directly from the shaft of a lance, just below the lance head.

Great Horse: a specially bred war horse of the western knights that could endure heavy weight and the clash of battle. It responded to leg commands so the knight could fight with both hands.

halberd: a cross between a battle-ax and a spear.

heraldic: a family insignia worn on the helmet, gonfanon, or shield.

jess: a soft leather thong attached to the falcon's legs.

keep: the stronghold of the castle, used as a watchtower and arsenal. The thick walls were laced with arrow loops. Usually there was a well beneath. The storage and eating rooms were above, and sleeping quarters were on the top level.

mace: a favorite weapon of warrior-priests; was sanctified and carried in ceremonial processions, slung on a loop on the right wrist. It was made of wood with quatrefoil-shaped head.

morning star: a type of mace; a round ball studded with spikes and attached to a handle by a chain.

Patriarch: head of the Eastern Church at Constantinople.

scimitar: a curved single-edged sword of eastern origin.

Seigneur: the trusted commander of a castle, a term of respect.

"Song of Roland": the epic poem about Charlemagne's Christian victory over the Moslem Moors of Spain. It was an early model of knightly chivalry.

> His right hand gauntlet to God he offers it.
> Saint Gabriel from his hand has taken it.
> —Song of Roland